DAUGHTER
OF THE
DRAGON TREE

DAUGHTER
OF THE
DRAGON TREE

SUSANNE AERNECKE
TRANSLATED BY ELKE LEIKHOFER-SCHMIDT

Bear & Company
Rochester, Vermont

Bear & Company
One Park Street
Rochester, Vermont 05767
www.BearandCompanyBooks.com

Bear & Company is a division of Inner Traditions International

Originally published in German under the title *Tochter des Drachenbaums* by Alyna Verlag
First U.S. Edition published in 2018 by Bear & Company

Library of Congress Cataloging-in-Publication Data

Names: Aernecke, Susanne, author. | Leikhofer-Schmidt, Elke, translator.
Title: Daughter of the dragon tree / Susanne Aernecke ; Translated by Elke Leikhofer-Schmidt.
Other titles: Tochter des drachenbaums. English
Description: First U.S. edition | Rochester, Vermont : Bear & Company, [2018] | "Originally published in 2015 in German under the title Tochter des drachenbaums by Alyna Verlag"—T.p. verso.
Identifiers: LCCN 2018014205 (print) | LCCN 2018023265 (ebook) | ISBN 9781591433156 (paperback)| ISBN 9781591433163 (ebook)
Subjects: LCSH: Time travel—Fiction. | Fantasy fiction, German. | BISAC: FICTION / Occult & Supernatural. | BODY, MIND & SPIRIT / Spirituality / Shamanism. | GSAFD: Voyages, Imaginary. | Fantasy fiction. | Occult fiction.
Classification: LCC PT2701.E63 T6313 2018 (print) | LCC PT2701.E63 (ebook) | DDC 833/.92—dc23
LC record available at https://lccn.loc.gov/2018014205

Printed and bound in the United States by Versa Press, Inc.

10 9 8 7 6 5 4 3 2 1

Text design by Debbie Glogover and layout by Priscilla Baker
This book was typeset in Garamond Premier Pro with Noyh Geometric used as a display typeface
Maps designed by Hauptmann & Kompanie

To send correspondence to the author of this book, mail a first-class letter to the author c/o Inner Traditions • Bear & Company, One Park Street, Rochester, VT 05767, and we will forward the communication, or contact the author directly at **www.amakuna-saga.com**.

*Love is the bridge
that overcomes time and space
and connects us to everything,
what was, what is, and what will be.*

UNKNOWN AUTHOR

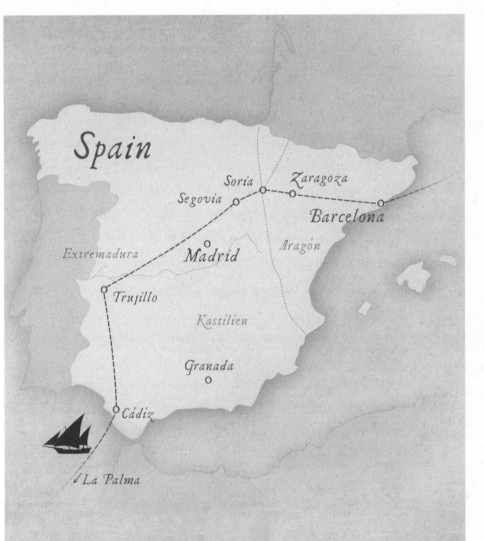

Spain

Soria
Segovia
Zaragoza
Barcelona

Extremadura

Madrid
Aragón

Trujillo

Kastilien

Granada

Cádiz

La Palma

Iriomé's Route

CAST OF CHARACTERS

PRESENT-DAY

Romy Conrad: *Laboratory doctor at Biotex*

Thea Sinsheim: *Romy's best friend*

Hannes Berger: *Romy's boss, owner of Biotex*

Professor Hattinger: *Specialist in the field of mycology and Romy's former teacher and mentor*

Tom Sattler, also known as Alexander Merten: *A man with a mysterious past*

Sam: *Hippie on the island of La Palma*

Ricardo: *Tour guide on La Palma*

Nic Saratoga: *CEO of Forster's Health*

Antonio Borges: *Chief of Security of Forster's Health*

Gerald Forster: *Owner of Forster's Health*

Jennifer Saratoga: *Forster's daughter and wife of Nic*

Chapter 1

Romy was traveling solo. Free solo. Without hook, without rope, and without Thea, her climbing partner. Everything within her was eager to finally start climbing, to dive into that world in which the rules laid down by people no longer held any significance; one in which higher laws applied. The law of gravity, the dictatorship of wind and weather, the challenge to retrieve one's skills and experiences at the right moment—when life depended solely on one's own fingertips. Perhaps in this way she would manage to not think of Thea's disease, at least for a while. Out of overwhelming concern about her best friend, Romy had spent another night without sleep and had set off spontaneously at three o'clock in the morning.

She decided on the lower part of a familiar training track that was clear of snow and ice despite the onset of winter. That meant about ten meters on a near-vertical climbing wall, crossing a ridge to the right, and back to the ground via a shale slope. For somebody with more than ten years' climbing experience, it was a calculable risk. Even without a partner. She knew each foothold and each handle.

After a few stretching exercises to warm up her muscles, Romy sat on a big stone sticking out from the fresh snow cover and changed her shoes. *This stone could split my skull if I fall,* popped into her head, but Romy dismissed that thought immediately.

She stowed her backpack in a small cave and chalked her hands. An icy wind was biting through her colorful Peruvian wool hat with earflaps. Expectantly Romy turned her face toward the sun, which was pushing like a glowing ball of fire over the craggy summits of the Karwendel Mountains at that exact moment. The pink of the dawn had given way to a fresh blue against which the now partly snow-covered limestone cliffs stood out bright white. She took in the colorful image and was glad about her decision to come here. It was Monday morning, so she would probably have the wall all to herself. And that's just what she needed.

The first two limestone flakes were no bigger than a matchbook. Romy spread her fingers like hooks and shifted her weight on the ledges while tensing her upper body. Then she put the tip of her shoe on a slight bulge in the rock, tensed, and pushed herself upward. Next she reached with her other hand above her head and put two fingers in a slack in the wall that was the size of a golf ball, pressed both fingertips in the concavity, and climbed higher. This procedure was repeated step by step, grip by grip. Yet no movement was like any other.

When she was about eight meters above the forest floor, a flock of jackdaws began screeching above her, interrupting her flow. The icy wind was tugging at her jacket harder than before. Romy suddenly felt her heartbeat and glanced down.

A feeling that she had not experienced for a long time flooded her body like a wave. An inner voice that she also had not heard for a long time whispered: *Something is going to happen!* She felt hot and cold at the same time. Her head was pounding. An invisible noose tightened around her neck. Her breathing came only intermittently; rapidly, every single muscle in her body tensed. Although her hands lay tightly around two secure handles, she was standing in exposed terrain with the wind hissing in her ears. She loved this toe dance over the abyss. It was her personal drug, her own special medicine to treat the panic attacks that had agonized her in her youth. It was the perfect balance to her life as a doctor, now functioning interminably in the monotonous routine of the lab.

But suddenly, something changed, and the panic she thought to have long since overcome was returning, despite trying to fight against it. Thoughts pounded her rhythmically like a percussion drill: *Now you're going to fall down! Now it will catch up with you! Now you have gone too far!*

Her fingers became stiff; she could hardly hold on any longer. Soon she would have to let go. Relinquish all. She closed her eyes, pressed her face against the cold rock, and forced herself to breathe evenly. Usually, she loved to feel the rough rock on her cheek. But now the touch of it pushed the panic even deeper. What had induced her to engage in this venture? Was she tired of life? Was there something in her that no longer wanted to carry on? Was it because Thea had been lying in the hospital for weeks and perhaps would die of cancer? That she couldn't imagine a life without her friend?

Fear clenched her stomach like a ball of lead. Romy was trembling all over, no longer able to control her arms and legs. Like the dark maw of a predator beneath her, the depth was waiting to devour its victim. She pressed her belly against the rock to find a grip and tried not to trigger any jolting that would endanger her already unstable balance. But her fingers slid over the rough rock, finding no purchase, and she lost her footing.

Romy heard her own shriek echoing from the cliff walls and flailed her arms about as she plunged into the depth. Her last thought was: *Don't fall on the big stone!*

Chapter 2

Waves of mist were drifting like white veils over the giant volcanic crater honeycombed with cavities. Their openings looked like the open mouths of dead people loved ones had forgotten to close. In the largest cave, the leaders of all twelve tribes of the small island of Benahoare had come together.

Iriomé, who had seen her seventeenth winter, let her eyes wander over the bearded crowd that had settled on the bamboo mats. The men had fixed themselves up for the occasion by braiding their long hair. The beards, usually wild and disheveled, were hanging down to their suntanned chests in good order. Some wore sandy leather garments embroidered with colorful seedpods; others had stitched-together goatskins tied around their loins.

It was the shortest day of the year, the day on which Tichiname, the supreme medicine woman, would transcend the limits of time to learn what the gods had predetermined for her people. She was sitting motionless, eyes closed, in front of a mighty fire in the midst of the cave. Her face, wrinkled by wind and weather, framed by curly white hair, was painted with blue spirals, the sign of infinity and the eternal recurrence of being. Around her neck she wore a string of dried lizards, and in her hand she held a roughly carved staff, at the top of which was mounted a goat skull with two pointed horns.

The tribal leaders hoped to learn from Tichiname what the coming year would bring. Whether their herds of goats would grow and whether the women would find enough roots, fruits, and edible leaves to build up stocks for times of privation. They were anxious to know whether enough children would be born. And whether Guayote, the hellhound, living deep inside the fire-spewing volcano, would remain peaceful and not desire one of them.

Without notice the wise woman made a shrill whistling sound that died away on hitting the stone walls of the cave. Iriomé took a deep breath. The time had come! For the first time she was allowed to be witness when Tichiname drank the sacred potion *amakuna*. She had cooked the brew as instructed by the medicine woman until the shadow of the rod of time had moved from one stone to the next. And even though Iriomé did not quite understand what the potion actually should bring about, she fervently hoped to travel someday in those mysterious worlds of which Tichiname told her over and over again. But so far she was only the youngest of seven disciples among whom the medicine woman eventually would choose her successor.

A low hum filled the air. The seven young women were standing side by side at the walls of the cave raising their arms. Their long cloaks made of bleached vegetable fibers spread out like the wings of seagulls. Their lips were painted blue. Each of them wore around her neck a small leather bag containing dried herbs.

Iriomé closed her eyes while the hum turned to a kind of song in which she and the other six disciples repeated a single word, always in the same rhythm. "Amakuna, amakuna, amakuna . . ."

Despite the barely tolerable volume, Iriomé perceived the sound of small bells that hung on Tichiname's leather garment. Apparently, the medicine woman had stood up. Three knocks on the rock floor of the cave from Tichiname's heavy wooden stick silenced the singing.

Iriomé opened her eyes, brushed her long reddish-blonde hair out of her face, and stepped forward to fulfill her assigned tasks. Proud and upright, she strode to the rock shelter in which a dish with the mysterious concoction was standing. It was not hidden to her that the dark eyes of one of the students were pursuing her with a look that promised nothing good. She knew that Guayafanta was eaten up with envy because she believed herself entitled to Iriomé's privileged position.

Two tallow candles illuminated the rock wall in which triangles, squares, and concentric circles were incised: symbols by which the initiates could connect with the spirits.

Iriomé took the lid from the bowl and stirred the oily yellow film on the surface with a wooden spoon. Then she took the vessel in both hands, knelt in front of the supreme medicine woman, and held the bowl up in offering. Eagerly she watched as her teacher brought the bowl to cracked lips.

Iriomé thought she could smell the slightly putrid, earthy flavor of the syrup as if it was running down her own throat. After a few breaths Tichiname's pupils rolled upward. Only the whites of her eyes were still to be seen. She must have arrived in the other world.

Suddenly there was a dull bang. The shell fell to the ground, shattering into several pieces.

Iriomé winced and looked in horror as Tichiname's body began to tremble, rearing up and twisting as if possessed by a demon. Her face distorted into an ugly grimace. Foam was seeping out of her mouth. She gasped as if fighting someone. Then she stumbled backward.

Iriomé jumped up to catch her. But the body, shaken by convulsions, slipped from Iriomé's hands and crashed into a cliff edge. Tichiname howled with pain and rolled across the floor out of the cave. Blood was oozing from a head injury, dying the medicine woman's white hair red. Outside she pressed herself against rough bark, seeking help against the gnarled trunk of a huge tree, which with its mighty crown towered into the pale moonlight.

From the frightened eyes of the leaders Iriomé concluded this could not be the normal running of the ceremony. The girls had turned away in horror; only Guayafanta's broad face with its dark, impenetrable eyes showed no emotion.

Iriomé was not able to imagine what the medicine woman had seen in the other world that would cause such an outburst. No one dared to approach her. Finally Iriomé could not stand it any longer. She ran to Tichiname, clung to the still trembling body, and tried to unclasp her arms wrapped around the trunk like strong ropes, but to no avail. Only after some time the old woman finally let go. Her mouth was close to Iriomé's ear so she could hear what her teacher whispered with her remaining strength, "Men with ships will come, men who only care for power and wealth. These men know no love. They will destroy everything that is sacred to us. But one thing must never fall into their hands: the secret heart of the island that beats in the cave of the highest mountain! Only when people are free from the greed for power and wealth will its secret be safe to reveal." Her voice became weaker. "It is your task as my successor to preserve amakuna until that time has come." Exhausted by the effort of speaking, her head lolled, forcing Iriomé to support it.

"Tichiname!" she screamed with fear.

"Swear," the dying woman panted with the last of her strength.

Iriomé took Tichinamé's wrinkled hand and laid it on her heart; "I swear."

A deep breath filled the chest of the old woman. *Vacaguaré,*" she breathed in the language of her people. "I want to die." And then again, "Vacaguaré!"

"No," Iriomé whispered, desperate. "No, don't go."

Tears were running down her high cheekbones. The blue color on her lips was smeared, her hair disheveled. She pressed her back against the trunk of the tree as if it could give new power for life, looking for help in the faces of the others who had formed a circle around them.

But the breath of the old medicine woman became shallower, until it completely ceased and her old body slid to the ground.

Iriomé collapsed over her, sobbing. It was as if something inside the young girl had died as well.

Chapter 3

Hesitantly, Romy opened her eyes. Overhead was nothing but rock. The rushing of water. It took her long minutes to finally orient herself. *Where am I? What happened?*

Slowly the memories welled up inside. The panic. The fall. The thick stone. This noise must be the rain beating down outside the cave entrance. "Strong rainfalls later in the afternoon," Romy recalled—the weather forecast she heard in the car on her journey from her apartment in Augsburg, Germany that morning. She had intended to have been back for a while by this time.

Cautiously, Romy moved her head and noticed a weird feeling and an earthy flavor in her mouth. She spat, but the taste on her tongue persisted. Her eyes fell on the small backpack with her winter boots, both of which she left here in the cave next to the climbing entry. *But how on earth did I get here? Did I have a total blackout?* Romy searched her mind for a clue. But there was nothing. Nothing but the fall . . .

Cautiously she tried to move her limbs. First her fingers, then her hands, arms, and legs. Amazingly, she was even able to get up—without feeling any pain. Obviously, the production of the body's narcotics was in full swing to dampen the pain. Was this the golden half hour Mother Nature gave to all injured that should enable them to take life-saving measures despite injuries? Impossible. It was already getting dark. A glance at her watch told Romy she had been lying there for at least seven hours.

Even without having studied medicine, it would have been clear to her that one did not just get up and walk away after having fallen on firmly frozen forest soil from a height of twenty-five feet. Limbs should be broken, ligaments torn, muscles bruised, not to mention suffering from internal injuries. She should be a paraplegic, if not dead. In no case, however, could she have been able to trudge into this cave. And by no means should she be able to stand. Yet she was on her own two feet, albeit slightly bent in order not to bang her head on the cave ceiling. Someone must have caught her! But how? And who? This was impossible. And why then had the person left her alone here? It made no sense at all. In addition, Romy did not feel a bit cold. After the many hours on the floor of the cave, she should be stiff as a frozen pizza.

Did I dream the fall just like I dreamed the experiences in a strange Stone Age world? But dreams felt different. Both the fall and what she saw through the eyes of a young girl with a strange-sounding name appeared utterly real, even though Romy had not the slightest idea in what part of the world or in what period of time that creepy ritual she had witnessed could have taken place. The language had been completely alien to her, yet she had understood every word. And also the people, especially the old medicine woman, had been somehow familiar.

She needed to talk to Thea about it. Certainly Thea would have a plausible explanation for the entire episode. Her best friend had worked as a neurologist in the same hospital as she.

At the thought of Thea, Romy suddenly saw the cup with the toxic brew in her mind's eye. Had she perhaps invented the girl who gave the death potion to the wise woman out of hidden guilt? Fear for her friend might have played a role. Thea had also been administered a kind of death potion after all. And it had been Romy herself who had ultimately persuaded Thea to undergo chemotherapy. But why the Stone Age ambience, the strange vegetation? Romy had never before seen such an archaic tree as the one under which the medicine woman died.

Romy felt completely unable to organize any thoughts or to distinguish what was imagination and what was reality. Something that normally was not difficult for her at all. Both in her private and in her professional environment, she was a woman who had both feet planted firmly on the ground. But at the moment her brain was playing games with her—the rules of which she was not familiar with.

Whatever had happened here, she had to get away. Preferably as fast as possible, because soon it would be dark.

She searched in the pocket of her anorak for her cell phone. It was broken in several pieces. That at least proved that she actually had fallen. *How can I get help now?*

Romy stood at the cave entrance. The rain had somewhat subsided. Carefully, she took a few steps. Her knees were a bit weak, but she would make it to the car. Perhaps it was better this way. What could she have told her friends from the mountain rescue service? That she started to climb the cliff without securing herself, was having a panic attack, and fell off the wall like a dead beetle? That someone caught her and laid her down in a cave, where she then set off on a little trip into the Stone Age? They would probably institutionalize her right away, and not even Thea could get her out of that easily.

Sighing, Romy took her winter boots out of the backpack and slipped them on. This also did not cause her any trouble. She stowed her climbing shoes in the backpack, threw it over her shoulder, and cautiously felt her way along the cliff to the place where she must have fallen. The snow there was trampled down and melted away by the rain in a number of places. Nevertheless she thought she recognized footprints of foreign shoes in addition to her own tracks. Somebody had been here.

෨෨

Romy knew only too well the feeling of being boxed in and the creaking noises as the CT cut her body visually into slices. She was not lying in "the tube" for the first time, and this was not even her first climbing accident.

She had not slept a wink all night. She just could not get this girl with the mysterious characters on her cheeks and the blue painted lips out of her mind. She had googled "amakuna," entered all possible spell-ings, with k, with c, double-m, with h, and yet had not received a single matching result. The Stone Age ritual was going round and round in her mind like a merry-go-round.

At two o'clock she was ready to believe that she had been this Iriomé in a previous life and had taken part in the ceremony herself. At three o'clock she even suspected that the girl from the island or someone else from that period had rescued her. At four, she decided to drive to the hospital to have a computerized tomography made. Perhaps something was wrong with her head after all.

Romy was lucky. Angie, her only friend in Augsburg Hospital, was on morning shift and instantly agreed to put her under the tube with-out filling out a heap of forms, even though she was shaking her head.

A long buzz signaled the end of the scan. Angie freed her from the claustrophobic apparatus smiling. "I'm going to send the pictures directly to the evaluation room for you. You can have a look at them there, taking your time," Angie said in her thoughtful way.

"I'll be right there." Romy stepped into the dressing room and took a look in the mirror at her thin face, free of makeup. Searching, she ran her tongue over upper and lower lips, where she still perceived a putrid, earthy taste. She quickly pulled her jeans and sweater on, tied her long strawberry-blonde hair into a ponytail, then headed out.

In the evaluation room Angie was grinning at her broadly. "You're lucky again. At first glance I couldn't find anything. Skull, shoulders, spine, pelvis, all's okay so far."

Actually Romy had expected nothing else. Nevertheless, she was happy about Angie's first assessment.

"I don't get it, why you're always exposing yourself to such a risk," she said, shaking her head, while Romy viewed the photos on different monitors, particularly those of her head, with a trained eye. Nothing remarkable.

"There are plenty of sports that aren't as dangerous as climbing. If you keep this up, you'll be sitting in a wheelchair—or worse."

Real concern could be heard from Angie's words. She was a kind soul. Most of their colleagues were so overworked that only on rare occasions was a private word spoken.

"I can only explain it to you this way," Romy replied seriously. "Up there at the crag, I've a better grasp of myself. I feel strong because I know who I am and what I'm capable of."

Angie looked her over in amazement. "You are strong. I only know a few people as brave as you."

"Not everything's as it seems." Romy played it down with a movement of her hand.

"You risked your job because it was important to you to speak the truth about the working conditions in this dump."

"I still feel little and helpless sometimes," said Romy. "It's not easy to understand, but it's true."

Angie hugged her spontaneously. "Yes, I understand that. And I believe we all feel like that now and then."

"Perhaps, but it really hurts me." She disentangled from Angie's embrace. "Thanks anyway. Thank you for everything."

"Any time. You know where to find me."

By now, it was six o'clock in the morning. Wake-up time in the hospital. She could visit Thea. Perhaps her friend had a sympathetic ear for her—and maybe even an explanation for this trip to the Stone Age.

The corridor of the oncology department smelled of fruit tea, which was kept warm in thermos jugs on a food cart. Next to them, covered plastic plates piled up, each with three slices of pink sausage, a packet of jam, three slices of grayish bread, and a small packet of butter. This had not changed over the years. Already, at this ungodly hour, breakfast was served on all wards, something that Romy had never understood. For her, there was nothing more relaxing than to sleep in. But here this leisure was not granted to anybody—neither the patients nor the staff—like so many other things. Angie was right. It had been brave to draw attention to staff grievances and to propose certain changes, even if it had proved futile in the end. She was no match for the power of the hospital administration and finally had no other choice but to go. Since this defeat she worked as a lab doctor at Biotex, a medium-sized company performing drug research. Avistan had been developed there, a new treatment for a particularly aggressive form of breast cancer. Currently, the last of seven clinical trials was running. This meant the drug was nearing authorization. That's why Romy recommended Thea participate in the study.

Even before she could open the door to Thea's room, Anton Feistner, who led the study, was coming toward her. Under the fluorescent lighting the doctor looked pale, as if he himself was on chemo. He was a head shorter than Romy, wore a crew cut, and always took a bolt upright posture when he faced her.

"Good to see you. Did you already hear? Acute renal failure. It happened last night. She died during dialysis," he said with the neutral voice of a doctor who uttered such phrases often.

Romy gasped. Her stomach tightened painfully. Her eyes filled with tears. The floor threatened to give way beneath her feet. Feistner just managed to grab her. "Relax. No! No, not Thea. Her roommate!" He said quickly when he realized what had been implied.

Slowly Romy regained her poise. She would have liked to slap his face.

"She was a high blood pressure patient, and the kidneys were already heavily affected. Definitely has nothing to do with Avistan."

Romy wiped a tear away that had got caught in the right corner of her mouth.

"Everything okay with you?" He didn't wait for an answer. "Thea is thinking that she'll be next. Try to reassure her somehow!" He looked embarrassed and turned on his heels. "See you later then."

Still unsettled, Romy opened the door to Thea's room. It was empty. The window was tilted, letting in cold air. Probably Thea could not bear to stare at the empty bed where until recently a fellow sufferer had lain.

Romy took the elevator down to the cafeteria and discovered her friend hidden behind an overhanging rubber tree, sitting at one of the blue plastic tables. She was wearing an expensive jogging suit, which could not hide how thin she had become. Her face, on the other hand, was slightly bloated from the medication, causing her to look older. Her once full auburn hair had become thin.

"So much for your miracle cure," Thea said in a low voice, raising her head briefly.

Romy pulled up a chair and sat down. She still did not want to accept that her best friend, who, though smaller, had always been the stronger of them, actually could die. Up to now Thea had managed to come to grips with the situation with a sense of humor. Only in very rare moments had the deep despair shown through. Now seemed to be such a moment; Thea's face showed a seriousness Romy seldom observed.

"They have a bad thing going on," she whispered and moved closer to Romy. She looked around carefully, to see if anyone was nearby to overhear. But except for an old lady in a flowered bathrobe with an oxygen bottle suspended on a rack beside her, no one was in the cafeteria yet.

"I overheard a phone conversation Feistner had last night with your boss," she continued in a low voice. "They still want to bring Avistan on the market and even manipulate the study, if necessary. They've put too much money into its development. If the drug is not authorized, your frigging laboratory will finally be absorbed by some U.S. company."

Romy took a deep breath. "Are you sure? Perhaps you've got something wrong?"

Thea shook her head. "Definitely not. I can still hear his words clearly." She leaned back in her chair. "To die this way—as a guinea pig—is not exactly what I imagined for the end of my life," she said.

Romy suddenly thought of Iriomé, who had handed her teacher that death potion. She shivered.

"I'm backing out of the study in any case. And I'm not going to stay another day in this guinea pig farm."

Romy understood her friend all too well. They had often discussed corrupt doctors and drug trials funded by the pharmaceutical industry and thus pressured to show the desired result. And now Thea might become a victim of this corruption herself. They could not let that happen.

"Okay," Romy said without further thought. "Let's go to your room and get your things packed. For starters, you'll come to my place."

Chapter 4

The morning rain passed into snow as the friends headed for the city in Romy's Golf. The car was a bit dated, but at least the CD player was intact and belting out *What a Wonderful World* by Louis Armstrong. Romy was about to press the forward button, but Thea blocked her access. "Don't bother. The world *is* beautiful. In spite of everything."

Romy looked at her friend. Without a word of accusation Thea had packed her belongings and informed Feistner in no uncertain terms that she was no longer available for the dodgy dealings of the pharmaceutical industry. Romy wondered where Thea found this strength and peace of mind. And all this without real support. Her boyfriend quickly disappeared after the cancer diagnosis. Thea had broken away from her family, which counted among the richest in Augsburg, years ago. They owned nearly a quarter of the city, but when Thea decided to be a doctor instead of joining their real estate empire, they turned their backs on her.

Thea and Romy met while studying in Munich and had replaced each other as family. Romy's parents were killed in a car accident when she was a child, so she grew up with her grandmother in southern Spain. Without Thea, Romy never would have survived those first years in Germany. The friends were each other's one and only.

At that moment Romy saw the tree!

She stepped on the brakes with all her might. The driver behind them honked indignantly.

"What?" shouted Thea, trying to loosen the seatbelt, which pressed her firmly into the seat.

Instead of answering, Romy turned into the next driveway. Was she being plagued by hallucinations again? "I'll be right back," she said quickly, got out, and trudged through freshly fallen snow on the sidewalk a few meters back to the display window of a travel agency with the poster that almost caused a crash. No, it had not been a hallucination. Despite all the emotions, she still could rely on her five senses. The tree on the poster in the window looked exactly like the one under which the old medicine woman died.

Without hesitation, she entered the store. A woman the same age as her with poorly dyed red hair sat behind a messy desk and smiled in a businesslike manner.

"Hello, what can I do for you?"

"That tree, out there on the poster . . ."

". . . is a Canarian dragon tree," the red-headed woman informed her. "You want to book a trip to the Canaries?"

"Uh?"

"Those trees don't grow anywhere else. You find most of them on La Palma, the most beautiful and greenest of the islands. A little paradise." She handed Romy a brochure in which the natural beauties of the island were displayed in vivid colors: exotic flowers, black beaches, bizarre volcanic landscapes with craters and caves.

One of the pictures caught Romy's eye immediately. She felt dizzy. Closing her eyes she tried to resurrect the images from her vision. There was no doubt. The ritual must have taken place right there in one of the caves.

"Where's that?" she asked excitedly, pointing at the photo.

"This is the Caldera de Taburiente, the large volcanic crater in the center of the island. A gorgeous region to go trekking. Especially at this time of year. Still pleasant temperatures. Not as hot as in the summer. Do you already know when you want to fly out?"

Romy looked confused. "No, no, not at all."

"I could offer you a pretty *finca* with an overwhelming view of the sea and two dragon trees on the plot," the travel agent went on, undeterred. "If you decide quickly, I'd even have two cheap flights for you tomorrow. Just yesterday, a young couple canceled so you can have a deep discount on the price."

That's perfect! Romy thought. It seemed as if some alien force wanted her to fly to this island.

"And? What do you think?" The woman already was punching up forms on her computer.

"Thank you, I'll think about it," Romy said, somewhat taken by surprise, and made a step back.

"Be quick. La Palma is very popular in the winter. I can reserve the flights until lunchtime . . ."

A loud honking on the street interrupted the tempting offer. Romy looked outside through the large glass window. A large truck wanted to turn into the driveway blocked by her Golf. Romy rushed out of the travel agency, ran to the car, and jumped in. Her attempt to maneuver past the truck sparked even more lengthy honking.

"Did you book us a climbing tour through the Andes, or what have you done in there?" asked Thea while Romy tried to pull out into traffic. She didn't answer.

"What's going on? You look strange."

"Something funny happened to me," she replied. "Let's go home; I'll tell you everything over breakfast."

෨෧

The forty-year hulk of a man with blue eyes, a scar on his forehead, and a blonde beard was looking thoughtfully out the window on the twenty-fifth floor of the Holiday Inn over the rooftops of Augsburg. His muscular, tanned body was dressed in a military jacket, which he had kept since he had begun his fight against the powerful as a young man, a fight against those who were insatiable and got rich at the expense of the powerless.

Now, at last, he saw a light at the end of the tunnel, because from now on he would no longer be on his own. He had set the course. A new era had begun. A new chance. He, the warrior, and she, the healer. Soon they would see whether the great plan would come true. Whether the time was ripe. Whether love would triumph or people would continue to be driven by the greed for power and wealth.

Germany was a dangerous place for him to be, but he had no choice. He had been forced to come here in order to initiate everything that was going to happen. So it was predestined hundreds of years earlier. His role in this great plan was to protect *her* life. To ensure nothing intervened that prevented her from fulfilling her task. But he was not allowed to influence her directly in any way. She had to find her own way, make her own decisions.

He turned away from the window, went to the phone on the bedside table, and pressed the 0 button. "Is this reception?" he asked in a throaty voice. "Will you book me a flight, please?"

∽

Romy told Thea everything she had experienced the previous day without leaving out a detail. They were sitting at the old oak table in the kitchen of Romy's cozy prewar apartment, eating whatever was in the sparsely stocked fridge. Fruit, yogurt, honey, and a heel of Pfister sunflower bread. Both of them were wearing thick sweaters and socks, although the old stove did its best. Romy had wanted this apartment in the old Welser Kontor pretty badly and thus put up with the disadvantages uncomplaining.

When she finished, Thea looked at her thoughtfully. She had not interrupted Romy a single time, but Romy knew her well enough to know that she had already formed an opinion. And so it was.

"I think your falling was a hallucination," she said in the typical, friendly-compassionate tone of the neurologist that she was.

Romy shook her head. "I did fall. Definitely. And someone caught me. The tracks in the snow . . ."

"You said yourself it had begun to thaw."

"And the story with this Iriomé?" Romy defended herself.

"Some kind of hallucination, triggered by adrenaline overproduc-tion, which—as you know—occurs after a shock and makes the syn-apses in the brain go crazy."

"But if I didn't fall at all, why should I have had shock?"

"It must be related to your panic attacks, and those are caused by stress. Whether it's old stress or new stress."

"But I haven't had one in years. And in career terms I've a lot less stress in my new job than in the hospital. The only thing that's wearing me down is . . . that you . . ." She fell silent.

Thea disregarded Romy's embarrassment. "Who do you think this Stone Age woman is anyway, and what did she want to tell you?" Thea was again using her sympathetic neurologist's tone.

Had Thea not been her best friend, Romy would have abandoned the conversation now. She hardly recognized herself. Normally, her arguments were rational, like Thea's, scientific. But something had changed. She had an urgent feeling that she had to defend Iriomé's existence.

"I imagine that she called to me for some reason."

"From the Stone Age?" Thea asked, frowning.

"Perhaps? Maybe I was even once this Iriomé, in a former life. Thea, I don't know how to explain it to you, but it was all so incredibly real."

"I do believe you, sweetie. This is typical of hallucinations. And Romy sounds almost like Iriomé."

"You're kidding me!"

"No, I'm just trying to figure out what's wrong with you."

Romy suddenly felt as if she were the sick person, not Thea.

"Strong emotions, self-reflection, and feelings are mental states and their neurobiological correlates consume plenty of oxygen and sugar. I think you've collapsed for some reason, which caused a blackout and subsequently these hallucinations."

Everything in Romy was reluctant to accept this theory. "Normally

I'd agree with you. But . . . have you never, at least briefly, considered that our souls could reincarnate?"

Thea grinned. "Truth to be told, no. As I've just explained, for me all mental functions are connected with mechanisms and centers within the brain. And if it's dead . . . well . . . everything's dead."

"But what about the old religions? For Buddhists, reincarnation is quite normal. And the Hindus are convinced that there is a life after death."

"And the Earth is flat! People believed that for centuries."

"Call me crazy. But somehow through this experience I've gained the impression that death is not the end. Perhaps it's really like that, and our soul undertakes a journey time and time again. I'm even convinced that it's just like that."

Thea now was really worried. "This isn't like you, Romy!"

Her friend was absolutely right. *Was that really me? My voice speaking? My opinion?*

"Well, in view of my own situation, I can actually only hope that you're right," Thea said suddenly with a changed tone, taking another sip of tea and then staring into the cup for a while as if a solution could be found there.

"Be honest. You think I'm seriously disturbed."

"No, I know you too well for that."

"What should I do now?"

Romy's cell phone rang, so Thea was spared answering. "Where have you been?" came from the handset. "Berger is fuming because of your friend and wants to see you immediately."

"I'll be right there," answered Romy, as composed as possible.

She ended the call. "Kyra, my boss's secretary. He wants an explanation for your withdrawal from the study."

"I'll gladly provide it," said Thea. "Do you want me to call him?"

"Let me talk to him first. Actually I should already be in the lab."

"Then go to work and make clear to him that he must withdraw Avistan no matter what."

"I understand. Nevertheless, you have to get together with an oncologist as soon as possible to have a new treatment plan drawn up," Romy appealed.

"Don't worry. I'll be fine here. Let me get a few hours of sleep first and I'll deal with it tomorrow."

Chapter 5

With numb fingers Romy slipped her ID card into the security scanner. Buzzing, the heavy door opened as if by magic and shut in the same way behind her.

She took the stairs to the second floor, again opened a security door to her lab with the ID card, and turned the ceiling lights on. The main Laboratory for Medicinal Plant Research was located in an adjacent building, so she and her two colleagues here were pretty much left to themselves. Both of them had worked late the night before and would come to work later that day. Her office, which could also only be opened with an ID, was separated from the work area by a glass wall. The display on the phone already showed five calls, presumably from her boss's office. Nevertheless, she first got her white coat out of the closet, went back to the lab, and checked the surveillance monitors of the synthesizing robots.

KL13 split the DNA of a recently discovered root from the Amazon into its individual components and reviewed the potential effects and possible matches with already known compositions. It was a laborious business with large financial expenses. Unfortunately, it was still far too rare that a new, effective plant substance was discovered to declare war on incurable diseases. No wonder, then, that the pharmaceutical industry now mainly put their money into genetic engineering and chemistry and swept the side effects under the carpet. Romy was convinced that nature itself offered a remedy for all disease. It just had to be found. This new job filled her with far more satisfaction than she ever would

have thought. During her time at the university she had had little interest in research, but now it almost seemed to her as if her disputes with
the hospital had been necessary to find her true calling.

Romy had gone through a quarter of the protocols, when the phone
rang and Kyra summoned her to Berger.

His Cerberus, who changed her hair color once a week and as a
matter of principle wore clothes that did not match, looked up only
briefly as Romy entered.

"He's pretty pissed," Kyra remarked, turning back to a screen on
which she moved around the displayed cards with incredible speed.

Berger looked red-eyed, as so often lately. Probably he had slept
on the office couch. He was unshaven, and his thinning blond hair
fell in greasy strands on the collar of his shirt. Romy looked away. On
the wall hung pictures of historic military vehicles from the First and
Second World Wars, which Berger collected with great passion and
restored in his spare time. Like a little boy he loved to drive through
mud, over boulders, and across rivers. Shortly after her recruitment
he had invited Romy to come along, but as she held an extreme aver-
sion against anything that remotely smelled of war, she had turned
him down.

"Take a seat," he said with a slightly hoarse voice. "I'm sorry about
what happened last night. But such a particular case doesn't necessarily
mean the end of Avistan and justifies no such panicked reaction. I don't
know what's gotten into your friend. She's a doctor after all."

"That's exactly why she got out."

"That's a mistake she's going to regret. You know as well as I do
that she has no alternatives left."

Romy had to admit he was right. Thea had already tried everything
after surgery: two different chemotherapies, irradiation, a complete
change of diet, mistletoe, and immunotherapy . . . But the tumor continued to spread, as if it wanted to mock her about running against it
with such weak weapons.

"Avistan will kill her faster than the cancer," Romy said softly.

"That is mere speculation. The patient, who sadly died last night, was beyond remedy anyway."

"Then you shouldn't have let her participate in the study! That makes no sense. It would falsify the results from the outset, which is in nobody's interest, surely." Romy actually had intended to stick to the facts when talking to Berger, but when he presented her such hypocritical excuses, she found it hard to keep herself in check.

"Things don't always turn out as planned."

"That's exactly why you have to recall Avistan. Obviously it is not ready for application yet. Thea looked at the file of the patient that died. She was by no means a high blood pressure patient," she said in a cutting voice.

"This assessment is not your responsibility," Berger replied with an equally sharp undertone.

So far, Romy had appreciated her boss and knew him as a fair and competent scientist. This was out of character for him. "Is it because of Forster's Health?" she asked him. "How many millions have they actually put into the development of Avistan? Four, five, six? Or ten?" Romy knew he was drip-fed by that U.S. company. Apparently they put him under pressure, and in the end he had to push Avistan through at the Federal Office for Drug Approval. This being the case, a dead volunteer only played a minor role. Feistner covered it up for him and in return surely got a decent salary increase. Had he not driven up in a brand new Jaguar last week?

"If you eventually take on more responsibility, I'll gladly continue our wee talk. At the moment you can only ensure that your friend comes to her senses. This conversation is over."

Romy wouldn't be put off so quickly. "What're you going to do when I turn to the press or the Federal Office?"

"You'll hardly be that stupid. You already lost a job once because you went out on a limb. And this situation is a little more serious than better care or working hours for hospital staff. A company this size is powerful and reaches far up into politics, the press, and the public. This is a hornet's nest. Whoever begins poking around in it will inevitably be stung. And each sting is fatal."

"You want to frighten me?" She knew, of course, that he was right. If Avistan wasn't approved here in Germany, the Americans would try somewhere else. In London, in New York, in Abu Dhabi . . . Somebody was always on the "payroll" of such companies someplace where they could exert pressure. And they would hire a few luminaries who would praise Avistan to the skies at congresses and in medical journals. For a decent sum in an account in the Bahamas, these figureheads would do anything. Sometimes even a nice holiday trip was enough.

As if he could read her mind, Berger suddenly looked like a picture of misery. He took a sip from his coffee mug and looked at Romy in disillusionment. "In the end, everyone is bribable, Romy. You, too. Imagine someone offering you a lead on developing a new anticancer agent in your field. Wouldn't you snap at the chance, even if you had to make a pact with the devil?"

Romy was silent.

"I once was as idealistic as you. Wanted to defeat fatal diseases. Cancer, AIDS, MS. Save humanity. But these ideas have been knocked right out of my head by now. First a multinational allures you with large sums of money and promises, and then they tighten the noose on your neck until you become short of breath. These guys are like vultures. They're going to gobble up this place. One way or the other." He put his coffee mug back on the desk. "In the next few weeks Señor Nic Saratoga, CEO of Forster's Health, will turn up at our doorstep wanting results. And the man is not to be trifled with. He's a native of Colombia. Old cartel school." Berger laughed bitterly, but it was clear to Romy how serious the situation was and that her boss was in real trouble.

"I've put all my money into this company. I've got nothing else, you know! What will become of my family? I've got two children to put through college soon."

As mad as she had been with Berger just now, she suddenly felt compassion for him. She knew this painful feeling of being exposed to a higher authority against which one felt helpless.

At that moment, her cell phone rang. Romy saw it was Thea. Instinctively she took the call.

"You won't believe it!" Thea blurted out. "I did some research on the internet. These Stone Age people you've described actually existed at La Palma, as close as five hundred years ago. When the Spaniards conquered the island, they found people dressed in skins and living in caves. This is historically proven. This would also be in line with what your medicine woman foresaw!"

Romy closed her eyes for a moment taking a deep breath. *Men with ships will come, men who only care for power and wealth.*

"By men she meant Spanish conquistadores," Thea said excitedly.

"That means it was not a hallucination?" Romy asked and caught Berger's eye. "A second," she signaled him.

"I've no idea. I know only one thing: we need to go to this island."

"We?"

"Yes, we. If there really is such a thing as reincarnation, I want to know." She paused for a moment, only her breathing could be heard. "It would reassure me somehow. Inform good old Berger that you'll be on vacation the next three weeks. I'm going to book our flights now."

She was gone. Romy had to grin. *This is the Thea I know! Thinking clearly, moving, so full of energy despite it all.*

"Was that Thea?" Berger asked. "Everything okay?"

Romy nodded.

"And? Did she think it over?"

"No. She wants to fly with me to the Canaries tomorrow. Would you give me a three-week holiday?"

"This comes somewhat out of the blue, doesn't it?"

"Yes." She looked at him expectantly. "Don't you think we owe this to her?"

Berger took a deep breath. His gaze was difficult to judge. "That probably isn't the worst thing. When you're back, everything will have calmed down a bit and perhaps Thea will think it all over again . . . if it's not too late."

"Thanks," Romy said with clenched teeth.

"Drop the anger, and take care of your friend."

Romy said goodbye and returned thoughtfully to her office. Berger was not a bad fellow. Just got greedy. And now Forster's Health had him in their grip. They would swallow Biotex and enforce their interests and policies. Her stomach tensed at the thought.

ᥬᥩ

The man with blue eyes was not wearing a military jacket this time, but a blue windbreaker, trousers from Jack Wolfskin, hiking boots, and a backpack. He had shaved and looked like most of the other passengers in line in front of the check-in desk for the flight to Santa Cruz de la Palma. When his eye fell on the two young women that had just checked in at the counter, his expression became almost affectionate.

Pulling a cell phone out of his pocket, he typed a Spanish number.

"*Hola*, Ricardo . . . Yes. Everything is going according to plan. The airplane is on time."

Suddenly, someone tapped him on the shoulder. "Alexander Merten?"

He turned to look into the expressionless face of a civil cop. He knew these guys all too well and would recognize one in a crowd. So he also knew immediately that he had no chance to escape. There were at least five other civilian police officers in the immediate vicinity.

"Ricardo, there is a problem. You need to take care of the women. Don't let them anywhere near the caldera," was all he could say before his phone was jerked out of his hand.

"You're under arrest. I must ask you to come with us." The policeman pulled out a badge.

Alexander Merten remained motionless, expressionless. The officer became nervous. "Please, let's leave the airport without attracting too much attention. We don't want to spoil the day for all these people who are looking forward to their holiday, do we? May I ask why you wanted to fly to La Palma?"

Merten did not answer. People were already turning their heads to stare. He threw Romy and Thea one last anxious glance and then yielded to fate. He held his hands out to the policeman for the handcuffs.

"Let's go. You don't have all the time in the world either."

"I think we can do without handcuffs." The policeman took the backpack off the giant man and guided him toward the exit. "You know what? Basically, I can understand you. There's also a lot that goes against the grain for me. Sometimes I think about creating havoc. But there are still laws."

"I stick to my own laws," said Merten and lifted his chin.

Chapter 6

Shortly before landing the clouds cleared. Romy leaned over Thea, and both looked excitedly through the window at the landscape below. The volcanic island, which was abundantly covered with vegetation up to the rocky peaks, was rising mysteriously from the sea. To Romy it seemed like a green primeval creature. She leaned back again. *Will I really find something about these Guanches here?* Guanche was originally derived from Guanchinet, meaning the original inhabitants of only Tenerife. In the Berber language *Guan* means person and *Chinet* was originally the name of Tenerife. The natives of La Palma were called Benahoares. Today, for convenience, all natives of the Canary Islands were called Guanches. Romy and Thea had been surfing the internet half the night to get more information about the Canary Islands and their history. It was massive. In antiquity they were already described by Homer as the isles of the blessed—an earthly paradise, which was said to lie somewhere in the Atlantic near the Western end of the then known world, a kind of Elysium, that no ordinary mortal could ever find. Those islands, it was told, were intended only for a few heroes, those chosen by the gods to achieve immortality. And this, according to legend, could only be reached by eating golden fruit that grew in gardens there and were strictly guarded by the Hesperides, the daughters of Atlas. All just legends, and yet Romy felt as if there was some connection to that potion from her vision. Was Iriomé perhaps even immortal and only living in another dimension now? Had she perhaps broken through some time barrier in order to give Romy insight into her life? But if there actually was such a thing, then a question remained: *Why?*

The seat belt sign was blinking as the plane slowly descended. The airport of Santa Cruz de la Palma was considered to be one of the toughest in the world. The runway was extremely short, and strong downdrafts could smash an Airbus against the steep rocks. Romy noticed how her hands went moist and her breathing quickened.

Thea put a hand on her shoulder soothingly. "Everything okay?"

Romy nodded and concentrated on breathing. Obviously, panic was still lying dormant in her, like a volcano from which one never knew when the next eruption would occur.

With a severe jolt they touched down and braked so sharply that they were both flung forward into their seatbelts. The passengers clapped loudly. Romy had always thought that was ridiculous but now could understand it only too well. She took a deep breath, undid the belt, and helped Thea get down her heavy backpack from the overhead compartment, which was apparently crammed with books. Normally, her friend devoured at least two each week. Even during their last vacation into the Andes, Romy had caught Thea with three thick books in her backpack.

A pleasantly warm wind received them when they walked down the gangway to the airport building. On the Atlantic, right next to the runway, small whitecaps were dancing. What a contrast to Germany! There the thermometer was minus three degrees with frost in the mornings; their plane even needed to be deiced before they could leave.

Thea had slept most of the flight and now was shivering despite the springlike temperatures. She pulled a woolen scarf tighter around her head but otherwise seemed quite cheerful.

"Well, how does it feel to touch the soil of your ancestors for the first time?" she teased her friend.

Romy didn't answer. Because it indeed seemed to her as if she was breathing this air not for the first time.

The airport building, a block built of practical dark gray concrete, unfortunately did not look at all like the gate to paradise. Modernity in its worst excesses had struck here with all its might. Setting off, however, went like clockwork. Their suitcases appeared almost first on the baggage carousel, and the formalities for the rental car were finished quickly, except for the additional charge for collection, which had not been mentioned in the bargain offer from the internet, as usual. Romy benefited from her still solid knowledge of the Spanish language to get them on their way.

The little white Citroën, which they finally located after a long search in the vast parking deck of the airport, seemed brand new. At least it smelled new, which gave hope that the brakes would work. This was essential for survival on the island; the travel agent had stressed this fact.

After a few kilometers it was clear what she had meant. As soon as they left the coast road to get to the west of the island crossing a high crest, they were facing one hairpin turn after another. Thea opened the side window and, just to be on the safe side, lay the barf bag from the plane on her lap. Romy tried to drive as slowly and smoothly as possible, so they had sufficient time to take in the impressive scenery.

Gigantic rock walls to the left, deep canyons to the right, and the same vice versa around the next bend. Mountain masses up to seven thousand feet high and surrounded by clouds plunged down to huge banana plantations by the sea. Most of the steep slopes were divided into cascaded terraces by countless walls of thick virgin stones.

"Well, I don't know whether the original inhabitants of the Happy Isles really had such a carefree life. Several generations must have piled all that up stone by stone with tireless energy for centuries," mused Thea.

Romy had to agree. Somehow she had imagined paradise a bit differently. Not so steep and wild. This illustrated how much stories and legends often differed from reality. Nonetheless she liked the landscape with its lush vegetation, changing texture and color from place to place. At the coast mostly different cacti and succulents were growing, thick plants with fleshy leaves. Higher up they found pink flowering almond trees and poinsettias that were several feet high. Then they drove through sun-drenched, spicy-smelling pine forests. And of course throughout the island, the Canary island date palms were prolific.

As recently as the day before yesterday she had "dreamed" of La Palma, and today she was here. Reincarnation or not, there was a reason for this! Romy had to find it.

"Look," Thea interrupted her thoughts, pointing to a town sign with the name of Tazacorte, which was half hidden behind a bush. "I've read somewhere that the Welsers owned vast plantations there in the Middle Ages. Wait a minute."

"The Welsers? Here?!"

Thea dug one of the books out of her backpack and soon found the right page. "Listen, in 1492 Spanish troops under the command of Alonso Fernández de Lugo landed at the coast of Tazacorte, to initiate the conquest of the island. In memory of the brave head man of the Guanchen, Tazo, who fell in battle there, the area received its name from the derivative Tazo and Corte—Tazo's court. The land around Tazacorte—which gets its water from the caldera, the huge volcanic crater in the center of the island—was later used for the cultivation of sugar cane. A competitor of the famous Augsburg Fuggers, the Welser trading house bought large parts of the territory in 1509, carried on commerce in the Canaries for a short period of time, but then oriented themselves more toward the New World." Thea looked at her friend triumphantly. "I knew it. My brain isn't eaten up by metastasis yet."

"As a native of Augsburg I find that interesting. But wait a minute . . ." Romy hesitated, then threw Thea a quick glance. "Are you thinking what I'm thinking?"

Thea nodded. "You wanted that old den in the Welser Kontor at all cost, it was freezing cold in winter. And I even needed to temporarily reconcile with my mother, so that you could get it."

"This can't be a coincidence, can it? There must be a connection." Romy suddenly became very excited. So many coincidences at once could not be possible. There was something going on. But what?

"Perhaps there's something around here like a museum with an island archive or an old convent, where records on former land tenure are kept?" Thea prompted.

"Glad I've brought you along," Romy said, grinning.

"That's right, and you should take advantage of every minute."

Romy pulled over and stopped the car. She could not help but take her friend firmly in her arms. Minutes later they were following signs past a malodorous sewage treatment plant, through a settlement of housing projects, then down to the beach, which made up for everything. Black lava sand formed a noble contrast to the deep blue sea and white surf. Along the boardwalk, seafood restaurants were lined up, in front of which tables and colorful sunshades were set up.

"It's hard to imagine that Spanish vessels once moored here, spitting out men in armor with swords," Thea said as she got out.

Romy agreed. For a brief moment she thought about being in Iriomé's shoes, who must have witnessed the conquerors landing and extinguishing her people almost completely. Much of that experience, Romy already knew about. The conquistadors showed no pity. With sword and Bible they subdued not only the Canary Islands, but large parts of the world. Those who did not convert to Catholicism had their heads cut off. Romy shivered, even though the sun was burning in the sky. Her head began throbbing again.

"You okay?" Thea gave her a questioning look.

Romy nodded. At the moment she didn't want to talk with Thea about her anxiety, which seemed to plague her more often again. "Shall we take a short walk along the beach?" she suggested instead.

They took off their shoes and socks, letting their feet sink into the fine black sand with the waves swirling around them. The water was a pleasant temperature. Numerous tourists were splashing around in the surge. Both women were letting their thoughts run free and just enjoying the warmth.

Thea linked arms with Romy and squeezed her hand. "I haven't even thanked you yet that we're both here now. It means a lot to me. Even though I can't explain it."

"There is actually something that you can't explain?"

They laughed. Romy hugged her friend again. For a brief moment they both were able to forget about Thea's illness and that the stay here could perhaps be their last time together.

A little later they were sitting in a small restaurant with wood instead of plastic tables, right on the waterfront. Romy ordered mineral water, table wine, grilled calamari, and a bowl of salad in flawless Spanish. Her stomach actually had been rumbling since landing.

As on the plane, most of the tourists in the restaurant were fifty plus. Mainly Germans, but also a few Dutch tourists. But at the bar stood a young native in his midtwenties having a cup of coffee. He looked friendly. Romy believed she had seen him at the airport. But perhaps she was mistaken. He kept looking over at them, but when she made eye contact, he quickly looked away, paid for his coffee, and left the bar. Thea seemed not to have noticed anything. Her eyes were closed as she enjoyed the sun on her face.

In a small grocery store and a health food store, they bought supplies for the next few days before setting out on a winding road to the northwest where they had rented a finca. After having followed the well signposted way up the coast for half an hour, they reached their destination.

Even from the driveway one had a fantastic view over the cliffs to the azure sea. The two women got out of the car simultaneously and stood still, thrilled by the magnificent view. They could hardly get enough of the vast ocean spreading out before them.

"This is really paradise," Romy said softly.

Thea smiled. "The island of the blessed. Now we only have to put the gods in a conciliatory mood so that they admit us to the number of the immortal heroes."

Romy sighed softly and then unloaded the luggage. She rolled their two suitcases down a stone path lined with tree-high cactuses to the finca. Thea followed with their shopping bags. The key lay as arranged on the door frame of the thick-walled, whitewashed square cottage whose corners were interspersed with dark natural stones in the typical Canarian style.

The old wooden door was opened after several futile attempts and gave a loud creak. . . . Curious, they entered the inviting space with an open roof truss. Through the cracks in the closed shutters, the sun was trying to come in. Romy immediately opened them.

The furnishings were simple but tasteful. A kitchen and dining area had an old, massive wooden table, a comfortable sofa, and a large, old-fashioned iron bed with pristine white bedding.

The second room was a bit smaller and also equipped with a double bed. Thea dropped onto it, exhausted. "Isn't it the custom in Spanish countries to have a little siesta after lunch?"

"Absolutely!" Romy helped her friend take off her shoes and covered her with a blanket. But Thea no longer noticed. *Perhaps a miracle will happen, and she'll recover here,* Romy thought, while looking at the sleeping woman. *Perhaps this is the reason my vision sent me here.* The next moment, however, Romy scolded herself for her wishful thinking. It was unrealistic. Thea was suffering from a highly aggressive form of cancer that had already spread. A cure was extremely unlikely. Quietly, she closed the door and went into the kitchen. As described on the leaflet at the door, she switched on the fuses so that the refrigerator turned on, then settled with a deep-drawn sigh in a deck chair on the terrace. She could unpack later.

Before long she fell into a peculiar state. Everything suddenly moved into the background. Berger, Avistan, the American company, concern about Thea, her fall, the Guanches, the island of immortality. The carousel in her head was turning, but not so quickly, and Romy felt it might come to a complete standstill. Something she had not managed to achieve for years.

Apart from the noise of the lizards, which were whizzing back and forth between scrub and stones making strange whistling sounds, and the chirping of a small, yellow-bellied canary, no sound was to be heard. No near or distant traffic noise, no radio or television, no police siren, no phone. Romy felt like sitting there forever. No need to do anything. No hours spent with the calculations of test series, no waiting for sensational research results that did not come, no turning nights into days writing reports.

"Strong vibrations around here, huh?" A warm male voice interrupted her thoughts. From behind a stone wall bordering the terrace, a tanned, slightly spent face appeared, framed by long, dark dreadlocks bound together at the neck. The smell of marijuana penetrated her nostrils.

"*Cannabis sativa,* the main active ingredient of tetrahydrocannabinol," she stated.

The hippie looked nervous and stubbed out his joint reflexively on the stone wall.

Romy laughed. "Don't worry, I work in drug research."

His face showed noticeable relief. "Hi, I'm your neighbor." Romy looked around but could not make out a house in the immediate vicinity. "I'm living down there . . . in the cave."

She spotted below the terrace, between cacti and wild fennel, a cave entrance with a wooden door and an old truck windshield as a window.

"Romy Conrad." She stood up and stretched out her hand to the Rasta. He wore wide Indian harem pants of an indefinable color, a faded purple batik shirt, and no shoes. She reckoned him to be in his late forties. She had believed guys like this were extinct.

"Sam!" He ignored her hand and hugged her instead, snuggling her at least half a minute.

"You're under stress, sister," he said. "But this is a good place to relax. I've just made fresh lemongrass tea. You want a cup?"

Romy glanced through the open bedroom window and heard Thea's regular breathing. *Why not?* Maybe he could even give them some useful tips, and definitely they would need some neighborly help sooner or later. She followed Sam down a small footpath to his cave. At the entrance, there was a high dragon tree.

Romy froze. Exactly the kind of tree in her vision! She could not help but lay her hand on the silvery bark, which felt rough under her fingers. Romy looked up into the mighty crown. The gnarly branches above her were rising up to the sky like the spokes of an open umbrella. At their tips long, sword-shaped leaves were hanging down in dark green tufts. Whether she wanted to or not, she could not escape the power that emanated from this tree.

"Aren't these trees cool? It's definitely two hundred years old, if not more." Sam peeled off a little of the red resin that stuck to the trunk with his finger. "When I have a toothache, I just lubricate my gums with it. That helps, at least for the time being. I'm not insured, and I can't afford a dentist anyway."

Romy gave him a compassionate look. "Do you know anything else about these trees?"

"What do you mean?"

"Well, in connection with the natives?"

"With the Guanches?"

Romy nodded.

"Yeah, for them they were holy trees. The leaves were used for weaving baskets, and they built their boats with the trunks."

Romy leaned against the trunk and actually believed she felt a certain familiarity and even security from the touch. Or was it all in her imagination?

From a tiny Moroccan pot Sam poured two bowls of tea and put them on a ramshackle wooden table outside the cave entrance.

"It's not so common in the twenty-first century to live in a cave," Romy stated, amused.

"Here it is," replied Sam. "Those who don't have enough money for a house simply rent or buy a cave."

"And live in it like ancient natives?"

Sam laughed. "Not quite. They didn't have solar power or a satellite dish or internet. If you're interested, feel free to take a look around."

He didn't need to offer twice. Romy stepped through the entrance and was pleasantly surprised. She could easily stand upright. Though the stone ceiling was rough, it had been whitewashed and was obviously waterproof. From flat stones and cement he had designed a cozy, snug berth, on which there were mattresses, colorful scarves, and countless pillows. It almost looked like a nice living area. This seemed to also be his bed, because in the corner lay a rolled-up blanket.

Several niches were carved right in the cave wall as shelves for books and all sorts of odds and ends. To the right of the entrance there stood a neatly polished gas stove; a sink, which was fitted into the wooden frame of an old table; and a shelf full of jars that were carefully labeled. Romy had to admit that one could comfortably live here.

"A cave is ideal," enthused Sam. "It's almost always the same temperature. In summer it is nice and cool, and in winter it protects you from the rain. In addition, I'm only paying fifty euros rent per month."

"That's really low." Romy thought of how much she had to shell out for her cold flat in the oldest part of Augsburg, plus utility costs.

"And apart from that you don't need much here. The avocados almost grow into your mouth, next month the oranges will be mellow, and bananas you get for free anywhere on the plantations."

Romy could understand him well. For someone like Sam this was the ideal place. Truly a paradise! A hippie probably wouldn't be able to live elsewhere anymore. In the hectic pace of a big city, in the shark pool of global wheeler-dealers, he would have no chance.

"The island of the blessed," cited Romy from her research.

"I don't know. But it's a special place, that's for sure. I've been to many magical places. To India, Ireland, Peru. But it's awesome here in the north of La Palma, energetically speaking."

"What do you mean?"

"Don't know how to describe this energy. Has something to do with the volcanoes, the magma, the past. It does something to you. The Guanches definitely felt that, too. You should visit their caves down in Buracas; they're quite unusual. Those who have a sense of it can still feel something there." He smiled at her. "You've noticed it yourself when you touched the trunk of the dragon tree just now, right?"

Romy felt called out and realized she was blushing. It was not easy for her to accept her feelings and not be ashamed about them.

"Down there we've already celebrated a couple of full moon parties where we drummed until the early morning. Eventually you're in such a trance that you no longer think this time is the real one."

"Especially if you had plenty to smoke." Romy grinned and decided to return to safer terrain.

"That goes without saying."

By now they had gone outside again. Sam pointed to a sunny, somewhat hidden corner behind a stone wall, where several six-foot-high hemp plants were neatly lined up. "I'm self-sufficient."

"And when is the next full moon party going to take place?" Romy thought perhaps she should engage in such an event. What could happen, after all? In the best case she would have some visions from the past and maybe understand the meaning of it all.

"I'll let you know," replied Sam.

"That would be nice of you."

"Want to give it a try?" He held out a joint, which he had lit as they drank their tea. "Best quality. Everything's organic."

Romy hesitated briefly but then accepted it. *Why not?* She inhaled deeply and felt the smoke filling her lungs. It had been an eternity since she'd smoked weed last. At first she felt a slight dizziness, but then her senses sharpened as if at the push of a button. The smell of fresh soil and fermented prickly pears rose to her nose. The cries of the crows, the humming of the bees, the chatter of the lizards was penetrating her ears much louder than before. As if she was summoned elsewhere. To another time.

After a further puff she passed the joint back to Sam. "Do you think the Guanches also used any drugs? They're said to have been a very spiritual people," she said, as casually as possible.

"Sure, all archaic peoples got in contact with their ancestors, spirits, and gods with the help of psychotropic plants." Like most hippies he was well versed in this field. His voice almost sounded as if he were giving a lecture. "In South America the Indians celebrated their rituals with peyote, curare, or ayahuasca. In Europe and northern Asia druids and witches used to take hallucinogenic mushrooms . . ."

"And the Guanches? What did they take?" Romy looked at him intently.

"I've no idea," Sam replied with regret in his voice. "In any case, nothing that's still growing here today; otherwise I'd have already discovered it."

Romy laughed. Then she glanced at the house. "I think I'll have to go now and look in on my friend. She doesn't even know where I am."

"No problem; we'll surely meet again. You can take the joint along with you and give it to her," said Sam. "As a welcome gift, so to speak."

Romy gratefully accepted. Of course she knew that cannabis was used in some countries as an official treatment for cancer. It stimulated the appetite and had an analgesic effect. It would do no harm to Thea anyway. "Oh, one more thing. Have you ever heard of amakuna?"

Sam shook his head. "No, what's that?"

"Never mind, forget it. And thanks again."

"No problem. Wait, take a couple of avocados; they're already ripe, and I can't eat them all." He thrust a few of the solid green fruits into Romy's hands and then made the peace sign with his index and middle fingers.

Romy grinned. "Thanks, that's really nice. I hope we'll be able to return the favor soon."

"Certainly, I'm not worried. Who gives, will receive," he was laughing.

Odd fellow, but kind of nice, thought Romy while slightly swaying. She walked up the small trail to their vacation home. Thea was already waiting for her on the terrace stretched out on a deck chair.

When Romy held out the joint toward her, she took it dumbfounded. "Since when do you smoke weed?"

"Opportunity makes devotees. We've got our private dealer right next door."

"What?"

"It's just a harmless hippie who's growing a little hemp."

"I can't even remember when I last held such a thing in my hands." Thea grinned and leaned back in her deck chair. Appreciatively, she inhaled the smoke, looking across a group of dragon trees out to sea.

Chapter 7

The next morning Romy woke up early. It took her a moment to remember where she was. No loud slamming of car doors, no garbage collection or emptying of bins with loud hooting and noisiness at an ungodly hour.

She stood up, slipped into her flip-flops, opened the patio door, and enjoyed a clear view of the Atlantic Ocean. This was something quite different from the early morning view from her bedroom window in Augsburg. The first rays of sunlight peeked over the mountains. They threw a gently shimmering light on the dragon trees in front of her, illuminating their reddish flowers. A hawk took to the skies right before her eyes, staying for a while at the same spot by moving his wings back and forth at high speed, then suddenly shot down like a rocket, probably to pick up his breakfast in the form of a lizard or a mouse. Romy also felt hungry but preferred a different kind of food.

The fridge was filled, and her mouth watered when she thought of the freshly smoked goat cheese they bought. She went to the kitchen and put the pie-shaped cheese on a plate with a good amount of red, shiny jamón serrano from the paper as well as some salted butter. Fresh spelt bread from the health food store completed the meal. In addition, she had raided the orange tree behind their house the night before.

With a sharp knife Romy cut the fruit into two halves and squeezed the juice into two glasses. She took a glass and drained half of it at once. Delicious. As sweet as sugar. Then she split Sam's avocados into two halves and decorated all with the yellow and red flowers of the nasturtium that grew rampant on the terrace and some lemon wedges. Finally, she got the simple clay plates from the dish drainer over the sink; laid knives, forks, and orange cloth napkins beside them; and viewed her work.

"That looks great," Thea's voice came from behind her. She wore a turquoise linen dress, had wrapped a cloth of the same color around her head, and stood in the doorway looking the very picture of health. For the first time in a long while she had rosy cheeks.

"And you look great, too."

"That's how I feel. I can only say thank you to these Guanchen, or Iriomé, or whoever called you."

Romy grinned. "Come, sit down and enjoy."

Thea actually had an appetite. Whether this was owed to the joint or the ocean climate did not matter at all. Romy felt grateful.

"Would you rather just relax today, or do you want to go on an outing?" Romy asked, while she smashed an avocado with a fork and sprinkled it with lemon juice.

"We should go to Santa Cruz. There's a former monastery, founded by the Franciscans, that now houses a museum of the island. The Spanish conquerors had monks with them, and they were the only ones who could write. Perhaps we'll find some original documents there with information about the Guanches. I think we should first study up on them before we venture into the terrain and inspect one cave after the other. It could take forever before we find the one from your vision. The more knowledge we have, the more we'll be able to narrow down the search." Thea had always been good at organizing. Here on the island her energy seemed to have come back.

"And if we actually discover the cave, what do you think we will find there?"

"Some kind of hint of amakuna. This potion is the key! I'm rather sure about that. I've been giving it a lot of thought. If the medicine woman of the Guanchen has traveled through time with its help, perhaps this can be done today as well. Who knows? Tichiname foresaw the Spanish conquest. Maybe you can travel back into the past instead of the future and contact this Iriomé."

Romy almost choked on her orange juice. "You've got some nerve! The medicine woman died in agony after she emptied the cup."

"I don't think the potion was responsible; after all, she had used it before. She died because she didn't want to experience what she foresaw and because she knew no solution to avert the bitter fate of her people."

"You mean she killed herself?"

"Yes, sort of." Thea lowered her eyes. "When you can't stand against a destructive power, it's sometimes easier to die than to experience the whole horror that's going happen to you, I think."

Romy eyed Thea attentively, contemplating what her friend figured out. And after having claimed only two days ago that it all had merely been a hallucination. On the other hand, Thea's situation was, to a certain extent, comparable to Tichiname's. Ultimately she was facing an invincible power in the form of cancer. Perhaps she also wanted to die before the disease destroyed her body like the invaders had destroyed the inhabitants of the islands.

"If the old woman killed herself, she probably took the secret of amakuna with her to the grave forever," Romy said thoughtfully.

"Or Iriomé as her successor has kept it somewhere."

"But that was over five hundred years ago. How can we find any traces today? Plus, these are all mere assumptions."

"And yet we're here! In for a penny, in for a pound. We can't back out now. Let's go. After all, I haven't got forever."

Just outside Tijarafe, a small village with box-shaped white houses, on the right side of the road a young man thumbed for a lift.

"Shall we offer him a ride?" Thea suggested.

"If you like." Romy pulled the car over and started. *Isn't that the young guy from the restaurant in Tazacorte?*

"*Hola,* where are you going?" he asked in pretty good German.

"To Santa Cruz," Thea answered.

"You give me a lift?"

Romy tried to catch Thea's gaze to signal she was not thrilled about this idea, but it was too late.

"Sure, no problem," Thea called to him cheerfully and thumbed toward the rear door.

"*Muchas gracias.*" He got in and made himself comfortable in the back.

In the rearview mirror Romy watched his alert, dark brown eyes. He actually looked quite friendly, but one never knew.

"You speak German well; are you a native from the island?" she asked skeptically.

He nodded. "From Tijarafe. I've taught myself to speak German because I've always liked the language. My name's Ricardo, by the way, Ricardo Cabrero."

"Haven't we met before?" Romy persisted.

"That's quite possible. I sometimes work as a tourist guide, pick up people from the airport and take them to nice fish restaurants."

Romy saw in the rearview mirror that he was winking at her. For some reason she didn't trust him. He had not said a single word about why he needed to go to the capital.

"If you want, I can show you Santa Cruz."

"A great idea." Thea ignored Romy's dismissive glance and sounded thrilled with the idea.

After a good hour's drive they parked the car between containers and trucks at the harbor, because according to Ricardo it was almost impossible to find a parking space downtown. On the quayside only three ships were anchored: the *AIDA,* a large German cruise ship, and two car ferries that connected La Palma with the Spanish mainland and the other Canary Islands. Apart from these, the whole port area seemed deserted.

"It wasn't always like this," Ricardo told them while they headed for the historic city center equipped with sun hats and cameras. "After the conquest of Benahoare, today's La Palma, and the foundation of the capital Santa Cruz de San Miguel de la Palma, the port very quickly became the main transshipment center between Spain and the New World."

"San Miguel de la Palma?" Thea asked stunned.

"Yes, after the archangel Michael. He's part of the coat of arms of the island. However, not slaying a dragon, but with a palm tree in one hand, the symbol of peace, and a scale in the other, on which the souls were weighed before entering paradise."

Paradise again. It was curious that this term appeared time and again in connection with the island, Romy thought. Even the belligerent invaders seemed to have noticed that this speck of land was special.

"Michael's also the patron saint of Germany, since the battle at Augsburg on the Lechfeld," Thea remarked.

Romy nodded and was again amazed at how much her friend knew.

"Almost any vessel plying between the Spanish mainland and the New World, which then had just been discovered by Columbus, made a stopover here," Ricardo said. "The island shortened the route across the Atlantic by almost 1,000 kilometers, which otherwise would have to be traveled without additional provisions."

"Then the conquest of the Canaries was a strategic move for further raids of the Spaniards in South America."

"Not quite. Columbus discovered America in 1492, the same year when La Palma was subjected. Thus it fit well into the concept of the Spanish crown. Later the Spaniards that were located in the capital received the privilege of using the new possessions to trade in the overseas territories. And in addition they did good business with the abundance of timber on the island. The woods then extended down to the sea, which was more than convenient for shipbuilders. Most of the frigates and caravels were built at that time in Santa Cruz. Later, however, all the ships on their way to America had to register in Tenerife and pay taxes there. Therefore the shipping traffic here came to a complete standstill, and the former commercial metropolis turned into the tranquil colonial city of today."

"But at least the authenticity of the island was preserved," Romy said firmly.

They had left the port area by now and were strolling along the Calle O'Daly. The historic buildings in Spanish colonial style now housed small boutiques, restaurants, and bars.

"And the Guanchen?" Romy asked. "What has become of them?"

"Those who survived were employed as workers by new Spanish settlers, unless they ended up in the slave markets of the mainland. They possessed no rights, and of course they did not participate in the new wealth of the island in the least. Many of the women also later married Spaniards."

I wonder if Iriomé escaped with her life? And if so, was she enslaved, or did she make it into some cave in the caldera where she could hide?

"They were very beautiful, the women of the Guanchen, tall and blonde with blue eyes, a bit like you." He threw Romy a searching glance. She felt that she blushed as if he had caught her doing something wrong.

"Then they must have originally come from northern climes," she said quickly.

"Not necessarily. There exist various theories. The most credible is that originally Berber tribes from North Africa settled the island. Berbers are often blond, since they mixed with the Vandals, a Germanic people that conquered Spain and North Africa in the fifth century."

Thea laughed. "The Germans—always looking for the sun. Nothing much has changed."

Ricardo smiled politely. "But there are also historians who believe that true northerners were involved: Vikings or slaves from Greenland that were settled here by the Portuguese. No one actually knows exactly."

"But you do know quite a lot. Is this taught in school here?" Romy asked warily. Somehow her suspicion that it was no coincidence that Ricardo showed up to guide them was reinforced.

"No, I'm just interested in my home island."

By now they had reached the Avenida Maritima. Romy remembered having seen pictures of it on the internet. In fact, the promenade looked even better in reality as far as the colonial architecture was concerned. Here stood the oldest Canarian town houses with the richly ornamented wooden balconies that gave the street its unique flair, especially when, as now, the waves came thundering over the embankment, their surf almost splashing up to the house entrances.

Thea took a few photos while Romy walked to the end of the road to the ruins of an old fortification. Lost in thought, she looked at the iron guns in their loopholes directed toward the sea.

"If the Guanchen had possessed such means of defense back then, they might have been spared the expulsion from paradise," she said to Ricardo, who had followed her.

"That's true. With their clubs and wooden spears they had no chance."

Romy gave him a sidelong glance. Was there genuine regret in his voice? It almost sounded as if he had been there at the time. They sat for a moment in one of the empty, sun-warmed loopholes. "It's a shame that we know so little about this people," Romy mused.

"Maybe it's a good thing," he said.

"What do you mean?"

"Because this knowledge should only be revealed to certain people."

"Who are you talking about?"

"Those who feel a connection to this people."

Romy looked at him. *What gave him this idea? He could not possibly know about my vision. I haven't told anyone except Thea.*

"The time will come when you understand everything . . ." he said, his gaze directed at the ocean.

Why was he so mysterious? Was it possible that he knew the reason for their stay on the island? But from where?

". . . and until then I just want to prevent something happening to you," he continued.

"What could happen to me?" she asked, worried.

He hesitated a moment before answering. "I hope nothing."

Despite this more than strange direction their conversation had taken, Romy felt they were finally on the right track. Somehow things seemed to fall into place, albeit slowly. Perhaps she just had to have a little faith—something she generally did not find easy.

Ricardo seemed relieved. Thea joined them, interrupting their conversation. "Want to move on? I think I've taken enough pictures of colonial architecture for an entire photo book." She linked arms with Ricardo and walked ahead a few steps with him. Romy caught up with them on the placeta, a small, picturesque place on which the tourists were toasting themselves in the warm midday sun in a variety of cafes. Ricardo ordered a *cortado condensada*—a small glass of coffee with viscous sweet condensed milk—for each of them plus churros, fresh spritz biscuits fried in oil. Actually, the churros were traditionally dunked into thick drinking chocolate, he explained, but considering the calories, coffee was the modern choice.

When Romy told Thea in the restroom about her suspicions that the meeting with Ricardo had been no coincidence, her friend agreed. Somehow, he must be connected to this odd adventure. Thea guessed that he had been instructed to not let them out of his sight. But by whom and why? She also had not succeeded in worming further details out of him yet.

Having paid the bill, the three set off for the monastery. They crossed the main square of Santa Cruz, which was tellingly called the Plaza de España and still gave an idea of the former power of the Spanish colonialists.

On the right side, it was bordered by the impressive Ayuntamiento, the town hall; on the left by the Iglesia del Salvador, whose mighty bell tower made of lava stone soared against the sky like a fortress. Even the wide staircase, which led to the artfully crafted door of the church, would have suited a cathedral. A unique exhibition of power, nothing more than what today's conglomerates were doing when they built gigantic skyscrapers with luxurious entrances for their headquarters.

The monastery, on the other hand, only a few streets farther away, looked relatively unpretentious from the outside. As they walked through the portal and entered the square patio paved with ancient flagstones, a comfortable silence welcomed them. The clean lines of the architecture and the strong contrast between the whitewashed walls and the balconies and cloisters crafted from dark teak conveyed immediately the typical severity of the Spanish Middle Ages.

Inevitably Romy had an impulse to lower her voice, although they were the only visitors. They followed signs to the exhibition room on the second floor, going up a wide, well-preserved wooden staircase, creaking at every step. In the former refectory, the dining room of the monks, stuffed animals that lived in and around La Palma were displayed: huge sea turtles, all kinds of seagulls, fishes, and lizards. In a small side room hung drawings and engravings of the endemic flora. Romy looked carefully at the inscriptions below each picture, in the unlikely hope of coming across amakuna. Even if the term really referred to a plant or fruit that formed the basis of the potion, the Guanchen word would hardly have been adopted into the Spanish or Latin languages.

Thea and Ricardo had already gone to the next room when a friendly, white-haired man in a dark suit and tie addressed Romy in German with a strong Spanish accent.

"You're interested in the plants that grow on our island?"

"Mainly in medicinal plants," Romy replied spontaneously.

"Are you a pharmacist then?" the friendly man with warm eyes asked.

Romy smiled. "Something like that. I work in herbal drug discovery."

"This is surely beneficial for mankind. My name's Manuel Gutiérrez. I'm the curator of this museum."

"Pleased to meet you; I'm Romy Conrad." She was about to shake hands, as was usual in Germany, but suddenly felt a bit awkward. "Are there any records at all of the plants that the natives used for healing or rituals?"

He shook his head, smiling. "I'm sorry. I think the Spaniards had little confidence in that. The Guanches were a rather primitive people, after all. They still lived, how should I put it, as in the Stone Age and were lagging far behind the rest of Europe regarding their developmental stage."

Romy felt the urge to defend Iriomé's people, but this surely would only perplex the nice old islander. Obviously, he identified more with the Spanish conquistadors than with the former inhabitants of this island.

"Have you ever heard of amakuna?" she tried anyway.

"What did you say?" The old man put his hand behind his ear the way older people do when they have not heard clearly.

Romy repeated the word, speaking louder, without success.

"No, I'm sorry. What is this supposed to be?"

"I'm not sure; it has something to do with the Guanches. I was hoping that I might find some information about it here."

He shook his head. "Unfortunately not; from this early period we have only a few original exhibits."

"But the monks who once lived here must have written down their impressions of the original inhabitants," Thea, who had joined them, chimed in.

Señor Gutiérrez looked from one to the other and suddenly made a mysterious face. "Perhaps I have something for you. Come with me!" With surprising speed he walked ahead, followed by the two women and Ricardo. They passed through a second smaller cloister, in the middle of which orange trees were in full bloom, whose sweet smell was downright overpowering. In the corridor one floor up, several technical achievements of the Middle Ages were displayed. An old grinding machine, a small weaving loom, a plough—equipment the Spaniards had brought to the island and that must have been completely unknown to the Guanches.

Señor Gutiérrez opened a high wooden door with iron fittings through which they entered a small library. Shelves filled with books reached from floor to ceiling.

"We have here probably one of the largest collections of books on the history of the Canaries from the conquest till today," he said proudly.

Thea and Romy decided to spend at least a full day in this library. Even at first sight, they spotted countless titles dealing with the original inhabitants. Gutiérrez had walked ahead and unlocked a door at the other end of the library leading to a small room. He turned on the overhead lights. In the middle of the chamber stood a glass cabinet with a nondescript book wrapped in an envelope made of brown, shabby fur.

"That's so typical of these museum folks," Thea whispered to Romy. "The most precious things they let gather dust in some back room, as if they want to keep the special things for themselves instead of displaying them. Reminds me of my mother." Even though Thea spoke little about her family, Romy knew that her mother often curated exhibitions in museums in Augsburg.

"With this *he* has led the savages to the true faith," Gutiérrez said in a low voice, which was charged with a good deal of respect. "Frai Hieronymus de Torremar, the first Franciscan to set foot on this island. It's due to him that the conquest ended without great bloodshed."

"That's not what I've been reading," said Thea, who the night before had devoured a book on the history of the Guanches, slightly indignant. "It must have been a terrible battle, in which many of the natives died."

Gutiérrez nodded. "Yes, but only in one battle. It was the last battle against Tanausú. He was the leader of the tribe from Aceró, who lived in the caldera, and was the only one who put up a fight against the Spaniards. But in the end of course they caught him."

"But not alive," replied Thea.

"That's right," Señor Gutiérrez answered. "When the great conquistador de Lugo wanted to take him to Spain to present him to Queen Isabella as a trophy, he's said to have killed himself on the ship." He shook his head uncomprehendingly. "To kill oneself is a mortal sin. What can you say?"

"Perhaps he preferred death to a life without freedom," Thea said. "I read that during the last battle many jumped to their death from the cliffs."

"Among the rural population suicide is widespread, even today."

Gutierrez leaned toward the two women, and there was fear in his voice. "Some still feel deeply connected with the Guanches and allegedly even perform their ancient rituals on certain days." He shuddered. "You should keep away from this, even if you're interested in culture. I, for one, want nothing to do with this! The house of a writer, who wrote a book about the natives, was set on fire and some scientist even murdered."

Romy didn't know what to make of this. She certainly was not indifferent to Gutiérrez's remarks. Before he could dredge up more scary stories, she asked if she could take a closer look at this Bible.

Señor Gutiérrez hesitated for a moment, but Romy beamed at him so trustingly that he finally picked up the glass dome and gently handed the old book over. When Romy opened the first pages of the fine parchment, she discovered records written in precise handwriting with pen and ink. Ricardo looked curiously over her shoulder. It took Romy a moment to decipher the old font, but the islander seemed to have no trouble with it.

"This is a vocabulary," he said excitedly. "Here, look! On the left it says *sol* and *magec* on the right. That's the Guanche word for sun. And here: *barco* and *naramotanoque*. This means ship."

"The monk tried to learn the Guanche language," concluded Thea.

"Definitely. And since he had no other paper at hand, he used the blank pages of his Bible!"

"Or he taught a Guanche the Spanish language," said Romy. "But how do you know that this is the Guanche language?" Romy turned to Ricardo.

"What else could it be? Also, some of these words are known. Their language hasn't been fully explored yet. But recently archaeologists have deciphered characters here on the island that resemble the Tamazigh or Tamashek, the Tuareg language."

Romy looked at him attentively. The guy really knew what he was talking about. Carefully she turned the page. The following pages also contained vocabulary. With difficulty she tried to decipher the words to get a feeling for the language. Then suddenly she caught her breath. The word on the left side was *Hieronymus* and to the right *Iriomé*. Beneath *takit* and *nombre*: name. She swallowed and looked closer. No, she was not mistaken. A person with this name actually existed!

Romy felt her knees become weak. Any doubts she still had were completely erased in that moment. She took a deep breath and tried not to let on anything was happening. Not in the presence of Ricardo. They were actually on the right track. Once she was alone with Thea, she would tell her about it.

Romy closed the Bible and handed it to Señor Gutiérrez. "Thank you very much. That was rather interesting," she said as casually as possible.

"If you want to learn more about the Guanches, you should pay a visit to the Museo Arqueológico Benahoarita in Los Llanos. It's open until 6 p.m. There you'll definitely find much of what interests you."

"Thank you very much. We'll do that," Romy said. "It's been very enlightening to talk to you."

"I'm glad," said the curator. "Feel free to come back, whenever you want."

After having said goodbye to Señor Gutiérrez and left the library, Ricardo turned back again as if he had forgotten something. Romy paused and heard him ask the curator in fast Spanish whether he could come back tomorrow and copy the handwritten notes of the monk.

"*Porqué?*" she asked him, now also in Spanish, when they were walking back to the car. "Why are you interested in what this monk wrote? What've you got to do with the Guanches?"

"I did not know you speak Spanish," he replied. "I'm interested in them because they're my ancestors. What's so weird about that? I think it's much stranger that you as a German want to know so much about them. What's *your* purpose?"

Romy decided not to continue the conversation at this level, at least not before she knew Ricardo better and knew that she could really trust him. Something was not fitting together. If he really worked as a tourist guide, he should have known Gutiérrez and probably known of the Bible. It was a small museum, after all. "Sorry, I'm a little mentally stressed and not as relaxed as the people who live here permanently." She struck a conciliatory tone.

"It will come with time," he grinned. "You've only just arrived."

Chapter 8

Los Llanos, the second largest city in La Palma, lay at the center of the island. Though almost twice as many people lived here as in Santa Cruz, at this time of the day the town was deserted. It was siesta time, so most shops would not open their doors again before five in the afternoon. *Actually a good idea to enjoy a little nap after lunch and tackle the second half of the day with renewed strength,* thought Romy as she threw Thea a worried look. Her friend was wiping sweat from her forehead. Even during the winter months it could get quite hot on the islands. They even had needed the air-conditioning during their ride into town.

The sun beat down on the square in front of the museum, a modern rotunda with glass surfaces. Next to the entrance rock fragments were arranged, into which different symbols had been carved—spirals, concentric circles, interlocking wavy lines forming a pattern.

"They're imitations, of course," said Ricardo. "But the real petroglyphs don't look much different."

"And it's not known what they mean?" asked Romy.

He shook his head. "At least the scientists don't."

"Who knows then?"

"Well, the Guanches themselves."

"But they're not around anymore."

He shrugged. Romy traced the symbols with her finger. Suddenly she saw in her mind's eye the alcove of her vision in which the bowl with the mysterious potion was standing. In the cave these very symbols were carved into the stone.

"Do any of these symbols exist in the caves?" she asked Ricardo.

He nodded. "Mostly they're found at former cult places and where there once were springs. The spiral is now something like the symbol of the island and is printed on T-shirts, mugs, and all that has remotely to do with the island."

Romy got the impression he was not too happy about this, as if the old culture was defiled somehow. "And what is the meaning of the spiral for the Guanches?" she asked.

"The same as for almost all archaic peoples. It's the symbol for infinity, for the eternally recurring cycle of nature."

"Even for reincarnation, maybe?"

"That I don't know."

"Have you ever heard of amakuna?" Romy didn't take her eyes off him.

"No, what's that?" He really seemed to have no idea.

Romy waved in dismissal. "It's not important. Let's go inside, it certainly won't be so hot in there," she said and went ahead.

In the museum lobby a school class that definitely had not come here voluntarily was roughhousing around. The teacher, a South American–looking, full-figured young woman, made a genuine effort to bring them under control. Some of the boys had folded paper airplanes from advertising brochures, which they shot wildly through the room. The young teacher was obviously on the edge of despair when the cashier finally gave her a sign that the wild pack of children could go in.

"*Venga, venga,*" she called in a loud voice, dragging a plump boy behind her, who absolutely did not want to move along.

Romy gave her a sympathetic smile, which she returned beaming. "You get used to it. I hope you weren't too bothered by the children."

"No, don't worry," Romy answered in Spanish, which she spoke more and more fluently now. Thea bought three tickets, and they entered a recreated world of that forgotten people who had lived here in La Palma, in one of Europe's outermost regions, until five hundred years ago.

The first thing they came across was a replica of a cave, which vividly depicted how domestic life was organized at that time. At the front was the hearth, in the middle lay thick slabs of stone to eat and work on, and farther back in the cave were the sleeping places. Next to the large cave there was a smaller cave in which the food was stored.

The information panels said that the Guanches cultivated corn, oats, beans, and lentils but also ate wild growing fruits such as dates or strawberries. They had herds of goats, a particularly strong race that was still farmed on the island. Their staple food was *gofio,* a mash of roasted fern roots and barley. The tribes of the coastal regions also lived on seafood. They especially loved the firm flesh of the *lapas,* marine gastropods which are found on the menu of almost every Palmerian restaurant, Ricardo explained.

In the next room there were mainly showcases with clay bowls and plates decorated with fine patterns, as well as necklaces and bracelets made of bone and shell. Romy couldn't get enough of them. She had always had a soft spot for relics and antiques. The older they were the more beautiful and more mysterious. That this had been a primitive Stone Age culture, as Señor Gutiérrez had called the Guanches, was definitely not the case.

"Their taste was good," said Thea, who especially liked the jewelry. "You could easily wear this today."

"The Guanche women had a very special position," Ricardo said. "Unlike the rest of Europe, they had a voice in all decisions and could keep up with the men physically. They were warriors and even participated in stone-tossing competitions. But mostly they acted as healers and visionaries, the so-called *harimaguadas,* who were highly respected and acted as advisors to the leader of the tribe."

Again it seemed to Romy that Ricardo was speaking about his own people, as if they were still alive. "A leader," he continued, "had to be of a high rank, into which one, however, was not born, but one had to work up to by an exemplary life and good deeds. Those who acted badly were reduced in rank."

"This should have been introduced all over the world; people would have escaped many despots," said Romy.

"The ruling class would never have allowed it," said Thea. "Those who are in power are usually unwilling to let it go. Nothing has changed in that regard."

Romy knew exactly what she was referring to. Suddenly a chill ran down her spine, and she thought of Forster's Health and her boss, Berger. She had hardly finished that thought, when the voice of the nice teacher reached her ear. The young woman apparently still had not given up trying to awaken the interest of her pupils for their ancestors. Though Romy could not understand everything because the noise level was rather high, a word caught her attention: *harimaguadas.*

The teacher said that not long ago four mummies had been found on the island, probably medicine women. The oldest had died one thousand years ago and the youngest five hundred. Romy could hardly believe it.

"Yes, that's right," said the woman, as Romy asked her to repeat what she had said. She was delighted that at least one person showed some interest in what she was talking about. "Mummies of harimaguadas!"

Romy swallowed. "And how do you know that they were harimaguadas?" She did not find it difficult to pronounce this word completely unknown to her minutes before.

"Because only they were mummified, they and of course the male tribal leaders. Furthermore, their stomach contents have been examined and remnants of an unknown psychotropic substance were found. So it seems likely."

Romy felt like she was suddenly in a mystery thriller. "How do you know all this?"

"My boyfriend was there. His hobby is rock climbing, and he helped the archaeologists retrieve the mummies from a difficult to access cave in the caldera."

Romy's face was glowing. This was just not possible! Thea had been right with her assumption: Tichiname must literally have taken the secret with her to the grave.

"Do you think your boyfriend would show us this cave?" she asked excitedly.

The teacher looked at her slightly puzzled. "I don't know, but he's not here anyway."

"Where is he?" Romy kept at it undeterred.

"He's in Ecuador on a climbing tour and won't be back for a couple of months."

"I was there, too, with my friend two years ago." Romy pointed to Thea, who was just coming up to them with Ricardo.

"These are Thea and Ricardo, our . . . guide. I'm Romy."

"Pilar," the teacher introduced herself and gently pressed her cheek against Romy's, once left and once right. "*Encantada*, pleased to meet you."

Romy told Thea briefly what she had just learned. Thea immediately wanted to hear more, while Ricardo's face darkened.

"Is there anyone else who knows the way to the cave?"

"*No lo sé*," said Pilar, shaking her head. "But I can ask Manolo when he calls me tonight."

"That would be great. My friend and I are passionate rock climbers, and we're also very interested in the culture of the Guanches."

"In stark contrast to the bunch here," she sighed. "Manolo says it is a most extraordinary, magical place. He wanted to show it to me several times, but so far I couldn't bring myself to go. These things scare me. My grandmother's from Garafía, in the secluded north of the island, and has told me about the creepy death rituals of the Guanches when I was a child. This imprinted firmly on my memory. Also, I'm not very athletic." She looked herself over, laughing. "I'd probably have to slim down a bit; otherwise the rope probably would break right away."

"It would be great if he could tell you the way at least roughly," Romy said in a happy tone to keep the subject alive.

"The caldera is a nature reserve," Ricardo interjected. "To go climbing there you need a special permit, which only scientists get. What do you want there? The mummies have been brought to the museum in Gran Canaria long ago. And now, in the winter, it's far too dangerous to climb there, especially when it has rained as much as in the past month," he added.

"Unfortunately, I need to check on my little monsters," Pilar apologized. "They have probably turned half of the museum upside down by now. It's suspiciously quiet. Here's my phone number; feel free to call me." She handed Romy a piece of paper, which she tore from a notepad and quickly followed her class into the next room. "*Oh . . . mi madre!*" they heard her cry.

Thea looked at Romy questioningly.

"Probably the kids have taken apart the caves, undressed the dolls, and dressed in their furs."

Before they could drop off Ricardo in Tijarafe, he cautioned them again against a tour into the caldera, described the dangers in colorful detail, and even worked in the cost of the rescue helicopter if they needed to be flown out. And suddenly he discouraged them, just as Gutiérrez, from digging deeper into the culture of the Guanches.

Romy and Thea promised him faithfully to go nowhere without letting him know, with which he finally contented himself. Meanwhile, it seemed more and more strange to them that he was so keen on playing their nanny. The real reason for his behavior was a mystery, but they knew there was something deeper going on.

At home on their terrace they decided to finish off this exciting day with a glass of red wine from La Palma. Thea especially was exhausted. Romy wondered how she hung on so well.

"To Iriomé." They clinked glasses.

"So?" posed Thea.

"What?"

"When do you call Pilar?"

"Tomorrow."

"Good. After all, we've conquered other mountains. This volcanic crater should not really be a problem. A rope and a few hooks can definitely be found somewhere," Thea said, so full of verve and energy that Romy could only look at her in amazement. "I'll see this through with you, and neither you nor this Ricardo or anyone else is going to stop me."

Romy looked at her friend thoughtfully. "What do you expect to gain by it?" she asked.

"Formerly, I'd have asked myself that, too." She laughed. "But look where my pragmatism has got me in life. Perhaps not everything is what reason dictates to us. I don't know. I just know that since your vision, or whatever it was, it all kind of . . . sorts itself out?"

Romy nodded. Actually, nothing surprised her anymore. Since they had landed on this island, she no longer had a grip on herself. It was as if someone else had taken over. The only question was where the path would lead.

Meanwhile the sky glowed in all imaginable shades of orange, creating a spectacular sunset. The touchdown, as the friends called the moment when the fireball touched the horizon, was in the offing. They looked over the sea in order not to miss it, when Sam's dreadlocks pushed into the picture.

"Hi, I don't want to bother you, but I have good news."

Romy groaned inwardly. He destroyed a magic moment. She was sure she had just seen Iriomé's face in the setting sun. Of course, it had been only an illusion, wishful thinking. But still.

"You've come to bring us more pot?" Thea said amused.

"No! Yes! You'll get some. But what I wanted to say is that tonight the moon is full, and there's going to be a full moon party down in the caves of Buracas. Maybe you'd like to come along?"

He vaulted over the low terrace wall, and this time Thea also got a hug lasting at least two minutes. "A few Rainbows from the last gathering will be there too. That's going to be cool."

"What on earth are Rainbows?" Romy asked, a little bit irritated.

"Don't you know the Rainbow legend?"

Romy shook her head. Another legend; there seemed to be no end.

"It comes from the Hopis and says that there will be a new tribe composed of people from all parts of the world, their colors as varied as the rainbow. After an era of exploitation and war, it will be this tribe that reconciles man and nature and heals the Earth."

"And you believe in that?"

"No," he replied smiling. "I live it, just like all the other hippies, environmentalists, artists, travelers, and dropouts."

Romy gave him a skeptical sidelong look.

"So you coming along?"

"Sorry, I'm exhausted," Thea said. "It's been a long day. I could fall asleep right now. But it's okay if you want to go." She winked at Romy. "You'll definitely get some new insights."

"Yes, certainly," Sam agreed.

Romy looked from one to the other uncertainly. "Oh well, I'll tell you everything afterward."

"I'll pick you up in two hours. Dress warmly; it gets cold at night around here." Sam had already disappeared behind the terrace wall.

"Well, to the hippies!" Romy raised her glass to Thea. "You know what they seem like to me? A bit like the Guanches from the museum. They're against technology, against violence, don't care for power or money, and live surrounded by nature."

"That's right. It's probably no coincidence that so many of them are running around here. On this island everything seems to come together somehow, as if there was a precise plan behind it," said Thea thoughtfully.

Romy marveled at how Thea's rationality had melted down. They both dwelled on their thoughts for a while and let themselves be captured by the tints of red and purple in the sky that now, just after sunset, were glowing intensely. Romy felt as if she was pulled away from her familiar world more and more. But where? *Where is this going to take me?*

The stony path on which she followed Sam down to the caves of Buracas offered a view so beautiful and unreal it surpassed imagination.

Almost like in her dream. A full moon bathed the rugged landscape, blossoming almond trees, cacti, and dragon trees in silvery light. Except for some dilapidated, thick-walled houses made of natural stones, nothing indicated civilization.

It was so bright they didn't need a flashlight to find their way. No wonder fantasies and thoughts of the supernatural were taking root here. The shadows the rocks were casting under the moonlight looked to Romy like alien beings that appeared at night to show people there was another world beyond theirs. A world that had its own rules. Maybe even a better world.

From a distance she heard the waves of the Atlantic thunder against the cliffs, and when the muffled sounds of drums and the bright sounds of flutes drifted up to them, the scenario was perfect. Fifty yards below the path a large fire was burning in a *barranco,* a deep gorge. Romy spotted cave entrances of various sizes in the rock walls around her. The smaller ones were partially blocked with wooden doors; the large ones looked like open mouths. It gave her goose bumps. Somehow all this seemed quite familiar. Like déjà vu. If a Guanche in fur clothing appeared in one of the cave entrances now, it wouldn't have surprised her in the least.

However, when they arrived, all she heard was a mixture of English, Spanish, German, and some Eastern European language. Neither the word *magec* nor *aramotanoque* reached her ears. Someone handed her a mug of hot chai from a boiling iron kettle over the fire. Romy nodded thanks, sipping the sweet liquid flavored with cloves and cinnamon. She sat down by the fire, stretching her feet toward the heat, and looked around. The men wore wide pants and the women long skirts with chunky knit sweaters or ponchos. Almost all were barefoot. Most had long hair, many of them dreadlocks like Sam, some decorated with beads and colorful threads. Two young women carried babies in wide cloths wrapped around their upper bodies. All were very friendly and peaceful. Everyone here seemed to have a task, but no one was in charge or gave instructions.

"You're also from Germany, right?" one of the young mothers asked, sitting down beside Romy in front of the fire. She said her name was Salima. She was at most in her midtwenties, was very pretty, and wore a funny hat.

"Yes, I'm here on holiday with a friend," answered Romy.

"We're always on holiday," Salima laughed. "Three hundred and sixty-five days a year."

Obviously I'm doing something wrong, thought Romy and grinned. "What do you live on?"

"It's no problem. There's always something left for us somewhere. And when we need money, we make music or juggle on the beach for the tourists. I sing, my boyfriend plays the guitar, and Amina, the girl over there, plays the flute."

Romy remembered hearing people play in Tazacorte outside the fish restaurants by the sea. And now she also recognized Salima's hat. "And that's enough to live on?"

"The less you have, the less you need."

"Do all Rainbows think like you?" Romy asked.

"Essentially, yes. We simply have no desire for so-called society. Being conformist, always having to catch up regarding money, status, friendships . . . And then the falsity of the powerful in politics and business."

Romy understood what the young woman meant, but she felt the urge to object. "And what about the responsibility one has to do something against this hypocrisy? Dancing and drumming won't change anything. Hippies already tried this back in the sixties and seventies. And look where we are now."

"But at least I can protect my child from this world, as long as possible. She's learning something valuable here. Among us, everyone's there for everyone. Everything's shared. There is no hierarchy; we decide everything jointly, no ego games, no one feels superior to the other. Of course there are arguments from time to time, but we try to resolve them peacefully and with respect for the other."

The island of the blessed, even if what the young woman was saying was true, seemed rather idealized to Romy. How on earth would the children get along later, when they left the island?

"You're going to find out," a tall, lean guy with long hair that almost came down to the waist chimed in. His gold-rimmed glasses were the only remainders of a previous, obviously bourgeois, existence.

"What do you mean?" Romy asked.

"Well, you don't look like someone who always keeps her mouth shut and dutifully marches in step. But that's what they want from you in the world out there. If you protest or even mess with those who hold the reins of power, you will have to run as fast as you can or be destroyed."

"And hide in a cave," Romy added, grinning. She was not sure whether the guy was a nutcase and suffered from paranoia or actually was on the run.

"They don't waste any time, you know. First you lose your livelihood, then you lose your family, and when they still haven't gotten you down, then it's off with your head. I'm George, by the way." He embraced her, but not quite as long as Sam had.

"So you're not here of your own free will?"

"No, but that's a long and especially ugly story," he replied seriously.

"Why La Palma?"

"This island's something special," Salima cut into the conversation.

"You mean because of the Guanches?" Romy was not quite sure what kind of people she was dealing with.

"I think it goes back before their time. The Canaries were once Atlantis, the legendary continent that disappeared beneath the waves of the Atlantic. Legend has it that the people there lived in a golden age of peace and harmony with nature. And some of it has been preserved here."

This was a bit much for Romy. However, she didn't want to disillusion the young woman. That would happen soon enough. On the other hand, she had encountered much on the island so far that had been of some relevance. Perhaps George's words were meant as a warning, which she'd better take seriously. Maybe this young mother could show her a new way.

Romy stared into the fire and suddenly wished she could share the attitude of this young woman. How awesome it would be if people could live in harmony with nature again. No more pollution. Respect for all living things. Healthy food and exercise in the open air. Many of the so-called lifestyle diseases would no longer exist. Both pharmaceutical companies and all connected industries would be superfluous in their present form. Doctors could really tend to their patients and would no longer be forced to make fast diagnoses and prescribe drugs. What a beautiful dream. But who could implement it in reality? She herself had already tried and failed when she wanted to enforce a few innovations that would have meant only minor financial loss to the hospital.

"Could you please look after my daughter for a minute?" Salima interrupted Romy's thoughts. "I'd like to do a bit of drumming, and she's fast asleep." Without waiting for an answer, Salima pulled her sling, including child, over her head, put it into Romy's arms, and ran off.

"That was quick," laughed Sam, who suddenly appeared next to her. "Looks good on you. You've got no children, I suppose?"

Romy shook her head.

"And do you want some?"

"I don't know. I've always thought it's not very responsible to bring children into this world. Besides, there are already enough. And honestly, I haven't met a man yet I think is suitable to be the father of my children."

"Uh-oh, that sounds like bad experiences."

"Well, we all have them, don't we?"

"You want to talk about it?"

Romy took a deep breath. "Better not."

"Come on!" Sam sat beside her at the fire and gave her an inviting look.

"Well, I've trusted the men, and then they went their separate ways all the same."

"And why?"

"I think I'm too complicated and not conformist enough. Maybe because I haven't said what they wanted to hear. I've no idea."

"And that's what always happens?"

"Yes."

"Then that's karma."

She couldn't help laughing. "Perhaps." For a brief moment the thought flashed through her mind that Iriomé might have had similar experiences, even though the women of the Guanches, in contrast to the rest of Europe, enjoyed a rather emancipated position. Allegedly. "I think my expectations regarding men are simply too high. Probably no one will ever meet them."

"Never say never."

Sam gently stroked her back; Romy enjoyed it. Of course, she was longing for a partner, and she also had not abandoned the desire for a child completely. A few times she had even tried to adapt, against her nature, to expectations, but in the long run she had never succeeded in playing the good girl.

"So you don't believe in true love?"

"I probably wouldn't even recognize if it were two feet from me," replied Romy, looking into the fire.

"You'll recognize the love of your life immediately," Salima said, who had heard the end of their conversation as she took her baby back. "Hey, why don't you two join in?"

Romy noticed that most of those gathered were dancing to the rhythm of the drums now. Though it was not techno or trance, the music types Romy preferred for dancing, the acoustics were still phenomenal. Sam took Romy's hand and pulled her up. She closed her eyes and, without even thinking about what she was doing, she began to move first her legs, then her hips, and finally her head to the rhythm of the drums echoing from the cliffs. She had never danced in the open air under the full moon before, but she liked it. After a while, she stopped worrying about the meaning of it all.

Eventually, there was only the music and the rhythm. Then suddenly a gentle flute melody snaked through the archaic tones. It penetrated her skin and made its way through her whole body. For the first time in a long time, Romy felt connected with herself. And in some way also with Iriomé. The more she reveled in this feeling, the more ardently she wished to finally be reunited with her.

Chapter 9

The next day, Thea's condition deteriorated dramatically. She felt weak and spent most of the day in bed asleep. Even worse, she felt severe pain in her bones, which could hardly be soothed by drugs. She also had no appetite, despite Sam's gifts, which he had brought as promised.

Romy was sitting by Thea's bed drawing up an injection of morphine. She administered it to Thea as carefully as she could, and the effect was almost immediate. Thea's face relaxed, and she sank back into the pillows. "Thanks," she said softly. "I feel better already. Fortunately the morphine still helps."

Romy had to restrain herself from crying on the spot. "We can always fly back, Thea. I just need to call Berger. He's got friends in medical repatriation. They'll be here in no time."

"I won't go back!" Thea turned her head to the window and looked out at a dragon tree and the blue sea. "Or do you actually want me to die all alone in an ICU?"

"Of course not." Romy stroked her friend's head gently over the thin hair. She had seen many people die during her time in the hospital, but to watch her own friend getting weaker and weaker was something different. She prayed to have the strength to be at Thea's side till the end.

"Have you already called Pilar?" Thea asked in a weak voice.

Romy shook her head.

"Get a move on."

"I won't leave you alone and climb into some volcanic crater just because . . ."

"Remember Iriomé. Her name is in the Bible of this monk; you told me yourself. And in the stomach of one of the mummies from the caldera, there was a psychotropic substance. What else has to happen before you take action and follow her call? That's why we came here."

"But you're not well," Romy said desperately.

"Right. But you are. And I may not have a lot of time left, so . . . please . . ."

Romy closed her eyes for a moment and took a deep breath. "I can't climb there alone."

"Take Sam along. He's a good guy. Certainly he must've been to the caldera more than once. This volcanic crater is not the Nanga Parbat. If you don't do it for yourself, then do it for me."

"All right, I'll talk to him," Romy said softly.

Thea smiled. "Thanks."

The medicine took effect, and she dozed off. Romy carefully arranged the blanket around Thea's shoulders and stepped out into the garden. She sat under one of the two dragon trees, leaning her back against the rough trunk. At that moment, like an unforeseen thunderbolt, a thought flashed through her mind. She actually winced. *Tichiname died under a dragon tree. Maybe there really is a connection between the medicine woman and Thea. Is their fate repeating itself? Is this why Thea wanted to come here to the island with me? Is this the reason Thea is so interested in visiting this burial cave? Perhaps she is wondering whether she and Tichiname share a history. What an obvious and at the same time absurd idea!*

What is wrong with me? I've never dealt with things so far removed from reality before. After all, I'm a scientist and not some airy-fairy esoteric.

But since falling off the cliff her life had taken a complete U-turn. What was yet to come? What had made this Iriomé show up and call her to the islands?

Never before had Romy had less control. She had never felt so unsafe. Even though she had failed in life now and then, and especially in her relations with men, she had always managed to regain some control over her life. This was probably due to the fact that she grew up without parents and had been forced to learn to hold her ground at an early age, even without backup. She developed a strong assertiveness leading to realizing her goals. But this seemed of no help at the moment. And her best friend, who had become the closest thing she had to family, would soon no longer be around.

Romy went back into the house and once again opened the door to Thea's room. She watched her friend for a while, almost as if she wanted to fix those features in her mind forever.

Sam wasn't particularly surprised when Romy later told him Iriomé's story over a pot of lemongrass tea. She deliberately left out another reference to amakuna. She was beginning to feel obliged to the oath Iriomé had sworn and nervous about mentioning it too often or to too many people. They were sitting on the terrace in front of Thea's open window so they could hear if she needed something.

"Here on La Palma the most fantastic things occur," Sam reassured her. "Most people you ask would say they've seen a UFO, not to mention ghosts and voices from other worlds. So don't worry about having a vision."

Romy had kind of figured it was like that here. She nodded, and he continued.

"I'm convinced there are things between heaven and earth that we can't explain. Not yet. Maybe later when we've lost our strong attachment to material things."

Romy looked at him thoughtfully. The people who lived here were definitely more connected with the true existence of the universe and also more autonomous. They could spend more time thinking and did not need to boost the economy every day, come hell or high water. Perhaps this was also the reason her thoughts here on the island drifted in realms that had nothing to do with her actual living environment.

"I'd love to come with you to this cave," Sam said. "I've climbed before when I lived in the Bavarian Forest and was trying to go through with my bank apprenticeship for my parents' sake. That was a while ago, but I can back you up in case you need it."

"And what are we going to do with Thea? We can't leave her alone here." The very idea, she would return and Thea . . .

"I've got a friend I can ask to come and stay with her for the day. For a few euros, he'll definitely do it."

Romy looked at Sam skeptically. "Who?"

"He's one of us and absolutely reliable."

Romy decided to throw her prejudices to the wind. "Thanks, I'm really glad for the help."

"Hippies are sometimes quite useful," Sam laughed, tossing back his magnificent dreadlocks.

"They're amazing people," Romy said, smiling. "Even though they don't pay taxes or contribute to the increase of the GNP. There should be more of them." She poked Sam in the ribs, stood up, went into the house and got her cell phone and the slip of paper on which Pilar had scribbled her number.

૭૦

"What's she doing?" the man with blue eyes and the scar on his brow whispered into the phone available for inmates of the remand prison in Munich.

"Her friend is very sick. But I think they're still pursuing the plan to go into the caldera," Ricardo replied.

"Stop her at all costs. In two weeks, I'm coming up for review; maybe I'll be released on bail. Probably they will already be back in Germany. Then we'll see. Thank you for your help."

"What's all this really about?" Ricardo asked.

"I can't tell you now. You have to trust me."

"I trust you," replied the young man from the island.

Chapter 10

Five o'clock in the morning, and the moon had just sunk into the sea. Romy made her way up to the driveway with the help of a flashlight. Sam was already waiting. He put his backpack beside the other stuff in the trunk.

Pilar had not only spoken with Manolo but even got the hand-drawn map from the archaeologists. And she had organized two complete sets of climbing gear.

The adventure could begin. Fortunately, there was only one road that led to the entrance of the caldera because the local guide fell asleep after a few kilometers and was snoring untroubled. With his dreadlocks under his woolen hat, he reminded Romy a little of Alex, the first man who took her climbing ten years before and who now was a sought-after surgeon.

She had first met him in the mountain rescue hut in Little Walser Valley and before long was spending almost every weekend with him in the mountains. After several months, however, all that was left were discussions about where to go for climbing or who should lead. For Alex, both the fun of climbing and of being with her had been lost.

When was the last time I went on holiday with a man? Must have been quite a while. Ages ago. After her relationship with Alex ended she had tried another with an orthopedic surgeon, then with a bank employee, and finally with a lawyer, but none of these lasted longer than a few months.

Romy startled when the noise level of Sam's snore reached an unbelievable high. Maybe men like this were more suitable for her. But if she was honest, she could hardly imagine living cozily in a cave without her iPhone, her computer, and buying shoes at least once a month. She especially could not imagine a life without her job. But what did she want instead? A man who might meet her expectations did not seem to exist. She simply had to face it.

Just beyond Los Llanos Sam was awake again and guided Romy to a place where they could park the car and climb into the volcano crater after crossing a wide and stony riverbed. Even though there had been a lot of rain during the winter, the bottom of the canyon was dry. They distributed the equipment on both backpacks and set off, Sam taking point. The sun had not yet made it over the hill, and Romy was glad that she was wearing a warm fleece jacket under her anorak. She loved these early hours—the mood of new beginnings and to still have the whole day in front of her, without knowing what it held in store.

"Did you know this is the famous Barranco de las Angustias, the valley of mortal fear, as the Spaniards called it? It is the only access to the interior of the crater without an arduous climb up the crater wall. The conquistadores got squashed here in their first foray against the Guanches."

Romy's gaze wandered over the steep, partially vegetated cliffs and she tried to imagine what had happened then. Probably the Guanches had thrown stones from the edge of the gorge at their adversaries to prevent them from entering the heart of the island. In this rough terrain it must have been almost impossible for strangers to find their way.

"Forty years later, Lugo tried it again, this time with more men and heavy guns, and then the same thing happened as in South America. True to the motto, off with your head if you don't want to be baptized. But many of the natives saw the conquerors as sort of supermen anyway and bowed to them voluntarily."

"Apart from the tribe of Tanausú." Romy had learned extensively about the leader of the tribe of the Aceró, who had once lived here in the caldera. Iriomé could have belonged to his tribe. If so, she must have moved about in the caldera, gathering herbs or food; perhaps she was even on the run. Or a captive of the conquistadores with her hands tied. This thought let a heart-pounding panic well up inside her. Romy forced herself to breathe consciously and regularly. Sam noticed something was wrong, but he asked no questions and did not mock her. He was a really pleasant companion.

After a while they heard a faint rushing. The riverbed became moister foot by foot. On a narrow path they walked up the river bank and were soon surrounded by a dense, fragrant pine forest and lush ferns.

"Look over there." Sam pointed at a huge stone pillar towering into the sky some distance off. "That's Idafé, the famous speaking soul stone of the Guanches. It is made of basalt and over one hundred feet high. Tanausú is said to have communed with it quite often."

"But it could not tell him what to do to get rid of the Spaniards," Romy replied thoughtfully.

"Perhaps."

"What do you mean?"

"Many of the Guanches jumped to their death from the high cliffs to escape slavery. *Vácaguaré,* they cried. That means: I want to die."

Romy stopped abruptly. "That's impossible!"

"What?"

"Repeat that word!"

Sam shrugged. "Sure. *Vácaguaré.* Or maybe *vacáguare.* I don't know the exact pronunciation. What about it?"

"If I'm not mistaken, it is exactly the word that this medicine woman said when she died in Iriomé's arms."

Romy repeated the word stressing the last syllable. Vacaguaré. It came from her lips easily and sounded exactly as Tichiname pronounced it shortly before her death. Romy closed her eyes for a moment. More and more things were falling into place. Like a jigsaw puzzle coming together. What the final image would look like, however, she could not imagine.

"Do you know the legend of the *guerreros sagrados*?" asked Sam.

She shook her head. "I know a couple of legends that are connected to this island, but I haven't heard of this one."

"The guerreros sagrados are holy warriors who are considered immortal and appear over and over again in different centuries to fight against evil and destruction in the world."

"You mean immortal heroes, like those that lived here thousands of years ago according to the ancient Greeks?"

"I haven't a clue. I don't know much about antiquity, but did you see the film *Highlander*?"

Romy vaguely remembered the movie with Christopher Lambert and Sean Connery. It was about an immortal Scottish warrior from the Middle Ages, who in the present encountered his deadly enemy from the past. This subject seemed to exist in many archaic cultures. "And what made you think of it? Do you believe the Guanches had their own type of Highlander?"

"Or even have one today! A Palmero told me so at a fiesta; however, he was already pretty drunk. When I wanted to know more, he was rather mysterious and didn't breathe another word about it. So I did some research on the internet but without much success."

"And you believe that?"

"I think it all depends on how you interpret it."

At the moment Romy no longer knew how she should interpret what had happened during the last four days. "Do you actually believe in reincarnation?" she asked Sam, who had walked on.

He stopped and turned to face her. "I don't think that all is over after death. In nature there's a kind of cycle, and everything starts anew. I can well imagine that certain things are brought to light time after time because their development is not yet finished."

"Yes, I know, but I mean in concrete terms."

"You mean, if you could be the reincarnation of this Iriomé?"

"Yes." It was still a bit embarrassing to express this thought.

"I've only heard of children who recall earlier lives. Most adults would never admit it if they actually did remember for fear of ending up in the loony bin. But go and have a look in an esoteric bookstore; they have yards of books on this subject."

He stopped in front of a rusty screen door, which closed a cave entrance that was partially bricked up with concrete blocks. "Look. Supposedly this was the cave of the great Tanausú."

Romy tried to peer inside through the iron bars, but except for a few old boxes and a large chain saw she could not see anything. She looked at Sam, disappointed. "Looks more like the storeroom of the forest administration. There's not even a sign. What a shame."

"I know. Today's Palmeros don't necessarily consider themselves the descendants of the Guanches; they feel connected to the Spanish conquistadores. But recently they've begun to raise monuments for the original inhabitants, and streets, shops, or schools are named after them. But I'm not sure if that comes from the heart or is just for marketing purposes."

Romy thought of Señor Gutiérrez from the museum. He had called the Guanches primitive Stone Age people. Even Pilar did not seem to be proud of her heritage. Although her parents were from Garafía, the northernmost community, where most of the families lived who still had some Guanche blood in their veins, she felt in no way connected with them. And Ricardo? Romy still could not figure him out. He seemed proud of his heritage, but somehow he did not want to show that.

೦ನಿ

Three hours later Romy and Sam had advanced deep into the caldera. The path along the crater wall became narrower. They could only progress sideways, their backs pressed against the wall. Beneath them pieces of rock broke off repeatedly and clattered into the depth. Romy was used to it, but Sam flinched each time and was constantly looking for a hold.

"We're almost there," she reassured him, studying Manolo's map. And indeed, soon afterward a large platform opened before them, from the rear end of which a gigantic, almost vertical wall rose up to the sky. In its upper part yawned a dark cave entrance surrounded by several smaller openings. "There it is," she said excitedly. There was a buzz in her ears, and she felt slightly dizzy. "That's it, the cave from my dream!" It almost seemed as if she had returned to a place from her childhood after many years.

"Wow. Then you're here, so to speak, at your destination."

She just nodded.

"Means we need to climb up there," Sam sighed.

Romy could see he was far from feeling comfortable at the thought. "In the past the caves were connected with ladders made of tree trunks," Romy recalled from her vision.

"What a pity they're no longer there; that would've been convenient."

"Don't worry, we could do this blindfolded," she tried to calm him. "But something's different . . ."

"What?"

"It's missing! The dragon tree where Tichiname died."

"Dragon trees don't grow up here. It gets too cold in the winter."

He was right. Farther down there were still some pines; here only low windswept shrubbery covered the rough rock. Maybe the tree was indeed specially connected to Tichiname, and only she had been able to grow it here.

"Let's get it over with." Sam opened his backpack and got out a rope and hook while Romy checked the condition of the wall. "Someone has recently been climbing here. There are relatively new hook holes," she stated with an expert eye.

"Maybe this Manolo came up here again and showed someone the cave."

"Perhaps." Romy put on her climbing harness, hooked up with the carabiner at one end of the safety rope and examined whether it was tight. "I'll climb first, okay? Can you handle backing up?"

"Sure. Don't worry." Sam took the other end of the rope, checked the guide plate and then gave Romy enough play to go onto the wall. She was immediately in her element again, felt neither panic nor any uneasy emotions rise inside her. After about six feet she set the first hook.

The basalt rock, soaked by the sun, was slightly crumbly. She hoped the hooks would hold. She'd had enough of tumbling down.

Without much effort, she instinctively found the right grips and footholds, although she had never been here before. In no time she reached a ledge, which, though it was a foot wide at the most, seemed to hold her weight. "Okay, stand," Romy called from above. She saw Sam hesitate.

"Don't worry, you'll be all right," she encouraged him. "Just take the same route as me." She vividly recalled her first attempts at climbing and the fear, which lessened the more often she overcame it. Foot by foot Sam made his way up while Romy watched attentively from above. He slipped only once, but the rope held him without any problem.

When he finally reached the edge of the cliff, Romy helped him pull himself up and patted him on the shoulder appreciatively. Sam was breathing heavily. He hardly dared to look down. "And all this because of a vision," he gasped. "The things I do!"

Romy shrugged. "Now since we're here, we'll figure it out together."

He nodded resignedly. After she checked his stand, she set out for the next leg. From there they would reach the cave without another stopover. While Romy pulled herself up along the wall bit by bit, an absurd thought crossed her mind: *If I fall now, I might meet Iriomé again.* Since they were on this island, the longing for a reconnection with the Guanche woman had become ever stronger. She had become almost something like a soul sister. But before Romy could analyze this thought, she reached her destination and pulled herself with all her strength over the edge onto a small open space in front of the cave entrance.

The view from up here was staggering. Before her spread a green primeval landscape that now, in winter, was crossed by little streams and waterfalls that meandered like glittering snakes around the bizarre rock formations. When she looked over the crater rim out at the sea, she could see in the distance the peaks of other Canary Islands, Tenerife, Gomera, and El Hierro, peeking out of white clouds. It was exactly the perspective she recalled from her dream. Romy sat down at the very place where the dragon tree must have stood and waited for something unusual to take place. But nothing happened. Only the whispering sound of the wind and the cawing of a few jackdaws reached her ear. Almost *déjà vu*. And all this had started just a few days ago.

"What's up?"

"Oh!" She almost had forgotten Sam. Romy got up, secured the rope, and stepped to the edge again. "Everything's okay!" She pulled him up more than he climbed for the rest of the way. She was really glad to have him. How silly of her to have treated him a bit disdainfully at the beginning.

Sam was out of breath and needed to sit down for a moment. He seemed to find it a bit embarrassing because he turned his back to her, unfastened the rope from the harness with trembling fingers, and took a deep drink from his water bottle.

"Just get some rest," she said. "That was quite a challenge for a beginner."

"Oh, and just a moment ago you said everything would be easy."

Romy smiled. "What else could I have said?"

"All right." He straightened himself and took a few steps toward the cave entrance to distract from his dizzy spell. "Come on, let's dive into the past. Maybe the mummies have returned."

Men are all the same, thought Romy. *Whether in dreadlocks or short corporate hairstyles.*

The sunlight was enough to light up the rock walls in the cave entrance. Fascinated, Romy looked around, then got out a flashlight and followed Sam.

"Look, everything here is full of symbols," he said, impressed, illuminating large spirals, triangles, concentric circles, and diamonds with a flashlight. With a lot of imagination Romy could recognize a dog among the carvings. If this was really the right cave, the bowl with the potion that made Tichiname travel into the future had been placed somewhere close. Romy photographed each detail, no matter how small, for Thea. Who knows what her meticulous friend would discover.

"I've never seen so many petroglyphs at the same place," Sam said. "They're certainly original. It's a pity no one knows what they mean."

Almost reverently Romy traced a finger over the rough outlines of a spiral from the center outward. The sign of infinity—the eternal recurrence of being. Did this cycle of life really exist? Didn't all things come to an end eventually? If she was honest, she could imagine neither the one nor the other.

"Come on, let's try to find the burial cave and then head back before it gets dark," Sam interrupted her thoughts. He was right. After all, that's why they were here. Romy got the map out of her pocket and turned it round a few times to find her bearings. In doing so the map slipped from her hand. When she bent down to pick it up, she suddenly stopped short and remained sitting on her haunches frozen. A shiver came over her; she got goose bumps.

"What's wrong?" asked Sam.

Romy didn't answer. There it was—the little niche where the bowl with the mysterious potion once stood! The symbol on the walls had been deeply engraved in her memory. No doubt, this was the right place.

"Nothing," she answered Sam, since at the moment she didn't feel able to express her feelings in words.

From the main cave two passages branched off that led into the interior of the mountain. According to the map, the right passage was the one they needed to follow.

The ceiling was relatively low, so they needed to stoop. In some places water was running down the walls, giving the basalt a dark and shiny color. Romy shivered. The deeper they got inside the mountain, the lower the temperature became. A slight cooing came from niches where pigeons had built their nests.

Suddenly Romy stopped. In the beam of her flashlight shone a white pile of bones. She was almost frightened to death.

"Just a goat that didn't find its way out again," Sam remarked soberly. "However, the question remains how it got in here. Certainly not with the climbing rope. This means there must be a less arduous entrance somewhere."

"Do you have fresh batteries in your flashlight?" asked Romy, who wanted to escape the fate of the poor goat.

"Sure, I'm a cave dweller with regular power failure myself, after all."

They followed a stone shaft that pushed forward in a straight line for about twenty meters and then made a sharp right bend. Behind it the initial darkness turned into a kind of fog. It seemed to Romy as if they had left the present time. For some reason she felt no fear in here; rather the opposite: she gained confidence in what had brought them here and a kind of security being deep in the bosom of the earth.

Just beyond the bend the passage ended in a second cave whose ceiling was much higher than the first one and with a hole in the ceiling through which daylight was coming in. The high walls gave Romy the impression of being in a cathedral. The goat had probably fallen down here and then had trudged as far as it could.

A startled bat brushed Romy's cheek. She looked after it as it disappeared into the depths of the cave.

"What's taking you so long?" she heard Sam's muffled voice up ahead.

"I'm coming," she called, and the echo carried the words back to her ear. "I'm coming, I'm coming."

As if in a trance, she walked on and nearly collided with Sam. He stood in the middle of the passage illuminating the rock walls with his flashlight. "According to the map, it would be right here." He pointed to a bare rock face. "But I don't see anything!"

"Let's look closer at the map." With focus Romy studied the drawing in the light of the flashlights and came to the same conclusion as Sam. "It must be here. We've followed the passage shown on the map exactly. First the narrow passage, then the small atrium, then the cathedral, and now this left turn."

"I don't get it either."

"The grave can't simply have vanished into thin air," Romy said, almost defiantly. They were so close. This climb just could not be for nothing.

Sam again illuminated the damp walls. Suddenly he stopped. "Look!" In the light cone of the flashlight about fifteen feet high they discovered a small niche that obviously had been closed by humans with piled-up stones. "That must be it!" he said excitedly.

"Someone must have closed the grave again," Romy speculated. "It's funny, Pilar didn't say anything about it."

"She also didn't mention it's so high up," said Sam, who began to realize what would follow now.

"I'll go back and get the hammer, hooks, and the second rope from the backpack," Romy said.

Sam was less enthusiastic. "Maybe there's a good reason the grave is closed?"

"What?"

He just shrugged his shoulders.

"You just don't want to climb."

"Exacto."

"Then I'll do it alone!" Without paying any further attention to Sam, she walked back to the cave entrance, where they had left their backpacks. Thea would never forgive her if she gave up now, so close to their goal, not to mention her own self-guilt.

Upon her return, Sam was cooperative and promised to belay her from below.

"Ah, there you go," she said, grinning at him. She only needed to set two hooks to pull herself up to the bricked-up grave.

Her hand trembled as she firmly hit the hammer against the stones. Nothing stirred. This wall definitely had been erected by a Palmerian master of wall construction, because the stones were cleverly wedged into each other as if mortar bound them together. Romy tried again. Nothing.

"Let me do it; you won't manage alone," the macho in the hippie called up.

Romy stepped down and handed him the hammer. "Thank you."

Shortly afterward, his admittedly more powerful blows were echoing through the dark passages. After the third blow the first loose rock came crumbling down. Romy hoped fervently that the cave would not collapse. Hadn't this been the ending of *The Mummy*? She had watched the horror movie one night on pay TV, and as far as she could remember, almost all of the researchers had been buried alive in that scene.

There was a cracking sound. Romy winced.

A stone had popped off the wall and dropped on the ground right next to her. "Watch out!" Sam cried too late from above. Now more stones were crumbling down, and a small opening appeared. Sam pushed himself up with both arms and shone his flashlight into it.

"What do you see?" asked Romy excited.

"You won't believe it. Unbelievable!" Sam eased himself down and handed her the lamp. "See for yourself."

She hesitated. Suddenly she was afraid of what she would encounter. Sam handed her the rope. She took it, supporting herself with her feet against the wall and pulled herself up rapidly.

What she saw was overwhelming. The floor of the grave chamber was covered with a fairy ring of long-stemmed white fungi with tiny cones, like a spiral of infinity. It had to be a kind of sac fungi, but a variety that Romy had never seen before. How unusual that it was growing here in complete darkness. Slowly she let the beam of the flashlight wander from one side of the chamber to the other, discovering several cavities, probably the resting places of the mummies. Pilar had said nothing about fungi. Maybe they grew only in a certain season; namely, now in winter. Otherwise they would have been found when the mummies were recovered.

"Do you have a plastic bag or something?" she called out to Sam.

"I do." He buttoned his empty lunch sack on the rope so Romy could pull it up.

With extreme caution Romy took some mushrooms and let them slide into the bag. They were soft and velvety to the touch—as if they were not from this world. The thoughts in her head were in turmoil. *Are these mushrooms amakuna, the heart of the island that beats in the cave of the highest mountain, the secret of the Guanches? Am I about to make a revolutionary discovery that could change the world? Perhaps the way Alexander Fleming did when he discovered penicillin, only on a different level? But how is this connected to Iriomé's and my lives?*

Carefully she tied the bag and eased herself down on the rope, landing but not feeling as if she had solid ground under her feet again.

"Hey, what do you think, I bet this is some kind of magic mushroom." Sam was quite exhilarated as he took the rope off the hook and rolled it up. As an expert Romy knew various sac fungi contained the hallucinogenic drug psilocybin, but these normally didn't grow in caves, but on cow dung or molding wood and also did not have this snow-white color.

"I bet that those medicine women used these mushrooms for their magic rituals. I'm going to make a soup tonight." The anticipation in his voice was obvious.

"Take it slow," warned Romy. "Those are not normal magic mushrooms. You know as well as I do. Maybe they're highly toxic. The medicine woman in my vision might have died from them."

Sam's euphoria deflated just a bit. "Well, you're the specialist," he admitted. "What will you do with them?"

"I'll take them to Germany and examine them in the lab."

"They won't last that long," he said skeptically.

"In their dried form, it shouldn't be a problem."

"How do you know they will still have the same effect dried?"

"Because the DNA doesn't change even after a long period of time. Also the substance in the stomach of the mummy could still be identified after more than five hundred years."

"You really think it contained these fungi?"

Romy didn't answer.

"So if the stuff is really hot, you'll have to tell me, I'll come up here again and get me more of them."

"Promise. But until then, we'll keep it to ourselves. Agreed?" Romy asked as insistently as she could.

"My lips are sealed," Sam said with mock seriousness.

Romy was well aware this would not be their last discussion on the topic, but under no circumstances did she want Sam to give the mushrooms a try. If they really were the secret of the Guanches, this secret should be preserved. Bad enough there was still this Mister Unknown, who apparently had been in the cave before them and bricked up the grave. Things felt out of control. She wanted to make sure they covered their traces.

"All the stones back up again? Is that really necessary?" Sam was getting really annoyed. "Then it will be pitch-black when we get back," he said in an attempt to cut short this new effort. But Romy persisted.

"The mushrooms obviously grow only in winter. The mummies were found last summer, and apparently nothing was growing here then; otherwise we would have heard of it."

"Or not. If they really are hallucinatory, it wouldn't be broadcast. Otherwise streams of hippies would pilgrimage up here."

He had a point. Nevertheless, she felt uneasy. "If we put it all back into its original state, no one will notice I've taken some. Officially, we can't climb here at all and could get into a lot of hot water if the forest rangers find out."

Sam admitted defeat. "If you insist." Grumbling, he hooked the rope in again, getting ready to climb. "Throw one stone up at a time so I won't have to climb up and down all the time."

In no time, Romy mastered a technique to throw each stone almost precisely where Sam needed it.

"You really have it; have you ever been German champion in stone throwing?" Sam's bad mood improved as things went quicker and easier than he expected.

"Maybe," she answered. "In a previous life."

Romy was surprised how easy it was for her to lift even heavy chunks and know exactly how much momentum was needed to toss each one. As soon as they closed the niche they set off for the cave entrance. Romy stowed the bag with mushrooms in her backpack and watched Sam climbing down the crater wall first. After a last look at the caves she followed him into the depths of the canyon.

The way back took much longer than expected, and it was well after dark when they reached the car. Romy tried to call Thea on her cell phone once they had reception, but Thea didn't answer.

Sam's friend met them at the driveway above the finca. Unlike Sam he was bald and wore a full beard made into a little plait at his chin and decorated with a red bead at the end. Warm, gentle eyes contrasted sharply with his wild exterior.

"She's just fallen asleep. At sunset she was in pain and was sick. So I gave her the pills you left and made her a joint. After that she felt a little better." He smiled slightly embarrassed. "As a nurse I'm probably a lemon."

"No, you've done everything right," Romy reassured him. "Thanks for the help."

"No problem, but . . . I think she . . . she's really not well."

"I know." Romy handed him fifty dollars, which quickly disappeared in his colorful bag printed with Indian gods.

"Thank you. So, I gotta go."

She turned to Sam. "Here, you don't have to go empty-handed." She tried to give Sam a fifty-dollar bill, but he declined.

"It was a pleasure to help you, but I want to have a share of the find, once you have studied it. Don't forget."

"Of course not," she said. No way she wanted to get into a discussion with Sam at this hour.

After he walked off, she ran to the house and looked in on Thea. Thanks to the strong pain killer she was fast asleep. Romy would tell her everything tomorrow morning and share all the finds.

The mushrooms were still white when she spread them neatly on the old wooden table in the kitchen. At the edges, however, they already had a slight yellow tinge. Iriomé had gathered amakuna at the right time and then cooked it over the fire until the shadow of the time bar had wandered from one stone to the next, Romy recalled.

Maybe the fungus only took effect when freshly cooked? *Until the shadow of the time bar had wandered from one stone to the next . . .* that meant possibly an hour? Had it perhaps lost its effect already? And how many mushrooms had Iriomé used? The right dose could mean the difference between life and death, particularly in plant medicine.

Do I really dare to carry out an experiment on myself? Romy's reasoning as a biochemist advised her strongly against it. The scientifically correct procedure was to dry or freeze the mushrooms and make a comprehensive analysis in the lab back in Germany.

Romy was pacing up and down the kitchen, unable to take her eyes off the mushrooms. The yellow tinge had already become stronger. That worried her. She lied to Sam. Subsequent laboratory tests could not in all cases determine the effect the mushrooms would have when fresh. Finally, she made a decision. She had taken ten fungi. She would cook five right away and dry five in the oven at a low temperature.

After she had brought a small pot of water to a boil, she put the mushrooms that now were dyed yellow into it and let them simmer over low heat. Excited, she kept looking at her watch. She almost felt like she did before her first experiment during her first biochemistry semester at the university. There was a slightly earthy odor. Romy opened the kitchen door in order to let some fresh night air in.

She stepped outside and looked at a starry sky of the kind one would actually expect only in the desert or far out to sea. A shooting star fell into the sea, and she took that as a sign. Today was December 21. Winter solstice. The same day on which Tichiname wanted to travel *beyond the limits of time* using the mushroom. Would she also be able to look into the future or maybe even into the past? Would she actually survive this experiment? Perhaps she should leave a kind of written statement in case something should happen? *What nonsense!* She didn't update her will every time she wanted to go climbing. Impatient, she looked at her watch again. The hands seemed to move forward in slow motion. She went back into the house and again checked on Thea, who was fast asleep. Should she wake her friend? Romy was torn. No. She had to face the music alone, so to speak.

Finally, the time had come. The mushrooms had dissolved in the water and formed familiar yellow streaks on the surface. Romy stirred them evenly with a wooden spoon, just as Iriomé had. Then she poured the brew into a small porcelain dish and put it in front of her on the kitchen table. She was overwhelmed by a feeling she knew too well. It was the same inner vibration felt when she attacked an unknown rock face of a high grade of difficulty. A sense of insecurity willingly accepted that gave her this special kick. The kick of being part of the free play of natural forces and not knowing how the game would turn out. Giving it her all to win.

She took a deep breath, held the cup in both hands, and drank the first sip. And then another. There it was again, the earthy, slightly putrid taste. She was still curious how it appeared in her mouth after the fall days ago, but then a strong dizziness stopped all thoughts. The cry of a night bird reached her ear. It seemed as if somebody called her.

Far in the distance, in a blue mist, she saw Iriomé. Iriomé held her head in her hands, and in her eyes tears glittered.

Chapter 11

Tichiname's body was laid out on a bed of skins in the middle of the cave. The seven students of the medicine woman were sitting at the head end keeping vigil. Their high laments echoed off the rough rock walls and penetrated the starry night. Nearby a little owl shouted, as if it wanted to chime in.

The facial features of the medicine woman were now smooth and radiated a peace that seemed to come from a world in which evil did not exist and where there was no danger.

Iriomé would have preferred to follow her there. Why had her beloved teacher left her alone? Tichiname had meant everything to her. After her parents perished in a severe storm at sea, Tichiname adopted her and became a mother, teacher, and mediator to the otherworld rolled into one. Together with six other students she taught Iriomé the application of medicinal plants, midwifery, the embalming of the dead, and astronomy. Not only that. From Tichiname she learned to become one with nature and to understand the language of the spirits. The older woman explained to her how *abora*—the power of life—originated, how it could be preserved, and how it had to end. And now she had passed away. Much too soon. The young woman was overwhelmed by deep despair and feelings of loneliness.

Having seen only seventeen winters, she didn't feel ready to succeed Tichiname and take the responsibility that went with that. For the benefit of all the tribes of the island, final judgments always rested with the highest harimaguada. Whether it was a dispute between two tribes due to cattle rustling or how to help a woman who was desired by several men: her word was law. Her orders had to be followed by everyone. In addition, she was the only one who had permission from the spirits and ancestors to wander through time to receive their advice and messages. This also was a task Iriomé was not prepared for yet. Tichiname had often told her about her journeys into other times, and one of them had been etched in Iriomé's mind as deeply as if she had actually been there.

The medicine woman had traveled to a time when the ancestors of their people were still living in the desert, where the baking sun burned their skin and thirst and hunger tormented them. The leaders decided to abandon the inhospitable land and to embark on a dangerous sea voyage. In a violent storm their boat overturned and was driven against the rock of an island, where it eventually crashed. Iriomé had believed she heard the howling of the storm and tasted the salty water which adhered to their eyes and made their throats ache. Tichiname let rise in her mind's eye images of people and animals that escaped onto the island with the last of their strength and eventually discovered they had landed in a heavenly garden with gushing springs, edible plants, and habitable caves offering coolness in summer and protection from the rain and storms in winter. The people were so happy that they swore the gods an oath: they promised to honor everything that had been given to them and to sustain it the way they had found it. And to defend it with life and limb, if necessary.

Iriomé loved this story. It gave her strength and a sense of pride that she belonged to this happy people. But now everything seemed to be in danger. At this point, she had told no one what Tichiname whispered into her ear before she died. She wanted to speak first with Tanausú, the leader of the Aceró, who lived in the village below the cave shrine. But she would not set forth before the other harimaguadas had fallen asleep, overwhelmed by their grief.

At dawn the next day she fearlessly climbed down the ladders made of tied up logs, which led from cave to cave, until she reached the level from which a narrow rocky path along the crater wall led to the village.

She knew every bush and every stone here. A hawk circled over the river, and on the rocky hillsides the goats of the villagers were grazing on roots and herbs. Their bleating gave a touch of the ordinary to this surreal morning.

Tanausú awaited her in front of his cave. His large, strong figure was silhouetted against a sky that had turned brighter now. The two of them bowed to each other, touching the other's forehead, as was the custom among the *menceyes,* the tribe members of superior rank. In doing so they whispered simultaneously, "*Chusar axhoran, magoc, e cel.*" Hail in the face of the sky, the sun, and the moon.

Tanausú smoothed back his thick blond hair, which came down to his bare shoulders, so that the scar over his bright blue eyes became visible. "What did Tichiname say?"

Iriomé had stopped wondering a long time ago how he always was one step ahead and knew exactly what others thought or planned to do. An art that, apart from the old medicine woman, was mastered by only a few people on the island.

"She has seen foreign men coming across the sea in their vessels. Men who are only interested in power and wealth. They will destroy the people of Benahoare and extinguish abora for all eternity."

"And she did not see how we can stop these men?"

Iriomé shook her head. "I think otherwise she wouldn't have decided to go to the other world."

Deep concern clouded the blue eyes of the tribal leader. The scar on his forehead turned dark, also a clear sign of impending danger. The scar always reminded Iriomé of that night at sea when Tanausú saved her from the deadly waves that had dragged her parents out of the boat. The rudder hit his head and left this deep fissure.

"The old ones say men from the other side of the sea came here. Before this, they occupied our neighboring island Gomera. But the brave tribes of Benahoare put them to flight."

Now Iriomé remembered. Some nights by the fire, stories of this battle had been told, which dated back quite a few generations.

"So far they have not dared to attack us again," Tanausú said in a defiant voice. "But I've heard that they repeatedly invaded islands, captured the inhabitants, and traded them in their mother country for valuable stuff."

"We must warn the other tribal leaders before they return to their villages," Iriomé exclaimed excitedly. In that moment she believed she literally smelled the danger that was in store for them. Death cries reached her ears, but in the sky only a swarm of crows circled, insulting each other loudly.

"We're all going to convene *tagoror* and discuss what to do."

Iriomé knew only too well what Tanausú was about to do. As long as he still had an arm to throw a stone or hurl a spear, he would fight until the last drop of blood. Deep down she hoped there still was another solution. One that claimed fewer lives. Maybe Tichiname had not been able to see such a way for a reason.

"I'll go down to the coast to lay down offerings at the holy well and ask the ancestors for advice," Iriomé said. "Last winter Tichiname gave me permission to do this."

Tanausú nodded. "Guayafanta shall accompany you. It's too dangerous alone."

"You mean the men are already here?"

෧෨

The air had a smell of wet earth when the first rays of sunlight entered the dense laurel forest and cast flickering light on the rampant ferns that lined the muddy path. The humidity of the night had made the steep path slippery, and the two young women had to be careful that they did not slip in their thin leather soles. Both wore tight-fitting dresses made of finely tanned goatskin embroidered with colorful seedpods.

Guayafanta was slightly older than Iriomé and of robust build. Her skin was darker and her hair the same blue-black coloring as the solidified lava flows that covered large parts of the island. Her dark, flashing eyes gave her the look of the sharpness of a blade of obsidian, the stone from which the islanders built their knives. She carried a basket woven from dragon tree leaves with offerings for the spirits in it.

There was silence between the women. Iriomé knew it was not easy for Guayafanta to accept that Iriomé, and not her, was going to be Tichiname's successor. After all, Guayafanta was older and more experienced and had assisted Tichiname in difficult healing ceremonies. In addition, she was physically stronger and more robust. In the last competitions in stone throwing, Guayafanta defeated all the women and even a few of the men.

"We'll show these conquerors how our people can fight. They'll pull back just as empty-handed as last time," said Guayafanta as she resolutely kicked a stone aside.

"Tichiname wouldn't have left us if she anticipated a victory," Iriomé replied softly.

"She left us because her time had come, and because she was against any kind of violent defense. But sometimes there is no other way."

"Violence is the little brother of death," Iriomé repeated, words from their common teacher.

Guayafanta gave her a disparaging look and ran past her down to a crag from where one could overlook a part of the tribal territory called Tazo. A long black pebble beach was one of the few beaches the island offered, otherwise surrounded almost entirely by cliffs. She let out a little scream.

In the calm waters of the bay three ships were bobbing up and down, like black monsters lurking over prey. Iriomé had followed, and the two girls looked at each other, startled. The ships were made of dark wood and many times bigger than the dragon tree boats the islanders used to fish. From each of the ships three logs loomed in the sky, and from the highest a colorful cloth was blowing. Some men had already reached the beach in small rowboats and built a camp. Snippets of a foreign language and the smell of fried fish drifted up to the girls.

Iriomé grabbed Guayafanta's hand. Tichiname's prophecy had become reality. A reality one could see, hear, and smell in this world.

Something had enraged Guayote, the hellhound, who sat in the lowest abyss of the fire-breathing mountain waiting for those who had done evil in their lives.

They lost no time and climbed as fast as they could from their vantage point back to the path that led to the holy well. Soon they heard the familiar ripple that, however, had no reassuring effect on Iriomé at all. On the contrary, she felt fear rise inside her. It was the fear of failure. As a budding harimaguada she had learned to ask the spirits of the ancestors for help and to use their forces, but so far only in the presence of her teacher. Never before had she been on her own. She looked over at Guayafanta, whose eyes had narrowed to slits from inner tension. No help could be expected from her. All her senses were focused on combat and defense.

A light breeze gently touched Iriomé's cheek; her fear disappeared, and she knew the spirit of Tichiname would always help her, and not only that, but earth, water, plants, animals, and even the wind were joined with her and would share their wisdom.

Focused, Iriomé turned to the well that gushed from a crevice into a small pond. All around spirals of different sizes were carved into the stone. Iriomé touched the cliff and gently followed the circular lines from the center of the largest spiral up to the outside—the symbol of infinity, that this well might gush forever, but also of eternal transformation and recurrence.

Whenever Iriomé left the well she became a different person. She always learned more about herself and the mysteries of life. There was so much between heaven and earth that she did not understand yet. So many relationships she wanted to understand, starting with the course of the stars and the change of the tides with the different seasons. Everything was connected somehow, even if she did not know how and why. The miracle of life, healing, death, and birth called to be unraveled. But one lifetime was not enough for that.

Iriomé knelt down, bowed, and gently touched the ground with her forehead. Slowly, she closed her eyes and enjoyed the smell of the earth.

"Tara, Mother Earth," she murmured, "the inhabitants of Benahoare thank you for everything you give them. For the fruits with which you nourish them, the flowers with which you please them, and for the herbs with which you heal them. We thank you for the water that makes everything grow, and for your love, which makes everything possible."

Guayafanta followed suit. For a while the girls remained in this position. A group of sparrows came so close that Iriomé could look into their small, dark eyes. They knew no fear. When the girls got up, the birds flew a few yards away and alighted on one of the mighty pines that lined the clearing.

Guayafanta unpacked the basket and was pouring goat milk from a clay pot into a small channel that had been carved into the stone and filled up quickly. Into a rock niche next to it she laid some goat butter, and right at the top of the sanctuary she placed a wooden bowl with the entrails of a goat. The girls went off and waited at a respectful distance for the arrival of the birds. If they came to get the offerings, they were no longer hawks, eagles, or crows but messengers from beyond that delivered the message of the ancestors.

Iriomé closed her eyes. Tichiname had also taught her to listen to what the wind was whispering. The wind from the north always told different stories from those of the south, west, or east winds. Also the earth and the sky could be asked for a message.

She lay down on the ground, doubled up like an unborn child in the womb, closed her eyes, and waited. But nothing happened. The veil between the times was not lifted. It was as if Iriomé was facing a thick layer of fog. No voice, no word came from the other side into her world of thought. The wind was silent. Likewise, the earth. The sky. The ancestors did not speak. Nor Tichiname. Something must have changed; things were no longer in harmony. Iriomé felt like a spider whose web had been destroyed and that now frantically sought the missing silk that had connected it to its environment.

The cry of a hawk made her open her eyes. He grabbed a piece of liver and flew away. Iriomé looked at Guayafanta questioningly. But she shook her head. She also had not been able to penetrate the wall of silence. "It's the strangers down at the beach," she said in a rough voice. "As long as they're here on the island, the ancestors will be silent."

Guayafanta was right. The men were responsible for the dividing wall that both women clearly felt.

"Then let's go back," said Iriomé. "It will be dark soon. We'll have to walk part of the way in darkness anyway."

"And that's good," Guayafanta said. "The darkness will give us protection."

Only then did Iriomé realize the men might not only be down at the beach, but perhaps also in the inner part of the island. Startled, she looked around and tried to adjust her sense of hearing to perceive sounds from a great distance. Everything seemed calm.

When they reached the entrance gorge to the caldera, through which the river bed was meandering, dusk was already approaching. On both sides steep rock walls grown with knotty spruce towered into the sky, and the sharp shadows made the rock formations appear like grim figures. An eerie feeling came over Iriomé. She thought of the stories the old people told. Were the ghosts of the dead still here? Were they, for some reason, not able to leave this world? Was this the reason the strangers had come back? To avenge their dead? Time and again the two women stopped to listen. But except for the rustle of fleeing lizards they heard nothing. Looking both ways, the women walked on.

Iriomé felt his hot breath even before she was grabbed from behind and pulled to the ground. She immediately knew that it could only be one of the strangers, as there were no wild animals on the island. An unknown clinking sound came to her ear, and she felt a thud on the back of her head before darkness fell upon her.

"*Hakanamahé!*" Guayafanta let out a battle cry that brought Iriomé back into the light. With all her strength she rammed her feet into the genitals of the man forcing himself between her legs. He collapsed groaning in pain. Using that short respite, she jumped up. Only a few feet away Guayafanta was fighting with a second man who unmistakably swore in a foreign language. Iriomé looked around quickly. There seemed to be only two. Without effort, she lifted one of the heavy boulders that were lying all over the place and launched it with full force at the skull of the man who had just thrown Guayafanta to the ground. With a dull noise he collapsed next to her. Guayafanta straightened up quickly, grabbed for the stone, and cried a warning. The man who had attacked them first had picked himself up and was about to grab Iriomé from behind, but Guayafanta's stone hit him right in his back and felled him like an ax on a tree. With an animal-like cry that echoed back from the cliffs, he seemed to crumble and showed no sign of life.

Silence. Even the rustle of the lizards stopped.

Guayafanta's eyes flashed with anger. She was breathing heavily. Her robe was torn, one of her eyes already swollen, her fists clenched. Iriomé rushed to her side and put her arm around her shoulders. The two women remained like that until their breathing calmed. Then they had a closer look at the two men.

One looked at them with lifeless eyes. His shimmering headwear lay beside him. From his skull, blood and a whitish, gelatinous liquid were oozing. He had a round, chubby face, short hair, and no beard.

Maybe they're not even real men, thought Iriomé. They had little in common with the men of their own people. Instead of vestments of animal skins or plant tissue, they wore a hard shell that looked as if they were covered with huge shiny fish scales. Their head gear was from the same material. On their feet they wore hoses made of dyed black animal skin that reached up to the knee. And something sharp and round was fixed at their heels that resembled the jagged edge of a lapa.

The other man lay motionless on his stomach. The two women turned him together. As Iriomé touched him, she winced as if lightning had struck her. Never before in her life had someone made her feel like this. It was an unknown, sweet pain that was spreading through her body. She looked in the stranger's face with great surprise. He had not seen twenty winters, possessed noble facial proportions and short, shiny black curls. His eyes were closed.

Iriomé took his wrist as she had learned from Tichiname and felt if abora was still in him. Barely perceptible, she felt the soft pounding of his blood under her fingertips, and this time a feeling sweet as berry juice flooded through her.

"He's alive," she whispered, and to her own amazement she perceived an expression of joy in her voice. Guayafanta quickly picked up a boulder in order to bring him to an end. Just in time Iriomé noticed what Guayafanta intended and pulled the man's head aside, which otherwise would have been smashed like that of the other. With a dull thud, the rock sunk into the ground.

"What are you doing?" hissed Guayafanta.

"The children of Tara never end the life of another human being without an immediate danger to themselves. Such an act is solely reserved to the gods. If they had wanted him to die, they would have seen to it. They still have something planned for him. And we have to respect their decision."

"The gods are silent," Guayafanta gasped breathlessly. "You've seen it yourself. They've left the island long ago. We need to rely on ourselves now."

Iriomé, who held the stranger in her arms like a child, shook her head. "The spirit of Tichiname will never leave us. And you know yourself what she thinks about killing."

"What are you going to do with him?" Guayafanta asked angrily.

"We'll take him with us and nurse him back to health."

Guayafanta stared at Iriomé blankly. "Despite the fact you know what these men wanted to do to us? I certainly won't help you. You can carry him alone." With a proud sweep of the head she turned away and slung the wooden tube, the dangerous weapon of the strangers of which the old people had spoken, over her shoulder like a trophy.

"You'll help me now," Iriomé replied in a firm tone. "For I am Tichiname's successor, and I'm telling you."

Guayafanta winced. And Iriomé knew that from now on they would never be friends. Open hostility spread like stinking smoke between them. But Guayafanta obeyed. With pursed lips she knelt down beside Iriomé. Together they tried to remove the armored garment from the unconscious man. It was not easy to open the closures of leather and the hard clips; they succeeded in pulling off the bulky shells that protected his back and chest only after several attempts. Underneath he wore another large-mesh, heavy robe that they pulled over his head.

"I wonder how they can even walk with all this, let alone fight," Guayafanta muttered indignantly. Each movement was difficult for her, and each touch of the stranger's body gave her a feeling of disgust. He now wore only a thin white shirt that made him look small and vulnerable. Guayafanta looked down on him contemptuously. "These worms will never defeat us. Just look at him." She spat in the stranger's face.

Iriomé had to admit she was right. Without the armor the young man looked completely harmless, like someone who would keel over at the slightest breath of wind. Nevertheless Guayafanta insisted on tying up his arms and legs in case he regained consciousness and gave them trouble. With ropes made of plant fibers, which the girls wore around the waist as belts, they tied him like a stubborn goat. Then Iriomé put his legs over her shoulder while Guayafanta picked up his upper body. The injured man groaned softly, without recovering his senses. He was much smaller than the men of Benahoare and wasn't an excessive load for these two women.

♾

In Aceró not a single fire was burning, unlike other nights.

"Tara," Iriomé whispered, full of foreboding. "Please, let them all still be alive."

As quietly as possible, the two women crept closer.

"If anything has happened to them, I'll kill this man, and no one will stop me," hissed Guayafanta into the darkness.

Still no voices could be heard, not even a baby crying. Iriomé gave a low whistle, like the goatherds who communicated in this way over long distances. Nothing. Only the chirping of the crickets.

Suddenly someone grabbed her from behind. But this time it was no stranger in a glistening fish-scale robe, but Ertoma, one of the villagers. All three of them were relieved when they recognized each other.

"We deliberately made no fire, so the smoke and light don't betray us," he said. "The leaders of the other tribes have gone to their villages to fetch their women and children. Here in Aceró they are safer than down by the coast." Questioningly he looked at the stranger, who was still unconscious.

"A prisoner," Guayafanta announced. She dropped him unceremoniously, so that Iriomé almost fell to the ground with him.

"The tagoror has not made a decision yet. Tanausú wanted to wait for you to hear what the ancestors say," said Ertoma.

"They're silent. Besides, what's there to decide?" snorted Guayafanta. "Just look at him." She pointed to the tied-up stranger on the ground. "A worm, no more and no less. These men have no chance against us."

"We should take him to the cave for the sick," Iriomé interrupted.

Guayafanta shook her head vigorously. "My duty ends here." She turned around and walked away without another word.

"The man's going to die if I don't dress his wounds," Iriomé told Ertoma. "He's already lost a lot of blood."

Ertoma shook his head thoughtfully, making no attempt to help, so Iriomé could do nothing other than to shoulder him alone and carry him to the lowest cave in the rock wall intended for the sick. There she laid him gently on one of the fur beds cushioned with pine needles. She poked the fire that glimmered only dimly and removed his shackles. Then in the bright light of new flames she pulled off his blood-soaked trousers. Intently she looked at the gaping laceration, which ran from the waist down the right thigh. The man's most valuable parts had remained uninjured, though swollen and stained purple. The pelvic bone was not broken. Without touching his body, she sensed him and inhaled his scent as she had been taught by Tichiname.

Iriomé did not need to think about what to do. She recalled what had always been in her memory: the knowledge of the art of healing.

It was transferred mysteriously from one supreme harimaguada to the next. Iriomé had been born with the same gift that all her predecessors had possessed. Tichiname had only taught how to access this knowledge. It was not much different from remembering experiences that she had had herself. Once the path to her memories had been smoothed, it would never become overgrown again.

From the medicine bag around her neck she took some dried iris root and a few daisy petals, put them together with fresh aloe meat in a clay bowl, added some water, and placed the whole thing over the fire. Doing this her eyes fell on the strange rigid headgear of the stranger. Guayafanta had insisted on bringing it with them. The cup-like object must have fallen from his head and rolled into the hearth when she laid him down. Using a leather flap Iriomé fished it from the embers and was surprised to find that the material showed no changes. It was only a little blackened by the soot. It could be possible to heat liquids in it up to a very high temperature without the material bursting, as often happened with her pottery, she reflected.

Who were these people? And why did they have materials and weapons that were completely unknown to her people, and probably superior? For a while she studied the features of the young man as if they could tell her. His eyes were closed, but his chin expressed determination and willpower. His lips were soft and gently curved. To her surprise she liked this face and felt like caressing the young man's cheeks. She didn't understand herself, considering he had planned to do violence to her.

The bubbling sound of the boiling medicine interrupted her thoughts. She poured off the water, cleaned the wound, and then dribbled the rest of the brew over it. From another vessel standing in a rock niche, she scooped a green pulp prepared from nettles and distributed it evenly on the bruised spots. She hesitated briefly before she took his maltreated genitals and applied the ointment there as well. Her touch flashed through his body like lightning strikes.

He opened his eyes. To Iriomé they were like two deep, dark lakes. For a moment, she felt the need to dive into those lakes, all the way down to their very bottom. The stranger did not move but held her gaze. It did not befit a virgin harimaguada to look a man in the eyes, and Iriomé felt a faint blush flitting across her face. He must have noticed it, because suddenly he smiled at her, which gave his face a completely new expression.

He pointed to himself, and his lips formed a strange sounding word. "Joaquín."

She guessed that it must be his name and repeated it, as best she could. "Akin."

He nodded and smiled back at her, so that she could hardly hold his gaze. With a slight movement of his head, he seemed to ask: And you, what's your name?

"Iriomé," she replied softly.

He repeated her name, which out of his mouth sounded as strange to her as his.

"Iri," he said. And then again. "Iri. Iri. Iri." Nobody had ever pronounced her name in this way. He tentatively reached for her long blonde hair and let a curl slowly slide between his thumb and index finger. Iriomé didn't try to get away.

Suddenly she realized what she was still holding in her hands. Startled, she continued to apply the rest of the sticky plant pulp. She felt his eyes on her neck, her shoulders, and her hips, penetrating her skin like grains of sand during a storm. Feelings were spreading inside her, which she as a harimaguada should suppress. Her force belonged to the sick and needy, and she had learned that the connection to a man would weaken this force forever.

Though Akin must be in a great deal of pain, she could not help noticing how the blood collected in the middle of his body, which made his penis bulge even more. He turned his head aside and whispered something that she did not understand but which sounded like a mixture between a curse and an invocation to the gods.

"Iriomé," a woman's voice came from the cave entrance. The healer winced.

Nesfete, an older harimaguada, entered the healing cave. Around her friendly round face short gray curls were crinkling. Curious, she came closer to have a look at the stranger. Iriomé leaned forward a bit, so that she could not see the man's belly.

"Tanausú wants you to come to the tagoror at once," she said. "I can take over here."

Iriomé shook her head. "Thank you, but I want to finish the treatment myself." She tried to give her voice a firm tone. But Nesfete, who knew Iriomé well, noticed immediately that something was wrong.

"Are you sure?" she asked.

The sandstorm on Iriomé's skin slowly calmed down, just as was the case with Joaquín. She straightened up and finally could look Nesfete into the eyes. "Everything's fine. I'll come with you."

Nesfete smiled, as if she knew what had happened.

Iriomé checked if the green paste, which now covered the injuries of the stranger as a healing protective skin, had solidified. Then their hands conducted a series of flowing movements over Joaquín, whose eyes were closed now. It was a petition to the spirits to help the patient recover. One last look, and she got up. When he still held her curl for a brief moment, she felt a little pain.

⌀

Down in the village the members of the tribes of the coast and the Aridane Valley had arrived. Bulging leather bags with their most important possessions and baskets made of dragon tree leaves were leaning against the rock walls. Dogs barked in a frenzied chaos. Mothers called for their children, who ran about playing tag.

Iriomé welcomed some acquaintances and then followed the path that led to the meeting place. The small rock plateau was just above the village; she saw from afar that many people had gathered there. The atmosphere was more than heated. A young man from Atogmatoma's tribe had the floor. He spoke quickly and in agitation. Nesfete told Iriomé he had been caught by the strangers but managed to escape.

"They chained us to trees with ropes consisting of hard, intertwined rings that one can neither tear nor break with the teeth. They gave us food and something to drink. And then a fat man in a brown robe with hair that grew like a wreath around his head came to us. He was accompanied by an old woman who knew his and our language. His name was Frai Hieronymus, and he told us that he was an emissary of a very special god, who had died on the cross for us humans. Those who believe in him will live in eternal peace. Then he murmured strange spells while looking at a quadrangular thing in his hands, which was coated with animal skin and according to his words contained all knowledge of this god."

Silence. Tanausú broke it first. He cared neither about this god on the cross nor the knowledge jammed between animal skins. He had only one question. "What are these men doing here?"

"They showed me small, hard, shiny yellow stones and wondered if any of these can be found here. I told him I've never seen such stones."

Atogmatoma, the leader of Tijarafe on the west of the island, chimed in with an anxious voice. "They're thieves! Just as they have stolen Gomera, Esero, and the islands in the east, they now want to steal our island. They were successful there. The leaders of the tribes from the south and the middle of the island have subjected themselves: Mayantigo from the Aridane Valley, Echedey from Tihuya and Echentire. The strangers gave them presents, and the old woman made fine promises. Her name is Gazmira. She was born in our village many moons ago and was with her father on Gomera when the iron men—as she calls the strangers—raided the island. They've no regard for abora. A person's life has no value for them. The old woman told me that they cut off the head of everybody who opposed them. Those who managed to flee were persued until they were caught. And they spared neither children nor women."

Iriomé turned away and looked at the jagged rocks of the crater rim. On Benahoare they did not kill each other. She thought of Akin. He was one of these iron men.

As if Guayafanta read her mind, she stepped forward and shook her curly black hair in a self-confident gesture. "The man whose life Iriomé has saved is not worthy to be spared. He wouldn't have spared us either," she cried with a loud voice. "I suggest we kill him and then drag him at night to the camp of the strangers. They might then understand that we're not afraid of them and won't surrender."

Iriomé winced. Guayafanta's proposal was more a declaration of war than a possibility to reach an agreement with the strangers without bloodshed. But most raised their fists and agreed with Guayafanta vociferously. With a single movement of his hand Tanausú ensured silence and asked the young man from the tribe of Atogmatoma to continue.

"The strange item, in which the knowledge of this god is contained, actually plays a big role. The men of the conquered tribes formed a long line and swore an oath on it. Afterward, they were splashed with water by that Frai Hieronymus."

Tanausú snorted. "There's only one oath, and this our ancestors have already taken. Each of us, whether man or woman, today swears it anew once they enter adulthood: to honor nature and to take only what we need to survive. This is the only way to preserve the balance of life. Besides, do we not have our own gods? Tigotan, the one god of heaven, and Tara, the eternal Mother Earth? I don't understand why the other tribes bow to an unknown god."

"They believe that this god has more power and will give them what the strangers have," Atogmatoma said. "Larger ships, more powerful weapons, more robust clothing, and better tasting drinks."

"Why?" shouted Tanausú angrily. "To live in bondage? The price is too high! Why ships? We have everything and don't need anything from other islands. Why strange clothes? Why weapons? In order to wage war and be guilty before Tigotan, Tara, and the other ancestors?"

Iriomé knew he was right, but she also knew that the balance had already been disrupted; the enemies had come to the island. Something that had been changed could never be returned to its previous state. She remembered something Tichiname had often said to her: fate behaves like a stone rolling down a mountain. Only very rarely something stands in its way that can stop it.

"I cannot allow the people of Aceró to break this oath," Tanausú continued and turned to Bediesta, the leader of Tegalgen, the northern-most tribal area of the island, as he spoke. He was a strong man with a thick red beard who had remained silent so far. "Shall we leave to the strangers all that has belonged to us since the time of our ancestors, so that they can destroy it and their gods dominate ours? Shall our people stand back and watch our men and women being taken away on their ships and sold in their country without a fight?"

"No, we won't," Bediesta sided with him.

"And you, Juguiro," he now spoke to the leader of Tigalate, "do you want to see how they make our women their own? How the children are increasingly losing our spirit and accept theirs? How our people will get lost in theirs?"

Juguiro struggled to his feet. His hair was white and straggled down over his shoulders. He spoke slowly with the soft voice of an old man. "They possess weapons that are superior to our spears and clubs made of wood. They have protective clothing and animals with high legs, on which they are faster than any man of our people."

Tanausú looked at him sternly. "The good life on the coast has made you sluggish, Juguiro. The sun has burned the fighting spirit from your brain. The inhabitants of Benahoare are a brave people and will put to flight these men, as they have done before. If you're not of this opinion, then join the row of those who take an oath on that knowledge that is pressed between the goatskins, but do so immediately, because then there will be no place for you anymore here in my country. Only if those who are left hold together will we have a chance," said Tanausú gravely and in the hope that in the end, all would stick together. He needed the other leaders if it should come to a battle with the strangers. Although Aceró could resist a long time due to its location within the crater, this would be of little help if the neighboring tribes bowed to the enemy. He saw it as a major drawback that current power was no longer in one pair of hands. He never would have tolerated the tribes from the south throwing themselves at the strangers.

"Our gods are alive! The Atagon, the Great Spirit, will lead us to victory," Ertome now confirmed Tanausú's words. "He didn't die on a cross like the god of the strangers. Just look at them. They're small and thin. Even women were able to knock two of them to the ground, although they were armed." He looked at Iriomé and Guayafanta, who clenched her fist and agreed with him.

When the night proceeded and no agreement had been reached, Tanausú again raised his voice. "Let us ask amakuna," he said, "just as we always have done, when a decision had to be made." No one could object to that. For the spirit of the mushroom had always foreseen what would happen, even before it happened.

"The spirits have nothing more to tell us," Guayafanta chimed in. "They have left the island."

Tanausú gave her a reproachful look. "How can you talk like that?! The spirits may perhaps be silent for a while, but as long as we're alive, they will always be part of us and help us with their advice."

Guayafanta lowered her eyes and said nothing. Iriomé, however, felt an ardent hatred emanating from Guayafanta that almost smothered her.

"Amakuna will speak through Iriomé and bring about a decision," Tanausú said in a voice that tolerated no dissent.

Chapter 12

The next morning, preparations for the upcoming ceremony and the associated feast began. All members of the four tribes were grateful for this unexpected distraction. It seemed as if they were given a brief moment of normality. The women set off to gather roots and tubers. Wild fennel, asparagus, legumes, and mushrooms were already simmering away in pots.

Several goats lost their lives. Their skins were hung on the appropriate racks to dry and their flesh put on spits and soon roasting over the fire. The children spread out to pick sweet berries, of which there were plenty at this time of the year. The smell of fried chestnuts was in the air, mixed with the smell of roasted fern roots.

Iriomé wondered if Tichiname actually anticipated that her successor would so soon set out on a journey to the after time herself because she had prepared twice as much amakuna as needed for her final journey. Only thus could Iriomé perform the ritual at all. For no one except Tichiname knew where the fungus grew, and it was strictly prohibited to give away this secret in her lifetime. Only at her funeral it would be revealed to her successor by the spirits.

But before Iriomé could bury her teacher, her body had to be embalmed so that it could outlast eternity together with her mind. Since ancient times, this procedure had always been carried out by a certain harimaguada in a cave at the very edge of the sanctuary to which nobody else had access. Iriomé felt the need to go there, even if it was not she who was entrusted with the embalming. She felt there was something the medicine woman still wanted to tell her. Something that was so important that she had to defy all rules and prohibitions.

She was lucky. Nesfete, who kept vigil, was not present because she was also busy preparing for the amakuna ritual.

Tichiname's body lay on a flat-hewn stone and was covered with goat skins, into which it would be sewn later. It smelled of pine needles that filled the body along with heather and grated pumice, so that it would not decay. Later, it would be rubbed with goat butter and dracaena blood to convert the skin into leather. Iriomé dared not take off the fur that lay on the face of the dead, but she could sense the wise smile of her teacher without seeing it. She knelt down, closed her eyes and tried to get in touch with Tichiname's spirit. It took a while; then a strange whistling sound became noticeable, which became louder and louder. When it was so loud that Iriomé could not bear it any longer, she believed she heard Tichiname's voice behind it. "The time in which amakuna was under the protection of virgins alone is over. Its future depends on love. The love between a wise woman and a man who has power."

Then there was dead silence. Iriomé opened her eyes. She felt as if she had dived into the sea and her ears were full of water so that she now perceived all sound as muffled and distant.

The love between a wisewoman and a man of power—Tichiname's words echoed in her head. Suddenly Akin's face appeared in her mind. Had she saved him from death for this reason? Was it their love that would protect amakuna? Was he the man and she the woman? Was it all predestined?

When she first looked into his face as he was lying on the ground half dead, she sensed his fate was intertwined with hers. Yet he was one of the men Tichiname had warned her to keep away from. This she had kept in mind. *These men know no love. They will destroy everything that is sacred to us. But one thing must never fall into their hands: the secret heart of the island that beats in the cave of the highest mountain! Only when people are free from the greed for power and wealth will its secret be safe to reveal.*

What should she believe now?

"Iriomé!" Nesfete stood at the entrance of the cave looking at her reproachfully. "I've been looking for you everywhere."

Iriomé turned to her guiltily. "I couldn't help it. I simply had to come here."

"It's time to go to the well," was all the old harimaguada said.

Iriomé took a deep breath and then stepped out into the warm sunlight. "You're right. Would you accompany me?"

Nesfete nodded. For a while they walked in silence because Iriomé did not know how to put into words what Tichiname's spirit had just told her.

"You need not be afraid of decisions. That which is predestined to happen will happen," Nesfete finally said. "Whether we understand it or not. The gods have their own plans, which we humans mostly don't understand because we only have the ability to look over our present life, nothing else."

Iriomé sighed deeply. "I envy you your wisdom and the peace that rests in your soul."

"That's why Tichiname asked me to watch over you," replied the old woman and put her hand gently on Iriomé's shoulder. "You're still very young, so sometimes it's good to know someone's by your side who has a little more experience."

Iriomé gratefully took Nesfete's hand and only let it go when they reached the well. Just a few days ago she had assisted Tichiname with her ablution. Now it was up to Iriomé to wash away all that could affect the force of amakuna.

Fresh water from the mountains gushed into the small rock pool that was just large enough to lie full length in. Nesfete had brought some soapwort and drew it through the cool water; fragrant foam formed immediately. Iriomé took off her clothes and basked her slender, naked body in the sun for a while before she stepped into the stone tub. The old harimaguada gently rubbed her with a sponge from plant fibers humming a soothing melody. The familiar voice made Iriomé feel safe and protected. It gave her the strength to make a decision and ask for a favor that would require a lot of courage. "I'd like to ask you if you could do something for me that might be very dangerous," she said in a low voice.

The old harimaguada fell silent and looked at her in astonishment. "What is it?"

"While all the others attend the ceremony, you must help Akin to escape and show him the way down to the coast. Ouch!"

Nesfete had just started to untangle Iriomé's hair with a comb made of toothed wood and pulled it out of terror.

"I can't do that!" she exclaimed in dismay. "He'll lead the iron men here, and they're going to kill us all."

"He won't," Iriomé declared.

"How can you be so sure?"

"I'm not sure. All I know is that it's wrong to kill him. Tichiname wouldn't have wanted it."

Nesfete let the comb drop and sat on the edge of the rock basin thinking. "So the time has come."

"What do you mean?"

"She entrusted me with something a while ago. Something I didn't understand until now. But now I know what she meant by it. That you'll be the first supreme harimaguada that will strike a new path."

Iriomé straightened. "She told me, too."

"She probably anticipated I wouldn't speak to you about it."

"Why not?"

"I'm too old for such new thinking. I believe in what has stood the test of time. But in the end Tichiname has always been right." She began running the comb through Iriomé's hair again, and it took a while before she spoke again. "No one will notice if I don't take part in the ceremony tonight," she said in a toneless voice.

"The foreigners are not all bad, just because they're different. Love must live somewhere in their hearts. They're just not familiar with it."

Nesfete looked at the young harimaguada, smiling, "I hope you're right."

૭౿

Joaquín received Iriomé with his eyes open. The light of the stone lamp reflected in his pupils. Again she realized how much she liked those eyes. How much she wished to drown in his eyes and escape reality and the fear that her people would go down and everything would be different.

Joaquín took her hand, and Iriomé felt that a cloud of sadness had lain on his soul as well. She felt infinitely close to him, although they had been together only a few moments. He opened the door to his heart for her, and she boldly stepped across the threshold. All violence and everything destructive she had recently seen in his facial features seemed extinguished. He had changed in a magical way.

With a smile Iriomé handed him a wooden bowl with gofio. When their hands touched, immediately a sandstorm swept up her arm and conquered her body in a flash. Akin, who had noticed it, smiled and gently stroked her shoulder and back. Only then did he turn to his meal. When he had tasted the first bite, his face spontaneously split into an amusing grimace. Iriomé laughed. She quickly handed him a wooden cup with sweet berry juice, which he tried with pursed lips. But then he was beaming, poured the entire contents into the bowl of porridge, and emptied it in no time. He then sank with a deep sigh back on his bed and closed his eyes languorously. Iriomé had waited for this. She softly hummed a simple melody and soon sleep took over. When his breathing came calm and steady, with a jerk she pulled the sticky dressing off his thigh so he had no time to scream. He just opened his mouth briefly and then closed it again.

This time Iriomé suppressed a laugh and then washed the remains of the gelatinous green mass off the wound, which had already closed. She was pleased to see how quickly healing had set in and silently thanked Tichiname for all her wise teachings. Akin would be able to walk tonight. Not fast, but fast enough.

She handed him a goatskin that he wrapped around his loins and taking his hands lifted him up carefully. For the first time they looked each other in the eye level with each other. Joaquín stumbled and had to hold on to her. Their bodies touched. Iriomé would have loved to stay in this position for a while, but time was short. He had to walk. She supported him under the arms and signaled him to slowly put one foot before the other.

Akin looked at her doubtfully yet began to hobble forward. Step by step. And with every step he became more confident. He did several laps around the cave, then stopped in front of Iriomé relieved and looked at her with deep gratitude. But there was something else in his eyes. A desire that she could not escape. He pulled her into his arms, pressed her to his body, and gently pressed his lips on hers. The sandstorm rose to a hurricane, so that she almost lost balance.

But this time Joaquín stood firmly on both legs holding her tight and kissed her again, this time wildly and full of passion. Iriomé thought she would merge with him forever, and this touch that was completely new to her felt like a vow of love, which burned deep into her heart.

Only yesterday this stranger seemed weak and powerless. Now she could feel the fire that burned in him and his strong desire to kindle the flames. She took a step back and slowly ran her finger over her lips. "You must leave Aceró tonight," she said, pointing at him, and then to the exit of the cave. "Nesfete will go with you and show you the way down to the coast."

For a moment Joaquín gazed at her blankly, but then he seemed to have understood, because he looked down at his lower body only dressed in a goatskin. Iriomé smiled. "I'll get you something to wear." Then she hugged him again and pressed her lips courageously on his.

◌◌

At the large banquet Iriomé was so nervous that she could not swallow a bite. Nesfete practically had to force her to eat a little gofio and goat meat as a base for her stomach, anticipating the venture that was in store for her. The others, however, feasted and enjoyed the sumptuous meal as if it were their last. Fermented goat milk served in clay jugs pushed their sorrows into the background and ensured a relaxed atmosphere.

The moon shone so bright that she practically blinded the eyes. She bathed the crater in an unreal, silvery light, creating exactly the right atmosphere to let amakuna speak. A piercing sound that a young man coaxed from a colorfully painted nautilus shell announced the beginning of the ritual and gave the tribal leaders and harimaguadas their starting signal to climb the wooden ladders up to the big cave.

Iriomé was already sitting inside the cave in front of a huge fire. Nesfete painted downward triangles on Iriomé's forehead and cheeks with blue powder. There was a different atmosphere from that in previous ritual ceremonies. There was more at stake. Tonight was about the life of all.

A clear, thin sound now replaced the dark tones. A harimaguada was playing a flute made from the bone of a bird leg. She charmed a simple melody out of the finely honed instrument, which like a very thin thread was wiggling at first only through the cave and then through the souls of the men and women present. It had scarcely faded away when down below at the feast the men with their drums began to play. Carefully crafted instruments from the hollowed trunk of a dragon tree, strung with tanned goatskins. The drummers increased the beat until it was in unison with the dull stomping of the timber rods of the tribal leaders in the cave above. Together they created a furious, unique rhythm, which carried them away to a world where everything was one.

Iriomé leaned forward and threw a handful of chopped pine needles into the flames, which flared up crackling and sputtering. Then she got up and called the spirit of Tichiname. "Tichiname, highest harimaguada of Benahoare, I beg you for a sign of your approval that I'll be your successor."

To show the deceased the way, the harimaguadas now raised a long-drawn, clear sound. When one woman was running out of breath, the next took over with neither a pause nor an interruption to be heard. After a while a transparent figure with long white hair appeared at the entrance of the cave surrounded by a bright glow. Her feet did not touch the ground as she came closer and softly stroked Iriomé's hair and back down to her feet. All this seemed like an eternity, but only a few moments had elapsed when the spirit of the old medicine woman dissolved in the smoke of the fire.

Iriomé raised her arms to the sky, letting out a shrill whistle, which she repeated three times. The harimaguadas also put their arms up and burst forth into a tone from which clearly could be made out the word *amakuna*. At a signal from Iriomé, Nesfete stepped to the alcove where the clay bowl with the potion of wisdom stood. Nesfete stirred the yellow streaks and offered it with both hands to the new supreme harimaguada. Iriomé thanked her and with eyes closed put the bowl to her lips. She thought the earthy flavor familiar when the first gulp was running down her throat. The effect was not long in coming. Part of her seemed to disengage, and she saw everything around her from an ever greater distance. Colors and sounds changed. The cave walls, the wood logs in the fire, and the people around her took on unnatural, elongated forms. They became more and more distorted, until everything dissolved into a spiral and disappeared into the fog of memory.

Iriomé saw a purple sun coloring the sky red, then the sea and the earth, too. But the light was transformed into blood that gushed from countless wounds. A thunder and crack echoed from the rock walls, followed by shrill death screams. A stone ax split the skull of an unknown man. Eyes wide open were staring into the sky. Bodies clashed. Wheezing turned into a dying gargle.

The madness of senseless killing tugged at Iriomé like a dangerous storm that uprooted a tree. She had to grab hold of something to avoid being carried away into the dark nothingness from which there was no return. Into the inner volcano, where Guayote was ready and waiting for his victim. She desperately grasped for a hold, but she grasped at nothing. Just when she had nearly given up, in a blue light a female shape appeared. At first she thought it as Tichiname, but as the shape came closer, she recognized it as a young woman with long strawberry-blonde hair, wearing strange clothes. The woman put out her hand, and Iriomé reached for it at the last moment. The dark powers that had been tearing at her slowly left her alone, and the roar subsided.

And suddenly Iriomé felt safe. She felt trust in this woman encouraging her from a world in another time who seemed to tell her that things would go on. That the disaster she had seen was not the end. That there was nothing, not even death, that could deter her from defending amakuna against the iron man now and for all eternity.

Chapter 13

"Wake up, sleeping beauty!" Romy heard Thea's voice as if from far away. It was not easy for her to let go of Iriomé's hand. But she felt that even the brief moment of contact had been important for the Guanche woman. How she would have liked to tell her that amakuna, even now in the twenty-first century, was growing in the same cave, and the hostile invaders had not got hold of it—neither those of the past nor the present.

But too late. Romy slowly opened her eyes. Thea was sitting in front of her dressed in a bright green nightgown. "That must have been an exhausting hiking tour if you could fall asleep at the kitchen table."

Romy stared at Thea. Just as after her first encounter with Iriomé, she noticed the earthy, slightly putrid taste in her mouth and on her lips.

"What's wrong with you?" Thea, who knew her too well to not notice, asked.

"I've been there again," Romy said in a low voice.

"Where—there?"

"I was with Iriomé and the Guanches."

"What!" Thea sank into the chair next to her. "How?"

Romy pointed to the bowl with the rest of the mushroom brew. "With this. With amakuna!"

Thea gave her a puzzled look, then took the pot and sniffed it. "Doesn't smell very appetizing."

"Doesn't taste it either."

"And how do you know . . . where did you get . . . I mean, what is this?"

"A fungus that grows in the burial cave of the former harimaguadas. You were right; you can travel to the time of the Guanches by drinking it. It's totally crazy! Definitely not logical."

Thea looked at her triumphantly. "I knew it. But then you must have swallowed the stuff when you first met Iriomé."

Romy nodded. "I can even remember the aftertaste. It was the same as what I have in my mouth right now."

"Maybe Iriomé quickly overcame the limits of space and time to get to you and helped you ingest the stuff when you fell?" Thea grinned.

"I don't know what to think anymore," said Romy, her elbows on the table, her head held thoughtfully in her hands.

She sat bolt upright. "But one thing I know, or rather, I'm pretty sure of now."

Thea looked at her questioningly.

"The mushroom has an additional effect."

"Yes?"

"It heals, and in a way that I can no more explain than anything else."

Thea looked at her as if she had finally begun to doubt her friend's sanity.

"No, think about it a minute," Romy said excitedly. "I survived this fall from about twenty-five feet without a break, a bruise, or even the slightest scratch. This is counter to logic, the laws of gravity, everything we understand to be true. And I had the same taste in my mouth as now. What does this tell us?"

"That you're crazy?" Thea suggested and pulled the nightgown tightly around her slender body.

"I'm not!" Romy put the bowl with the rest of the amakuna in front of Thea and stirred the yellow streaks, which had once again formed on the surface. "Drink!"

Thea looked at her doubtfully. "I don't know."

"Please," Romy begged. "Nothing will happen to you. Look at me—everything's just fine. All you need is trust. The worst thing that could happen is that you also travel into the past."

"But . . ."

"Drink!"

"Well. It doesn't matter anyway." Thea took a deep breath, took the bowl, and downed it in one gulp.

The sun forced his way through the shutters as if he wanted to be present at what was happening now. For the first time in her life Romy felt the desire to pray. She did it quietly, without moving her lips, while her friend slowly collapsed on the kitchen table.

Romy carried her without much effort into her bedroom and laid her on the bed.

She spent the next few hours in a state of hope and self-doubt. What if something went wrong? What if she simply had been hallucinating? Her first hallucination had been so intense, and her stay on the island had enhanced the mental pictures. No wonder she read something into all she experienced. And what if Thea woke up in a few hours and nothing had changed? Or even worse, if the effect of the mushroom was too much for her weakened body? As a friend, but above all as a medical professional, she had acted completely irresponsibly.

Time and again she quietly opened the door to Thea's bedroom, but her friend lay in bed sleeping soundly. Her eyelids twitched as if she was having a haunting dream. Romy wondered what she was experiencing right now.

To give herself something to do, Romy ground the dried mushrooms from the oven into a fine powder and filled a hermetically sealable glass tube from her drug case. Then she sat in the garden beneath one of the two dragon trees and waited. She was not able to read anything or even to open her laptop and check emails. She just sat there listening to the chirping of the birds, the rustling of the lizards, the buzzing of the bees, and the distant sound of the sea. Eyes closed, she tried to think back to the time in which Iriomé lived. Everything was so much more magical, so much more deeply connected with nature and the supernatural. The art of healing was not to be compared with what medical science taught today and with which most doctors agreed. The healers of that time relied on their intuition. On the experience of their predecessors, which they could access in some way and which then worked through them. At least that's how she understood it. The harimaguadas did not need statistics, diagnostic robots, and especially the pharmaceutical industry.

But why had Iriomé not used amakuna to heal Joaquín? Was it possible that she did not know anything about the healing effect of the mushroom? Or did it only exist in Romy's imagination? What had made her so sure earlier in the kitchen?

Of course, Romy was also interested in the love story between the Guanche woman and the Spanish conqueror. Could Iriomé really trust Joaquín? After all, the conquistadors had not left much of the culture of the islanders. This was at least what the history books said. Was he really the one who would help her to protect amakuna? From her own experiences with men she would have strongly advised Iriomé against it. But unfortunately it was too late. Iriomé had lived her life a long time ago.

Around noon Sam came over. He vehemently claimed his share of the mushrooms and said he would climb into the cave again with his friend to secure himself a small supply otherwise. Thus Romy had no choice but to bag some of the powder for him. That she had already carried out a self-experiment and that Thea, this very moment, was traveling somewhere between the times, she preferred to keep to herself.

"I'd still wait and see what I find out in the laboratory," she warned, although she knew that it was pointless. Knowing Sam, she was sure he would make his own experiment with the mushroom no later than this evening. On the other hand, it was definitely quite thrilling to wonder if he would also end up in the time of the Guanches. Probably the mushroom had a different effect in every person, depending on his or her frame of mind. Or maybe depending on former lives?

Romy was impatient for Thea to finally wake up to share her experiences. She looked at her watch. Only 1 p.m. She herself had traveled in the other time for seven hours. It was strange how normal it all sounded to her already. As if it was nothing unusual to make a short trip to the late fifteenth century from time to time. Within a week her whole world had been turned upside down. Nothing would ever be the same again.

Finally fatigue overcame her. She woke with a start when Thea called her name from the bedroom. Romy rose noisily from her chair and almost fell flat, excited as she was. Thea, in contrast, sat peacefully on her bed beaming. If angels really existed, then they must look like her friend in that moment. It was as if everything that had ever aggrieved her, that had ever been done to her, or that she had done to herself had been lifted from her. As if a dark curtain that had been closed for a long time was opened to reveal a glistening bright sunny day. Romy could only stare. She could not utter a word. Tears filled her eyes. Something had changed. Thea was cured. Romy felt it. No, she knew it! Even without laboratory tests, without CT scans, and without her body needing to be cut open. She just knew it, although she had no proof at the moment. And she knew even more. Thea had become Thea. She no longer was the outcast daughter of a rich mother, the stubborn neurologist, or the cracking rock climber. All she was now was Thea, a part of the boundless universe, a cog finally turning at the correct speed in the wheel of infinite existence.

Romy was witnessing a miracle for the second time. She had to digest this first. Although she still had no clue how everything was connected, she promised herself she would find out. She would not rest until the mystery of this mushroom was revealed and she could understand why it had been she of all people who had found it, why she had been chosen by Iriomé, and what task she was meant to perform in this mystery. Romy hugged her friend silently and sat next to her. She felt the urge to ask Thea immediately what she had experienced during her journey, but Thea's face told her it was premature to talk about it. The two of them silently looked out the open window at the dragon tree, the sea, and the infinite horizon.

Chapter 14

Three weeks later, Romy was waiting in line at the check-in counter for the flight to Munich with mixed feelings. It was hard to leave. The island, with its fragrant pine forests, volcanoes, and steep cliffs, against which the raging sea had been breaking for millennia, had become a piece of home to her. The same was true for Thea, who spontaneously decided to stay. Just a few days after her experience with amakuna, she was certain: the island was the place she wanted to be. This was where she belonged. She wanted to live here. As soon as she found a nice home for rent or sale, she wanted to have her belongings shipped over.

Nothing would make her go back to Germany, back to a family that rejected her, and back to a health-care system that had not lived up to its name in a long time. No, her place was here on this island, where she had gotten her life.

Romy tried several times to get Thea to talk about her time travel, but without success. Thea didn't want to talk about it. She eluded Romy's requests whenever she could. Something had changed between them. Their common experience with the mushroom had inexplicably pushed them apart instead of forging them together for eternity. And just like Iriomé, Romy felt abandoned by the person who played the most important role in her life, the one she trusted most of all. Thea vehemently opposed Romy's dream to put amakuna at the disposal of all humankind. Because of that, they even had a dispute. Thea never tired of underlining Tichiname's last words: *Only when people are free from the greed for power and wealth will its secret be safe to reveal.*

126

Furthermore, she was convinced that once the pharmaceutical industry found out about test results that could be taken seriously they would make sure that both Romy and amakuna disappeared for good. The health-care business flourished on disease so the companies would not let it be pried out of their hands.

Although Romy knew her friend was right, a fire of curiosity was burning inside her. She was a scientist and simply had to solve the mystery of the mushroom. Maybe Iriomé had reached out to her through the times exactly in order to make amakuna available for humankind?

"*Su pasaporte, por favor,*" the Spanish receptionist behind the counter interrupted her thoughts. Romy handed her the document, heaved her suitcase on the scale, and received a boarding pass.

By the time she got to the gate, she felt abandoned once more. But she also knew that it was her business alone to follow through with what was in store for her in Germany. Was this the reason Thea had withdrawn from her?

Munich received her with black ice. The cold winter air that she was no longer used to took her breath away. Romy slipped with her luggage down an ice-slicked street in front of the airport arrivals building between parked cars and impatient taxi drivers. When she was distracted for a moment, it happened . . . Despite the excellent tread of her walking shoes she fell hard on her bottom and slid against the bumper of a Jaguar XF limousine, the tires of which missed her by a hair. An elderly woman behind her let out a little scream, and a young man rushed to her, but in a flash a hand in an elegant suede glove was held out to her.

"Everything okay?"

Romy looked into a tanned male face with deep black eyes. It took her only a second to realize this man would readily be able to trigger the feeling of sandstorms on her skin. His pleasant voice sent chills down her spine. She liked his smell and his face. But she also immediately recognized the warrior in him: a well-paid sword for large economic battles; instead of armor, elegant designer suits were worn.

"Yes, I think so. I'm fine," she said bravely, although one of her butt cheeks hurt quite a bit.

The stranger helped her up. For one fleeting second their faces were so close they could have kissed. Romy felt how the skin on her cheeks contracted in a pleasant way. Perhaps no sandstorm, but a strong wind in any case.

"Can I give you a lift?" he asked politely. The man spoke German well but had a slight Spanish accent. "I'm going to Augsburg but can also drive you somewhere else."

This was really a bit too much. "Thank you, but that's not necessary," Romy stammered, perplexed.

"What a pity." The stranger gave Romy a last smile, climbed back into his limousine, and ordered the driver to go on.

Romy watched in bewilderment as the car left, then shook her head at herself. *Have I taken leave of my senses? What is wrong with me?* He surely would have driven her home. Or at least she could have asked for his business card. Now he was gone. Just as quickly as he had walked into her life. *Well done!* Due to her suspicions another really nice guy had probably slipped through her fingers. Hastily she patted the dust off her pants and strode to a bench where the bus for the railway station would be leaving. To make matters worse, the bus was full to bursting. With difficulty she squeezed through baggage, people, and their odors to the back of the bus. How much more comfortable her trip could have been! A temperature-regulated limousine, probably with a bar and heated seats in addition to a handsome, good-smelling, interesting man. Would she ever see the guy again? She had not even made a note of his license plate.

Thankfully, she soon was occupied with the practical matters of the journey. The train from Munich to Augsburg was not running because of frozen switches. This meant rail replacement transport. While she tried to figure out where the bus departed and more importantly when, she momentarily forgot about those dark eyes that had fascinated her so much.

Totally exhausted, Romy arrived home shortly before midnight. In her apartment, it was hardly less freezing cold than outside. Winter had relentlessly eaten its way into the old walls, and although her beloved cockle stove did its best, the room did not get warm. Romy was sitting on her couch wrapped in a blanket and wearing thick socks, a bottle of Teneguia Tinto on the table in front of her. As expected, it didn't taste as good as on the island. Just like the smoked goat cheese, which she could not get enough of there. She longed to be back and suddenly felt out of place in her own apartment. Everything seemed weird and unreal, the ticking of her grandmother's old clock, the flush of the toilet on the floor above her, and the motorcycle that drove past her window with a loud roar. Romy missed the particular silence of the island, when at night only the wind softly swept around the house, carrying the distant sound of the surf with it. How she had enjoyed being lulled to sleep by it. Of course she could understand Thea. She would have loved to stay there herself. Just like Thea, she enjoyed, for the first time in her life, the feeling of finally being in a place where she felt at home.

But Iriomé had not called her without reason, of this Romy was convinced. Why else should she have discovered the mushroom if not to make it available to the whole world? If people never again had to endure suffering through illness, perhaps they would change their behavior. Their greed for power and wealth might eventually be a thing of the past, and a kind of golden age could begin again. Maybe then times would dawn like those the islands had blissfully known. At the thought Romy smiled to herself and realized that the bottle of red wine was almost empty now. No wonder she had lost herself in such rosy pictures of the future.

The ding of the washing machine brought her back to reality. Romy got up with a sigh. Before going to bed she would hang her laundry, even though her legs were heavy as lead and tomorrow an exciting day awaited. In her lab she would be able to get a better understanding of the mushroom. She was a scientist, and maybe she was on the verge of making a great discovery. Nothing better could have happened to her!

While hanging her summer clothes on the clothes rack in the bathroom one by one, she was whistling a little tune.

ᐧᐧ

Once the heavy door of the jail in Munich had closed behind him, he could breathe freely again for the first time. The sun on his face was hot. It had not been his first time in prison, but this time it was different from before. Losing his freedom was always like death to him, but since he knew about his former life, the time had not been so hard for him. Instead, another responsibility now rested on him that muddled up his whole life. He could no longer only do what he wanted to. A new task was waiting for him that demanded more from him than anything he had done so far.

Chapter 15

With an ugly sound the security terminal at the front door of Biotex Company ate her ID card. Outraged, Romy banged away at it with the flat of her hand, as if this would cause the box to spit it out again. Nothing happened. She could do nothing else but go to the main entrance and check in like some visitor.

"Girl, you look great. I am green with envy!" Kyra greeted her. Strangely she was behind the reception desk instead of in front of Berger's office. "How was your holiday?" Kyra did not wait for the answer.

"There have been some changes here, as you might have already noticed. We have new security, new ID cards. And in other respects a completely new wind is blowing around here."

"Good morning, to begin with," Romy tried to interrupt Kyra's tirade.

"Oh sorry! Good morning. I just don't know whether I'm coming or going." Kyra handed her a new ID card, and Romy acknowledged the receipt.

"By the way, a little warning. You don't have your office to yourself any longer. *She's* sitting there now!"

"Who's she?"

"The controller from Forster's Health. Yes, as I said, a new wind is blowing here, a wind that is pretty hot. And maybe it will breeze us all out soon."

Slowly it began to dawn on Romy. Berger's fears that Forster's

Health could swallow Biotex had obviously come true. "Is Berger in?" she asked in dismay.

Kyra shook her head. "He only shows up once in a while now. Honestly, I don't even know if he still owns the business at all. A lot of rumors are circulating, but so far no one has told us what's going on."

Romy thanked Kyra and pocketed her new card. As she took the elevator up, she felt a mild panic rise inside her, which she got under control with a few breathing exercises before entering her office through the open door.

"You must be Romy Conrad. I've heard a lot about you," a deep voice with a slight Spanish accent welcomed her. It belonged to a pretty dark-haired woman who sat at Romy's desk and was getting up to shake Romy's hand. She wore a red skirt and jacket cut to emphasize a beautiful figure, black stockings, and high heels. "I'm Juana Marquéz. I'm glad to finally meet you. I've heard such great things about you."

All Romy could utter was, "Hello, I'm also pleased to meet you." Now she understood what Kyra had meant by a hot wind blowing.

"I've assigned myself to your office because it seemed to me that yours is the quietest. We've temporarily moved your desktop to the wall and packed your stuff in the boxes there," Juana Marquéz said while she returned to her seat. "I hope you don't mind. Since you've been on holiday during the last weeks anyway . . ."

Romy's puzzled look stopped her. In fact, all her shelves had been restocked with someone else's folders.

"I won't be a burden to you very long. Just a few weeks; until I have sorted through everything. After all, Forster's Health wants to know exactly what business we saddle ourselves with."

"No one forces you." It slipped out of Romy's mouth.

"No need to tell me. I'm just responsible for accounting. But if it makes you feel better, Forster's Health has no plans to make reductions on a large scale," the Mediterranean beauty said with a patronizing tone.

"How reassuring," Romy answered. How could she work on the

mushroom in peace in the presence of this snoop? If a company like Forster's Health learned about it at this stage, precisely what Thea had predicted would happen.

She went to her laboratory, greeted her two coworkers, who seemed equally as surprised as Romy herself, and then opened the door to the animal room. The terrarium of Cleo, the cobra, was kept there. Cleo's poison fangs provided sought-after neurotoxins for Romy's homeopathic research, a field of study she had built up in accordance with Berger. By now, Romy had grown quite fond of Cleo.

The snake recognized Romy by the way she walked; more specifically, by the vibration of her footsteps on the linoleum. It lifted its head immediately. Its amber eyes with narrow pupils stared at Romy blankly. Romy thought she could definitely read the word *hunger* in them. The calendar above the glass box showed that today was feeding day. Only every three days Cleo was fed a white mouse that was grown in the laboratory just for this purpose. This was enough for the snake. If it was not hungry, the little rodent presented a serious hazard to the snake. The tiniest bite could mean death, since reptiles were highly susceptible to all mammalian infections. A fact that Romy liked somehow. Thus, at the right moment, even a small, harmless mouse had a chance against a large, highly venomous snake.

But this morning there was not the slightest chance that the rodent would survive. No sooner had Romy placed the mouse in the terrarium than the snake focused its eyes on the curious animal standing on its hind legs, poking around sniffing. Then the snake shot forward and snapped at it. Romy had gotten used to the sight and didn't mind so much anymore, unlike when she had started working here.

"Certainly not pleasant to look death in the eye this way." She heard Berger's voice behind her. She had not heard him come in.

"How was your holiday; how's your friend doing?"

"She's just fine," Romy said.

"That makes me happy. Still she needs to get in touch with Feistner. All Avistan test persons must . . ."

"Does that mean the study is actually still going on?" Romy interrupted him, horrified.

"This is no longer my responsibility." Berger watched the cobra as it choked the mouse.

"Thea didn't come back with me," Romy said.

"What's that supposed to mean?"

All the excitement of the last weeks had completely pushed the Avistan study into the background. Romy wasn't prepared for this conversation with her boss. "She wants to spend the rest of her life in La Palma," she said, somewhat more sharply than intended.

Berger's face showed concern. "She'll manage at most a few months, if at all. I would like to speak to you in private in my office."

Romy followed, her feelings in turmoil. Should she let Berger in on it? She needed his lab and perhaps also his expert advice. Besides . . . perhaps Biotex could be saved by amakuna? It would at least give them a chance. On the other hand, Forster's Health was already in the house, and according to Berger, it was best to stay clear of its CEO. What options did she have? She had to go through with it. She needed to trust Berger, even though it was difficult for her.

"Thea is fully healed," she said in a calmer voice now, when they were alone in his office.

"What do you mean by that?"

"Very simple. There's nothing there anymore. She's had a scan, and the MRI showed no signs of metastases. You're free to see the clinical findings."

"Who gave the scan? Some island doctor?" Hannes Berger looked at her doubtfully. "Besides, I must tell you, that Avistan has failed—in every aspect. At least that's my opinion. Forster's Health wants to launch it anyway and with a lot of fanfare." Resignedly, he let himself drop into his shabby leather office chair.

Romy thought for a moment; then she put the tube containing the mushroom powder on his desk. "This cured her." Briefly she told her boss how she found the mushroom and discovered its phenomenal effect. She left out the story of Iriomé and the Guanches, as this would certainly have been too much for him. Even the "cure-all" mushroom must have sounded like a tale from the Arabian Nights. Needless to say, it did.

After she finished, he smiled at her benevolently. "Romy, I appreciate very much that you want to help me. But what you're talking about rather reminds me of Chinese magic mushrooms, mistletoe therapy, or magical roots from the Amazon. You know what I think about that."

"Give me a few days, and we'll know more," Romy urged him. "Maybe we can use it to defy Forster's Health. It would be worth a try, don't you think?" Berger furrowed his brow. He had never looked so bad before.

"What have you got to lose?"

He looked at her with resignation. "Only because I cherish you and because our mutual friend Hattinger goes into raptures about you." The professor had been her thesis supervisor and helped place Romy with Berger. "Maybe you should call him; after all, mycology is one of his fields of study."

"I think we should keep it to ourselves for the time being. You have to promise me!"

"Fine. But nevertheless, you should definitely convince Thea to come back."

"Why? So that Forster's Health nails her and claims that Avistan healed her?"

Berger took a deep breath and then sank deeper into his chair. Romy really felt sorry for him. It was certainly not easy to watch one's own life's work pass irrevocably into other hands and not be able to do anything about it.

When Romy was about to leave his office, he stopped her.

"Yes?"

"Thank you. I really do appreciate your loyalty."

৩৩

Around 6 p.m. the lab workers got their things together and called it a day. Only Juana Marquéz seemed to do overtime and had brought down two thick folders from the shelf.

Romy thought hard about how she could get rid of her so that she could finally start what she had come for; then the problem fortunately cleared itself. Juana's cell phone rang, and after a while she said, looking annoyed, "Chez Julienne, at 7 p.m. *Bueno.* I'll be there." She hung up and turned to Romy. "I really don't know what Berger wants from me . . ."

Romy secretly sent him a big thank you. They were still a good team. Perhaps everything would ultimately come up roses and the snake would spit out the mouse again.

Once Juana left, Romy got the tube containing the mushroom powder from her bag and set to work.

Shortly after midnight, she got the first decent result. Romy recorded a molecular structure that confirmed she was dealing with a hallucinogenic alkaloid. Romy could very well imagine certain regions in the brain where signals were stimulated by the mushroom and sent to diseased cells, triggering a kind of self-healing process. This could mean the mushroom created a link between mind, matter, and a particular environment. Exactly what scientists in the field of alternative medicine had long been searching for. Along the way it probably set in motion temporary changes in consciousness, similar to substances from the same family of alkaloids. This was basically how it seemed to work.

Excited, Romy scoured through all accessible internet archives for chemical compounds. But she could not discover any alkaloid that in some way resembled or even corresponded to amakuna in its structure. It seemed to be as yet unknown.

Romy opened a window, letting some cold winter air in. Her heart pounded. It was a very similar feeling to what she'd felt in the cave where she had come across the mushroom for the first time. Even then there was no doubt she was tracking something huge. After she had closed the window and made strong coffee, she decided to forget her original intention and call Professor Hattinger. She simply had to be sure before she seriously talked to Berger about further measures. If a luminary like Hattinger confirmed these results, this first evaluation of the mushroom could be a real opportunity for Biotex.

The professor was a night person and surely was still sitting at his desk. He had been a friend of her parents and had often lent Romy support during her studies. Certainly he would do it again. Nevertheless, she hesitated for a moment before picking up the phone. Hattinger would then be the fifth confidant along with Thea, Sam, Berger, and her. Not to mention the unknown person whose traces they found in the cave. It made her slightly uneasy. But what other path was there?

The professor immediately answered. Romy told him briefly what they found and how Thea had been cured. To be on the safe side she dropped the Guanches part of the story again. When she finished her account, all she heard for a while was the old man's heavy breathing on the other end of the line.

"I don't want to frustrate you, and perhaps Thea's really been cured," he said. "But in most of these so-called miracle cures it turns out afterward that there has been another reason for the healing," he said in his own quiet, authoritative way.

It was clear he had the same doubts as Berger. He was also a thoroughbred scientist who didn't believe anything without sevenfold double-blind tests. Nevertheless he would not leave her in the lurch. "Send me a sample, and mail me your preliminary results. Then we'll see what happens. It is probable that your mushroom can't be synthesized anyway. Most fungi only spore in their natural surroundings and cannot be reproduced artificially."

"I think this fungus is very special," said Romy, who suddenly felt like a stupid little student. "The original inhabitants used it."

"Well then . . ." Hattinger's ironic undertone was hard to miss. "If you send me your results right now, I'll have a look at them at once. You know I can't sleep before four in the morning anyway."

"Can we please keep this to ourselves for the time being?"

"Of course," replied the professor. "Don't worry."

Romy compressed all files in a zip file and was just pressing the Send button as a black uniformed guard from the security service entered the lab. His athletic body was striking, as well as his bright hair and sparkling blue eyes, above which there was a clearly visible scar. Romy stared at him, aghast.

"Did I frighten you? I'm so sorry."

Slowly she regained her poise but was unable to utter a single word.

"My name's Tom Sattler. I've only been working here for a few nights."

"Romy Conrad," she said in a flat voice. His handshake was warm and strong and gave her a feeling of security.

"May I ask what you're working on?" he asked with apparent interest.

Romy shook her head. "Company secret," she said, as composed as possible.

"I see. Don't be afraid; we have everything under control. There's no need to worry."

Again she looked into his striking blue eyes. They reminded her of someone, as did the scar. *Tanausú!* Was she seeing ghosts now? Did all men from Iriomé's life suddenly turn up in hers? Involuntarily she thought of the man at the airport, who had triggered similar sandstorms on her skin as Joaquín had on Iriomé's. And now this watchman. *What is going on? Am I just completely exhausted?*

For a mad moment she considered asking this man if he perhaps had been the leader of the tribe of Aceró on the island of Benahoare once in a previous life. She took a deep breath. "I'm convinced you're doing a good job," she said instead as cool as possible and then shut down her server, but not without first activating the encoder.

"Thanks, we do what we can," he said.

Even his voice sounded familiar to her. She wanted to call Thea immediately but somehow was not sure about receiving support there. "Good night! Probably we'll see more of each other from now on. I've got quite a lot of night shifts ahead," she said as jovially as possible before she put on her winter coat and left the laboratory.

This time she was glad about the cold air that hit her face on the way to the parking lot. It cleared her head and made her feel sane again. The temperature was definitely below freezing, because the snow under her winter boots was crunching. No, she was not overtired. Perhaps life was just showing itself from a side she had not known yet.

൭෨

The cozy café where Romy used to go for breakfast was just two blocks away from her apartment. As a single person, it was not worth the effort to fill the fridge for the little she ate in the morning. In the Petit Café they knew exactly how Romy preferred her latte and which jam she wanted with her croissant. For a brief moment, it felt as if the events of the past few weeks had never taken place. She inhaled the scent of the coffee and enjoyed the atmosphere. She knew almost everyone who came here in the morning. Those who comfortably sat at a table to read the daily paper in detail and also those who quaffed off an espresso at the counter. Romy belonged to the former. This half hour in the morning was sacred to her. No one was allowed to disturb her. But apparently this no longer applied. Her cell phone loudly announced the receipt of a text. Romy fished it reluctantly from the depths of her purse: *Beware of the CEO. Greetings from T.,* it said.

Instantly the perfectly ordinary morning was over. Romy felt an almost painful uneasiness well up in her. Who was T? Tanausú? So this meant these guys from the past could also text? *Soon I'll really be ready for the funny farm,* she thought.

Romy tried to calm down and took a large sip of her latte, her hand trembling when she brought the cup to her lips. *Perhaps the message was not for me at all?* She glanced at her cell phone. The sender was anonymous. *How is that even possible?* An inner voice told her she should go to the lab immediately. She left her croissant untouched, got up, paid at the counter, and hurried back to her house in the Welsergasse, where her car was parked.

There, the next surprise was in store for her. The front door to her building stood open. Romy knew she had closed it behind her when she left the house, if only because Mrs. Bieber, who lived upstairs from her, complained about it. Clearly there was something wrong. She ran to her apartment on the ground floor and put the key into the lock. The door opened after one turn, although Romy always turned the key twice. She thought feverishly. *Should I call the police?* She fumbled for her mobile. Too late. From inside the apartment she heard someone opening the living room window and obviously fleeing. As fast as she could, she ran through the long hallway into the living room. The window was open, but out on the street no one could be seen. She looked around in panic. All the drawers of her small secretary desk inherited from her grandmother were pulled out. Romy kept her jewelry there, but nothing seemed to be missing. *What on earth had the thief been after?*

Then a shiver ran down her spine. Manolo's map! Frantically she rifled through the drawer in which she had put the map. Nothing! Whoever was just in here had taken it. He must have been specifically looking for it. But who knew about it? Only Berger. He was the one she had told about the cave search operation yesterday. He knew where she lived, and he knew that at this time she was always in the Petit Café.

Her heart beat faster. She had to sit down and take a breath. Had she betrayed amakuna already? Had what Thea warned her about already happened? She jumped up, ran to her car, and put her foot down hard on the gas as soon as her tires touched the road.

A short time later she stood in her lab breathless. She tore open the door to the laboratory fridge. Empty! Romy's heart skipped a beat again. Not a single petri dish was still in its appropriate compartment. Stunned, she started her computer and with flying fingers opened the files she created the night before. The folder was completely empty. Despite the encoding nothing was left.

Romy forced herself to stay calm, even though her heart was thumping. Berger was the only one who knew the decryption code on this computer. Or was this Forster's Health señorita behind it, who had just walked into the lab with a neutral expression?

Romy pushed her aside and ran up the stairs to the office of her boss, taking three steps at a time. Ignoring the protests of his new secretary, she tore open the door. "What did you do with my samples?" she cried, beside herself with rage.

Realizing that Berger was not alone, she paused. A well-dressed man sat on the visitor's couch. It was the stranger from the airport. He smiled at her in bewilderment.

"May I introduce: Nic Saratoga, CEO of Forster's Health Europe. And that's one of my best employees, Romy Conrad," Berger said for appearance's sake.

Brushing this forced politeness aside, Romy pushed on, "I want to know who hacked into my computer and what happened to the files I created last night!"

Nic Saratoga stood up and walked slowly toward her. "I'm glad to see you again," he said in a dark, warm voice. He gently laid his perfectly shaven cheek against hers, first right, then left. And whether Romy wanted it or not, the first grains of sand pierced into her skin.

"You know each other?" Berger asked, surprised.

"The young lady almost fell under my wheels at the airport. Or rather, under my car. But apart from that she's right." He fastened his dark eyes on Berger. "You've got immense security vulnerabilities here. The new security company that you've engaged allegedly employs a certain Tom Sattler, who's said to be in reality Tanausú, an eco terrorist."

Romy gasped. "What? Who?"

"Pardon, who?" Berger also asked, worried.

"You should be better informed, Mr. Berger." Saratoga got his iPad out of his pocket, called up an article in the Sunday edition of the local newspaper and read it aloud:

"Ecoterrorist released from custody. Evidence was not sufficient for a hearing in Germany. The ecoterrorist Alexander Merten, known under the pseudonym Tanausú, was released from custody in Munich yesterday. His specialty is the uncovering of scandals in the pharmaceutical, chemical, and food industry. Furthermore, he supposedly has been involved in several attacks on global companies in Switzerland, the United States, and Germany. But the evidence was too scant for the Munich investigator.

"As has become known in the meantime, until five years ago he led a notorious unit of FARC rebels in Colombia under the name of Comandante Leandro ..."

He looked up. "Need more? The man is extremely dangerous and stops at nothing," he said to Berger with a sharp undertone in his voice.

Romy tried as best she could to unite the pieces of the puzzle that were known to her into a full picture. Involuntarily, she remembered the legend of the guerreros sagrados, the holy warriors, about whom Sam had told her in the caldera. Didn't people say that they reappeared in different centuries to fight against the powers of evil in the world? Was this perhaps not a legend at all? What about the text? Had Tanausú been the author? It was all out of hand. She was dizzy. She seemed to be caught in a maelstrom of past and present, in which she was almost drowning. She must have triggered something that she could no longer control. As if all that wasn't enough, this man, who was still standing next to her, drove her out of her mind.

"I'd like to make a suggestion." Nic Saratoga now turned to her with a winning smile. "I'd like to invite you to lunch; I owe it to you anyway. This surely will help straighten things out."

Chapter 16

The Don Quixote was simply but tastefully furnished with dark wooden tables and chairs. Over the bar air-cured ham was hanging from the ceiling. It was still early, and the two of them were the only guests. Saratoga ordered a light cava, a Spanish sparkling wine, which could be enjoyed without guilt at this time of day. It was served with black olives, Serrano ham, several kinds of Manchego cheese, and *gambas al ajillo,* whose smell of garlic soon filled the whole place.

He raised his glass and looked into her eyes. "I'm very happy to have met you again, even if I wish it were under better circumstances."

Romy agreed, although it was clear it had been precisely the right circumstances that had brought them together. Actually, she could imagine that what they just experienced was, so to speak, volume 2 of a five-hundred-year-old story. And it seemed to be up to her to bring this story to a favorable conclusion. But she was far from achieving that, considering the fact that she didn't even know what a happy ending might look like.

"*Salud,*" she said, clinking glasses with him. Despite how much he appealed to her, she took heed of the warning that Tanausú or whoever had sent that morning. Was this ecoterrorist perhaps even the thief? But why? If he really was a holy warrior, then he certainly wanted to protect the amakuna. Could it be from this man who sat opposite her?

"I want to be honest with you, Señorita Conrad. Your boss, whom, by the way, I appreciate very much, told me of your find after he received an email from Professor Hattinger with the confirmation that you pretty certainly have made an important discovery—whose further development you can't possibly shoulder alone. You're now in mortal danger already."

Romy stared at him speechless. Although she had asked both Berger and Hattinger for discretion, *both* ignored her wish without batting an eyelash. "My apartment was broken into this morning," she said angrily.

Saratoga looked at her in alarm. "And did you still have some of the mushroom at home?"

She shook her head.

"Has something been stolen from you?"

Should I tell him about the map? Something kept her from it, and she shook her head.

"This probably is already our competition," speculated Saratoga. "Hattinger may have started his own research on controlled sites and thus called into action the first vultures. Who knows where your results have ended up by now. Romy—if you don't mind that I call you that— you can't cope with such a discovery alone. Please understand that. And with Berger or an old man like Hattinger you are basically alone."

Romy began to understand this situation. Too many people already knew about the mushroom, making it so much harder to protect. Nic Saratoga was right. She would never manage this alone.

"I, on the other hand, can provide you with whatever you need," he continued. "A laboratory with the most modern facilities, and the financial resources of a global company. But above all, I'll take care of your safety and make sure the mushroom won't fall into the wrong hands. This is what matters to you, isn't it?"

She still was unable to speak. Had it not also been Iriomé's destiny to protect the mushroom together with Joaquín? She recalled the scene between the two harimaguadas. *The time in which amakuna was under the protection of virgins alone is over. Its future depends on love. The love between a wise woman and a man who has power . . .*

Saratoga was the CEO of a pharmaceutical company and definitely a man of power. Just as Joaquín, the Spanish conquistador, had been one. And power was required to protect something as valuable as amakuna.

But how was she to trust him? She could imagine only too well what methods corporations like Forster's Health used to generate their profits.

As if he had read her thoughts, he took her hand. He had the sensitive hands of a pianist, a thing she had always found attractive. "I wouldn't want anything happening to you, Romy! Come with me to my private property in Spain today. There you'll be safe for the present."

෬

For the first time in her life Romy could stretch out her long legs in an airplane and recline the seat as far as she wanted without anyone complaining. The food deserved at least three stars and the champagne even one more.

Across from her sat Nic Saratoga with his eyes closed. Despite the late hour, he was clean-shaven. He had loosened his tie and put his jacket on the seat next to him. A perfect figure, Romy noted. Not the beginnings of a belly and no double chin. The snow-white shirt was tailor-made, the shoes of simple elegance and the same color as his socks.

Despite all her reservations she decided to take Nic Saratoga's invitation and fly to Marbella with him in his private plane the same evening. She was well aware that he was one of the vultures, the iron men, as Iriomé would have said, yet she could not help but entrust herself to him. She understood only too well why Iriomé had healed the conquistador and helped him escape. She had been in love. And Romy was, too, and realized she had been since their first encounter at the airport.

"We're almost there," he said in a pleasant voice, opening his dark eyes. "Unfortunately I'll be away for an appointment in Puerto Banus on the yacht of the Sheikh of Bahrain first thing in the morning. He's planning a new hospital, and Forster's Health will support him. But at noon the two of us can have lunch together and discuss all further issues."

So this was his world. A world of private planes, villas in Marbella, and appointments with sheikhs in marinas. And in addition he was extremely handsome. A mixture that probably only a few women in the world could resist. Romy, of course, had known successful men before, but not at this level. She had always found excessive luxury and showing off with status symbols to be obscene. Still, she could not deny that at the moment everything that had to do with Nic Saratoga fascinated her to some degree.

The Learjet landed softly at the airport of Málaga. A silver Jaguar stopped right next to the small gangway. A chauffeur in a dark blue suit took her travel bag and opened the door for her. As Nic Saratoga sat beside her in the back of the car, briefly their thighs touched. Pure sandstorm feeling, right down to her toes and up to the roots of her hair. More and more Romy was aware of what she just let herself in for. *Had there been another choice for me? Should I have waited until the ominous ecoterrorist turned up? And then?* The lights of Costa del Sol were moving past them. In the distance Romy caught sight of the sea. Nic offered her a Spanish brandy from the well-stocked bar of the car and to be on first-name terms.

"I hope we'll be friends—not just business associates. Call me Nic. Nicolo is actually my name. My mother's from Colombia, my father from Panama, but our ancestors were of course Spanish. I studied in the US and the name Nic stuck." They clinked glasses.

"I grew up with my grandmother just a few kilometers from here in Fuengirola and even attended the German school in Marbella for a few years."

"*Hablas espanol,* so you speak Spanish," he said delighted. "This makes everything easier. You could work in Spain or South America and would be out of the line of fire for a start."

Romy looked at him doubtfully. Suddenly the picture of the snake and the mouse crossed her mind. *Am I walking into the same trap as Berger?*

"A steep academic career awaits you," she heard Nic saying. "Detailed articles in the *Medical Journal, Science Report,* or *Medicine Today.* I see it in my mind's eye. Alexander Fleming discovered penicillin; Romy Conrad, a mushroom to cure cancer. You'll see, we're making history in medicine."

Somehow it sounded okay. But she had not brought the mushroom to Germany to make history in medicine. What she wanted was to make it available to all humankind.

"Do you like classical guitar music?" asked Nic, as if he could hear her doubts and wanted to distract her. He did not wait for an answer but pressed a button on the console in front of them, and immediately the back of the car was filled with the virtuosic sounds of Paco de Lucía.

Romy enjoyed the music, into which all her excitement, doubts, and fears dissolved. The brandy caused a warm feeling in her stomach. After the second glass her body relaxed, and after the third she felt safe and secure. Her gaze rested on his lips, and she was not even surprised that at this moment she wished nothing more than to kiss him.

The next morning Romy was awakened by a pretty Spanish girl in a maid uniform with a beaming smile and a friendly *Buenos días* handing her a steamy cup of latte. Then she opened the curtains, letting in bright winter sun. It took Romy a moment to realize where she was. Last night she had not observed much of her new environment but had just flopped into bed dead tired.

While she was sipping the hot coffee, she looked around. She was in a tall room with whitewashed walls, a dark wooden ceiling, and antique Spanish furniture. Over the huge bed there hung a canopy of red brocade. To her right and left were double draped curtains made of red silk. What a difference from her bedroom at home with its furniture from the discount store. Romy looked at her watch. It was already after lunchtime!

"I've run you a bath," said the housemaid in the melodious Spanish that was typical of the Andalusians. "Enjoy it. You'll meet Señor Saratoga for lunch in the winter garden within an hour."

Romy began to remember. His invitation to come here with him suddenly appeared almost like kidnapping. Or rather like a seduction? She had to be on guard and must not allow herself to be taken in, either by all the luxuries or Nic Saratoga himself; at least not before she knew for sure whether she really could trust him. Finding out seemed the biggest challenge at the moment.

Frowning, she went into the adjoining bathroom, which was as large as Romy's living room in Augsburg. The tub had room for another three people. She stretched out in the warm water while the wheels in her head rattled on.

It was by no means the sheer goodness of his heart that had prompted Nic Saratoga to bring her here, she was sure of that. He wanted to keep her under control because she knew where the mushroom grew, which he wanted to secure for Forster's Health—hardly for commercialization, but rather for the drawer in which it would stay until the day the cows come home. Because what would become of the pharmaceutical industry if a remedy existed that grew for free and that healed everything and everyone?! Thea had foreseen this.

Suddenly she noticed the bars that were installed on the bathroom window, almost like a prison. At that moment she felt like she was in a live trap into which she had run with her eyes open. And Nic was the bait. What if she never got out of here? What if he kept her prisoner until she told him about the cave in the caldera? Had it been a mistake to trust this man? Just as it had been a mistake that Iriomé healed Joaquín and helped him escape? The very young Guanche woman could not have known what kind of a person Joaquín was. Romy, on the other hand, had had many experiences and was accordingly prejudiced. But who this Nic Saratoga actually was and what means he would employ to get what he wanted, she did not know.

She wrapped herself in the terry towel that had been laid out ready for her and that was so thick and soft she could have remained curled up in it forever. With mixed feelings, she put on jeans and a simple white blouse and left the room. She stepped into an endless hallway with a light marble floor covered with a red carpet. On the walls dark oil paintings of Spanish noblemen were displayed, almost all in armor and with weapons. Were they Nic's ancestors? In wall niches stood man-sized frames decorated with different armor, breastplates, and chain mail. A huge glass cabinet housed rifles and pistols.

It was like a museum. Some of it definitely dated back to the time of the conquistadores. Why on earth had he gathered all this stuff? Out of an attachment to Joaquín, who was a part of his soul, and to whom he unconsciously felt close? All this seemed pretty crazy. Romy was afraid that sooner or later she no longer would be able to distinguish between present and past. Bravely she walked down the hall until she came to an open double-winged door behind which there was a huge library. The shelves were full of modern books and old folios reaching to the ceiling. In order to get one of the books farther up, one had to climb a ladder that was fastened to the ceiling via a peripheral rail. The Franciscan monastery of Santa Cruz seemed terribly small in comparison. What treasures had Nic Saratoga amassed here? She took one of the leather-bound folios from a shelf. It was a chronology of the recapture of Spain from the Moors.

"Are you interested in Spanish history?" his voice came to her ear. Nic stood in the doorway. He wore casual beige linen trousers with a white sweater that underlined his dark complexion and black curly hair, which showed some silver streaks.

"No, but at the German school in Marbella I had a Spanish history teacher whose hobby was the Moors and the Spanish Reconquista," Romy replied, secretly thanking Señor Méndez that he had made the lessons so exciting that she actually remembered quite a lot. "Here in Andalusia the Moors held their ground till the end of the fifteenth century," she said, in an attempt to impress him a little with her knowledge.

"Unfortunately, then the cultural high time of this country was over. After the recapture by the Spaniards, it was all about power and gold from the New World."

"The age of the conquistadores," Romy said softly.

He nodded. "It was the golden age under Isabella of Castile and Ferdinand of Aragon."

"But it was also a cruel age." Romy was thinking of the conquest of the Canaries, the beginning of it all.

"That's true. They were not exactly humanists at the time. But let's think about something more pleasant. Like the wonderful meal that's waiting for us."

Romy took a deep breath and put the book back onto the shelf. How was she to find out if there really was some sort of connection between Nic Saratoga and Joaquín? She could not very well ask him directly. The mere fact that he was interested in Spanish history and collected paintings, weapons, and armor from the time of the conquistadores wasn't proof of Joaquín's reincarnation. If such a thing existed at all. Though she had no other explanation for all that had happened to her lately, there might be some other logical reason for it.

Nic gallantly linked arms with her and guided her through a glass door to the terrace. In that moment, she felt like she was on autopilot, as if Saratoga only had to pull a string, whereupon he could make her do anything he pleased—a thought she did not like at all.

Crossing a manicured lawn, they came to a glass pavilion, which stood in front of an oval, turquoise-painted pool that was empty now in the winter. Romy took in the huge size of the luxurious property, modeled after an old *castillo*. It was built from light sandstone, but instead of medieval loopholes, the architect had fit in large, modern doors and windows, all of which were barred. Three huge round towers formed the vertices of the triangle-shaped building. Here Saratoga had built himself a kind of modern fortress with medieval treasures that were probably worth a fortune.

Lunch smelled of freshly grilled fish and roasted garlic bread. The very sight of it made Romy's mouth water. Only now did she realize how hungry she was. The table was stylishly laid. Too classy for a lunch for two: a white china set with chiseled gold rims and a coat of arms on the bottom of each dish on a dark red tablecloth.

"Unfortunately, not the original," Nic, who had followed her gaze, said regretfully. "It's the emblem of the Order of Alcántara, the largest independent Equestrian Order of the Extremadura, at least until in the fifteenth century King Ferdinand of Aragon made himself leader of all equestrian orders and thus extremely limited their freedom of action." He said this in such a regretful manner, as if he himself had been affected. Perhaps Joaquín had been knighted and personally had suffered from this acquisition.

Nic pulled a chair out for her. "I hope you feel comfortable here," he said, smiling.

Comfortable was perhaps not the right word. Romy felt something like nervous anticipation. As if watching a thrilling movie, she wondered what would happen next and how the main character, in this case, she herself, would react to it. An odd situation. A little of it reminded her of a climbing adventure in an exotic country when one did not know what was waiting on the next hundred feet of altitude gain.

"Come on, let's clink glasses. There's something to celebrate." Nic raised his glass to Romy. "Khalifa Bin Kayid Al Tahan, Emir and Prime Minister of Bahrain and at the same time President of the United Emirates, has just signed a 400-million-dollar contract with Forster's Health."

Romy swallowed hard—400 million dollars! Well beyond her league. Obviously, a deal encompassing such a sum was something special even for Nic. The faceted crystal glasses, also with gold rims, gave a sonorous sound as they clinked.

"He's having a party tonight on his yacht. I would be pleased if you'd come along with me. Up in my wife's closet hang plenty of clothes for such an occasion. Take your pick. The two of you are about the same size. I'll inform Esmeralda to help you."

Romy took a deep breath. Not that she had something against worn clothes, on the contrary. She loved to spend whole Saturday mornings in her favorite second-hand shop in Augsburg. But the fact that there also existed a lady of the castle, she had successfully not considered so far. Now she remembered having learned from Kyra that Nic Saratoga was married to the daughter of the main shareholder of Forster's Health.

"Don't you think she would mind?" Romy asked cautiously.

He laughed out loud. "I don't think she even knows how many dresses she has and definitely not which dress is presently on which continent. Besides she's not here at the moment anyway. But if you have a problem with it, we can also have a new dress delivered from a boutique in Marbella."

"No, no. That is certainly not necessary," Romy said hastily.

He smiled at her benevolently as he blithely let his eyes wander over her slim figure. "If it was up to me you wouldn't have to wear anything. But on an Arab ship . . . well, I don't know . . ."

Romy was blushing like a thirteen-year-old girl. Incredible. With such a blunt phrase the guy actually had succeeded in beaming her back to her hardest times as a shy teenager. Thank god at that moment an appetizingly sizzling fish was served on a silver plate. A domestic worker in a white jacket and bow tie filleted it with incredible speed. Fresh spinach and garlic bread were served as side dishes.

"*Buen provecho!* Enjoy your meal," Nic said before they began eating.

The white, juicy flesh of the freshly caught *loup de mer* melted on the tongue. Romy indulged in it. Fresh fish was seldom on her menu in Augsburg. At lunchtime she usually grabbed a kebab from the Turkish takeaway or sometimes simply had a sandwich.

Nic watched her smiling. "I'm really happy that you've decided to come here and work directly together with Forster's Health."

This interrupted Romy's culinary experience abruptly so that she almost choked on her food. Until now she had made no commitment whatsoever. But Nic Saratoga obviously took her compliance for granted. He certainly was not used to anybody dissenting with him.

"I want you to feel at home here. Esmeralda, whom you've already met this morning, will satisfy your every wish, even if I'm not here."

Romy put aside the silver fish cutlery and looked directly into his face. "That's very nice of you, Nic. But I don't even know what all this will come to. It all happened really fast. First of all, I must get straight what will be best for me. After all, I can't stay here forever."

"Why not?" he said, beaming at her. "Joking aside, you definitely can't go back to Germany at the moment. The pharma mafia would be on your track in no time. You don't know this game. Profit's everything. And if this is in danger . . ."

". . . they're going to kill me?"

"After all, you're the only one who knows where the mushroom grows, right?"

"Not quite."

"Who else?"

"Is this an interrogation?"

"No, but I want to avoid something happening to people who don't even know they're in danger. Whoever they are, Romy, you'll need to warn them."

She blushed once more. He was right. For pros it would probably be child's play to spy out Sam and Thea.

"Best they go into hiding somewhere. On another island or elsewhere. At the moment I can only guarantee *your* safety."

Romy suddenly lost all her appetite. She wanted to call Thea on the spot, but her cell phone was upstairs in her room.

"Don't make any calls from your mobile. It could well be tapped," Nic warned her the very next second.

"But by who?" Romy asked irritated.

"By all those who don't want your discovery to ruin their businesses."

How would she ever be able to get out of this situation into which she had maneuvered herself so thoughtlessly? One thing she realized now: she would never be able to protect the mushroom on her own. She probably really needed Nic. He had, after all, the respective power apparatus behind him.

"Everything's going to be okay," he tried to calm her. "What our next step will be, we'll discuss later," he said in a businesslike tone and suddenly seemed in a hurry. He looked at his golden, extremely stylish watch and wiped his mouth with a cloth napkin made of white damask. "Feel free to continue your meal. If you'll excuse me, I still have to finish some documents for the lawyer in New York before the working day begins on the East Coast. I'll see you later."

After he left, Romy felt as if she had just come out of anesthesia. But instead of ether only the tart smell of Nic's aftershave was in the air. She gratefully accepted the fragrant espresso the nice server was bringing her and then also left the winter garden.

Back in her room she instantly called Thea from the house phone. But before she dialed the last number, she hung up in panic. *Have I taken leave of all my senses? Have the hormones and neurotransmitters finally shut down the last functioning part of my brain? I just voluntarily revealed information to Nic without him even asking for it!* What if he just wanted to frighten her and this so-called pharma mafia was not after the mushroom at all, but he himself was—or rather, Forster's Health. She tried to calm herself by breathing deeply. Now was not the time to panic. After all, there was still the internet. They could probably crack her emails, but as long as no one got his hands on her laptop that would be safest—at least she hoped so.

Via the house phone she tried to contact a member of the staff to find out the Wi-Fi password but unfortunately without success. Obviously siesta time was strictly adhered to. Well, then, she needed to ask Nic.

Romy had been wandering around the spacious, deserted castillo for at least ten minutes when she distantly heard his voice from the top floor of one of the three towers. She walked up an elegantly curved circular staircase made from light wood. The door to Nic's office stood open. The round bright room with unbarred windows offered a view of all directions, into the hinterland and the mountains and also at the sea. Unlike the rest of the house the study was modern and functional, a mixture of home, sweet home, Ambiente, and *Manager Magazine*. Nic fit into this picture as the perfect model. He was just hanging up the phone when she walked in. "You're just in time. I've got a message for you. Unfortunately not a good one." He pointed to one of the two designer armchairs that stood opposite his desk. "You prefer a seat?"

Romy shook her head.

"Professor Hattinger died of a heart attack last night. I'm sorry," he said softly.

Romy felt weak at the knees and now really needed a seat. "That's not true," she murmured. Romy closed her eyes. It was her fault. His death was on her conscience. This was murder!

"His daughter found him dead in his study this morning. According to police so far, no third party was involved."

"And you believe that? What about his computer? Is it still there? Are my files stored on it? How do you know this anyway?"

"From our security firm. We've got good relations with the police. On his computer, however, they couldn't find anything unusual."

"What does that mean?"

"No files from you were found. Either he deleted them himself, or someone else actually laid hands on them and then deleted them. Do you understand now why I urged you to come here with me, where I can take care of your protection?"

"Who could have done such a thing?"

"We believe it's possible that this Tanausú is behind it."

"Why?" exclaimed Romy. Impulsively she wanted to defend him but preferred to stay silent.

"The fewer confidants, the better, right?" said Nic.

Romy did not reply. She was far too shocked to think clearly.

"It could also have been someone from our competitors. But conjectures are useless now. All we can do is wait. I'll keep you informed." He gave her an empathetic smile and then turned back to his computer screen. "Excuse me, but I really need to finish this."

For Nic such an incident seemed to not be such a big thing. Was a power seeker like him even capable of emotions?

"Is there anything else I can do for you?" he interrupted her thoughts.

Romy remembered why she had been looking for him in the first place. "Actually I just wanted to ask you for the Wi-Fi password."

"No problem." He wrote a number combination on a notepad and handed it to her. "I'm really sorry," she heard him say as she left the room in a trance.

She found her room without getting lost. With trembling fingers she opened her laptop and entered the password. As she opened her mail folder, the first thing she discovered was an email from Thea.

Dear Romy,
I have thrown my cell phone into the sea, which is why I'm emailing.

This proved that Thea was the clever one!

Ricardo was here and got me away from the finca. I'm safe now. He's a close friend of Tanausú, whose acquaintance you will have made by now. You can trust him 100 percent. He will help you escape so that you can fulfill your task as guardian of the mushroom.
But first things first.
Yesterday Sam was visited by two sinister-looking guys. Since then he has disappeared from the face of the earth. I'm quite worried about him! The fact that you told others about amakuna puts those who know about it in serious danger. I've been aware of this fact for quite a while. After having consumed the mushroom I could look into the future and saw what horrible things are awaiting us. But I could not talk about it, just as Tichiname could not at the time.
The stone of destiny is already rolling. There will be death, and you're in mortal danger, too. This time I will not let you down. You, me, and Tanausú, we will ensure that our shared history is going to have a happy ending.
We have a chance to heal whose time has come to be healed.

But only if we ourselves have healed, we'll be able to work on the healing of the world.

Thea

Romy understood only half of what Thea had written. The healing of the world? What had happened to her otherwise rational friend? Yet another piece of the puzzle fit into the picture: Tichiname's fate was apparently just as closely linked with Thea's as hers was with the fate of Iriomé.

There had already been the first death, so Thea was on the right track! Amakuna must not fall into the hands of the pharmaceutical industry. Who else would have sent the men who threatened Sam? She could only hope that the hippie had consumed his share of the mushroom powder and was not forced to disclose the location of the mushroom. Hopefully he was still alive and had not been put down like Hattinger!

Thea seemed to completely trust Tanausú. Therefore he was not the one behind it. And Ricardo's connection to the Guanches had also become a little more transparent via the email.

It would be more and more difficult to protect the mushroom and to maintain Iriomé's oath. This was Romy's task. She could only hope that it was not too late and that it really had been Tanausú who had taken the Petri dishes in the laboratory and also Manolo's map of the cave. What had happened then was repeating itself now. The actors in the play only wore different costumes. The pharmaceutical lobbies were the conquistadors of today, the iron men. And Nic was one of them. He would always act in accordance with that group. How could she ever have believed for one single moment that he stood by her and backed her up with honest intentions? She had to get out of here as soon as possible. Someplace where she was safe from Nic Saratoga's charm and the power of Forster's Health.

But what was the business segment of this company anyway? Romy had to admit that she knew little about her host and the gigantic commercial enterprise he headed. Up to now she had only been interested in her laboratory work and had not wasted much thought on who was financing her research. Fortunately, there was the internet.

The website for Forster's Health showed a completely branched company whose product range extended from pharmaceutical products to baby food to medical devices for hospitals and medical practices. After some searching, she discovered a photo of Nic with the caption *CEO Europe / Arab Countries / South America*. When she entered the name Saratoga separately, she learned that Nic belonged to one of the richest families in South America. The Saratogas possessed numerous properties all over the world and played a major role in the bank league.

A photo showed Carmen and Enrique Saratoga, Nic's parents, with the former Panamanian president. Another photo showed Nic's mother together with an American property shark at the ribbon-cutting ceremony of one of his skyscrapers in Panama City. It gave her goose bumps. She had no chance against these people. High finance, real estate, and pharmaceutical industries. If she did not toe the line, they would squash her between their fingers like a bug. How could she stop the stone of destiny under these circumstances, or at least change the direction in which it rolled?

Now the question arose as to what role this Tanausú was playing. She clicked through the search results and finally found the following article:

From FARC Rebel to Ecoterrorist:
The Strange Life of Alexander Merten

Nobody really knows who he is—the man who today was arrested at Munich Airport and whose passport is issued to the name of Alexander Merten. The police consider him to be the man who on the internet has claimed responsibility for several attacks on pharmaceutical laboratories and executive staff of companies in chemical and pharmacological research under the pseudonym of Tanausú, in which, however, so far no one has been seriously injured. This may be a coincidence, because Tanausú's incendiary agents and bombs are not a particularly philanthropic means of providing information on the alleged "world conspiracy of the drug manufacturers."

Research revealed that his passport was issued to him only five years ago at the instigation of the German embassy in Colombia. In previous years he led, as Comandante Leandro, a notorious unit of FARC guerrillas in the southeast. When the Colombian government resumed the armistice negotiations with FARC in 2010, it offered some of the rebel leaders amnesty. Leandro obviously made use of it in order to see his German mother in Hamburg who, after several cycles of chemotherapy, died of cancer in 2012. Her son from a relationship with an unknown man of Spanish origin was born in 1986 on the Canary Island of La Palma. Which is why his nom de guerre Tanausú was a legendary resistance fighter of the Canarian original inhabitants, who led the last battle against the Spanish conquerors in 1492. Certainly a historical figure, with whom the fatherless Leandro could easily identify. So far it could not be clarified how he got to Colombia, where he joined FARC. Whether the police actually will succeed in proving his participation in the attacks of the recent months remains to be seen. As is heard from investigators, there is insufficient evidence—and were it not for the FARC past of Tanausú, he would probably be regarded as a harmless weirdo and copycat. But someone who has fought for years for one of the most murderous rebel groups in Central America must be kept a close eye on as a potential troublemaker . . .

There was a knock on the door.

"*Sí,*" said Romy.

Esmeralda, the housemaid, poked her pretty head through the door.

"Señor Saratoga asked me to show you the clothes of the Señora. Will you come with me?"

Romy nodded. *"Un momento."* Still completely under the influence of what she had just read, she closed the open tabs on her laptop and turned it off. *Once a warrior, always a warrior,* she thought. His resume was well suited to the legend of the guerreros sagrados.

Romy followed Esmeralda thoughtfully through the gallery of the Spanish conquistadors to the other wing of the castillo.

The only possibility for her to flee would be from this yacht tonight. She needed to talk to Tanausú. Also to Thea. They all were connected by the mushroom. And at the moment the mushroom only attracted damage. Tichiname had been right—humankind was not ready for it. The time was still not ripe.

Chapter 17

The chauffeur brought Romy and Nic directly to the wharf of the yacht of Khalifa Bin Kayid Al Tahan. The drive through the brightly lit marina of Marbella seemed unreal to her. One ship was more magnificent than the next, all of them with swimming pools and open-air cinemas. According to Nic a wharf of this size cost more than five hundred thousand euros per year just to operate. For this sum in Swabia you could buy a whole mansion with a large park. But all this did not really interest Romy. She had only one thought, and it said: *Get away.* This evening with so many people around her was her chance. And she was going to make use of it. Saratoga could not afford a scandal here. She wondered why he had undergone the risk to take her. What was his true intention? What had he planned for her?

The Jaguar stopped in front of a brightly lit yacht that looked to Romy like a medium-sized cruise ship. At the bow was written something in Arabic and beneath it *Alma del Mar,* the soul of the sea. Loud party music with an Arabian touch and multilingual voices echoed down to the pier, on which one luxury car was parked next to the other. Bored drivers were staring into the water, smoking, or talking together in small groups.

Nic took her hand. "You look magnificent. I'm happy that you came along. I hate these events," he whispered in her ear.

Romy agreed at least on this point. Even if she looked pretty good in Jennifer Saratoga's simple black and white Chanel dress with her hair nicely pinned up by Esmeralda, she felt uncomfortable. She was not a party girl. Lots of people she didn't know, loud music, and empty talk had never been her cup of tea.

The door of the limousine was opened from the outside; Romy looked into a tanned, angular face with a carefully trimmed silver-gray beard and dark-tinted glasses. The man wore a slim-fitting, dark gray, custom-made suit that suggested a well-toned body. "May I introduce myself? Antonio Borges," he said in Italian-sounding Spanish.

"Antonio is head of security at Forster's Health," Nic introduced him to Romy, "and also my best friend."

"It's a great honor to meet you, Doctor," he said demonstratively. "We'll take good care of you!"

"That's very nice, but I can take care of myself," Romy answered just as friendly. She took Borges's held-out hand. As their hands touched she flinched as if she had burned herself.

"Anything wrong?" he asked confused.

Romy was just as surprised. "I'm sorry, I'm a little jumpy."

"No wonder, considering all she has been through in the past few days," Nic came to her rescue. "She's just learned of Hattinger's death."

Meanwhile Romy got out of the car and was now face-to-face with the head of security. "Is there any news about the professor's death?"

"As far as I know, no further investigations were launched. The man was almost 80 and still spent a lot of time on the road. It could well have been a natural death. But as the three of us know, there was a good reason to kill him." Borges was still smiling at her. "But don't worry, as I said, you're in safekeeping here."

A shiver ran down Romy's spine. She hoped fervently for a favorable situation to escape her protectors. Nic put his arm around her shoulder and led her up the stairs to the yacht. Romy felt like a sheep being led to slaughter and had great difficulty putting one foot in front of the other, especially since Jennifer's elegant pumps were half a size too big for her.

"We will guard her around the clock from now on. I hope that's okay with you," she heard Borges say to Nic. *That's all I need,* Romy thought and wondered how she could escape. She trusted this Borges even less than Nic.

The deck, decorated with fairy lights, was bustling with the rich and beautiful: Arabs in caftans and galabias, Western businessmen in fancy tuxedos, and young women that mostly looked like models in haute couture gowns. From classy Africans to pale Nordic beauties, the invitation list left out nothing. This was Nic's world. In this world there was no room for her. How could she have believed even for a moment that he was interested in her on a personal level?

Nic offered her a glass of champagne. She refused at first, but then took it. "*Salud,*" she said softly. "To the professor."

"*Salud,*" said Nic. "I'm really very sorry."

"We were very close once, and he gave me a focus in life after the death of my parents. Without him I'd never have dared to study biochemistry."

"Don't you have any other family?"

"Only a very good friend."

"Does she know of the story with the mushroom? And more importantly, does she know that you're safe here?"

Romy nodded, though up to now she had not dared to email Thea where she was. Her friend definitely would have called her mad.

"Sorry, but I need to go instruct my men," cut in Borge. He also held a drink in his hand and wanted to clink glasses with her. "I'm really sorry that this evening is no longer as glamorous an experience for you as it could have been."

Romy looked at him suspiciously. She did not like people, especially men, feeling superior to her and showing it. "By a glamorous experience I picture something else," she scoffed. "All I see is the display of wealth, for which others have to work hard. Without our petrodollars the sheikh would be sitting in a tent somewhere in the desert."

Borges smiled with condescending kindness. "Don't be jealous, Doctor. But I agree with you. Wealth without influence and power is really just a farce. Power means to have things you can't buy for money."

Without looking at her, he took off his glasses and polished the spectacle lenses carefully with a small leather cloth. "Health for example . . ." He gave her a quick look that sent chills down her spine like the first touch had. Then he put his glasses back on, ". . . and love. Love is priceless, and the strongest power ever. Wouldn't you agree, Doctor Conrad?"

Before she could respond, Nic took her arm and led her to the buffet. "You mustn't take offense at Antonio's behavior. He's an old cynic and always gets a kick out of testing people and exposing their weaknesses."

"He gives me the creeps," said Romy while beholding a buffet decorated with delights from all over the world—from lobster to caviar to artfully arranged tropical fruits. But she felt no appetite.

"It just seems like that to you. He's a very loyal and obliging man."

"Like you?" she asked provokingly.

"Even if you don't think it's possible, yes."

Romy felt she believed this to be true at this moment. Or was it only his eyes that wanted to make her believe that? "How do you know each other?"

"We were at Harvard together, and being among the few Latin Americans there we allied and thus survived quite a few animosities. Juana Marquéz, whom you met back at Biotex, was also part of our team. And these friendships endured."

"Why study at Harvard when you want to work as security chief? Doesn't that require military or police training?" Romy wondered.

"He studied economics and management just like me. But you've got a point. His father was in the military, and Antonio served in the army as a young man. This is how he ended up in his current position. He has my complete confidence. Romy, your life is in good hands with him."

"Why is my life so important to you? Because I'm the only one who knows where the mushroom's growing?"

Nic took her arm and guided her to the bow, where there was not such a big crowd. "Romy, it's your discovery. I, rather Forster's Health, will provide you with the necessary resources to test the mushroom on its effect, its action time, its side effects, and its reproductive possibilities. Only then will we know what we really have. And I don't want something happening to you during this time."

She understood his concerns and realized at the same moment that despite her fears she was falling head over heels in love with this man. And this was the last thing she needed in this situation.

He took her face in both hands and kissed her softly on her forehead and cheeks. When he got closer to her mouth, she quickly turned her head aside, even though there was nothing more she wanted than to feel his lips on hers. Taking a step back she handed him her glass. "I need to go to the ladies' room," she apologized and asked a slender Eurasian beauty, who was dressed like a geisha, for directions. The girl looked at Romy and especially Nic and then asked her in strangely accented English to come along. When Romy followed she noticed Borges nodding to a man in a tuxedo with a radio button in his ear who then joined them inconspicuously.

"Do you know how I can get away from here?" Romy whispered to the Asian girl, who gave her a startled look from slanted eyes.

"Forget it. The Argentine has eyes everywhere." It took a moment for Romy to realize that she meant Borges. Right, this Italian-sounding Spanish was actually from Argentina. "You know him? What's the matter with him?"

But the young woman had already disappeared in the crowd.

The ladies room was overcrowded, and unfortunately there was no second door through which she could have fled. Probably Borges had positioned one of his men at the gangway anyway. Romy obviously would have no other choice than to jump over the railing into the water.

When she left the toilet, the man in a tuxedo, who had been waiting for her outside the door, followed her like a shadow. So much for fleeing. And in a soaking Chanel dress she would not get far anyway. She went back to the bow of the yacht, where Nic was talking to Borges.

"So did you have a look around the ship? Not bad, eh?!" He beamed at her.

Romy felt like strangling him.

"Do you want to dance?" asked Nic and pulled her onto the dance floor without waiting for an answer.

The band played Latin rhythms, and Nic was a good dancer. Romy could hardly remember when she had last danced, nevermind when she had danced with a partner whose smell and touch she liked this much. She could feel his warmth and his breath on her neck. And she particularly felt that she was finding it increasingly difficult to resist his male charisma. It had been over a year since she had been with a man, and that had only been a stopgap. No wonder she was about to melt like butter. His hands on her waist and the rhythm of the samba and salsa made her forget her good intentions one after the other.

When he began to distribute small kisses on her neck, she was ultimately lost. She could not help it. Nothing in her resisted this touch. On the contrary, violent gusts of sand spread out along her spine and flooded her body. She knew she could not trust him, she must not trust him. But this last burst of reason was not enough to put a stop to it. Romy permitted Nic to draw her to the edge of the dance floor and kiss her with a passion that allowed no resistance. The music, the voices of the distinguished guests, everything faded into the background. There was only she and Nic. He gave her little room to breathe, and she enjoyed this breathlessness. The gust of sand became a storm that could easily become a tornado. Never before had she felt her body in this way. Passion took over.

Confused she paused and looked in Nic's eyes. How was it possible that he caused such feelings in her? It was as if streams of lava were running through her body. From each pore heat emanated.

He led her below deck, opened a door behind her, and gently pushed her into a luxury cabin. The walls were decorated with silk wallpaper, the furniture made of precious ivory. In the middle of the room there was a round bed of at least ten feet in diameter. Nic eased her gently into the silken cushions, bent over her, and lovingly brushed her hair out of her face. Again he kissed her passionately on the mouth and then buried his face in her neck. His tongue playfully explored her left earlobe and then pushed further into the inner ear. Romy was catapulted from one chill to the next. Carefully, he unbuttoned her dress and ran his fingertips caressingly between her breasts. Romy felt the urge to embrace him, but he held her arms above her head with one hand. With the other he continued to undress her. He opened her bra with ease. Her nipples were stiff, as if they came straight from the freezer, and Romy could almost hear a crackling sound when they melted in his mouth.

Gently, he pulled down her underwear. She hardly knew what was happening when she felt his tongue within her. She had already come twice when Nic cautiously penetrated her, while his hands still seemed to be all over her body. Without ever having rehearsed it, they immediately found a common rhythm. Romy felt as if the ocean waves were carrying her far away—into another world.

Chapter 18

"Iriomé! Wake up!" Nesfete's voice sounded as if it came from far away, but the old harimaguada knelt right next to her.

Iriomé slowly came around. She had never had such a dream before. Was it a dream at all? She looked at Nesfete with a mixture of astonishment, shame, and guilt. "I dreamed about what a harimaguada never may dream," she said softly. "It was wonderful. But it was not I who did it. And it was not Akin who did it with me."

Nesfete stroked her tousled hair lovingly. "This was all too much for you. Tichiname's death, the foreign man, and amakuna," she said softly.

Iriomé shook her head. "This dream has a meaning. And this young woman too. I've already met her before. She saved me when I believed I would die in the last fight of our people against the Spaniards."

"Sure, she is a good spirit," Nesfete said reassuringly.

"She passionately made love to this man who was not Akin. What can this mean?"

Nesfete took her hand. "I think it has to do with what I have to tell you. There's good news."

"Tell me," she said excitedly, pulling Nesfete down to her, so she came to sit beside her on the soft fur bed.

"When we reached the camp of the strangers in the early morning, the sun had not yet risen from the sea. Akin asked me to come inside. I felt very scared, but then I thought about what Tichiname has said about love and that you gave him your trust. Therefore I followed him. We went to his leader, a man whom I didn't like, because in his eyes gleamed greed, a man who's never satisfied in life with what he has. I felt great pity for him."

Iriomé understood but was much more interested in the good news in store for her.

"Akin told his leader how well he had been treated by you," Nesfete continued, "although he and his companion wanted to do violence to you and Guayafanta. You didn't counter violence with violence, but with care and love. He said to his leader that you possess a high art of healing and that his people could learn a lot from our people, as well as vice versa. The Spaniards have much of what makes life easier and more pleasant. So it would be stupid to fight and kill each other. It would be much more useful talking to each other and to discover what one can learn from the other."

Iriomé smiled, and her heart was filled with joy. "How did you understand what they said?" she asked in surprise.

"Gazmira, the woman who speaks the language of the foreigners explained it to me," she said.

"Are you sure you can really trust this woman?"

"I don't think that she lied to me. She's a prisoner of the Spaniards and certainly hopes to regain her freedom by a peaceful solution."

"So what's going to happen now?" Iriomé asked excitedly.

"The leader of the Spaniards wants to talk to our leaders. He has invited them to come to his camp. Maybe this way bloodshed can be avoided and thus the stone of destiny be stopped."

Iriomé jumped up. "We need to speak with Tanausú immediately." Her heart was beating twice as fast as normal. Akin had not disappointed her. He wanted to give back what she had given him and thus would perhaps save the lives of many of her people. The love she had planted in his heart bore fruit and drove out the spirit of destruction and greed. Although they had been together only a short while, it seemed that the dark clouds had drifted away from his soul to let his inner light shine. She took Nesfete by the hand, and they climbed effortlessly down the wooden ladders from the caves to the village.

As usual, Tanausú knew what had happened before the two harimaguadas had even said a word. Yet he did not seem to like what they told him. His face darkened. "Why did you let him go without discussing it with me?" he rebuked Iriomé. "And what would the strangers want to talk to us about? They won't give us anything but will take away everything. What they have to offer we don't need. We've got everything we need. More would only lead to envy and jealousy and limit our freedom."

"But if we don't even try to talk to them, fighting will inevitably break out," Iriomé objected vigorously. "You know what amakuna has revealed to us regarding the last battle. Neither our spears and maces nor our slingshots will be enough to oppose the Spaniards. And even the great courage and strength of our people won't stop them in the long run. With their ships, they will come here in ever larger numbers and finally capture the whole island."

"And if it's a trap and they just want to make us come down to the valley, where we are no longer protected by the rock walls of the crater?"

Iriomé shook her head. "I believe that Akin wants to save the lives of our people, as we have saved his."

Tanausú raised both hands. "Remember Tichiname's words, 'these people have no love in their hearts.'"

"Then love must be awakened in their hearts. No heart is without love," Iriomé replied with conviction.

"And you think that it is our task to heal their hearts?"

"I believe that it is the duty of all human beings to first awaken the love in their own heart and then in the hearts of others," she said in a serious tone. "If people leave no space in their lives for love, there will be quarrels and wars to the end of time."

Tanausú looked at her a long time, thinking. "Well," he said. "You're the supreme harimaguada. You decide. This is how it's always been. And it's always been right like that."

They bowed to each other, and their heads touched for a moment.

"I'll take the ten strongest men of each tribe with me. If it's a trap, we'll fight to the death," Tanausú said. "Never will I break the oath of our ancestors, and I'd rather die than sacrifice my freedom and give up what I'm living for."

Iriomé understood only too well, but she also knew that the survival of their people and their ethos could never be based on fighting and killing. Tichiname taught her that people would never make any progress this way and ultimately even destroy what they themselves would need to survive.

While Iriomé, followed by Nesfete, thoughtfully walked back to the cave shrine, she felt the heavy burden of responsibility that pressed on her shoulders like a dead goat. Her heart told her that Akin was on her side, even if he belonged to the other side, but her mind expressed doubt. The more she thought about it, the more she had to admit how little she knew about him. Only what she had felt in the brief moments in the healing cave. Then his heart beat in the same rhythm as hers. But now that he had returned to his world and was among his own people, things might be different.

But what else could she do? Amakuna had shown her quite plainly the cruelty of the Spaniards and that the fight against them could not be won. These men represented an impenetrable wall of power and superiority, as she had felt on her first visit to the holy well. Of course she understood Tanausú's wish to tear down this wall forever, but she did not believe that was possible. Akin's proposal was sensible. Everything else amounted to suicide.

ಲ

The men left at the break of dawn the next day. They were armed with spears, slingshots, and clubs yet had dispensed with any kind of war paint. They wore short fur or leather garments to be able to climb unhindered over the rocks and, if necessary, to fight. Their hair was tied back with long leaves from the dragon trees.

Tanausú stood beside Iriomé on an elevated flat stone looking into the distance. He raised his arms to the sky and said in a loud voice, "We'll go to the camp of the Spaniards with peaceful intent. Since the ancestors remain silent, just like Idafé and Tichiname remained silent, only amakuna was left to grant the supreme harimaguada a look to the aftertime. And what she saw was terrible and cruel. Iriomé has experienced the downfall of our people in all its harshness. She says only one thing can avert this disaster. Love. Only love, mutual understanding, and honesty bring lasting peace."

Iriomé saw some men wince at Tanausú's last words, as if they did not believe in their power. Also Guayafanta, who together with the other harimaguadas was standing nearby, seemed frozen with anger. She would rather have fought, just as she would have preferred to kill Akin instantly. But Iriomé had saved his life. For the first time she felt a sense of power. It was her decision that her people followed now. Her responsibility, as would be all that happened if she had made a mistake. But she stood by her words and passed the strength she drew from them on to Tanausú and the men, as if she could thus slip a skin over each single man that would make him and his soul invulnerable for all eternity.

When this was done, Iriomé let out a shrill whistle, the signal to leave.

The men began to move. When Iriomé watched the men vault over the edge of the crater supported on their lances, she suddenly felt that this was the last time in her life she would see this picture. She was deeply frightened. *No, everything will turn out well,* she reassured herself. Love was the most powerful force man possessed, and nothing and no one could stand against it for long. Thus she had been taught by Tichiname. And this was the way to go.

The absence of their leaders paralyzed the people of Aceró. They only performed necessary work. Hardly anyone spoke, and even the children were quieter than usual. Only the birds and insects with their chirping and buzzing disturbed the silence that lay over the crater. Iriomé ensured that the harimaguadas prepared medicine for wounds and injuries in case it came to a fight. Guayafanta opposed everything. She was sowing hatred and discord wherever she could and split the harimaguadas into two camps.

On the morning of the third day, when the uncertainty was no longer bearable, the message arrived, which many of them had foreseen, but which in its impact hit everyone like a thunderbolt. A man from the tribe of Atogmatoma dragged himself with his last remaining strength to Aceró. He was bleeding from several wounds and could hardly speak.

Iriomé had already guessed what had happened; her faith in love and her hope were slowly dying now.

"They lured us into a trap. Many are dead. The rest in shackles," he gasped out while blood was running from his mouth and nose. "The foreigners are on their way here. I don't know if the rest are strong enough to stop them."

Akin had betrayed her. Betrayed her love, betrayed her people. It took Iriomé a moment to realized the scope of this disaster and to think clearly about what had to be done next. But she had no time left. One of the guards, who kept watch on the crater rim, announced with a warning whistle the approach of the Spaniards.

How could they defend themselves? Women, children, and old people?

The next moment she heard Guayafanta give a shrill battle cry. The harimaguada, her face painted with white, upward-pointing triangles, the sign of battle, was waving the wooden pipe she had taken from Akin over her head and rallied round her in a loud voice all men and women fit for action. Her plan was to throw down stones at the invaders from the spot above the narrow gorge that was the only access to the crater. Angrily she glared at Iriomé. All that had been making her seethe was now breaking out. Guayafanta stood on the same stone on which Iriomé had been standing three days ago and demanded the position of supreme harimaguada for herself.

"Iriomé has failed," she cried, so that her words echoed manifold from the gray cliffs. "She has been misled by the lust of her body. Something that is forbidden for any harimaguada. She has blindly trusted the stranger and laid the fate of our people in his hands. I'll now take her place as supreme harimaguada. Unfortunately there's no time for a ceremony, since we have to act. Does anybody want to put forward an objection?" Only a few raised their hands. Guayafanta threw Iriomé one last triumphant look, then climbed from the stone and took the lead of the group that set forth at once.

Iriomé felt frozen, just as the rock wall of the volcano crater, in which they were no longer safe. Akin knew the only path that led inside, and she had made sure that it was like that.

Nesfete came up to her and put her hand on her shoulder. "You can't give up now; everything's still ahead of you," she said in an insistent tone.

Iriomé slowly woke up from her mental paralysis and turned her gaze to the old harimaguada. Her eyes were glistening with tears. "You're mistaken, Nesfete. All is lost."

"No! Tichiname has made you and not Guayafanta her successor and this with good cause. Now act accordingly. You can't abandon the people here to their fate."

Iriomé didn't know why, but suddenly she felt the spirit of her old teacher, even though this time it was not visible. It led her slowly back to strength. Nesfete was right. Iriomé still bore the responsibility for her people. With the back of her hand she wiped the tears from her eyes and rose from the stone. Then she called in a loud, clear voice to the older children and the elderly who were still capable of it to drag as many big stones as possible to the caves of the harimaguadas in order to barricade them up. Ten to twenty people fit into each cave and could survive there for a while. When the Spaniards arrived, everything had to look as if for ages only the dead had been sleeping in those caves.

They formed a line of people stretching out over the wooden ladders up to the caves. And in no time all entrances were walled up except for a small slot to slip through. After that all existing food and water tanks were carried up into the caves. Without any instructions everyone knew what they had to do. After all the work was done, they were evenly allocated to the caves. They drew up the wooden ladders and filled the gaps from inside with the remaining stones.

The walled cave entrances now acted like burial chambers. The cave sanctuary had turned into a graveyard. Iriomé could only hope that the Spaniards would not dare to disturb the peace of the dead. As far as she was concerned it was impossible for her to hide with the others. She felt a great responsibility that almost smothered her. She had to find another way to survive. So she said good-bye to Nesfete, the only person whom she still dared to look in the eyes.

Once again she checked as carefully as possible that there was no sign that people actually lived there. No ash, no pottery, no forgotten child's toy. Everything had been removed. Then she slung a bag with ready-mixed ointments and painkillers over her shoulder and set off toward the coast.

Each step that brought her closer to the exit of the crater was harder to take. The sun was merciless today, beating down from the sky; her sweat dropped, painting dark spots on her leather garments. She knew that she was directly on the way into the volcanic pipe of Guayote. And it was not long before she heard the roar of the fire sticks and the anguished cries of humans and animals from the gorge that led into the crater.

Cautiously, always under the cover of a rock or tree, she crept closer, noticing a pungent odor. She climbed on a rock to get a clear view. What she saw far surpassed in its brutal reality anything seen during the amakuna ritual.

Down in the gorge several men were lying on the ground with broken skulls. Around them large animals with long legs were running in confusion, some of whom were injured. But the actual battle took place up at the crater rim. The strangers had climbed it and combated with the last defenders of the island. Guayafanta had succeeded in pulling a man to the ground and knocking him down with a stone. But immediately another grabbed her from behind, twisted her arms behind her back, and pushed her to the ground. Iriomé looked away. Although the harimaguada was her worst enemy, she did not want to witness her dying in such an inglorious way.

The scene broke her heart. Time and again people fell down from the rocky edge of the crater into the gorge. Mostly they were in twos. Courageous men and women of her people clung to one of the strangers and did not let go until both of them plunged into the depth. Their death cries were echoing from the rock walls. "Vacaguaré!"

The roar of the fire sticks, the screams of the dying, and the commands of the combatants became one eerie death song ringing in her ears. Iriomé let herself slide down from the rock, closing her eyes for an instant.

The stone of destiny had been unstoppable. Amakuna had predicted exactly what was happening now. Obviously these strangers were not ready for what she had wished so much. For what she had wanted to achieve together with Akin. The union of two different worlds in love, a communication in peace and mutual sympathy.

Pain, grief, and disappointment spread through her body like a giant octopus whose tentacles strangled all lifelines. And thus she hardly noticed as one of the long-legged animals came to a standstill next to her and a rider dismounted with a jingling noise. Only when a hand was put on her shoulder did she gaze up and look directly into Joaquín's dark eyes. They were filled with tears.

Iriomé felt neither anger nor hatred. Her heart now only beat to keep her alive, not to feel. Beside him appeared a second animal. It was armored from head to tail with shells made of that hard, fireproof material. His gleaming, white-rimmed eyes looked nervously at Iriomé. On his back a Spaniard with a pointed beard sat, exchanging with Joaquín a few words in their foreign language. His shoulders and arms were covered with moving scales of the same shiny material, so that he, despite his armor, was able to hold a lance and even stab with it. His chest and his belly were protected by polished plates that could fend off any strike. On his legs he also wore movably connected shells. To Iriomé he did not look like a man of flesh and blood. His icy glance seemed to be an equally deadly weapon as the ones he had on him. This must be the leader Nesfete had spoken of.

Another iron man came, dragging an old woman with tangled gray hair who was dressed in filthy rags. The leader barked an instruction to her, whereupon she crouched beside Iriomé. "My name is Gazmira. I speak the language of the Spaniards. They want to know where the elderly and the children of your tribe are."

Iriomé remained silent. She was not accustomed to lying. The leader became impatient and shouted at the old woman. His rough voice, coupled with that cold, contemptuous glance, petrified Iriomé completely. Joaquín stepped between them, raising his voice, and drew Iriomé up to him on the back of the animal and thus made clear his claim.

"Tell them the people of Aceró have all opted for death. The elderly first killed the young ones and then themselves," Iriomé said to the old woman.

Gazmira translated her words. The man with the cold eyes yelled something which made several men get on the long-legged animals and head out toward the caldera. "He thinks you're lying," Gazmira said. "His men are riding into the crater now. They don't want there to be survivors who could start a new tribe."

Iriomé felt Joaquín put his arm around her waist, and his animal began to move. From grief she closed her eyes and felt faint. When she awoke, she found herself in a sort of cave of a thin, unfamiliar material, through which soft sunlight came in. The structure was sewn together at the sides with ropes and was held by wooden poles. She was alone. From outside unintelligible shouts were echoing. Beside her was a pitcher of water. She drank a few sips, reviving her spirits. Slowly the memory of the terrible events of the last few hours was coming back. The yelling death cries of her people were still ringing in her ears, and the picture of the women who jumped from the rocks holding fast onto their enemies burned in her soul.

She only noticed Joaquín when he sat at the edge of her bed and silently took her hand. She let it happen. But her hand in his now only felt like a piece of dead wood. She knew no feelings anymore, wanted to see nothing, hear nothing. All seemed to be over. She had failed and betrayed her people to a man she still could not hate, whom she still allowed to touch her.

He sat there for a while looking at her sadly, then left the tent and came back with Gazmira. The old woman looked tired and apathetic. Iriomé noted signs of beating on her face and arms. Her eyes reminded Iriomé a little of Tichiname but lacked the kindness of a nonwounded soul.

Joaquín was talking at her with a desperate voice while Gazmira nodded patiently. "He wants to tell you how much he regrets what has happened to your people. He appreciates you more than anything and never wanted to destroy the trust that you gave him. There should have been no fighting, but peace negotiations. De Lugo, his leader, had sworn to him that this meeting with the tribal leaders of your people should serve the peace. But he broke his word and has used Joaquín only to make himself sole ruler."

Her words seemed to bounce off Iriomé.

"He speaks the truth," added the old woman. "I was there in person when this was decided."

Joaquín threw himself at Iriomé's feet and clung to her as if he were drowning.

"Are there any other survivors except me?" she asked quietly, without taking further notice of the Spaniard.

Gazmira nodded. "A few men and women. They're all in chains."

"And Tanausú?"

"De Lugo wants to take him aboard his ship and deliver him to his queen as a trophy, as the last opponent of this island."

How humiliating! For all eternity she would be burdened with this guilt. Though she had been true to herself and had acted on her heart, the stone of destiny had not been stopped. Tichiname had known this. That's why she had left.

"And you're now the slave of this man," Gazmira continued, pointing to Joaquín, who still embraced her.

"Slave?"

"This means you belong to him now. He can take you home with him and do there what he wants with you."

Was this her rightful punishment? Or would Nesfete's vision come true? But how should she ever be able to love a man who was involved in the killing of her people? The fact that she was inclined to believe that he had been betrayed by his leader would not change this.

Both their hearts had beaten in harmony for a short time. That's why he had been able to stand up for a solution of love and peace in the first place. Exactly as she had. But they had failed due to a power that had been stronger. At least for the moment.

Iriomé looked into Joaquín's dark eyes again for the first time, as if trying to discover something that allowed some hope. A tiny glimmer told her that this was not the end yet. He held her gaze. In it she read anger and despair, but also infinite compassion and love.

As unbelievable as it might seem to her, his eyes promised that there would be ways to meet their common destiny. Tichiname never made a mistake. She must have known why she had put the responsibility for amakuna precisely in Iriomé's hands.

"Tell him I have to go into the crater one more time, but that I promise to come back."

Gazmira explained it to Joaquín. His face showed neither suspicion nor anger, and he just nodded in agreement. "He trusts you," Gazmira said. "You can go."

He took a delicate chain that he wore around his neck and put it around Iriomé's. Attached to it was a filigree spherical amulet that shone as golden as the sun in the middle of the day.

Iriomé ran a finger over it, viewed it with surprise, and gave Joaquín a questioning look.

He cautiously took it between his fingers and firmly pressed his thumb on it twice, whereupon to Iriomé's astonishment it opened, revealing the portrait of a beautiful woman. "Who is she?" she asked.

"His mother. She gave it to him so that it may protect him. Now it is to protect you," Gazmira translated. Iriomé closed the amulet and rose.

"The ship will sail in three days. I hope you're on the right path. Tara, the earth goddess, may protect you."

"Thank you," replied Iriomé. "And what will become of you?"

"Vacaguaré. My time is up," said the old woman and left the tent in a bent posture.

Chapter 19

Iriomé did not take the path through the Valley of Fear, but climbed on all fours through rough undergrowth down into the crater, where only the goats traveled. It was the middle of the new day, and the sun was blazing down again. Blood from scratches and scrapes mingled with sweat. She ignored the pain. It had to be Tara who made sure she reached the cave shrine without major injuries. With each step that brought her closer to her home, fear grew of what she would find there. Had the Spaniards discovered the hiding places? Had they made it up to the caves? She found herself no longer able to imagine new dreadful images. Too many had become reality in recent days.

She pressed her back against the rough rock wall and crept cautiously along the narrow path leading to the cave shrine. At first glance, it seemed completely abandoned. Silence. Even birds and insects had fled to another place. Iriomé let out several whistles and at first thought there was an answer. But it was only her whistle echoing from the cliffs.

All cave entrances were still closed. Suddenly she thought she heard a muffled whistle that was not hers. Iriomé took off her shoes and climbed up the almost vertical rock face hand over hand.

When she reached the first cave and had a firm footing, she gently broke off a stone, which rumbled down into the depth. After a few moments, she got help from inside. Nesfete was the first to put her head through the resultant hole. She squinted into the brightness of the day and then grabbed Iriomé's hand, relieved. "You've come back, thank Tara!" Her voice sounded throaty. Nevertheless Iriomé noticed how glad the harimaguada was to see her alive. "The foreigners have been here briefly. I think a murder of crows that kept circling above the crater cawing loudly drove them off. They probably believed these were the souls of the dead of Aceró."

Iriomé saw behind Nesfete's back several children clinging fearfully to one another and three old men with narrowed eyes. They had been sitting tight this whole time in the dark, almost like being buried alive, without knowing what would happen next.

When the entrance was free, a little girl rushed into Iriomé's arms and would not let go of her. Despite the many tears that the young harimaguada had already cried, there still seemed to be more. And while the little girl was rocking frantically back and forth, she conferred everything that had happened without voicing it.

Later, when the others climbed down from the caves, she assembled them, explaining many had lost their lives and that the danger was still not over. Most of them kept calm, however, and even the youngest children understood that their parents were dead or in captivity and would not come back again. None of them cried, and none of the old people burst into wailing. The shock that their life of freedom, embedded in the generous nature of the island, was over now silenced them.

"Nesfete will take charge of the continuation of Aceró," Iriomé announced. "She will take care that the old ones will be father and mother to the young ones, as best they can. And she will pass on the knowledge of the harimaguadas. No one shall ever leave the crater and go to the coast. Because there captivity or even death awaits."

"And what will you do?" asked Nesfete.

"I'll return to the Spanish camp. If I stay here, they will look for me and kill us all, or take us prisoner."

The old woman looked at her thoughtfully. She knew that there was yet another reason for Iriomé's decision to leave. But this she kept to herself.

Iriomé spent one last, albeit sleepless, night in Aceró and before dawn went to the cave on the outermost edge of the sanctuary where Tichiname's body still lay. The harimaguadas had sewn it carefully into a goatskin; it gave off no smell. The face had shrunk and taken on a brownish color. Iriomé knelt down, picked the mummy up and cradled her in her arms like a sleeping child. She was lighter than Iriomé imagined, and it would give Iriomé no trouble to take her to her final resting place within the cave.

Iriomé knew the way. The medicine woman had once shown the grave chamber to her pupils, where the embalmed bodies of the previous supreme harimaguadas were resting. Iriomé vividly recalled the day. She had been only ten summers old then and felt deep compassion for the mummies lying in this humid darkness. However, the medicine woman had only laughed at her and told her that one day she would leave Tichiname's body here inside the mountain as well. This had frightened Iriomé so much that she had not been able to sleep for several nights.

Inside a hollow some moss glowed in an oily liquid, and she lit a readily available torch on it. The flickering light led her deep into the crater wall. For a short time a hole in the ceiling shed even more light on her way before she again had to feel her way along the slippery ground with only the light of the torch to guide her. Bats brushed her cheeks, and the moldy cold was seeping through her thin leather garment.

At last she reached the wooden ladder leading upward to the grave chamber. She carefully set her teacher on the floor, climbed upward, and illuminated the opening with the torch in her hand. She paused for a moment. An understanding smile flashed across her face. Now she understood why the supreme harimaguada always must be laid to rest only by her successor. In this way, the secret about the location of the mushroom could be guarded.

What grew here in complete darkness between the mummified bodies of several generations of medicine women might be the last harvest. Now that the island was in the hands of the strangers, they might perhaps not allow amakuna to grow here.

Iriomé reaped as many mushrooms as fit in her medicine bag, which she wore around her neck. Then she climbed down again to pull Tichiname up the ladder. With her knife made of obsidian, which she carried hidden in the inside pocket of her dress, she carved a shallow pit and gently laid Tichiname's body into it. A feeling of great tenderness flowed through her, accompanied by a deep sadness. She knew she was not just saying goodbye to Tichiname and the island. It was also the end of a happy time that would never come back.

The way back to the coast had never seemed so short before. Iriomé memorized each individual contact of her soles with the soil of her home island in order not to forget anything, in case she was never able to return. The world she knew was Benahoare. Although she knew that there were other islands that one could see from the highest mountain, her life had been so happy and busy that up to now she had never felt the wish to go elsewhere. That's why the thought of having to leave now filled her heart with fear. On the other hand she felt a certain curiosity for what she was going to learn in the country of the Spaniards.

The closer she came to the beach, the slower her steps. Still there was time to go back and lead the survivors of Aceró to the north of the island, where the Spaniards might not find them so quickly. But the view down to the sea from the rock where she had so recently stood with Guayafanta made her dismiss the idea outright: the Spaniards were driving the few survivors of her people, chained together like a stubborn goat herd, across the beach down to the sea in order to take them aboard the ships that were bobbing up and down there. Even from a distance she could see that many of them were limping and supporting each other. As fast as she could, she ran down the small path, hoping to be able to help at least some of them dress their worst wounds and relieve their pain. Once they were cooped up in the dark belly of the ship without clean water it would be much more difficult to treat inflammations, which often led to death.

Having reached the camp, she asked the first Spaniard who came across her way for Gazmira and Akin. But the men had their fun with sending her first in one direction, then the other. They laughed at her and tried to catch her and tugged her hair. One of them grabbed her and shoved her to his neighbor and this one to the next. All over her body Iriomé felt greedy men's hands. When she stumbled and fell down, she screamed.

"Alto! Locos!" suddenly a loud voice put an end to the ugly game.

The fat man with the brown robe of whom Iriomé had already heard helped her up and wiped the black sand from her face gently. Iriomé stared at him desperately and gasped the name "Gazmira."

His eyes took on a regretful expression. He pointed to the big rock at the edge of the beach, which was surrounded by thundering waves. She had chosen death over a continued life in captivity. But Iriomé could not allow herself to grieve for the woman. It was not the time. Instead, she took the hand of her rescuer and dragged him with her to the place where the Spaniards with loud screaming were still driving the chained group of prisoners into the water.

With words and gestures she tried to make the fat man understand that she also wanted to go on the ship, in order to dress the wounds of the injured. And Frai Hieronymus de Torremar understood. Less what she said, rather what her heart spoke. So he tried to explain to the Spaniards what she wanted.

Iriomé anxiously waited for a response as she was met by the contemptuous glances of the Benahoarias that went right through her. After a while de Lugo appeared, the man with the cold stare who had been sent for to make a decision.

Frai Hieronymus talked insistently with him. Repeatedly he pointed to the sky, as if a bad storm would come from there if he did not allow

Iriomé to board the ship. De Lugo gave him a startled look and finally relented. Hieronymus signaled for Iriomé to get into one of the smaller boats in which they were rowed to the big ship.

Cold Eye, as she now considered the leader of the Spaniards, also sat in the boat. He was blatantly staring at her the whole time. She felt that on the one hand he did not trust her but on the other was curious about her healing arts. Akin certainly had told him about it, and now he surely wanted to see it with his own eyes.

The prisoners were now all on board the vessel. They were sitting back to back or lying flat on the ground. Hardly anyone was able to stand on both legs. Some were groaning aloud as the saltwater burned in their open wounds. Their eyes had become dull. Only a few allowed her to apply the green ointment to their wounds so that a protective crust could form, under which all injuries healed quickly. Most did not want her to come near them. She felt intense waves of blame and hate, which hurt her just as much as the pitiful condition of the prisoners.

Guayafanta, whose body was covered with countless wounds, shook her fist at Iriomé from afar. Her fever-bright eyes cried for revenge. Nevertheless Iriomé walked over to her and knelt beside her. "We'll meet again," hissed the harimaguada. "And then I'll ensure that all the suffering that you've caused comes back to you . . . for all eternity."

She looked at Akin's amulet visible under Iriomé's gown when she bent down. Guayafanta laughed contemptuously and tried to grab it. But Iriomé was quicker. Bloody saliva that Guayafanta spat into her face with her last strength was their parting.

Hieronymus noticed her dilemma. After she put ointment on the head wound of a young woman, he took Iriomé's hand and helped her back to the small boat. She sincerely appreciated this. She could not stay here. The time in which she had felt protected and accepted among her people was irrevocably over.

With tears in her eyes, she looked back to the ship while they were slowly rowing to the beach. Would it now be Akin who would keep her going when she was not well? Would he be the one who gave her warmth and security when the storms of life were reaching for her? She was not sure, even if her heart wanted nothing more than that.

∽

The *Santa Cruz* sailed northward under full sail. Again and again clouds were drifting past the moon, dipping the sea into complete darkness. The bow of the small caravel rose almost vertically into the sky, just to dive into the next trough a little bit later. Iriomé stood at the railing, holding on to it tightly. The billowing sails caused a noise that frightened her, like all else since she had entered this swaying monster. Only at night did she dare to come on deck, when no one saw her and she did not cause a stir.

Here she recovered from the seasickness that never left her in Akin's small cave in the belly of the ship. He had built her a sleeping place there, which consisted of a net attached to a hook at each end. Through a round hole in the wooden wall fresh air came in, making the permanent rocking a little more bearable.

Iriomé was often on her own there, something she was not used to in her former life. Frai Hieronymus was the only one to stop by now and then during those long lonesome days below deck. During this time he tried to teach her his language and vice versa. He painted small drawings in his book and scribbled unintelligible characters beside them. Yet in this way she understood how the knowledge was put into the book. But how the god of the Spaniards should live in it and even his son, she still could not figure out. Hieronymus often told her about Jesus, who performed miracles and who had died for the people. The latter appealed to her not at all. Especially not since he had shown her the small colorful picture of the dead man covered in blood who was hanging from a cross. Much more important than this gruesome story was that they exchanged each day as many words as people have fingers on their hands. When they arrived at their destination, she might finally be able to talk to Joaquín. He was rather reserved toward her, and Iriomé guessed that he was just as wracked with guilt as she was. They lacked a common language; the language they once shared had quieted. He had never touched her again. Neither day nor night, when they were each lying in their rocking beds, had they gotten close.

When the moon was hidden behind a cloud again, Iriomé crept to the foremast where Tanausú was chained, constantly checking that no one could see her. They were the only Benahoarias aboard. The other slaves were on the other two ships. The spray trickled down through his long hair and beard. His naked body was shivering with cold. Next to him lay something soft and white, which the water had moistened and which the Spaniards called bread. He had not touched it.

"You need to eat," whispered Iriomé.

The wind in the sails rose above everything, so that she did not have to fear being heard by the guards who were sitting just a few steps away. She herself blended into the shadows of the mast. Tanausú opened his eyes, stuck shut from the saltwater, and showed with a barely perceptible nod that he had recognized her. He tried to speak, but only a faint croak came from his throat.

"Guayote will punish me for what I've done," whispered Iriomé and could have died right there in front of his eyes.

The proud leader of the tribe of Aceró, the brave fighter, the boy who had saved her life shook his head almost imperceptibly. "You were right," he whispered in validation. "But the time is not yet ripe for the love. But the day will come, and then we'll meet again."

So he also believed it. Had Tichiname spoken to him as well? Is this why he had agreed to Iriomé's proposal? "It's about amakuna."

Iriomé felt for Joaquín's amulet, which she still wore around her neck. Before returning to the coast, she had made a powder from the mushrooms so that she could always carry it with her. Nobody would suspect the secret of her people was hidden in there.

"You need to know one thing," Tanausú whispered with his last strength.

Iriomé came even closer and put her ear right to his lips so the storm could not carry away his words before they reached her.

"Amakuna not only lets the harimaguadas look into the future and the past. It connects the fate of all those who have ever taken it for all eternity in a chain that never breaks. But it also effects something else."

"What?"

"It defeats any disease."

"How do you know that?" she asked.

"Because Tichiname gave it to me when I was a little boy and broke my back in a fall and looked death in the eye, even though she actually never should have done that because amakuna is only reserved for the harimaguadas. That's why we'll meet again, little Iriomé, in another life. And then I'll stand by your side and make sure that nothing happens to you. I swear!" Exhausted, he collapsed, his body upright only by the shackles.

"Vacaguaré," was the last word that escaped his lips.

Now the guards seemed to have heard something. Iriomé noticed by the movement of the planks that someone was approaching. Quickly she hid behind a tower of ropes. But not quickly enough. One of the men grabbed her firmly, and she had to watch helplessly as the other spat at Tanausú and kicked him.

Then the two men turned to her. They had dirty, unkempt beards, stank of rot, and in addition Iriomé was confronted by a sharp nauseating smell. They dragged their prey away from Tanausú's body and held a transparent container in front of her face, in which a small flame was burning spreading some light. Satisfied about their find they laughed out loud and slapped each other on their shoulders and legs. Then they pushed Iriomé to the wet ground. She struggled with her hands and feet but had no chance to grab the knife hidden in a fold of her dress. One held her upper body and pulled up her leather garment. The second spread her legs by brute force and pushed himself in between, panting. The next moment he was met by a well-placed blow. He rolled helplessly aside. The other instantly let go of Iriomé.

Joaquín helped her up and put a protective arm around her shoulder. He barked a command at the two men, which made them withdraw to the rear of the ship like scared dogs.

Iriomé was still trembling all over when Joaquín took her hand and led her to their cabin. When her breathing became quieter, he stroked her tousled hair, trying to organize the sticky strands, and gently wiped the dirt from her cheeks. It was the first time since the devastating events that they had touched and that something else was budding between them other than pain and despair. The feeling of deep intimacy and mutual desire that had arisen between them in a single day in a cave shrine was rekindled. Were they on the right track despite it all?

Joaquín drew her close to him and brushed a gentle kiss on her trembling lips.

Suddenly loud cries destroyed this delicate moment. Men's fists were banging on the door, and someone was screaming. Iriomé heard the name de Lugo and immediately knew that this could mean nothing good.

Joaquín opened the door, and three men rushed in. They tore Iriomé from her bed and dragged her, despite Joaquín's loud protests, back on deck, right in front of the feet of Alonso de Lugo. He brutally kicked her twice, then grabbed her hair and turned her head to the mast to which Tanausú had been chained.

They had taken him off. His body lay on the wet planks, the eyes staring skyward where the first light of dawn already showed. He had made good his word and had quit this life.

Iriomé would have gladly followed him. Because it was true: the time of love had not yet come.

And thus the sound being made by the conqueror when he drew his deadly weapon from its sheath was almost a relief. She would follow

Tanausú into the realm of the spirits and ancestors. And she would be reunited with Tichiname and her parents. Iriomé closed her eyes and awaited the end. But nothing happened.

Joaquín's powerful voice again stopped the stone of destiny that was already rolling toward the abyss at high speed. He clutched the hand in which de Lugo held his sword and challenged him in a clear voice to a duel.

Although Iriomé understood only little of the language of the Spaniards, she knew what would happen next. When two men of her people had their eye on the same woman the decision was made by stick fighting, which, however, never ended fatally. What counted was skill and speed. But the weapons of the Spaniards were sharp and deadly. Should Akin lose, this meant not only his, but also her death.

De Lugo laughed scornfully and abruptly let go of Iriomé so that her head hit the planks. She blacked out, and when she looked up again she saw Joaquín drawing his sword and bringing himself in position.

The other men who had kept watch on deck came running up curiously. Even those who were due to sleep this shift were awakened by the cries and were staring, dazed, at what was happening in front of them.

The fight started. Iriomé was still lying on the floor, where she had a good view of the two men chasing each other from one side of the deck to the other. A little carelessness, a slip, an unpredictable movement of the ship, and one of them belonged to death. With the utmost attention she followed each of Akin's movements. Somehow they seemed to be her own. As he slipped, it was she who went to the ground, and when he came back up it was she who gave him the strength to do so. It was also she who looked death right in the eye when Cold Eye suddenly stood over Akin swinging his sword to give him the final blow. But Iriomé still saw a little chance. And Joaquín made use of it. A heartbeat later he rolled through de Lugo's legs, jumped up, and stabbed his opponent in the shoulder from the side. Blood gushed out, but the conqueror gave only a short cry of pain and still was far from giving up.

The first rays of the sun appeared on the horizon as the two fighters, exhausted and covered in blood, still fought for victory. Joaquín was the younger, which was an advantage the longer the fight lasted. As de Lugo paused to take a breath, Joaquín gave him yet another stab, this time in the leg. Cold Eye fell, struggled to his feet furiously, and tried to attack Joaquín from behind. Iriomé warned him again in her own way without a movement or a sound. He turned around jerkily and gave de Lugo a blow in the face, which knocked him to the floor for good. Akin raised his sword for the final flourish and then stopped. Iriomé had been able to help him this far, but no farther. A Benahoaria never killed someone who was lying helplessly on the ground.

The young Spaniard dropped his blade. A murmur went through the crew, which by now had assembled on deck in full force, including the cabin boy, to witness the spectacle. Joaquín turned to Iriomé. And this time it was she who gently took his hand and led him below deck. Nobody stopped them.

Down in their cabin she first cleaned Akin's wounds. There were only a few and not very deep. Iriomé took the rest of the ointment from her bag and gently applied it to the freshly coagulated blood, a familiar gesture that reminded her of the first time they had gotten close. It seemed almost as if they could build on this moment and push all those terrible things that had happened afterward to the back of their minds.

He took her hand and pulled her toward him. She let it happen. His breath was hot. His body smelled of sweat and blood. Iriomé felt his hands slide under her garment, grasp her backside, and gently caress her hips and her belly. Both their breathing quickened, almost synchronously. Somehow she knew what would happen next.

When his hands lay on her fluff, she was willing to give herself to him. She felt how she was getting wet. His fingers groped farther, stroking her gently. Ever larger waves of pleasure overwhelmed her, and she moaned. Both were breathing heavily now. He lay on top of her, penetrated her. A little pain she could barely feel. He continued to caress her while gently moving in her. She arched her back and enjoyed the unfamiliar feeling that was rushing through her body until she could not stand it any longer and screamed. She screamed herself free from all that weighed on her mind.

Chapter 20

Romy could no longer distinguish who was screaming. She or Iriomé. Space and time were fused together. Who was she? Who was the man who now lay beside her with his eyes closed? Nic or Joaquín, or Nic with the soul of Joaquín? Romy didn't know what to think.

"Best you don't think at all now," whispered Nic with his eyes still closed. "This just happened. It has nothing to do with our professional relationship." He opened his eyes and took her in his arms.

It was typical that he already had a clear head again while she still was asking herself in whose body she was at the moment. Obviously, she didn't need to eat the mushroom to get in touch with Iriomé anymore. The gate was opened. *Amakuna not only lets the harimaguadas look into the future and the past. It connects the fate of all those who have ever taken it for all eternity . . .*

Tanausú's last words were still fresh in her mind. But wouldn't that mean that Joaquín must have consumed the mushroom at some time— or eventually would? That Tichiname's story was continued in Thea's life? And that Tanausú lived on in the body of environmental activist Tom Sattler, alias Tanausú? They were all reunited. Those who took in the mushroom in this life got in contact with a previous life and now had the chance to smooth over what once had gone wrong.

It sounded mystical, like a fantasy. But that's how it must be.

This realization embedded deep into Romy's heart and gave her the feeling that she no longer was stumbling from one incident to the next. She was getting her feet on solid ground again. Even if this ground was totally alien, and until quite recently, she would have severely doubted it could exist.

"You're still thinking," Nic said, sitting up slowly. Romy smiled at him. He probably did not know about their common past; after all, he had not yet enjoyed amakuna. But perhaps he suspected something. The strong appeal he had toward her was at any rate the same as five hundred years ago.

"I think the party is over. We should be getting off this hospitable ship."

Romy became aware of the silence and the gentle lapping of the waves against the vessel's side. The band on deck had stopped playing.

"It's already 5 a.m.," Nic noticed amused while he put on his golden watch.

Romy had completely lost track of time. She had succumbed to Nic's skills of seduction as Iriomé had to Joaquín's. Or as Guayafanta had put it: *She has been misled by the lust of her body. Something that is forbidden for any harimaguada. She has blindly trusted the stranger and laid the fate of our people in his hands.* Was she now well on the way to doing the same? Was she on the verge of betraying amakuna, the secret of the Guanches, to the conquistadors of today?

Meanwhile, Nic found her dress and underwear between the rumpled silk sheets and handed them to her. "If you want, there's a bathroom." He pointed to a door embedded in the fine wood paneling of the cabin.

Such luxury was not available to Iriomé on Joaquín's ship, thought Romy and rose from the round dream bed. As she walked, she felt Nic's gaze on her bare back. Sandstorm feelings announced themselves again. She quickly closed the bathroom door behind her.

She looked in the mirror and breathed deeply. No man had ever triggered such feelings in her before and aroused such desire. When she had felt particularly close to someone, sometimes the thought arose whether she perhaps knew this person from a previous life. But this time it was reality. The idea was overwhelming, though not necessarily reassuring.

She would have loved to know what happened next in Iriomé's love story. Whether Joaquín continued to stand by her side. It was a pity that one could not just pull out one's cell phone and make a quick call to the fifteenth century.

She put on her dress and tried to fix the updo created by Esmeralda. But it was hopeless. A ponytail would have to do.

Nic had also dressed and come up behind her. He kissed her gently on the cheek and then took her hand. Like two thieves they crept over the empty deck to the gangway. Now Romy was hungry, but the buffet had already been cleared. A few party guests were still clinging to their last drink, but no one seemed to observe Romy and Nic. Only the man in a tuxedo, who had been instructed by Borges, had waited and nodded to them.

The ride home proceeded in silence. As much as she had enjoyed lying in Nic's arms, Romy now longed to be alone with her thoughts about Iriomé. She worried about her as if they were sisters, even though she knew that it was impossible to intervene in the events of the past. All she could do was to fathom the parallels and implications for her present life. Joaquín had saved Iriomé twice from death. But he was also responsible for the downfall of her people, which had brought his own people power and wealth. Nic also promised to save Romy's life. Yet at the same time he was chasing after the mushroom, which could immeasurably increase the power of Forster's Health.

Didn't a warrior always remain a warrior? Didn't a woman always make the same mistakes when she was in love?

The Jaguar drove up the avenue to Nic's property silhouetted against the pink-colored morning sky like a bronze fortress. The driver held the door for Romy. Nic said goodbye to her with a gentlemanly kiss on her hand at the bottom of the stairs. "I'd be happy if you'll accompany me tomorrow afternoon on a little trip in the Extremadura. In a monastery near the old castillo of my ancestors in Trujillo, writings from the Middle Ages were found during renovations, including a recipe book about plant medicine. That, of course, interests me and could be interesting for you, too."

Of course it was. And most of all she was interested in this castillo of his ancestors. Maybe she would find something about a connection between Joaquín and Nic. "I'd love to" she said. "If we don't set off too early. I need a good night's rest."

Nic chuckled. "I do understand that."

On the way to her room she was surprised that the thought that this could be a new chance to escape was actually of secondary importance.

୬୬

From the Dolby Surround system in the Jaguar, Latin jazz by Stan Getz soothed them while they drove northward. The more distance they ventured from the sunny coast, the colder it got. The sky went from blue to gray, and instead of wintry green vegetation, the snowcapped mountains of the Cordillera Central appeared on the horizon. From there an icy wind was blowing over the barren landscape, through which the scarcely traveled highway was winding its way. Every now and then ruins of old castles appeared out of nowhere, mostly near small villages with whitewashed houses.

"The Extremadura is still the poorhouse of the Iberian Peninsula," said Nic, who was sitting next to Romy in the back of the car, his arm around her. "The Spanish regained the area from the Moors in the thirteenth century. Most castillos you see here date from this time. Yet most were completely rebuilt by the Spaniards, which from an aesthetic point of view wasn't such a good idea."

Romy knew about Moorish architecture, which had been well preserved in Andalusia. Her grandmother had enthused her about it when she was still a child. They had visited the Alcázar of Seville, the Alhambra in Granada, and of course Cordoba, where they had played hide and seek between the columns of the most beautiful mosque in the world. She had, so to speak, inherited the Hispano-Moorish culture.

"The Moors were way ahead of the rest of Europe, not only in regard to architecture but also in the art of healing." Nic continued his lecture.

Romy grinned. "What's this supposed to be? A lesson in Spanish culture?"

"No, rather in the Moorish art of healing."

She looked at him in astonishment.

"I've just recently developed an interest in the beginnings of European medicine. Have you ever heard of the famous polymath Ibn Sina? He was also called Avicenna, which means king of all doctors. His most famous work, the *Canon of Medicine* was translated into Latin in the twelfth century, and later in the fifteenth century into Hebrew. It was the standard work in European universities up to the seventeenth century."

"I only took two semesters of medical history and don't know much about him, to tell the truth," Romy had to admit.

"I've just given one of his prescriptions to our laboratories for testing."

"Did you?" This Nic Saratoga surprised her more and more.

"Ibn Sina was convinced that powdered incense together with honey strengthens the mind. And indeed, a behavior test with laboratory rats has shown a significant pharmacological effect of this mixture on their capacity of memory."

"And you think this would help to overcome Alzheimer's and dementia?" She hadn't expected such an attitude from the chairman of the largest pharmaceutical company in the world.

Nic grinned. "I think it's high time to rethink things. Forster's Health is locked in a stalemate. Many products have side effects, which are increasingly less accepted by consumers. In addition, most profitable drugs reach the end of the time they're protected by patents sooner now. This makes it difficult to compete with low-cost generics, leading to annual revenue losses of several billion dollars."

So this is the way the wind is blowing.

"Last September, the patent protection of our anticholesterol drug

Lipitarum expired, which accounted for 15 percent of our total revenues and an annual turnover of over twelve billion dollars. On the same day on which the patent protection expired, an Indian pharmaceutical company was authorized by the United States Food and Drug Administration to dump a generic clone on the market for less than one euro per carton."

The problem was familiar to Romy. This was exactly the reason that ever more new products needed to be developed ever faster, which could be sold at higher prices—yet mostly were no more effective than the old ones.

"I think our future lies in the discovery of new herbal and other natural products, which have no or almost no side effects," Nic said, and he sounded very convinced.

Romy was now genuinely flabbergasted. Was he trying to suck up to her this way or did he really believe this? "And this will work out?"

"With the right recipes, the corresponding marketing, and worldwide sales, yes. I'm working hard on it, especially against the resistance of the hardliners in the company's top management. I currently fight for every penny to build this new segment. Thus, I'm also interested in your mushroom."

"And what about Avistan?" Romy could not resist this question.

"The company's management wants to establish it internationally, due to the high development costs."

"And you?"

"I'm against it."

"And you can't do anything?"

"Not at the moment." Nic had a serious expression.

Romy was keen to learn more about it, but unfortunately at that very moment Nic's mobile rang, and he spent the next two hours talking on the phone in the most diverse languages, including Japanese and Arabic.

Romy had to admit that she liked him more and more. A Mr. Right, who in his heart pursued the same ideas and ideals as she did. And who, even better, had the opportunities to implement them on a large scale.

They reached Trujillo before sunset. Even from afar one could see on the hill above the town the old Moorish fortress whose battlements were silhouetted against a red-colored sky like a paper cutout. The typical medieval village looked magical in the soft evening light. Nic finally switched off his phone and also enjoyed the sight.

The car stopped right in the middle of the Plaza Mayor, the main square of Trujillo. When Romy got out, the first thing she saw was a bronze equestrian statue of Francisco Pizarro, the most famous son of this town.

"Almost all of the great conquerors of South America came from this region, which is also called the cradle of the conquistadores," said Nic. "They all dreamed of power and wealth and of turning their backs on the Extremadura: Hernán Cortés, who destroyed the Aztec empire in Central America; Pizarro, who conquered the Inca empire in Peru; and Hernando de Soto, who seized Panama and Nicaragua for the Spanish crown."

And Joaquín, who was present at the capture of La Palma, Romy thought as she walked around the monument.

"They had the power of the Reconquista in their blood, hundreds of years of struggle against the Moors. And such a militant policy obviously had an impact on their faith," continued Nic, who seemed to enjoy demonstrating his knowledge in this field. "When the Moors had been expelled and the Jews emigrated or converted, the vigorous energy of Christian Spain turned to the conquest of new territory. And the cooperation between nobility, army, church, and court additionally promoted these ventures."

Romy's gaze was drawn upward, where the citadel built of light-colored limestone cast its shadow on the square. "And your ancestors, to which family of conquistadores did they belong?"

"De Alba y Santa Barbara," he answered, not without a certain amount of pride in his voice. "They did not belong to the nouveaux riches as Cortés or Pizarro. The latter actually was a swineherd here in Trujillo, a bastard from a liaison with a maid. The de Albas were old nobility," he stressed. "Even during the Muslim period they were regarded as the largest landowners in the Extremadura. Nevertheless, they also took part in the conquest later."

"Even on the Canary Islands?" Romy could not refrain from asking.

"That's quite possible. But the great conqueror of the Canaries was Alonso Fernández de Lugo, and he came, as far as I know, from Cádiz. This was, even then, Andalusia."

Romy instantly remembered Cold Eye, who would have killed Iriomé right away if Joaquín had not intervened so courageously. She wondered again whether Nic would also stand up for her. She gave him a sidelong glance.

"You don't trust me, Romy. Why?" He was more sensitive than she had assumed. "But I understand. Sometimes I don't even trust myself."

"What do you mean?"

He smiled. "Well, sometimes you find yourself doing things that don't fit in the picture, and suddenly you're on unfamiliar ground and need to reorient yourself."

Did he mean to say he was orienting in her direction?

Had Tichiname been right after all?

Nic gave the driver a signal to park the car and put his arm through Romy's. "The best thing about the Extremadura is not the conquistadors but the wine." He quickly changed the subject, as if he had gone too far out on a limb. He led her to one of the bodegas under the arcades that lined the medieval square on three sides.

There they were received by the typical smell of old wine barrels mixed with the ham hanging from the ceiling, along with it, a noise level that only the Spaniards were able to produce. Romy knew those pubs from her youth in Spain and felt immediately comfortable. The wine, a deep red Ribeira de Gurdiana, was pleasant to the taste, together with the typical ham from pigs that ate only acorns that was served. The well-hung, tasty meat melted in Romy's mouth. They touched glasses.

"*Salud.* I think I don't need to tell you how glad I am we've met,"

Nic said in his gentle voice and looked deep into her eyes. "You know, even though we've really only just met, I feel as if we've known each other forever."

Romy swallowed. She wished she could have told him that he was not so wrong about this. But it was clearly too soon. He would think she was completely weird and no longer take her seriously as a scientist.

Most local visitors of the bodega knew Nic and gave him a friendly slap on the back. He seemed to feel comfortable here, and the villagers had no reservations. "People here like me now," said Nic. "First there was a big scandal when my grandfather sold our old family home to an international luxury hotel group, but now the village has benefited a great deal from it and the protests have subsided." He showed his typical rascal grin. "But my grandfather was smart enough to ensure that the most beautiful suite is permanently available to our family. Let's drive up there, so we can have a little siesta before dinner."

The way he said the word siesta did not sound like a restful nap was the plan.

The atmosphere in the entrance hall of the Palacio del Conquistador was completely different from that in the simple bodega. From the gigantic vaulted ceiling of the medieval castillo hung iron chandeliers spreading their light over heavy, dark red carpets and rigid chairs padded with brown leather, which stood around a long table as if in a knight's hall. Romy shivered. It was chilly within the old walls; she felt uncomfortable in this environment as if she had once been here under quite different circumstances. She felt like turning on her heels immediately.

Nic must have noticed, because he laid his arm around her shoulders as if it were the most natural thing in the world. "What's the matter with you?" he whispered in her ear.

"Nothing; I'm just a little cold," she replied.

A forty-year-old Spanish woman with severe features and black hair tied back tightly, wearing a perfectly fitting dark velvet suit, welcomed them. She seemed not in the least surprised that Nic showed up not with his wife, but with Romy. And if she was, she did not let it show. She took the reservations for a table for dinner and then beckoned an employee dressed in a uniform to guide Nic up a narrow side staircase to a closed port wing to his suite.

Unlike the lobby this room was furnished in bright, friendly colors. The view from the small medieval stone balcony was breathtaking even in the gathering darkness. Below them, the village nestled against the fortress wall, and when one looked out into the distance, the horizon seemed infinitely far. *A perfect location for a fortress,* Romy thought. Enemies could be seen hours before they arrived.

The employee poured two glasses with iced Cava and handed them to Nic, who stood next to Romy on the balcony. "A sublime scene, isn't it?" he said softly.

Romy agreed. Had Joaquín and Iriomé also stood here? Romy wondered if he had married her. But had that even been possible? As far as she knew, a nobleman then could only marry a noblewoman and definitely not a savage from some distant island. The path of their love was certainly paved with many obstacles. That they had ever been able to live their love was more than questionable. This thought crossed Romy's mind like a sudden summer storm and made her sad.

"You're so absorbed." Nic gently stroked her lips with his fingertips.

"I'm just thinking," Romy said.

He took her face in both hands and kissed her on the mouth. Romy closed her eyes and enjoyed his tenderness; then she answered his kiss. "*Te quiero, mi amor,*" he whispered in her ear. "I've been looking for you all my life and never want to be without you anymore; do you under-stand this?"

His words sunk deep into her soul. Was this an old dream coming true right now?

Romy closed her eyes, snuggled in his arms, and got carried away on a wave of passion—far away from the thought that he was married to the daughter of the main shareholder of Forster's Health. And far away from the thought that there might be quite a different reason for which he was putting on this show.

Chapter 21

The Dominican convent of Santa Maria del Valle was nestled in a small hollow surrounded by rolling hills where sheep were grazing. The Romanesque church was still in good condition and appeared to Romy like a rock that had defied the eternal surf of time. The outbuildings, however, were partly encased with scaffolding and sheeting that looked like surgical corsets or bandages meant to keep an old body upright. Two orange cranes gave the whole scene a bizarre impression.

"The building was about to collapse. The roof is completely leaking, and there's mold all over the walls. But I think we can save the monastery," Nic said hopefully.

"We?"

"Yes, I've put some of my personal assets in the renovations."

Romy looked at him quizzically. "But not for religious reasons?"

Nic laughed. "No. The monastery was founded in 1490 by Lucía Pilar de Alba, and somehow I feel responsible for it still today. Even though I can't say why. Since I was here the first time, I've had the feeling of being familiar with this monastery in some way. And nowadays, I even think that I owe the place something."

Romy felt uncertainty in his voice. A completely new side to this man who was otherwise bursting with power and self-confidence.

"The Dominicans played an important role during the Spanish Inquisition, right? Weren't they like judges, who decided whether someone was of pure faith or should be taken to the stake?" Romy tried to remember the lessons of Señor Méndez. As far as she could tell, these terrible killings took place at the time when Iriomé sailed for Spain.

"But only the male part of the Order," Nic said. "And not because they scrambled to do it, but because their founder, Dominicus de Caleruega, had postulated an academic education for all members. And this simply predestined them for this bloody task. The nunneries, on the other hand, were a refuge for the ladies from the nobility, and the only way for them to learn something and escape marriages that only served to increase the family fortune and produce a legitimate heir."

Romy believed she heard something almost like compassion in his voice. Again the thought crossed her mind that Joaquín and Iriomé probably had had no chance at all. The social rules of that time would never have allowed such a connection. But was it really so much different today? Compared with the daughter of Gerald Forster, she was only a cute little nurse.

At the monastery gateway they were welcomed by a small, plump nun with mischief twinkling in her eyes. She introduced herself as Sister Philomena and wore the typical black and white dress of the Dominicans. Though she looked Romy up and down, she didn't say a word about her presence but guided them to one of the old, unrenovated buildings.

"If you just wait here, Señor Saratoga, I'll go and get the book for you," she said with a wink and disappeared.

In the sparsely furnished visitor's room there were only a few chairs and an old wooden table. On the wall hung an unadorned cross and opposite, on a pedestal, stood a roughly carved Madonna. She wore a blue cape whose color was just as washed out as the color of the face. The sun that was shining through the small window was not enough to expel the cold and the dampness.

Romy moved her toes in her black leather boots and zipped up her lined windbreaker.

"I'll encourage them to install a heater," said Nic, smiling.

At that moment the nun came back with a large leatherbound book under her arm. It was obviously quite heavy, because she groaned as she put it on the table. "That's it," she said proudly, as if she had written it herself. *"Liber Herbarum Medicinarum.* It dates from the late fifteenth century and was compiled by Hermana Guadalupe, a nun of this monastery."

Nic opened the cover and carefully turned the parchment pages. Romy looked over his shoulder. On the left side was a finely crafted drawing of leaves, flowers, and roots of the respective medicinal plant, on the right Latin text written in neat, small handwriting. Nic continued leafing through the book, while the nun watched his every move like a hawk, as if she was afraid he would run away with the precious oeuvre.

"And what do you think?" she asked, curious. "Do you think you can make use of it?"

"I don't know yet," Nic said.

"We've already got quite lucrative offers by some museums, and well . . . the renovation costs exceed what we expected by far," she said, friendly and determined at the same time.

Pretty brazen, thought Romy. After all, Nic had already forked out a nice sum for the old place.

But as always he kept calm and turned to Romy with a smile. "Why don't you use the opportunity and have a look at the monastery until I'm done here?"

Sister Philomena nodded in agreement, took out her cell phone, and asked a fellow sister to come over immediately. Shortly afterward a nun just about Romy's age entered the room and introduced herself as Hermana Felicitas.

"Please show the young lady our monastery," Sister Philomena said bossily and hustled the two out of the room. Obviously, she could not wait to negotiate a lucrative business deal with Nic.

"Unfortunately, everything's a bit chaotic at the moment, but there are still a few nice places, where everything is as it was," said the young nun with an unusually deep, rough voice, looking straight into Romy's eyes.

Romy took to her immediately. Her narrow face framed by the white veil of the novices conveyed calm and mental balance. Romy was currently far removed from that. The two women crossed the church square planted with ancient chestnut trees in the direction of the main building of the monastery.

Sister Felicitas ducked under a tarp, produced a thick bunch of keys from the pocket of her dress, and unlocked a heavy iron-studded wooden door. Before them opened a sunlit Roman cloister, in the middle of which was a well.

Their footsteps were echoing through the old walls. Romy felt a little out of place with her boots and tried to tread especially carefully. Sister Felicitas gave her a warm smile. "Don't worry. Sometimes it's good to break a little of the silence that has prevailed here for over five hundred years. This cloister is still original, from the fifteenth century."

"How long have you been living in this silence?"

"Until recently I've worked in a hospital in Madrid, but eventually I became sick there myself. Now I am responsible for the nursing and care for the older sisters here. In this place I can fulfill the task God has assigned me in his spirit in a humane way."

"I know what you mean," Romy said. "I'm a lab physician, and I also worked in a hospital before."

Sister Felicitas looked at her with interest. "Before?"

Romy nodded. "Recently I've been working in a pharmaceutical laboratory in the department for herbal drug research."

"Then you're certainly more interested in our herb garden than in the old walls here? It's quite unique and has a long tradition. A Dominican sister named Guadalupe planted it as early as the Middle Ages, and later here in the monastery the first pharmacy in the area was opened up."

"I just saw her book," Romy said. "It's wonderful!"

"An incredible find! We found it under the library in a half-buried room where books were probably kept during the Inquisition that were not intended for everyone, and certainly not for the inquisitors. Actually it was supposed to stay in the monastery, but with Señor Saratoga it will also be in good hands."

"I'm sure he will make a copy for the monastery."

"That would be nice," the nurse said with a smile.

They left the cloister and strolled through another mighty wooden door at the back of the west wing, which was also encased by scaffolding. From there, a trail along the old monastery wall led to a generously arranged herb garden. The individual plants were neatly separated and lovingly provided with small labels. While she was taking a look around, a small inconspicuous wooden gate in the wall attracted Romy's attention. "What's behind it?" she asked.

"An old hermitage that once belonged to the monastery. But it's dilapidated now."

"Can I have a look at it?" Romy asked with a determination that she could not explain.

"Why not? But don't expect too much." Sister Felicitas leaned resolutely with her shoulder against the old wooden door, which rendered fierce resistance and only jumped open when the nun threw herself against it with all her strength.

Romy saw a meadow dotted with flowers and at some distance at the edge of the forest an enchanting stone house with a sunken roof. As if drawn to it magically, she walked toward it. Sister Felicitas followed at some distance, puzzled.

The half-rotted door was completely off its hinges and almost fell off when Romy pushed it open. A number of pigeons flew up into the air, startled. Inside it smelled of mildew. On the muddy ground were broken roof tiles covered with moss. The windows had been barricaded with wooden boards. Only through the damaged roof did some sunlight enter, reflecting on the interior walls. Romy's eyes fell on a badly weathered piece of wall. She wiped off the lichen, and beneath it, beside several triangles, quadrangles, and miscellaneous large circles, a spiral appeared that had been carved into an especially flawless stone. Carefully Romy touched it with her fingertips.

At the same moment a stabbing pain flashed through her stomach, which became more and more severe. With the last of her strength she dragged herself outside and collapsed. The line between this and another world was blurring. She felt as if she were in a spiral vortex that pulled her up and cut the ground from under her feet.

Chapter 22

"Land ahead!" Although Iriomé did not understand the words, she could guess their meaning. The long journey full of privation was coming to an end. She heard the men running on deck and shouting for joy. Only Joaquín lay on his bunk and seemed not to be able to share this joy. Iriomé knew the reason.

Alonso de Lugo, the slayer of her people, was dying. Gangrene was raging, and severe bouts of fever shook his body. Joaquín and Frai Hieronymus had asked her to save his life, but every time she came near the sleeping place of the conqueror, she began to tremble. Then the noise in her head became as loud as the surf when it thundered against the rocky coast of Benahoare in the winter months, and she felt as though she was suffocating. She had let Joaquín have the rest of the green paste, even though she knew that it would be of no help anymore. He had treated Cold Eye with it, as well as with cold compresses and had been sitting at his bedside for hours. But why?

She felt that Joaquín suffered, as if he himself was dying. He ate and drank almost nothing and spoke to hardly anybody except occasionally Frai Hieronymus.

Iriomé shook the young Spaniard and pointed to the round hole in the ship's side. "Land," she kept repeating the word she had heard on deck.

He straightened up, pushed her aside, and looked through the hole to see for himself. Then he put on jacket and trousers and left their shared sleeping place without saying a word. Since Cold Eye had started fighting for his life, what had been between them vanished. Iriomé guessed that he secretly blamed her for the inevitable death of the conquistador.

She also dressed. As of late she helped herself from Joaquín's clothes trunk. Her own leather garment had repeatedly gotten wet and rubbed on the skin. The Spaniard's trousers fit her; all she had to do was to strap them around her waist with a leather belt so that she did not lose them. What he called "shirt" and "jacket" were a little loose, but that did not bother her.

She followed him without his noticing. As she had suspected, he went to his leader. The conqueror was resting motionless on his bed. His face was as white as the cloth on which he was bedded and formed a sharp contrast to the black, scruffy beard that grew profusely over his chin. Joaquín felt his pulse. He must have sensed that she was standing by the door and gave her a helpless yet completely desperate look that shook her to the core. She turned away just to collide with Frai Hieronymus, who was also on his way to the dying man.

"Why is Joaquín so desperate?" She asked him in a simple but now easily understandable Spanish. During the last weeks she had made much progress in the language of the conquistadors.

The monk took her aside and looked at her gravely. "If the Conquistadore dies, Joaquín will be accused of murder. He will be hanged, and that brings great shame to his family."

Iriomé did not understand all, but one thing was clear: the death of de Lugo would result in the death of Joaquín. She shuddered. He needed her help. Just as she had needed his when Cold Eye's sword had been hovering over her.

Between her and Akin there was a bond of mutual responsibility, as had been between her and Tanausú, a bond that must never tear. That was a law of her people that nobody had ever violated. When Joaquín went past them with his head bowed and without even taking notice of them, Frai Hieronymus followed him looking worried. In that moment Iriomé made a serious decision. She overcame her fears and crept back to Cold Eye's sleeping place. There she studied the dying man thoroughly. She felt neither hatred nor the desire for revenge. She only thought of the danger his death would mean to Joaquín. Then she opened the medallion, moistened her finger with spit and touched the content so that only a little of the powder stuck to it. After that she dipped her finger in de Lugo's water cup, supported his square head, and fed him the contents of the cup drip by drip while she avoided the foul breath from his mouth.

"Tara, Queen of the gods, Mother of the Earth, I invoke your power. Save this man. For the life of Akin, for he rescued mine." She had only whispered each word, but de Lugo must have heard her nevertheless. He opened his eyes, and his cold gaze hit her like the blade of his sword. She was not sure if he recognized her. Groaning, he fell back on his bed. Iriomé stayed with him for a while until she saw that he had fallen asleep and was breathing regularly. Only now she realized what she had done.

Again she heard Tichiname's voice. *These men know no love. They will destroy everything that is sacred to us. But one thing must never fall into their hands: the secret heart of the island that beats in the cave of the highest mountain!*

But Iriomé had no choice. She and Joaquín would henceforth ensure together that amakuna would never fall into the hands of the conquistadors. This was their destiny! And Cold Eye actually realizing that he owed his recovery to her medicine was doubtful. Somewhat reassured, she went back to Joaquín's cabin, where she lay in her hanging bed.

But something was different. It took a while; then she perceived that the ship no longer moved forward. It was only gently rocking and sometimes jerked like a goat that was tied to a stake and wanted to free itself. Through the small hole in the ship's side, she spotted the coast.

There was a flat bright beach where numerous boats of different sizes lay at anchor. Behind, lined up in rows, high white boxes with dark holes were rising.

The higher the sun was in the sky, the hotter and stickier it was in the small cabin. During the journey the wind had blown in through the small opening and brought coolness, but now the sun was transforming the ship into a fiery, stinking oven. Iriomé lay naked in her rocking net with her eyes closed. The sweat was running down her body in small streams while Tichiname's words were relentlessly echoing in her mind: *Only when people are free from the greed for power and wealth will its secret be safe to reveal . . . It is your task as my successor to preserve amakuna until that time has come.*

She woke up when the new day dawned outside and excited voices reached her ears. Through the hole in the ship's side, she saw a small rowing boat in which there were two men from the crew and a stranger who looked completely different from the Spaniards. He was small and plump and wore a strange twisted towel on his head and colorful clothes with strange patterns. She watched as they helped him on deck and caught a glimpse of his eyes. That was all it took. She recognized the soul of a harimaguada in the body of a man.

Joaquín greeted the man exuberantly and guided him immediately below deck. Iriomé knew where they went. Something better could not have happened. If de Lugo actually recovered, it would look to all as if this colorfully dressed man had healed him. No one would ever learn the truth. Reassured, she again fell into a doze that befuddled her senses and dissolved her concerns.

She only came to when Joaquín appeared calling her name and embraced her. All sadness and hopelessness had fallen off him. Tears of joy were sparkling in his eyes.

"Thank you for saving him. I don't know what you've done. But I'll never forget. Now I can go ashore and look my family in the eyes."

Iriomé freed herself gently from his embrace and saw that he had not come alone. Next to him stood the colorful man smiling at her with warm brown eyes. "Ali Ibn Musa Ibn Said," he introduced himself with a deep bow.

He reminded Iriomé of her home, where people welcomed each

other just as seriously and respectfully. She wrapped a towel around her body, stood up, and bowed also.

"I'm a *médico* and help sick people," he said first in Spanish and then in another language from which Iriomé only understood the word "sick."

"Did you cure the conquistador?" he asked quietly.

Iriomé shook her head vigorously.

"He says you gave him something that made him sleep for a long time, and now he suddenly feels like a new man."

"Just water," she said, pointing to a pitcher of water, standing near her on the floor.

"Nothing else?"

She shook her head. Despite the heat, she was shaking all over. So de Lugo had recognized her. He would leave no stone unturned to disclose her secret. He had watched her closely when she treated the prisoners and asked via the monk about the plants she used to prepare the green healing ointment.

Ibn Said understood without explanation the great fear that tormented her and did not press further. He said goodbye with a deep bow and left the cabin with Joaquín. She called her lover back, but he did not hear. Iriomé clearly felt he was already somewhere else—in his world. Was there a place for her at all? Had Tichiname actually been mistaken? Was it perhaps someone other than Joaquín who should be at her side? Was it all a big misunderstanding? Had she now betrayed amakuna for the same reason for which her people had fallen into the trap of the Spaniards? Due to false love and false confidence in Joaquín? But why did she feel so connected to him?

While she still tried to find an answer to these questions, Frai Hieronymus came in. He gave her a stony glance. All cordialness and warmth with which he had treated her before had disappeared. In his eyes she read only fear and hate. "Witch," he hurled at her. "You're in league with the devil. Only God has the right to decide who lives or dies!"

Iriomé did not understand. Only that he accused her from the depth of his soul and from one moment to the other had become her enemy.

"I'll have to hand you over to the Inquisition, once we've gone ashore." He held a wooden cross against her that he wore on a chain around his neck as if he could in this way prevent her coming too close to him. "You deceived me. The devil gave you your blue eyes. But now you can't fool me any longer." The last words he yelled at her, as if he were possessed by a demon. Then he left the small room bristling with anger.

Iriomé watched him, stunned. Though she could barely understand half of what he accused her of, his behavior made her realize that she had no time to lose. Her obligation toward Joaquín was fulfilled; now all was about amakuna. No sooner had the steps of the monk died away than she squeezed through a hole in the timber wall, jumped on deck, and crept unseen to the rear of the vessel. The wind once again blew Joaquín's voice to her ear, as he chatted nearby with the colorfully dressed man. Iriomé would have loved to stay with him, but finally she realized that he belonged to another world, to the world of the conquistadors and the false men of god. He could not possibly be the one who was destined to protect amakuna with her.

The medallion was just the right size to fit in her mouth. It tasted oddly of blood. She pressed her lips together and told herself not to open them again until she had reached the coast. A long way lay ahead of her that she could only master with the help of Tara and Tigotan. She knelt down and put her head on the planks of the ship to connect with Tara, the earth goddess. Then she looked up in the cloudless blue sky, asked the blessing of Tigotan, god of the sky, and closed her eyes. When she thought she had been heard by the two gods, she threw away the cloth and jumped.

The water was cold. The waves broke foaming over her, but she surfaced quickly. She had jumped from much higher rocks. The children of her people often swam before they could walk. Nevertheless, she had great respect for the sea. It had taken her parents. The current did not bring her to the beach but drove her parallel to it, and the coast now seemed much farther away than it had appeared from the ship. Fear rose in her. Would she make it? Had she acted too rashly?

With the setting sun a strong wind came up, and the waves slapped against Iriomé's face painfully, so that she could hardly breathe. The salt burned her eyes and throat. But she kept swimming, supported by Tara and Tigotan and the spirit of Tichiname, who would never leave her.

The darker it got, the more the waves merged with the shoreline, and she was not sure if the distance was ever less. She was cold and tired. At some point she no longer felt her body, and everything went black.

∾

Someone patted her on the cheek. Her first thought was Tanausú. He had come after her. At last. But then unfamiliar voices reached her ear. She felt wet sand beneath her body. Her head rang like the rumble of Guayote. The spirits had spat her out. They did not want to have her right now.

Two hands were trying to open her mouth, which she kept closed like an impenetrable rock wall. She opened her eyes and looked into a familiar face. The colorful man! The médico.

Gently he stroked her wet hair out of her face and wrapped her naked body in a soft cloth.

"Don't be afraid. You're safe now," he said softly.

Was she still in this world? If so, she owed that to the gods alone, who wanted her alive to fulfill her task. Tara had saved her. Had brought her to the one person she knew here and whom she had trusted from the very first moment.

When he was distracted for a second, she quickly took the amulet from her mouth and hid it in her hand under the cloth. Not a moment too soon, for the médico now held a bowl of water to her lips, which she sipped.

At a signal his companion, a strong young man with a muscular torso and a straw hat on his head, lifted her up and carried her across the beach toward the white boxes that were bathed in a rose light by the morning sun. She realized that she had spent all night in the sea.

Between the square white boxes there were lots of people. The men wore half-long pants, the women long dresses in different colors and tight headgear hiding their hair. All were talking loudly to each other or shouting over the heads of others something that Iriomé did not understand. Some carried wooden boxes with iron bars in which sat birds that Iriomé had never seen before. Others were driving before them animals with thick udders that were larger and clumsier than goats and who possessed much shorter horns.

Suddenly loud clatter and chatter penetrated her ears; she leeched on to the man who was carrying her. One of the long-legged animals she already knew from the conquerors trotted past her. It pulled a heavy load that was attached to round, rotating discs. Iriomé had landed in a new world, one that was completely alien to her and that overwhelmed her senses.

The médico who walked ahead of them stopped in front of a high wall with a small blue wooden door. He opened it and waved the man who carried Iriomé to follow him. The noise diminished after the door had closed behind them, and Iriomé breathed a sigh of relief. The man let her down gently but supported her until she could stand firmly on her legs. She wrapped the towel tighter around her body and thanked the young man with a faint, "Gracias." The médico gave him a small round disk and sent him away. Then he asked Iriomé, who was taller than he was by a head, to follow him.

Amazed, she entered a spacious patio paved with colored stones, in the center of which a star-shaped fountain was gushing. Next to it sat an old woman in a strange framework. She wore long skirts interwoven with shiny threads and around her head a dark, soft cloth.

"My mother," said the médico, pointing to her and him. "She can't talk, see, or walk." He accompanied his words with the appropriate hand signals and body movements so Iriomé could easily understand what he said. The old woman must have noticed that somebody else was present in addition to her son because she raised her hand and smiled in Iriomé's direction.

"Take a seat. I'll get you some clothes and something to eat. You must be terribly hungry by now."

Iriomé sat on a small stone bench and looked around. At her feet a small duct carried off the water of the fountain through an archway to another patio, from which slight bubbling could also be heard. The front was open and through three arches the view of a lush garden was revealed. She had never seen such carefully designed splendor. Orange fruits hanging on trees and blood-red flowers shed a beguiling fragrance. *What a contrast to the pungent odors outside the gate!* she thought. An island of good odor amid a churning, stinking sea.

After a while she saw the médico through the sparkling drops of the fountain heading back with a bunch of clothes over his arm. In one hand he carried a small bowl, in the other a device that looked like two intertwined knives. Even though she could guess what he was up to, she nevertheless hoped fervently that she was wrong. That he did not want to take away what on her home isle identified her as a woman and especially as a harimaguada.

But Ibn Said was relentless. With a compassionate expression on his face he cut off her first curl. Even if everything inside her cried out, she did not resist, because she understood why he did it. She did not dare to move. With each snapping noise, strand by strand of her long hair floated to the floor tiles with shiny blue-white stones. It was as if her past now finally dissolved. At home they would have ridiculed her if she had stepped out of her cave looking like this. Tears of despair and exhaustion welled up in her eyes. The mother of the médico must have sensed her feelings, because she suddenly began to whistle a song with a strange merry melody, as if to comfort her.

Several times Ibn Said stepped back to view her from all sides. After he had made some improvements here and there, he was at last satisfied with his work. He handed her a coarse shirt, a pair of trousers similar to Joaquín's, and a hat with a wide brim. Then he led her to the well and asked her to look into it. Iriomé did as she was told. She looked into the face of a young man, similar to the one who had carried her here.

The médico was smart. No one would recognize her now. Neither Joaquín nor Cold Eye nor the monk. Amakuna was safe for the time being, well hidden under her shirt. "Gracias," she said and laid her hand on the médico's shoulder as a sign of her respect and confidence.

He smiled and handed her the bowl, from which came a strange but appetizing smell. "*Buen provecho!* Enjoy your meal!" Then he packed the cut-off blonde hair in a bag and brought it into the house to bury later.

Chapter 23

Secretly Iriomé had hoped Joaquín would one day be knocking at the door of the médico and put his arms around her. Though she had been living in this house for more than three changes of the moon, he had not appeared. Only at night he visited her sometimes in her sleep, and when she awoke, she thought she could still hear his voice, feel his eyes on her and his caresses. She missed him, and she wondered if he had been looking for her at all.

Sometimes hope rose in her when she heard the drum of hooves at the gate, but this feeling often changed to fear that it might be Cold Eye who had come to get her. He would not stop looking for her, of that she was sure.

To reciprocate the courtesy of the médico Iriomé cared for his mother. She washed the old woman, helped her take her clothes on and off, fed her, and wheeled her in her rolling rack through the garden. At the place where it smelled best and the babbling of the fountain sounded like a melody, she let the old woman linger.

During this time she also helped the médico prepare the food in the kitchen. The walls of the small room with a huge woodstove in its center were, just as the walls of his treatment room, covered with shelves filled with dishes, pots, and jars full of powders and herbs. In this field Ibn Said was a master, and he explained to Iriomé patiently how the vegetables, the meat, and the sauces were tastefully prepared using various spices. Again a new world opened up for Iriomé. She would never have thought it possible that the addition of colored powders could transform simple food into ambrosia. More and more she loved the aroma of cardamom, coriander, turmeric, and cinnamon and even dared to use them herself. Gradually she lost her fear of the unknown and was eager to learn something new every day.

The médico was pleased with her curiosity. When he came back from his patients, he would give Iriomé two lessons. In the first lesson he taught her to speak Spanish, and in the second she learned to read and write Arabic. By teaching her the Arabic language he gave her the key to yet another new world; namely, the world of the books of which Ibn Said possessed quite a number and which he kept in a hiding place in the pantry next to the kitchen. Iriomé did not understand why he hid them there, but it had to be for similar reasons that the harimaguadas passed their knowledge on only among themselves.

Most of all she was interested in the works that dealt with the human body and the art of healing. For the first time she saw pictures of the skeleton, the muscles, and the inner organs. While she had up to now recognized diseases from experience, by intuition, or in conversation with the spirits she now had a new background.

When Tichiname explained the different diseases to Iriomé, she had never spoken of individual organs, but always of the whole person and the body's relationship with nature and the spirit world, Tigotan and Tara. The old medicine woman needed no book to know in which part of the body what demon had taken root and why. She just knew what addressed the diseases, at least those on Benahoare. If there was a book in which all these diseases were listed with the corresponding remedies, Iriomé pondered, everyone who possessed this book could learn the art of healing. But not everyone was chosen for it. Not everyone had the ability to look into another person's soul to identify the disease demons there and appease them.

Nevertheless, she spent almost the entire time in which Ibn Said visited his patients over his books. She could hardly wait to learn new words and letters of the Arabic language so that she could better understand the texts. Hour after hour she learned and practiced and surprised her teacher with new knowledge she had gathered.

Only the book that was most holy and important to him she did not touch. Because in it lived the god of the Moors, whom they called Allah. This much she understood by now. The médico believed in a different god from that of the Spaniards. And what for Christians was the Bible for him was the Qur'an. Five times a day the médico took it from the shelf, put it next to him on a prayer mat, and began to pray, always in the same direction and always the same words. So it seemed to her, anyway. One day a week, which he called Friday, he bathed at length after work, put on clean clothes, and went to the mosque to pray again, together with other people and to worship Allah.

Iriomé had not been in contact with her gods and spirits for a long time. It seemed impossible to perform the ritual of calling them here between the walls of Ibn Said's house. She missed the vastness of the sea, the jagged rocks of her island, the wind, and the smell of the pine trees and the wild herbs. Even if the médico by now had become her friend and she had become accustomed to life in his house, she still missed her home. Sometimes she wondered whether she would ever see Benahoare again and why she was still alive at all. What task should she fulfill here in a foreign land?

"Tomorrow I'll take you along to a patient, as my assistant," Ibn Said said one evening, when they were together in the kitchen preparing a lamb. For as Iriomé knew by now, Allah had forbidden his followers to eat pork. "I think even Captain de Lugo is now convinced that you have been eaten by the sharks and nothing of you is left. So I think we can dare it. And in your disguise no one will recognize you anyway."

Iriomé felt gleeful anticipation rise inside herself. On the advice of the médico she had never left his house, not once, even if she sometimes feared the high walls over which she could not look would crush her to death. But it was not only the prospect of escaping these walls for a while that made her heart beat faster, but also that she finally would be able to help the sick again.

Joyfully she packed the bag made of animal skin in which the médico kept vials of different sizes containing powders and liquids and left the house together with him early the next morning.

First they walked through the Moorish quarter, where people's lives mainly took place behind high walls, until they entered the barrio of the Christians through an archway that could be seen from afar. Their houses looked completely different. In front of the windows and doors were wooden structures on which one could step from the house. The beams were decorated with rich carvings, so smooth and fine Iriomé would never have thought it possible. She wondered what tools the Christians used and who had invented them. Were their minds really so much more powerful, and above all, what did the people have to sacrifice for it?

Ibn Said stopped in front of a particularly neat, stately house. Before he knocked on the locked wooden gate, he put his hand on her lips. "Don't speak!"

Iriomé immediately understood what he meant. Her female voice would give her away.

The elderly woman who opened the door wore a coarse robe made of linen with a clean apron and close-fitting headgear, which was held together under her chin with two cords. Before she pulled the two inside the house, she looked down the path with an anxious glance, as if she were afraid someone had followed them. Only when she had satisfied herself that they had come alone, she sighed and closed the gate.

Climbing a ladder the rungs of which were so wide that you could put your whole foot on them, Iriomé followed the médico into the upper part of the house. The smells that reached her nostrils differed greatly from those in the house of the médico. Instead of fine spices and the scent of roses from the garden the dark bars emitted old grease and mildew. Iriomé could hardly imagine living here and was all the more grateful that the gods had led her to Ibn Said.

Even the darkened room with a low wooden ceiling, which the médico entered determinedly ahead of them, was stuffy and hot. In dim light Iriomé recognized on a high sleeping place a girl, almost a child.

Her pale face was covered with large, scaly red patches. The woman stopped anxiously at the door, as if evil spirits could take possession of her in the room. Iriomé sympathized with the woman, even if she did not know the ghost who was walking abroad here and thus could not reckon how to defend against it yet.

Ibn Said fearlessly took the hand of the patient and felt her pulse, just as Iriomé knew from Tichiname. However, he did not compare the pulse of the girl with his own heartbeat but looked intently at a strange object that made ticking noises.

At his behest Iriomé opened the bag and handed him a shiny instrument made of metal, a material that was now familiar to her. He carefully scraped the scaly stains from the skin of the patient and then trickled a yellowish liquid from a transparent vessel on it. Then he pulled back the duvet and examined her body for more redness. Not finding anything, he covered the girl with the blanket again, nodding.

"You'll be well, my child," he said, stroking her cheek with a friendly smile.

"Thanks," she just breathed. "God may repay you."

The médico sat down at a small table at the window. The cracks in the shutters allowed just enough light through to write something down. He took a pen and parchment from a side pocket of the bag and set to work.

"These are the names of some herbs you'll get me." He turned to Iriomé. "I'll show you later how to mix an effective medicine."

The old woman, who was still standing in the doorway, looked at him fearfully.

"Don't worry," he reassured her. "Everything's as it should be."

"Leprosy," said Ibn Said to Iriomé when they were out on the street again. "Christians believe this disease is contagious and the devil has sent it to them. But this is not true. It mainly befalls those who do not keep clean. The Christians, unlike us, don't go regularly to the hammam to take a bath."

"Leprosy," repeated Iriomé, and then, "contagious." She knew now who the devil was. But how to get into a conversation with him in order to soothe him she still did not understand. Ibn Said had his own answer in the form of a pitying smile. He handed her the parchment on which he had written the things he needed for the mixture.

Iriomé looked at him, perplexed.

"You'll find all this at the market." He pointed down the alley. "Straight ahead, you can't miss it." Then he gave her some of the small shiny discs and nodded to her invitingly. "I'll see you at home."

Iriomé felt uncomfortable with the order. After all, she had never been outside the house and certainly not alone.

"You'll make it; you're a harimaguada after all!" The médico simply turned away from her and walked off.

Iriomé had no other choice than to get going. She hoped that she would find the way back to his house after her visit to the market.

Having walked down the alley according to Ibn Said's instructions, she heard human voices that grew louder and louder and that sounded scary to her. She slowed her steps but then joined some women obviously going to the market. They carried in both hands baskets filled with various fruits and vegetables. They chatted with each other, and Iriomé thought she understood that they hoped to get as many of these small round discs as possible for what they carried in their baskets.

When she turned around one last corner, a huge square lay before her. Everywhere stood small colorful stalls in which a wide variety of goods were offered in abundance. Fruits and vegetables, fabrics of all colors, fish and meat, and lots of items she had never seen before, let alone imagine what they were used for.

Iriomé walked through the streets between the stalls and just could not see enough. Both men and women loudly praised their treasures, pointed at them, and sometimes even held them up, so they were seen better. All over the place a smell was in the air that was unfamiliar to her nose, but which was not unpleasant and consisted of innumerable individual odors. Again and again she watched as the small shiny discs changed hands, and she began to understand: everything offered here could be exchanged for differing amounts of these disks.

A fat old woman who sold fish gave her a friendly nod and held a slimy squid in front of her face. Iriomé declined kindly and showed her the parchment of the médico, but the woman could not make heads or tails of it. With a shrill voice that went right through Iriomé, she called a younger man wearing a brown robe like Frai Hieronymus and a small wooden frame on his nose. He asked her if he could help her, but Iriomé remembered the warning of the médico to speak under no circumstances, pointed to her mouth, and shook her head. The young monk nodded his head understandingly, looked at what the médico had written, and then asked her to follow him.

He led her to the back of the tumult to a stand that looked different from the others. From the roof hung countless bunches of dried herbs. On shelves transparent tubes with colored elixirs were neatly arranged. In one of them Iriomé recognized a tiny man who swam curled up in a liquid, in another she saw worms of different sizes, and in a third a long scaly animal whose forked tongue peeped out between two danger-ous teeth. She shuddered. But the man selling all these things smiled at her kindly. He had a thorough look at the parchment she handed him, stroked his white beard, and then asked, "Have you been sent by Ibn Said?"

Iriomé nodded in relief. The bearded man studied the parchment again, slowly shaking his head. Then he put different dried herbs on a structure with two shells. As the one shell moved down, he equal-ized the weight with two stones, which he put in the other shell. This changed the semicircular background on which markings were applied that reminded Iriomé of her time bar on Benahoare. Fascinated, she watched the old man. He seemed to measure the amount of the herbs this way. On her island she had not needed such a device so far. She could always rely on her feeling that told her how much of any herbal species was necessary for a particular medicine.

Still lost in thoughts of her home, she suddenly heard a voice right beside her. "Iriomé!"

She froze. She knew that voice very well. And it meant nothing good. Slowly, she turned around. Two dark eyes in which cold hatred was reflected flashed at her. It was Guayafanta. She wore the simple garb of a slave.

"I'd recognize you, even if you were invisible, because you smell of betrayal," she hissed in the ear of Iriomé, who tried to stay as calm as possible, turning to the bearded merchant again. He handed her several bags and then held out his hand. She gave him all the small round disks and thanked him and the young monk who had brought her here with a smile. Then she pulled Guayafanta, who had not left her side, to a quiet corner behind a garbage heap.

"I'm glad to see you in good health," Iriomé said cautiously.

Guayafanta shook her head glumly. "How can I be healthy here in a foreign country where the people treat us worse than an animal? A healthy life means a life in freedom. You have taken this freedom from us."

"The stone of destiny was unstoppable; you know that as well as I do. I was just trying to prevent the worst." Iriomé tried to appease her.

Guayafanta laughed shrilly. "You were blind, blind with desire for this man. That's not worthy of a harimaguada." She looked Iriomé up and down contemptuously and then twisted her mouth into a snide smile.

"You're still blind. And on top of it you're carrying his child. It will poison your body as the man has poisoned your heart."

Iriomé could not prevent her face reddening, and she began to tremble inwardly. Perhaps Guayafanta was right. Her monthly bleeding would have been due some time ago, but she thought her rhythm got mixed up because she had been in the cold water for such a long time. The fact that she had put on some weight she had attributed to Ibn Said's good food.

"You're wrong," she said. "I'm not expecting a child."

Guayafanta looked at her with contempt. "Just keep on letting your lies confuse your senses. You won't escape Guayote. Soon he will come get you and burn you in his fire deep in the heart of the mountain."

Her words came like a curse. Iriomé perceived the wild force that Guayafanta still carried in her. "The man to whom I belong, de Lugo, has been searching for you for weeks," she continued. "He doesn't believe you've drowned."

Iriomé felt a chill running down her spine. Guayafanta's heart knew nothing but revenge. She would betray her to Cold Eye, there was not a doubt of it. Iriomé saw no other option than to run away, but the harimaguada grabbed her arm and dragged her with all her strength back to the stand of the bearded man. "For who are these herbs intended?" she asked in poor Spanish, pointing to the bundle in Iriomé's hand.

"Well, for Ibn Said, of course, the médico. The stuff is not suitable for cooking." The bearded man laughed at his own joke, then turned to a small humpbacked woman in whom Iriomé also recognized a healer spirit.

"Gracias." Guayafanta grinned, satisfied, let go of Iriomé, and disappeared into the crowd.

Iriomé felt as if once again the waves of the cold ocean beat over her body and tore her down to certain death. As fast as she could, she ran to the house of the médico to warn him. She had to ask the way a couple of times, which earned her some strange looks, but she did not know what else to do. However easily she might find her way in the woods on Benahoare, it was hard for her here to distinguish one house from the other. When she finally arrived at the wall with the small blue gate, she had lost precious time.

Ibn Said was not in his consulting room. She called out for him and searched all patios and premises for him. But not a trace of him was found. Only his elderly mother sat as always, silently smiling in her rolling chair at the fountain in the shady courtyard.

Iriomé pondered what to do now, when there was wild pounding at the gate. Several male Spanish voices demanded admittance. *"Abre la puerta!"*

She ran to the back door of the house, but there was already some-body rattling at the lock. She had to hide. But where?

The shouts of the men became increasingly demanding, the knock-ing on the gate more violent. They would break it down in no time. Someone was already hitting the thin timber of the back door with a hard object. Iriomé rushed through the garden, past the old woman as she heard the noise of splintering wood and a loud bang.

Footsteps were approaching dangerously fast, echoing on the flag-stones. At this moment the old woman raised her wide skirts, and Iriomé quickly took use of the hiding place that was offered. Not a moment too soon. Through the narrow slit between hem and bottom she saw the black boots of de Lugo coming toward her.

"*Dónde está la bruja*? Where's the witch?" He shouted at the old woman, who, however, did not move. De Lugo's legs were shaking in anger.

"Where is she?" He shouted again and again. One of the men pre-sented him a bag with Iriomé's cut-off hair, which the médico appar-ently had forgotten to bury. De Lugo opened it, inhaling the scent. "Find her!" he yelled like a madman.

His men invaded the house like a swarm of locusts. The conse-quences of their destruction assailed Iriomé's ears noisily. Each vase that broke, each cabinet that was split, each cushion that was slit open, made her flinch. It seemed as if the rampaging of the horde would never end. Without moving her lips, she asked Tara to ensure that Ibn Said might stay away for a long time.

De Lugo shouted again at the old woman, as if he guessed that the object of his obsession had something to do with her. And because he again got no response, he slapped her brutally in the face, so that the chair began to sway. Had Iriomé not held it with all her strength from below, it would have fallen over and her fate would have been sealed once and for all. But she managed to get the chair back into balance. She held her breath, not daring to inhale or exhale.

After a time that seemed like an eternity, there was calm. The voices trailed off in the distance. All Iriomé heard was her own heartbeat. Cautiously she poked her head out from under the skirts. Everywhere around her were broken things. The water flowed randomly across the floor of the courtyard, all fountains were destroyed, most of the plants uprooted. She struggled to her feet, took a deep breath, and turned to the old woman. Her head hung unnaturally backward. From the mouth and nose blood was running. She was dead.

Iriomé took her hand in desperation and fell to her knees. All this was her fault. How could she ever hope to repay this debt? She laid her head in the lap of the elderly woman. Had she given herself up to Cold Eye, Ibn Said's mother would still be alive. The mother of the man who had saved her life. A deep sob broke out of her but was drowned by the scream of the médico who had just walked into his ravaged home. Iriomé jumped up and ran to meet him. She threw herself in front of him on the wet ground like a beaten dog who expected the next swing. But Ibn Said lifted her up with tears in his eyes.

"You are not to blame. If not today, then the Christians would tomorrow, next week, or next month destroy my house."

Chapter 24

There was not much they took with them. After Iriomé helped Ibn Said bury his mother behind the house, they left after dark.

Silently they followed a narrow path along the city wall until they came to a mighty gate that was guarded by several men. They wore the armor that Iriomé recognized from Joaquín. Ibn Said spoke with one of them and gave him a vial of medicine.

"He's the father of the leper girl," he whispered to Iriomé. "He is letting us leave the town, without anybody knowing. We need to wait until midnight, when the guards change. For a brief moment the gate will be unmanned. That is our chance."

Although Iriomé did not understand every word, she understood enough that she was able to guess the meaning. She crouched beside Ibn Said in a corner of the city wall to wait. What had happened in the last hours reminded her painfully of the battle that had been fought on Benahoare. It was pure hatred that drove the leader of the Spaniards to commit such crimes. How could a man harbor so much destructive power?

It must be an evil demon giving him the strength for his misdeeds. But demons were beatable; she knew that from Tichiname. You only had to seize the right moment. And such a moment would come. Iriomé was not out for revenge; despite all, she still believed in the victory of good over evil.

Ibn Said looked at her thoughtfully and covered her caringly with a sheepskin that he untied from his suitcase. What a friend he was! She had destroyed his life, and still he protected her, as if she were his own flesh and blood. Had the spirits sent him to help her? For a moment she was struck by the terrible thought that he would even give his life for her one day.

The moon hid behind a cloud at exactly the right time to give the two fugitives the opportunity to escape through the city gate unseen. With quick steps Ibn Said turned north. Iriomé followed, puzzled about how agile and fast he was despite his advanced age. He must have seen more than fifty summers. He also slightly dragged his right leg, an injury that he had suffered early in his life during the defense of his native village against the Christians. She knew now that the Moors had just as little value in the eyes of the conquerors as her own people—something she had difficulty understanding. She had grown up with the idea that all people were equal before Tara. Each one had a particular gift, but none felt superior to the other or had the urge to brag about it through words or deeds all the time.

In the early morning light, a larger homestead could be seen on the horizon; only then did the médico slow his pace.

Even from a distance Iriomé could smell the long-legged animals she now knew to be horses grazing on lush meadows all around who welcomed them with a loud whinnies. A pitch-black stallion with a noble head came dashing straight to Ibn Said. The spirited animal did not slow down until just before the fence. Ibn Said patted his neck. For the first time since they had left his house in Cádiz something like a smile appeared on her friend's face.

"That's Nasir," he said in Arabic. "His name means protector."

Behind the stallion a gray mare with a black mane approached a little more cautiously. Ibn Said let out a low whistle, obviously a familiar sign of recognition, for she now trotted toward them and allowed him to pet her.

"Karima, the Generous," he introduced the animal to Iriomé. "She now belongs to you. We will stay here a short time, until you've gotten to know each other better and you know how to ride her."

Iriomé shook her head. She had her own two legs to walk. Why should she sit on one of these horses and possibly fall off and break all her bones? "I can carry my own weight," she said resolutely.

Ibn Said laughed out loud. "And what do you do when a Spanish cavalcade is after you? These are Arabian horses. Allah has bestowed on his own people the fastest horses in the world. No Christian nag can ever catch up with them."

As if the mare understood him, she put her head on Iriomé's shoulder and blew softly in her ear. The eyes of the animal were kind, and Iriomé decided to reconsider her negative attitude. Expectantly she followed Ibn Said, who strode determinedly toward the whitewashed homestead.

He pushed open the unlocked door and shouted, "Ali Ibn Bakr, son of a donkey and a cow, get out of your stinking bed and come down!"

Fortunately Iriomé did not understand every word.

On the landing a man appeared with shaggy hair and a sleepy expression on his face who was about the age of the médico.

"*Salam alaikum, Sabah el-chair.* Welcome to my humble home," he said, touching his chest, lips, and forehead briefly with his right hand before he held it out to Ibn Said.

"*Sabah an-nur.*" This reply, which meant beautiful morning light, Iriomé knew. She liked the flowery phraseology of the Moors much better than the dry, rather hard language of the Spaniards, but she had not yet learned to speak it.

Ali led them into a room where the only decoration was a magnificent colorful carpet on which several tables stood. He asked them to sit down, then clapped his hands twice. Two veiled women scurried down the stairs into the kitchen. Soon a pleasant aroma of fresh mint filled the house. Shortly thereafter, the two women returned with a large pot and a tray with glasses on it into which they poured the tea and then handed them to the guests. While Iriomé let the sharp yet sweet drink run down her throat, there was a knock at the door. One of the girls led in a bedraggled-looking young man.

"Médico, you need to come at once," he gasped breathlessly. "Not far from here a woman's giving birth. I don't believe that she'll make it on her own."

Ibn Said put down his glass and rose. Iriomé did the same. Again she felt a deep inner joy to be allowed to help a person in distress together with Ibn Said. Maybe she could in this way make up a little bit for the suffering she had caused.

The young man took them to a windowless wooden hut not far from Ali's homestead. Even from a distance they heard the cries of pain of the expectant mother. She lay covered in sweat on a dirty bedstead and hardly perceived Iriomé and Ibn Said coming in. It smelled of blood and feces. Time and again she was overcome by new waves of pain. Her reddish hair stuck in greasy strands to her head. Beneath a stained blanket her pregnant belly bulged with countless flies on it. The sheet was already soaked red. When she could breathe again, she opened her eyes briefly, grabbed Iriomé's hand, and gasped, "I can't take anymore. Save my child. Please . . ."

Iriomé wished she had one of the small clay figures of Tara with her that the women of her people held in their fists during the birth of their children to get the support of the earth goddess. But except for amakuna and the bag of herbs that she had depleted a long time ago, there was nothing she had taken with her from her island. She looked back for the young man who had come with them on the short walk, but he seemed to have disappeared from the face of the earth.

"He's not the father," Ibn Said told her. "She has been banned in this cottage at the edge of the village because she's not married and because there is no father for the child."

"And that's why they let her bleed to death?" Iriomé asked indignantly.

On her island something like that would never have happened. Every woman there banded together with a man who took care of her, and if that was not possible for some reason, another man from the tribe accepted this responsibility. But never was a pregnant woman left to her own devices.

Ibn Said shrugged. "Let's get down to work." He felt the pulse of the woman and asked Iriomé to fetch water and heat it on the fire. He had taught her not to trust the water of the ordinary people. They often threw waste into their wells and relieved themselves in creeks and rivers. This resulted in diseases that were completely unknown to her. But now she knew the risk and knew about the often fatal outcome.

When she entered the hut again, the woman's cries had subsided. She was motionlessly lying on her back with her eyes closed. Iriomé looked at the médico, startled.

"She's lost too much blood," he said in a low voice. He pulled the bloody sheets out from under the woman and spread clean towels, which he always carried with him, under her. Then he rolled up his sleeves, dipped his arms up to the elbows into the fresh water and rubbed in some pungent liquid. "The child lies upside down. I need to turn it around. A breech birth would be certain death for both."

The woman hardly breathed. Iriomé felt how abora, the power of life, slowly escaped her. Her contractions had stopped. Her body was too weak.

Iriomé put her hands on the woman's belly while Ibn Said was working in her body until he withdrew his arm covered with blood and mucus and a dark mop of hair became visible. Then the two of them pressed from the outside until head, shoulders, and finally the whole child came out.

It was a boy. Ibn Said cut the umbilical cord and Iriomé took the motionless baby in her arms. She sucked the mucus from his mouth and nose and breathed air in him, until she felt the first independent, weak breath of the child. He lived. A feeling of great happiness went through her. For the first time she allowed the thought that soon she would hold her own child in her arms. Guayafanta had been right. Iriomé carried Joaquín's child. She would not be able to hide it much longer, especially not from Ibn Said. She only hoped that she would not have to give birth to her child under similar circumstances as this poor woman.

Iriomé wrapped the little creature in the last clean cloth they had left and cradled him in her arms. The médico ensured that the after-birth came out, wiping the cold sweat from the woman's forehead and felt her pulse. "I don't think she'll make it. She will die soon. The child too. No other woman will agree to wet-nurse him." He shook his head sadly. "Give it to me; I'm going to choke it. May Allah have mercy on my soul!" Ibn Said took the child from her arms.

Iriomé stared at him. "No, you can't do that!"

"If you can't watch it, I'll go outside."

"Please wait," Iriomé said firmly.

The médico did not answer, just turned his back on her and left the hut.

Without thinking further Iriomé took the amulet out from under her shirt and opened it. If she had saved a monster like Cold Eye, it was impossible to let this pitiable woman and her child die. From outside she heard the little one cry. So he was still alive. She put a few grains of powder in one of Ibn Said's vessels, added some water, and gave the dying woman the drink.

"Tara, queen of the gods," she whispered. "Mother of the Earth, thy power I invoke. Save this woman, so that she can feed her child and raise him for the sake of the earth, the people, and the gods."

Iriomé sat on the edge of the bed and watched as the young mother's face slowly relaxed and she fell into a deep sleep. She sighed with relief and stepped outside where Ibn Said was sitting on a wooden bench, the child still in his arms. Tears ran down his cheeks.

"The will of Allah is not always immediately perceptible," he said huskily.

The little boy made soft chuckling noises and looked at her, his eyes dark blue, as with most newborn babies.

"The woman will live and will be able to suckle her child," Iriomé said softly.

Ibn Said raised his head and looked at her thoughtfully for a while. "Like Alonso de Lugo lives?"

Iriomé didn't answer. She took the child from him and brought the boy to his mother in the hut. Ibn Said followed her after quite a while. The complexion of the woman on the bed had returned to normal, and she was breathing regularly. Iriomé laid the newborn on her belly, and he began to suck immediately. Ibn Said felt her pulse again. "You're truly a great healer."

Iriomé shook her head. "It's a gift from Tara, the earth goddess. She helps women in distress. Especially the mothers, because they are the ones who ensure the stability of the earth. As they themselves were brought up by their mothers, they raise their own children. It is in their hands, how the people will develop in the future. For this reason, Tara grants them all the support they need."

"In our religion there are no goddesses," Ibn Said said pensively. "Only Allah! And he's great and powerful. Maybe he has also given his children something that's similar to the gift you possess, but I, Ali Ibn Musa Ibn Said, am not chosen to own it. That's why I don't want to get in touch with it. Do you understand this?"

Iriomé nodded.

"You mustn't tell anybody about it, because otherwise not only this Captain de Lugo is going to be after you, but also people who have far greater power than he. And they will torture you in the cruelest way until you betray the secret to them. Because the gift of being able to decide over life or death is worth its weight in gold. It allows the Mighty to become the Divine. And to gain this, man won't hesitate to kill and wage war. And once he is in the possession of your spells, he will fight even more wars. Because his soldiers will survive their injuries, but the soldiers of his enemy won't. So always remember: every time you save somebody's life, whether he has a good or an evil soul, you place yourself in great danger."

Iriomé looked at the médico wide-eyed with terror. She had never looked at amakuna this way. But now she understood why it was a taboo to talk about it. That was why only the highest harimaguada and Tanausú had known its secret. Perhaps it was better to destroy the amakuna?

At this moment they heard the drum of hooves and loud voices.

"Médico, come out of there!" The typical, snippy commanding tone of a Spaniard reached their ears.

Ibn Said remained calm. "You stay here. I go alone," he said to Iriomé in a low voice.

She checked again whether the amulet was safely tucked under her shirt, and then peered through a crack in the cabin wall. Two riders in shining armor were negotiating with Ibn Said. From what Iriomé could understand, it was about a high-ranking person who was seriously ill and encamped with his retinue not far from here. Her knowledge of the Spanish language had improved enough so that she could understand almost everything. She sighed with relief.

"Pack the bag," Ibn Said said when he returned. "Not far from here encamps His Excellency Frai Lorenzo de la Huerta, and he needs our help. It's important that you don't speak. And not a word about this woman!"

His voice sounded different. It lacked the joy and the energy that he normally exuded when he set off for a new patient. Iriomé knew him well enough to guess that something was wrong. But she also knew that now was not the time to ask him.

The two Spanish caballeros accompanied them back to Ali's homestead so that they could get their stuff. Ibn Said insisted on riding their horses, even if this earned him a horrified outcry by Iriomé. But it was to no avail. Under the supervision of the médico she saddled the gray mare and shortly afterward sat on the horse's back with a highly uneasy feeling. Ibn Said rode next to her holding a rope fastened to Karima's bridle securely in his hand.

With each stretch that they traveled, Iriomé felt a bit safer and soon lost her initial fear. She even succeeded in communicating with the animal in her own way, so that the mare was able to respond to her thoughts. When she wanted to ride a little slower, Karima tried for a leisurely gait and accelerated when Iriomé wanted her to move faster. It was almost as if they were one creature. Ibn Said smiled at her, as if he had known that the two would get along well.

"Frai Lorenzo de la Huerta is suffering from gout," he informed Iriomé about their next patient, "a disease by which only rich and stouter people are plagued." He now spoke Arabic, which the two Spanish soldiers could not understand.

"They eat too much meat and indulge in wine to a greater extent than is good for them. This leads to deposits in the joints and organs because the sickening juices cannot be excreted in the urine adequately. This causes so much pain that the patient eventually no longer can move. In a gout attack only one thing really helps: the extract of the autumn crocus. In its undiluted form it acts as a deadly poison, but in the right dose it's anti-inflammatory, analgesic, and promotes the excretion of the juices," Ibn Said explained. "When the attack is over, the patient should be sat in an anthill. The acid of the small animals causes the juices to be removed through the skin, and they no longer reach the joints through the blood."

Iriomé had listened carefully. The Arabic language still gave her a little trouble, but she could understand what the médico explained even if she had never heard of this strange disease.

What she still did not understand and had long wanted to ask Ibn Said was whether a patient who has been cured by him could get the same disease again.

The médico chuckled. "Many illnesses are part of the human character. You can heal them, but if the character is corrupt, then it will spoil the body again. I can relieve the gout but can't cure gluttony or alcoholism. Who never denies oneself a pheasant, a goose, or the daily consumption of wine will always remain his own grim jailer, his heart imprisoned between all the fat that has become his jail."

Iriomé found it quite strange that people purposely did things they knew would harm their body. On Benahoare nobody would ever have thought of such a thing.

The ride did not take long, and soon they spotted the campground of the travel group in the distance. A number of tents stood around a fire, above which a pig was roasting on a spit. The smell of fried food was in the air. Ibn Said turned away with disgust. The Spanish riders laughed sardonically. Iriomé knew from Ibn Said that Christians sometimes forced the Moors to eat pork in order to demonstrate their power. *These two would definitely be capable of this,* thought Iriomé.

The two caballeros led the médico and his assistant to the biggest tent. Cries of pain and fierce swearing came through the thin walls. Ibn Said briefly laid his hands on his lips to remind Iriomé to stay silent. The perfect servant, she took the bag she had fixed with a rope behind her saddle and followed the médico into the tent. The first look, which met her like a poisoned arrow, came from the green eyes of a beautiful woman with milky white skin. Maroon hair that was piled up in an elaborate hairstyle caressed her symmetrical face. She wore a dress interwoven with gold threads, and her waist appeared as slim as that of a wasp. She nodded to the médico yet did not rise to greet him. To his servant she paid no further attention.

"Greetings, médico," Frai Lorenzo de la Huerta said in a high falsetto voice, which did not fit at all with the round, puffy face and the massive body over which the black and white frock of a Dominican stretched. Two clumsy hands pale as pearls stuck out from under the garment. A magnificent ring with a red stone parted his fourth finger from the third so that they looked like two sausages. In his nearly black eyes agony and at the same time slyness could be read. Iriomé's eye fell on the almost bald head adorned by a narrow rim of hair. The monk reminded her of Frai Hieronymus, and she fought a shudder.

"I've heard that you abide nearby and sent two messengers. You enjoy a good reputation. I expect that you'll do it justice . . ." He writhed in pain, and it took a while before he could continue. "This is my niece, Inés de Perreira y Castellón." He pointed to the beautiful Spanish woman. "She tries to distract me a little, but in some cases even a woman's beauty fails. And now get out of here, everybody." He made a gesture that got his servants and even the doll-like beauty moving. "Go ahead, médico, do your duty, bring me relief."

Iriomé opened the bag assiduously, but the fat man shouted at her too. "You also! Get out!"

Ibn Said nodded to her, and Iriomé left the tent. Outside she ran across Inés de Perreira and could not stop herself from looking at her in amazement. She had never before seen a woman of such graceful beauty. However, she did not understand how one could breathe in such clothes, run, or even ride. She was glad about her disguise as a boy. *The life of the women in this country is not easy,* she thought. Either they were slaves of the men, tied to home and hearth, or had to walk around in tight robes that took their breath and coloring.

"You dare to stare at me like that?" the Spanish woman shouted at Iriomé, who immediately looked away and quickly went off.

"You could at least apologize," she called after Iriomé. "Have you ever seen such a lout?" she said to two women in similar, yet not quite so magnificent robes, who eagerly rushed to her, as if it was necessary to come to her aid.

Iriomé turned away, shaking her head. The neighing of Karima reminded her of her role as servant of the médico. She led both horses to a small stream where the animals of the Christians grazed. They were, as Ibn Said had told her, larger and more massive than the Arabian horses so that they could carry the Spaniards with their heavy armor.

A lanky boy with hair sprinkled with dust was grinning at her. His bony upper body was naked and he was wearing much too big stained pants tied with a rope around his waist to keep them up. "Hey, you, come along here!"

Iriomé laid her hands on her mouth and shook her head.

"That's okay," he laughed, grabbed her hand, and dragged her away from the tent camp where a few stable lads were dabbling in stone throwing. At some distance they had laid out a rope as a finish line, but so far it seemed that none of them had succeeded in throwing his stone to the other side.

The boy handed Iriomé a stone. She smiled. This was child's play for her. She had done quite well in stone-throwing competitions on

Benahoare, even if the gods on many a day had been more favorably disposed toward Guayafanta. She raised her hand high and threw the stone far behind the rope. Not all were impressed by her performance. A pudgy boy with freckles wearing only a shirt that reached down to his knees, urged her to throw again, and this time with a stone three times as large as the first. Without effort she flung this even a bit far-ther. However, instead of praise and recognition she earned distrust and envy.

"He's in league with the devil!" the fat boy shouted.

"A damned heretic!" The lanky one agreed with him and looked Iriomé up and down. "He also looks strange," cried a third party and ripped the hat off her head.

Iriomé picked it up and put it back on her head. This could get dangerous. Suddenly she was overwhelmed by a similar feeling she had toward de Lugo, although these were boys who were still mere children. And yet . . . their chief concern was also power. To be the stronger and make the other feel his weaknesses as painfully as possible. She had to get out of here.

But the fat boy grabbed her by the arm and handed her a pitcher of water. "Here; drink. Let's see if you pee as far as you throw!"

Iriomé hesitantly took the pitcher. What could she do now?

"Come on, drink," smirked the far boy, and the others joined in hooting. "Drink, drink, drink . . ."

She had to gain time. Slowly she put the jug to her lips and let the cool water run down her throat sip by sip until it was empty. The lanky boy took it from her, ran back to the stream, in order to fill it again and held it out to her once more. She drank as slowly as she could. However, no idea occured to her about how she could escape from this situation. Flight seemed hopeless. Right and left of her there stood two strong boys who would immediately hold her and throw her to the ground.

She returned the empty jug. The others drank also, one at a time. But beside her still stood the two strong ones, who did not let her out of sight. When all the boys had gulped down at least three pitchers, the fat boy made them line up in a row. While he only had to roll up his shirt, the others dropped their pants. They looked at Iriomé expectantly.

This was her chance. With their pants down they could not follow fast.

"Yours is probably so small that he can't even stand upright," the tall boy, who was standing right beside her, grinned.

She gave him a shove with her elbow. Then she ran as fast as she could back to the tents. Behind her the howling mob chased but did not dare to advance to the tent of the inquisitor, which she reached completely breathless.

At that moment Inés de Perreira stepped out of the tent. Iriomé did not manage to stop in time, and thus they collided. They both landed in a muddy puddle.

"This stupid brat again," shouted Inés de Perreira furiously and wiped the mud from her face disgusted. She glared at Iriomé, who first did not even understand what had happened. "How can one be so infinitely stupid," Inés ranted on, as she tried to get up. Doing so, she ruthlessly supported herself on Iriomé's breast. For a brief moment she seemed irritated, but then her attention was focused on her two maids, who had come running and were clamoring to aide her in any way.

Fortunately, now the médico stepped out of the tent. He immediately guessed the situation. "Doña Inés, I want in all humility to apologize for the clumsy behavior of my servant. He will receive his proper punishment today."

"You better had," she glared at him. "My dress is completely ruined. He shall clean it. And if even one spot is left, I'm going to have him flogged naked in front of my people."

"As you command, Doña Inés." The médico bowed even deeper. Iriomé had meanwhile also got up and tried to wipe the dirt off her pants. In a tone that would have no argument, he barked at her to take his bag and follow him.

"This could have been dangerous for you," he said with a worried voice when they were out of earshot and walked toward a small tent erected for the doctor and his servant for the night.

"You need to behave as inconspicuously as possible. These people miss no situation to demonstrate their power. Even I am nothing but a necessary evil to them, but you, as a savage from the islands, are worth less than air."

"But . . ." Iriomé was still upset.

"No buts! If you want to stay alive, you do what I tell you. The inquisitor insists that I stay with him until he has brought his niece to her fiancé. At the moment we're under his protection. He needs me to relieve his pain. But that's the only reason. Do you understand that?" He looked at her intently.

Iriomé nodded resignedly. Of course, Ibn Said was right. But after all, she had not bumped into the Spaniard on purpose.

Her friend held her by the shoulder, turned her around, and looked her seriously in the face. "Our patient told me that his friend Don Alonso de Lugo still has his men looking for me, and this is because of you. As I've predicted, he's obsessed with the idea that you possess a miracle cure that heals every disease. I told the inquisitor that something like this doesn't exist, and that the captain is mistaken. I said he has fought too long on the wild islands where people still believe in ghosts and witchcraft. He believed me of necessity, especially after I had relieved his pain a little."

Iriomé seemed to crumble. "What am I to do now?" she asked desperately.

"They still don't know who you are, but that could change very quickly. The inquisitor may be fat, but he's not stupid," said Ibn Said.

As if the Dominican had overheard their conversation, he let out a loud cry of pain. Both could not resist grinning gleefully, which reduced the tension a little.

"I filled a large tub with red wood ants. The monk's just taking a bath in it," said the médico, but at once became serious again. "I told him that you're a dumb castrato whom I bought a long time ago on the slave market. When they find out, however, who you really are, we'll both end up on the rack of the Inquisition."

"I've heard the word so often by now. What is the Inquisition?" Iriomé asked, confused.

"A kind of court and Frai Lorenzo de la Huerta is the supreme judge. He decides whether people are heretics," said Ibn Said.

"And what are heretics?"

"All those who don't believe in Jesus Christ, the god of the Christians, and don't follow his laws."

"So you and me."

"Yes, but especially persecuted are ones they call *conversos,* Jews and Moors who only pretended to be baptized in order not to have to leave the country but continue to practice their original rituals in secret."

It was not easy for Iriomé to understand all of this. Her head was thumping. These different religions with all their rules were incomprehensible to her. Why could people not agree on one god and one goddess?

"And what happens to them when they have been found out?"

"They're captured, interrogated under torture, and then usually burned at the stake," replied Ibn Said in a flat voice.

Iriomé thought suddenly about arriving at the abyss of Guayote. He also burned the souls of the wicked deep inside the volcano so that they did not return to the earth to do further mischief. But here it seemed to be reversed. The innocent, who wanted to live their faith, were burned. Only the Christians stayed alive.

"One of the boys who looks after the horses called me a heretic," Iriomé blurted out. "He said that I'm in league with the devil."

The médico gave a profound sigh. "You'll need to be very careful."

"But you're not a Christian. Why don't they hurt you?"

Ibn Said smiled. "I'm no converso and have never denied the faith of my fathers. Christians need my art. But if I do not let myself be baptized soon, I must leave the country."

"And you're leaving?"

The médico had no opportunity to respond because from outside a well-known tyrannizing woman's voice was calling for him. Inés de Perreira, surrounded by her two maids and one of the caballeros who had brought them, looked at Ibn Said accusingly.

"Médico, your servant stole from me!" she said coldly.

"This is a severe accusation. What makes you think that?"

"He ran into me and stole my chain with an amulet, which he's now hiding under his shirt on his chest."

Iriomé at first was not sure herself whether she had understood correctly. But when she saw how the médico began to tremble almost imperceptibly, her blood ran cold. Her heart cramped, and her head was about to burst. She wanted to run, but the caballero was much stronger and grabbed hold of her, tore down the chain with the amulet, and held it up triumphantly. Iriomé could no longer stand on her feet and fell to the ground. She was unable to make a sound.

"Don't thieves get their hands chopped off in your religion?" the Spanish woman said scornfully to the médico.

"He's not one of us," Ibn Said whispered, scared. "He comes from the Islands of the Blessed . . ."

Inés of Perreira was bursting with laughter. "That's how I imagine the blessed! Blessed, because they steal from others." She turned away with a haughty expression but turned around again and took the piece of jewelry off the caballero. With her fingertips she kept it away from her body. "I hope the sweat of the heathen doesn't poison my skin."

Before Iriomé could even react, Ibn Said pushed her back to the tent entrance and held her. "Most gracious Doña Inés, please forgive my foolish servant and show mercy once again. I will look into the matter and assure you that something like this will never happen again," he managed to utter, while again bowing to the ground.

Inés looked at him condescendingly. "Moorish vermin," she exclaimed, turned around, and left, head held high, with her two maids and the caballero in tow.

"I need to retrieve the amulet," Iriomé blurted out. "Even if I have to kill her."

The médico stopped her with an iron grip and then dragged her deep into the inner area of the tent. "I thought the decision whether someone dies is in your religion incumbent solely upon the spirits."

Iriomé looked at him in horror. Had she really just said that she would kill Inés?

Chapter 25

The next day, the group of travelers took off promptly at dawn. The vanguard consisted of ten mounted guards in chain-mail armor and helmets with a weapon they called a crossbow. Behind them drove two carriages, on the doors of which were emblazoned the coat of arms of de la Huerta: a fanned-out blood-red flower behind a golden trellis on a black background. In one vehicle sat Frai Lorenzo and his closest confidant, in the other Inés and her two *donacellas* without whom, as Iriomé learned from Ibn Said, she could not make a step. A second protection force, which the médico and Iriomé as his servant had joined, rode behind the carriages. The *mozos,* the stall lads, walked barefoot at the end of the train and had to make quite an effort not to be left behind. However, since they did not possess much more than the clothes on their backs, the risk that any muggers would hijack them was low.

After only two short breaks in which there was no opportunity for Iriomé to get closer to Inés or the amulet, they reached their destination before sunset: Trujillo. Even from afar the mighty castillo could be seen.

Iriomé saw tears sparkling in the eyes of Ibn Said riding next to her. "All that was once Moor country," he said in a sad voice. "The Spanish nobles have made the old Alcázar their fortress."

Iriomé looked at three high square towers forming the corners between high walls of chiseled light limestone. She had never seen such a large building before. From the outside it seemed impregnable, but in its interior people must feel like prisoners. How could they stand a life surrounded by such high walls? The enclosure of Ibn Said's house seemed to have the height of a blade of grass compared to it.

"Why are the walls so mighty? What are these people afraid of?" she asked Ibn Said.

He smiled bitterly. "The battles between the Moors and the Christians were especially bloody in this region," he explained. "The high walls were the only way to protect one's belongings and above all one's life."

What kind of life was this if it was constantly in danger? How could they ever feel happiness, love, and satisfaction?

"The fighting went on for many generations," Ibn Said continued to explain. "Most people didn't even know what peace meant. They only knew bloody battles, which brought heavy losses for both sides. When the Christians in the Extremadura emerged as winners, they believed, of course, that it was their god who had helped them. Therefore, people here are even more Christian than in the rest of Spain."

"And it really was their god?"

"Maybe it was their devil," replied Ibn Said. His last words were luckily drowned by a long tone, which became a little melody. It came from the battlements of the citadel where a man blew into a shiny, funnel-shaped tube. Karima pranced nervously. Iriomé felt that the mare would have preferred to run away. She herself felt more and more that behind those high walls danger was threatening. But Ibn Said smiled at her confidently, so she ran her fingers gently over Karima's neck, which settled the horse. She did not even flinch when with a loud, rattling noise a bridge was lowered over the wide moat encircling the castle.

How much time people here spend protecting themselves from others, thought Iriomé. *If only they took so much pains to get along better with each other.*

After the whole group had reached the courtyard, the bridge was pulled back and locked in place with a loud groan and a thunderclap. Once again the fanfare was resounding. The doors of the carriages were opened, and the guests got out and were welcomed by a number of people who came out of the castle. Iriomé looked around for the médico, but he was engrossed by the fat monk's attention.

"The accommodations for the servants are behind the stables," said a tall, overweight man with a red beard who put his heavy hand on her shoulder.

"I'm the servant of the médico." It escaped Iriomé before she thought. "He needs me for the treatment of the inquisitor." No way she wanted to meet the stall lads again.

The red-bearded looked at her in astonishment. Iriomé bit her lips. Had she now finally betrayed herself by her clear voice?

"Lo and behold, a castrato! Poor devil," the castellan only grumbled and ran the back of his hand amazingly gently over her cheek. Then he shook his head. "A skin like that of a girl. The lads will come down on you." Iriomé knew by now from Ibn Said what the word *castrato* meant and could only admire his foresight once again.

"I can't let you sleep in the guesthouse. I have a small bed above the feed chamber. Come with me."

Relieved, she followed the man up a narrow wooden staircase to a small shed directly under the roof. It was stuffy and dusty and smelled of pigeon droppings. But that was of no importance to Iriomé. The main thing was that she was not at the mercy of those boys. She thanked her rescuer with a deep bow, a gesture that she had learned from Ibn Said and which usually made the Christians peaceful.

However, the red-bearded man drew her up again. "It's okay. Your life is hard enough. If anyone gets too close to you, let me know. My name is Roberto de la Torre. I'm the castellan."

After he left, Iriomé locked the door and sat down on a straw mattress with a deep sigh. She was tired and desperate. Never had she wished more to return to her home island and give birth to her child there in the protection of the volcanic crater. And never before had this desire seemed so unrealizable than at this moment. She could not escape without bringing amakuna into her possession again. She had to get back the amulet before Inés de Perreira's curiosity awoke and she opened it—if she had not already done this and discovered the strange powder!

Despite all her worries Iriomé fell into a restless sleep, only to be awakened by loud steps approaching her room. They did not belong to the heavy castellan and also not to Ibn Said, who slightly dragged one leg. Overcome by anxiety, Iriomé looked around for an escape, but there was only a small skylight too narrow to have squeezed through. There was a knock on the door, and she heard someone call her name softly. "Iri . . ."

Was she dreaming? But there was another knock. "Iri, please open. It's me, Joaquín."

It was his voice. Without any doubt. She rushed to the door and pushed back the bolt. The first thing she saw was the chain with the amulet dangling from his fingers. The closure was unharmed. She could not help but reach for it at once.

"Thank Tara," she breathed and sank on her knees. Tears of gratitude mixed with the pleasure of seeing him again and unfulfilled longing ran down her cheeks.

Joaquín slid rapidly into the chamber and closed the door behind him. He also went to his knees, hugged and squeezed her shaking body, and held her close, as if he never wanted to let go of her. Iriomé put her head on his shoulder, but suddenly a cold shiver ran through her. He only could have taken the amulet off Inés de Perreira. Could it be he was the fiancé of the Spanish beauty?

After quite a while he released her, looked into her face for a long time, then took it in his hands and kissed away each single tear. "You're here. Now all is well," he whispered. "I've been looking for you everywhere."

He caressed her shoulders showing from her shirt, which had shifted during sleep. First the one, then the other. He ran his fingertips gently along her collarbone until he reached the soft dimple at her neck and finally pressed his mouth on it, which aroused in Iriomé dizzying desire.

She leaned back slightly and felt her body beg for more. Eventually, she no longer could resist, and her hands felt under the resistant fabric of his robe for his skin.

Joaquín quickly opened the leather laces of his doublet and slipped it over his head together with the undergarment. He kissed her lips, which were offered to him shivering and wet. It had been a few changes of the moon since they had last been united this way on the ship, but their bodies remembered vividly. And so they were floating away on a wave of pleasure which ended in an explosion, followed by a sweet death.

When they lay exhausted side by side on the narrow bed of straw, he beamed at her, as if life had again opened a door that he had long considered closed. "I'd have never thought that I would feel this way again," he whispered in her ear. His hands caressed her breasts and felt their way down to her belly that already bulged when she lay on her back. He stopped touching her and looked at her questioningly.

Iriomé smiled. "Yes, I carry your child."

Joaquín withdrew his hands and sat up jerkily. She could only imagine what he was thinking. He stood up slowly and dressed without a word, his back turned to her, without giving her another look. Iriomé's eyes filled with tears.

On her island it was always a source of great joy when a man learned of his impending fatherhood. Now it seemed to her as if suddenly a dark cloud had veiled the sun. After a few minutes, which seemed to Iriomé like an eternity, he turned around. "You'll need to give me some time. I'll find a solution. I promise you." His voice was strained.

The intimacy that had just been between them changed, and Iriomé felt a twinge of suspicion rise inside her.

Joaquín took her hand and pulled her up. "Come along," he said. "You can't possibly stay here."

She slipped into her clothes, and he led her gingerly down the stairs across the stable to a small hidden door. Above the door frame he groped for a rusty key and unlocked the door. On the floor an oil lamp was available, which he lit in order to light up the way.

"My ancestors had this secret passage dug," he said with pride in his voice as he led the way. "It offers the last chance to escape if an enemy has already taken the castle. The barn holds a hidden duct leading below the moat to freedom and can even be traveled with horses . . ." he paused. "Can you understand me at all?"

Iriomé nodded. The Christians definitely thought of everything. The narrow, wet duct reminded Iriomé of the dark cave passages on her home island, even if this one was man-made. After a while they came to a narrow staircase that led steeply upward. At the end was a door that Joaquín again unlocked with another key.

"Now we're in the castle without anyone having noticed us," he said in a low tone.

Iriomé entered a small room where a table, two chairs, and a kind of couch stood. Through a window in a wall some light and loud noises were coming in. Iriomé stepped closer and saw below her a huge hall, in the middle of which a long banquet table with chairs were arranged.

"Nobody knows this little hideaway except my father and me," said Joaquín. "From here we can secretly overhear people down in the great hall when we don't exactly know if we can trust them. Nobody will find you here."

By now nothing surprised Iriomé anymore. Meanwhile, beneath her, plates, bowls, and jugs were brought in and huge platters with fish, meat, poultry, fruit, and pastries. She could hardly take her eyes off the delicious food certainly not meant for her.

Joaquín seemed to notice her gaze. "Please excuse me, you must be awfully hungry. I'll get you something to eat right away." He seemed to have recovered from his shock and was able to look her in the face again.

"Please tell the médico that I'm safe," she asked him. "I travel as his assistant. He's probably already looking for me everywhere." Joaquín nodded and shortly engulfed her in an embrace before he left her alone.

Iriomé followed him with her eyes. Of course she understood that it was impossible for her to be attending the feast at Akin's side, especially in her current guise. Nevertheless, she felt neglected. Even though she carried his child.

At least it was fortunate that he had brought back the amulet; she could not thank him enough for that. She opened it carefully. The powder appeared unaffected. A relieved smile flitted across her face. No one, especially not Cold Eye, would ever know. She needed to make Joaquín promise not to disclose to him that she was still alive.

He returned after a short while and brought her a bowl of soup with a thick piece of meat in it and half a loaf of bread. He put everything on the small table. "What you eat on your island we unfortunately don't have here. But I hope you'll like it anyway. Enjoy your meal."

He did not have to tell Iriomé twice; she was already helping herself. She had not eaten anything since the day before; she had not left the tent on instruction of the médico in order not to attract further attention.

Joaquín watched her, smiling while she gobbled down her food. The meat was tender and the broth strong.

"Are you the one who is getting married to Inés de Perreira?" Iriomé finally asked.

He laughed bitterly. "That's what is planned. I've seen my future wife for the first time in my life today, and I think she's terrible."

Iriomé could only agree with him. "She said that I stole the amulet from her, just to annoy me," she told Joaquín indignantly.

"I know. She's vile, arrogant, and cold. But she's the niece of our Queen Isabella, and a connection with her will secure the possessions of my family for a long time," Joaquín said in a sad voice.

"I don't understand that."

"I'll try to explain it to you," he replied and sat beside Iriomé. "My and other great noble families have freed Spain from the Moors with our knights. For this the crown gave us lands in the former Moorish regions, which they see as their property. But now Queen Isabella claims it was all just a loan that can be taken away from us at any time. By my marrying Inés de Perreira and having a male heir, our possession would always be associated with the royal family. It's called marriage policy."

"And what kind of position would our son have?" Iriomé asked in a quiet voice.

"A rather uncertain one. The crown could take him and all that has been in my family's possession for many years. But be reassured, we'll find a solution." He stepped to the small window and for a while silently watched the buzz down in the yard. More and more people arrived, all talking loudly and at once.

"I have to go, but I'll be back." He hugged her briefly and then left the secret room at a quick pace.

Find a solution, echoed his words in her ears. *What did he mean by that?* Suddenly she felt alone and missed her friend Ibn Said, in whose presence she always felt safe and in good hands. She wondered whether he was also sitting at the banquet table. She stood up to walk over to the small window when she heard a loud voice she would have recognized out of hundreds. Startled, she looked down. She had not been mistaken. The butcher of her people, Alonso de Lugo, knelt before the fat monk and kissed his ring.

"Your Excellency, what an honor, to take part in this blessed event in your presence," Cold Eye's deceptive, submissive voice came up to her.

"Get up, de Lugo, and stop fooling about. Come and help me into that chair. Oh, the damn gout." He gave a cry of pain and then with the help of the conqueror sank in a particularly wide chair.

At that moment Iriomé remembered she had forgotten to make Akin promise not to inform Cold Eye of her presence. She cursed herself for it. It had seemed more important to her to talk about Inés and her child. How foolish of her! She again looked down in the banquet room, anxious to stay in the shade of the window frame.

"Sit beside me, conquistador, and tell me how many savages you've converted to the true faith on the Islands of the Blessed," said Frai Lorenzo after three servants moved his chair to the table so he could easily help himself.

"Just about all, Your Excellency," he chuckled. "But Frai Hieronymus can surely tell you more. After all, I'm no churchman, but only the one who makes the sheep bend to your will."

Iriomé saw the Franciscan, who had just entered the hall and now also went on his knees before the inquisitor and kissed his ring. "I can only agree with Alonso de Lugo, the large Canary Conqueror," he said humbly. "The herd is growing. We can be satisfied."

"Okay. Glad to hear that. Because we'll only rest when our work is done and there are only Christians all around the world. Am I right, conquistador!?"

"I'm always at your command. You know that you can rely on me."

Iriomé felt like fleeing through the secret passage back to the barn and galloping off with Karima. But when she tried to open the door, she found that it was locked. She went back to the window. Pure fear threatened to well up in her, but Tichiname had taught her how to deal with this demon. She directed her gaze solely on Cold Eye and looked over an imaginary line in the middle of his soul. What she saw there repulsed her but also filled her with compassion, and her fear subsided. Every soul had a story. Naturally she still had to become aware of his. But henceforth she was no longer at his mercy; she would know what to do at the moment of danger.

The servants had poured wine and water. Frai Lorenzo stood up with a groan, his voluminous buttocks got stuck at the armrests of his chair and then it fell crashing to the ground. Without even taking notice he raised his wine cup. "I would like to drink a toast to my enchanting niece Inés Pilar de Perreira y Castellón and the young Conde Joaquín de Alba y Santa Barbara and with the approval of both their families announce their betrothal and their upcoming marriage."

Iriomé received a soothing look, which Joaquín sent upward to her. He sat beside Inés, who wore an even more precious dress, blue as the night sky.

"That's a smart move," an elderly gentleman with thick, gray, wavy hair who had just stepped into the banquet hall rumbled. He possessed a tall figure, although he supported himself slightly bent on a stick. Iriomé took to him immediately. The expression on his face told her that he inwardly sneered at the odd bunch that was gathered here.

"Father, how nice that you've come after all." Joaquín got up and pulled out a chair for the old conde.

"You can be glad that your son has such powerful friends to protect the legacy of his family. So don't hold your stubborn head quite so high," the fat monk hissed to the old conde as everyone raised their cups to the young couple. "For this you owe me a favor, but more of it later." His greedy eyes fell on a large plate that was carried in by two servants. On it was a crisp fried pig dripping with fat with an apple in its mouth and lemon slices on the eyes. "Now we want to enjoy what the Lord gave us, and thank him for it." He said a prayer in Latin, the language of the Christian god, while the servants cut up the pig at an astonishing rate.

The monk finished the prayer with a solemn "Amen, praised be Jesus Christ," and then turned to the médico, who sat diagonally across from him. "Too bad that your god forbids such delicacies," he sneered.

"Yours would do well to forbid it also; then you would escape the next attack of gout," Ibn Said retorted in a friendly tone. Iriomé chuckled, hoping at the same time that Ibn Said would not meet with serious consequences for his apt remark.

"Then you'll treat me again, honorable Ibn Said. It would be a sin to refuse such a gift of God." The inquisitor smirked, biting with relish into a crispy brown crust.

De Lugo turned to Ibn Said. "As I have heard, you're the médico from Cadiz who hosted the witch from the Islands of the Blessed," he said coldly. "Where's she?"

Iriomé was almost frightened to death.

"I'm afraid you're mistaken, my lord. I've bought a castrato for ten silver coins in the port of Cadiz. That I already told your friend, the inquisitor," answered Ibn Said quietly and looked at the fat Dominican, who had just withdrawn from any conversation and intently tried to tear out a leg from a colorfully decorated pheasant he had been served on a wooden board. "And because of this castrato you have destroyed my home and killed my mother," Ibn Said continued in a sharper tone.

"Paw!" De Lugo got a coughing fit from sheer anger and had to cover his red-hot face with a napkin. "Where is the mysterious castrato? I want to see him myself at once," he said, almost as soon as his voice had returned.

"Calm yourself, dear friend. He has traveled with us. We'll let him come after our repast." The inquisitor patted de Lugo's arm with greasy fingers. "We should first devote our time to this divine feast."

"He seemed strange to me from the moment I saw him," said Inés but was immediately silent when Joaquín gave her a reproachful look.

"This witch has a miracle cure that has saved me from certain death," de Lugo said hoarsely. "One of my slaves, a dark-haired wildcat, which I brought from the islands, met her in the market in Cádiz and told me that your quack gave her shelter. After I encountered neither him nor the witch, I unfortunately had to torture the girl to see whether she knew something herself about this medicine. Unfortunately, she passed away when my servant poured a mere five liters of water in her stomach."

Iriomé felt sick, and she almost threw up. Despite everything, she felt pity for Guayafanta. Was she the first victim of amakuna? Ibn Said seemed to have been right with his prediction.

"Honorable de Lugo, torture is an art that you should better leave to the Inquisition; otherwise you'll learn nothing, but only have dead delinquents," the monk rebuked the conquistador while he attacked another dish of the pheasant.

"Torture is unworthy of a Christian. We have conquered this land by the sword and our faith and not torture," the old conde interrupted them, seriously upset, making clear that he no longer tolerated this subject at his table.

"Can such a miracle cure even exist?" asked an elderly, thin man with a long white beard and a nose that seemed to Iriomé downright huge.

"Since God is almighty, it will surely exist," said de Lugo hoarsely. "The fact that we haven't found it yet doesn't mean anything. We knew nothing of the West Indies until Cristóbal Colón discovered them for the crown. And if God calls us to discover new areas," he continued, "why should he not call us to find new remedies?"

The inquisitor nodded in agreement while Ibn Said vehemently shook his head. "I've read most of the books and writings from Greece, the Orient, and Asia, and there's no record of such a cure," he threw in with a confident voice. He got away with it because the inquisitor needed him and would hardly deliver him to de Lugo's arbitrariness. Iriomé would have liked to give him a hug for how bravely he fought to keep her secret.

"Dear médico, I entertain no doubt as to your knowledge, but I happen to have experienced this firsthand. Haven't I?" De Lugo turned to Joaquín who sat opposite him. "It was very clever of you, that you protected this witch. Maybe you even knew about the remedy. In any case, she saved me, and I owe my life to her and you."

"My dear friend," Joaquín said. "I deeply regret that a witch, as you call her, has made my blood surge through my veins to such a degree that I took up a weapon against you. An unforgivable mistake. And even if you don't allow yourself to be dissuaded from the opinion that my former slave has contributed to your rescue, it still can only have been the Lord's working." He looked to the fat monk for approval.

"In God, we can always trust, but not in humans; otherwise we wouldn't need the Inquisition." The Dominican was more than willing to pick up the thread. "Maybe the Jews and Moors already know such an agent and use it only for their own brothers in faith." The inquisitor was now completely in his element and even forgot for a moment to eat. "In this context, I wanted to discuss something with you anyway." He turned to Joaquín's father.

"By agreement between church and crown, we are planning to

build Inquisition tribunals here in the Extremadura, and we'll need your help."

The old conde looked at him contemptuously and raised his hands demonstratively.

"It's just to check whether the converted Jews and Moors actually stick to our Christian rituals." He smiled pointedly at the man with the long white beard, who mainly ate bread, soup, and desserts.

"With all due respect, I can't help you with that," rumbled the old conde. "And as for my treasurer," he continued, also turning toward the bearded man, "he has been suffering from indigestion for days and has no intention to worsen it by eating fat pork."

"Never mind," the inquisitor said in a sweet-and-sour tone. "Your stubbornness will wear off soon enough. Times are changing."

"The times may change, Frai Lorenzo, but I won't. Especially when my view of Christianity no longer conforms with church and crown," said the conde, annoyed.

"But church and crown are quite successful together," a young, slightly stocky man dared to chime in from the servants' table.

De Lugo and the inquisitor looked at him, surprised. "What do you mean?"

"I've heard that at the conquests in the New World with sword and Bible untold wealth and entire kingdoms can be captured."

"You're right," said de Lugo, pleased to find between church and old-fashioned nobility a man with a true conquering spirit. "What's your name?"

"Francisco Pizarro. I'm only a swineherd, but not for much longer." He stood up with great fanfare. "There will soon be new expeditions to the West Indies. I plan to take part."

"He will definitely become a real conquistador," de Lugo roared with laughter. "And how about you?" He grinned at Joaquín challengingly. "After all, we have finished off these savages of the islands together."

"We're really glad that you wrestled them down just before they would have conquered the whole of Castile with their slingshots and clubs." The old conde rose and leaned on his cane. One of the servants hurried to help him. "Pardon me, but I'll take my leave. I'm an old man and have neither time nor leisure to listen to the chatter of a swineherd. Have a nice evening."

Iriomé was also tired. It had demanded highest concentration to follow the conversation. One thing had now become completely clear. She could, under no circumstances, stay here. Joaquín had to get her away this night. Or could it be that he had imprisoned her here to deliver her to Cold Eye? A shiver ran down her spine. She still did not know if she could fully trust Akin. Her heart said yes, but her mind . . .

The sound of the key in the door interrupted her thoughts. Joaquín smiled at her, and her doubts melted as ice in the sun. He was carrying a dark green dress with a matching stole over his arm, which he put on the chair.

"De Lugo will search the whole castillo tomorrow morning to find you. You need to leave immediately. Here, put on this. The slave costume has had its day."

"Does he still want to thank me?" Iriomé asked sardonically.

Joaquín looked at her thoughtfully. "Then it's true! You've cured him with your magic remedy." Involuntarily he took a step back.

"Why is this man still your friend and eats at your table?"

"Because I owe him something. I fought in the battle at Granada side by side with him and was taken prisoner by the Moorish under dishonorable circumstances. He freed me, risking his life. My father never knew. And you're now the only person besides me to know about that."

Iriomé understood, although she was convinced that Joaquín's father would have forgiven his son and that Cold Eye had freed Joaquín not from pure philanthropy but calculatingly to use him.

"We're something like blood brothers. Why did you save him?"

"I did it for you! Because we both have a common task in this life."

He looked at her a long time, and Iriomé would have loved to sink forever in the depth of his gaze. "You mean the child?"

Still Iriomé could not bring herself to explain to Akin that it was about amakuna, the secret that henceforth could be preserved only by two lovers. As long as he held on to his friendship with de Lugo, she could not and must not initiate him.

He thought about it briefly. "If it's my child, then we have four to five months to take care of everything."

"Whose child could it be?" Iriomé asked shocked and tugged indecisively at the dress that still hung on the chair.

"Please excuse me. But it isn't easy for me to meet on the same day on one hand my future wife and on the other the mother of my child," Joaquín said.

Iriomé nodded but also asked him to sympathize with her situation.

"I love you, Iri, and nothing in the world will convince me otherwise."

"And your father, your family, your possessions . . .?"

". . . are of no importance. You are important and our son."

"But where shall we live, if they will take everything from you?"

"I don't know yet; maybe we'll go to the New World. There nobody asks for status and origin. Even a swineherd can conquer a kingdom there."

"And where is it, this 'New World'?"

"Far away in the west. Still much farther than the island on which you were born. But now please put on this dress."

"Wouldn't it be better if I stayed a boy?"

"Not where I am taking you."

She took the monstrous fabric in her hands and looked at him perplexed. "I do not know how to put it on. I have never worn anything like it."

"Neither have I," he said with a grin. "But together we'll manage somehow."

Iriomé pulled her shirt over her head. Joaquín helped her clumsily into a sort of camisole which was laced up at the back. After she put on the dress, he looked at her, pleased. It fit perfectly, even if it forbade taking a deep breath. Finally, he put a matching stole over her short-cropped hair which made her look like the perfect Spanish noblewoman. He took her by the hand. "You're beautiful."

When they left the castle of Trujillo shortly before dawn through the underground passage, the voices of drunks reached them from the banquet hall. Iriomé would have preferred to run even faster than was possible with the unfamiliar shoes that, like the camisole, had to be laced up and were cumbersome. This was not her world. It would never be.

When they reached the barn and Joaquín locked the door behind them, a figure stepped out from the shadows toward her. Iriomé started, but then she recognized her loyal friend.

"I can't let you go without saying goodbye," Ibn Said said, a little sadly. He blinked as if the not yet risen sun blinded him. "Allah doesn't always reveal at first glance the beauty he is capable of creating," he said with amusement as he gazed at Iriomé from all sides. Then he put his hand on Joaquín's shoulder. "Though your god is Jesus Christ and mine is Allah, it must be the same god who has brought women in their loveliness and their perfect beauty into this world, don't you think?"

The young conde nodded.

"Take good care of her!"

"I will."

Ibn Said looked him in the eyes for a long time. "I hope so, for you and for her." When he handed the reins of the gray mare to Iriomé, she saw that he had tears in his eyes. "Karima now belongs to you forever. May she carry you wherever you find your happiness." Then he quickly left the stable without looking around once.

Iriomé felt the pain of parting just like him. But Karima pushed her nose gently under her armpits. The familiar smell of the animal filled her with courage and confidence.

"You'll surely see him again," Joaquín consoled her while he helped her mount the horse, which turned out to be not so easy due to the woman's saddle and apparel. Iriomé longed to be back in her shirt and trousers that had made life so much easier.

They left the castle through the second underground passageway, which ended in a small wood just outside the *donjon*. From there they rode in a fast trot in a southern direction and shortly before noon reached a fertile valley in the middle of which a massive church tower pointed to the sky like a warning finger. Next to it were several gray stone buildings surrounded by a wall. Joaquín stopped his horse. "My mother founded this monastery in her lifetime. There you'll be safe for the time being."

Walls again, thought Iriomé. By now they seemed to her almost like a symbol for the people in this country. She did not know what a monastery was or what would be expected of her there.

"Let me speak to them," Joaquín asked and knocked on a wooden door with a closed hatch. After a long while, the hatch was opened from inside. From behind a lattice in the semidarkness peeked an old woman wrapped in a black and white dress that only revealed her pale face.

Iriomé stared at her in disbelief. If she already felt locked in this dress, what did this poor woman have to endure? She had of course seen veiled Moorish women in Cádiz, but this one seemed to have her whole head bandaged and still wore a veil over it that was tied under her chin.

"I'm the Conde de Alba y Santa Barbara and would like to speak to the abbess," Joaquín said firmly.

"She's on her way to noon prayers," the answer came from the semi-darkness. And as if to confirm this, at that moment the bells of the church broke the silence of the place. Even Joaquín's strict, commanding tone could not drown them. "It's urgent, very urgent," he nevertheless called into the hatch, but to no avail.

Only when the chiming of the bells had died away was the door next to the gate opened. The nun beckoned them in with an energetic gesture. They tied the horses to a tree and followed her along a narrow path to the church. From the open portal bright female vocals sounded that reminded Iriomé of the songs of the harimaguadas. She stopped and let herself be carried away to her island by the pure voices. She saw herself sitting under one of the sacred trees and looking out at the sea.

The nun smiled at her for the first time. "Our sisters are known throughout the country for their beautiful chorales," she said proudly, while she guided the two to one of the outbuildings. "I'll inform the abbess as soon as she comes from the church." The nun unlocked the door to the visiting room for them.

Iriomé's eyes fell on a wooden female figure in a deep blue coat. That smile made her think of her as a goddess. But not for long, because the thick walls radiated such an icy coldness that she began to tremble pitifully in her dress. Joaquín seemed not to notice; his mind seemed to be far away. Was he thinking of Inés de Perreira? His wedding? Of the advantages this marriage would bring him—and what he would have to sacrifice if he decided in favor of her and their child? Perhaps he wanted to just get rid of her now . . .

Iriomé scolded herself that she had not at least discussed other solutions with Ibn Said, but all had passed so quickly. And now she was here. On the way Joaquín had told her of the women here, who led a strict life ruled by prayers as the servants of god, but what did this mean for her? That she should worship the god of the Christians and had to deny Tara? And if not, would she then be burnt at the stake as a heretic?

The abbess of the convent of Santa María del Valle, Teresa de Angelis, was a lean, tall, middle-aged woman. Her simple, flushed face with clear, bright eyes showed great kindness but also wisdom. After she welcomed Joaquín and Iriomé, she immediately recognized the situation. She quickly realized that the young woman with the short blond hair was not a converted Jew fleeing the Inquisition, as the young conde tried to make her believe, but his lover.

"Why are you lying to me?" she asked Joaquín, as she looked him directly in the eyes. "I'm convinced the holy one would not like that. Especially not in a place like this."

Iriomé knew the answer. It was fear that made him lie. The anxiety about his future and the fear of not being able to keep the promise he gave her.

The abbess was inspiring confidence, so Iriomé decided to speak for herself despite Joaquín's previous request. "I'm from the Islands of the Blessed," she said. "I was a harimaguada there. A healer. Frai Lorenzo de la Huerta, the chief judge of the Inquisition, and the conquistador Alonso de Lugo believe that I have a magic remedy that can heal all diseases. But that's not true. Nevertheless, they follow me and will not rest until they've got me. Then they will torture me so that I tell them my alleged secret. For this reason I request your protection."

The abbess had listened to her quietly. When the two names were mentioned her eyebrows twitched suspiciously. Iriomé could clearly see how she was struggling with herself. Then, however, she put an arm around the shoulders of the young woman. "You're safe here. Mary, Mother of God, under whose protection this monastery stands, will also protect you."

Iriomé looked at her gratefully. Similarly to the médico, this woman was enclosed by visible walls, but not by invisible ones that put people out of reach of love.

The abbess threw Joaquín an appraising look. "You're very lucky to have met such a brave woman."

He nodded. "That's exactly why I brought her to you, Madre Teresa. You know how difficult the situation in Trujillo is at the moment. Once I've sorted everything out, I'll come for her."

"Then settle it quickly, Conde de Alba. The young woman here will be thanking you."

He nodded. "I'll visit you as often as I can," he said to Iriomé while following the abbess out into the warm midday sun.

Iriomé in contrast could find no words for him. The uncertainty of the future was weighing heavily on her heart.

"See you soon, Iri." He hugged her, then turned away quickly.

The abbess, who was not witnessing such a farewell scene for the first time, resolutely took Iriomé's arm and led her gently but firmly away from Joaquín. "You must now look to the future, my child," she said but could not prevent Iriomé from turning around for one last look at Joaquín.

He had reached his horse, swung onto the saddle, and spurred the horse so rudely that it nickered, frightened. For a last time Iriomé's and Akin's eyes met. All expression of happiness and joy seemed to have disappeared from his face. Instead he appeared to her like a tree that has lost all his leaves in a mighty storm.

"I think we'll put your horse in the goat house." The abbess tore Iriomé from her grief. She untied Karima and handed Iriomé the reins, and together they walked to the farm buildings. "A beautiful mare, she'll have a good life here, too," she said in a calming voice.

After the horse was fed and Iriomé was sure she wanted for nothing, the two women stepped into the dim entrance hall. A crucified Jesus in four-dimensional life size, who hung on ropes from the ceiling directly opposite the portal, was staring at her. Iriomé turned away from his bloodied face in fear. It was not the first time she had seen a picture of the Christian god, but each time he frightened her.

"Why did you kill your god in such a cruel way?" she dared to ask. This question she could not get out of her head, but even the médico had not known the answer.

The abbess looked at her seriously. "He has the suffering of mankind upon himself, has died for us, and has risen again."

"But the people here in this country are still suffering." This was at least her opinion, which became more and more set the longer she lived here.

"Only those who don't believe in him. But now tell me, what's your name?" Madre Teresa asked as they climbed a wide marble staircase leading to a long candlelit hallway.

"Iriomé," she answered but was not sure whether the abbess had understood the name because the door to a noisy room where several sisters were busy sewing was opened at the same time.

"This is Hermana Irina, a new novice," she said. "Please see to it that she's clothed." Reassuringly she put her hand on Iriomé's back as Tichiname had done so often. Then she beckoned to a young sister with warm, dark eyes and smooth olive skin. She rose with a smile and went up to Iriomé.

"That's Hermana Guadalupe. She'll help you change your clothes. Actually she works in the infirmary and cares for the sick," the abbess said, "but sometimes she also helps out here in the sewing room."

Iriomé felt immediately attracted to the young woman. Maybe because her skin color was more like hers and she was not so unhealthily pale like the Spanish women she had met.

"Then she will take you to my Holy Office, where you can tell me your story," said the abbess, stroking Iriomé's back soothingly once again, then leaving the room.

The young sister took her hand and led her behind a folding screen covered with dark blue fabric to get rid of her clothes. *Another person who is called to heal,* thought Iriomé. Another person whose touch and whose eyes she liked.

Patiently the young nun helped her out of the dress, but when it finally fell to the ground, she let out a surprised cry. Even though she immediately put her hands over her mouth, the others nevertheless had taken notice and came running, full of curiosity. Stunned, they stared at Iriomé's belly.

She covered it with her scarf; however, this did not improve the situation. Guadalupe was the first to compose herself, shooed the sisters back to work, and handed the pregnant woman a novice's habit.

After the abbess learned about her condition, she asked to find another garment for Iriomé because due to the fact that she was no virgin she could not be accepted as a member of the sisterhood. Yet she did not expel her from the monastery.

From the first meeting Iriomé had known that the abbess possessed a good heart and moreover that she, although generally women had little to say in this country, had a voice of her own. And if need be, this voice argued against rules and the men who made the laws in this country.

"Here, I give women the opportunity to lead an independent life," she told Iriomé. "That's how Doña Lucía, the mother of the young conde, wanted it. She herself married for love, but the most aristocratic women in this country are married for political reasons."

"The way this Inés and Joaquín are to be married?"

"The way the Condesa Inés de Perreira y Castellón and the young Conde Joaquín de Alba y Santa Barbara will be married," the abbess corrected Iriomé and gave her a look of understanding and compassion, which made Iriomé feel warm all over. "But for some women it's simply impossible to live with a man they don't love or sometimes even hate. And for those poor creatures Doña Lucía founded this monastery. God rest her soul. Unfortunately, she left much too soon."

Iriomé had been wondering why Joaquín's mother had not been present at the feast.

"She died many years ago after the birth of her fourth child," the abbess continued.

"So Joaquín has brothers and sisters?"

Madre Teresa shook her head sadly. "They were all stillbirths. The young conde was the only baby who survived. And his father loved his wife so much that he never married again."

Iriomé looked at the abbess sadly. On Benahoare, a child rarely died at birth, at least not as long as Tichiname had been near. Without thinking she anxiously stroked her belly.

The abbess felt the fear that suddenly overcame Iriomé. "Everything will be okay," she said affectionately. "You're not alone."

Iriomé gave her a grateful look and then followed Guadalupe, who was waiting to take her to her cell.

The sun was just setting behind the hill in the valley with a warm orange light. The birds said goodbye to the day with loud chirping. Iriomé, for the first time in a long time, had the feeling that she could stay at a place undisturbed, at least until her child saw the light of day.

When they passed the main cloister and turned the corner, Iriomé held her breath. Her face shone with joy. What a garden! Different from the one in the house of the médico, but no less beautiful. Mighty conifers, which gave shade in the summer, pink budding bushes, bamboo, palm trees, and roses . . . a secluded, flourishing idyllic spot. Behind this garden, bordering the monastery wall, she discovered a lovingly landscaped herb garden, before which an already slightly weathered stone bench stood. How beautiful it was here, how peaceful. Iriomé asked Hermana Guadalupe if they could sit there for a moment. The young novice had no objection and sat down beside her. Thus, the souls of the two young women were getting closer without their speaking a word. Almost simultaneously they stood up after a while, and Iriomé followed her companion through a small wooden door in the monastery wall to the outside.

Immediately she lost her heart to the small stone house in front of her. It reminded her a little of the balconies built from natural stones before most cave entrances in Aceró. Even the small dark room with a tiny window and a fireplace in the middle was like the caves on Benahoare. In any case, she felt much more comfortable here than between the high walls of Trujillo. Now she could only hope that Cold Eye would not find her here.

Chapter 26

Iriomé quickly got used to the quiet, steady life in the monastery, even if she missed the médico and especially the work at his side.

And of course there was Joaquín. Since she had met him again, not a day went by without her thinking of him. Missing him caused her deep emotional pain. But she accepted it as her fate. In her belly Joaquín's son was growing, and this would always band them together.

Twice a day Hermana Guadalupe brought her something to eat. She was the only one besides the abbess who exchanged a few words with her. The nuns had, as Iriomé understood by now, taken an oath of silence, which could only be broken in extreme situations. Iriomé respected that until one evening when Hermana Guadalupe brought her a pot of hot vegetable soup and half a loaf of bread, and she could no longer keep herself from asking about her previous life.

"My mother was a gypsy. She healed people and was murdered by the Inquisition."

Iriomé looked at her questioningly. "What are gypsies?"

"In the eyes of the church they are in league with the devil because they perform rituals of which the Christians are afraid."

"What kind of rituals?"

Guadalupe shrugged. "Animal sacrifices and the like."

"We also do that," Iriomé said. "After all, you have to repay the gods if they have helped you."

"You must never say that aloud again," the young nun warned her horrified. "Otherwise you'll be tortured and burnt. Like my mother!

Madre Teresa has taken me into the monastery. The rest of my family fled in order to escape my mother's fate. Madre Teresa taught me reading and writing and the Latin language. She belongs to the people who love every creature on this earth, whether he's strong or weak, or possibly doesn't believe in Jesus Christ."

"And you, do you believe in him?"

"Of course. He was the most wonderful man who has ever lived on earth and still stands by the people to this very day. To be a little bit more like him is my highest aspiration. Of course I'll never accomplish this." She laughed, and for a moment her face lost the expression of sorrow it normally showed.

"But you're also helping people. You're a harimaguada, a healer. You carry the gift to heal people," Iriomé said softly.

Guadalupe looked at her in amazement. "How do you know that?"

"You told me on my first day when we sat on the bench at the herb garden."

"I didn't talk to you then."

"But you did." Iriomé smiled.

Guadalupe answered her smile. "The abbess told me that they're after you because you possess a mysterious magic potion that heals everything."

Iriomé started, but her new friend took her hand and stroked it reassuringly. "Don't worry. No one will ever hear a word about it. Of that you can be sure." Iriomé felt that she could trust both the abbess and Guadalupe. "Who taught you the art of healing?"

"One day in the monastery I discovered in the library our Latin edition of a large medical work. It was written by the Persian physician and philosopher Avicenna. From then on I was hooked. Night after night I studied this book secretly by candlelight."

"I know the book of Avicenna," Iriomé said.

"Do you?"

"Ibn Said, a Moorish *hakim,* whose servant I was for a while, showed it to me."

Guadalupe beamed at her enthusiastically. "Then you certainly understand how important this knowledge is. You can help so many people with it who would otherwise be lost."

Iriomé thought of the young girl who had leprosy and most probably was living thanks to the formulation of Avicenna, even if it was a special gift and one needed a heart for healing people. She had to admit that books like this contained an additional knowledge that could be rather useful.

"We nuns actually mustn't read it," said Guadalupe in a conspiratorial tone. "Because the Holy Church says that it is solely in the hands of God whether the sick are healed. But I don't think so. For this reason, I've also started to plant herbs in the monastery garden that I've dug up secretly in the woods. Now I can make medicine to heal various diseases using Avicenna's formulations. So far, I haven't dared to begin."

"Why not?"

"If anyone here in the convent found out, or if even just a rumor got started about it, I'd be accused of being a witch like my mother, simply because of my skin color."

Iriomé thought for a minute. "If you want, we can do it here. I'm not a nun and live outside the walls. And except for you, nobody comes here anyway. The other sisters are afraid of me. It's also easier for me to go into the forest and look for new herbs than for you."

"But if someone out there recognizes you and betrays you to the Santa Hermandad?" Guadalupe exclaimed.

Iriomé smiled. "I can make myself invisible."

"Really?"

"No, that was a joke. But I'm good at hiding. So don't worry."

This idea appealed to Iriomé only too well. She would finally have a task and not just sit idly in her hermitage the whole day long. She felt how the various forces in Guadalupe were fighting each other: on the one hand the passion to discover new remedies, on the other hand the fear of the consequences if someone betrayed her to the Inquisition. But finally the voice of her heart won out over the fear. She hugged Iriomé with tears running down her cheeks.

"We'll do it! Although words are often redundant, sometimes it's a good idea to talk."

The next day Guadalupe brought, hidden under her habit, Avicenna's *Canon of Medicine* to henceforth continue her studies together with Iriomé.

Every time she brought food, she stayed for an hour longer in which the two young women discussed which remedy they wanted to produce next.

Iriomé learned quickly which Spanish herbs corresponded to those growing on her home island. Guadalupe used the bark of the holm oak instead of the bark of the resin and the fruits of the dragon tree, which only grew on the island, for bleeding wounds. For inflammation she used the stinging leaves of the nettle, which Iriomé did not know from Benahoare. Yet she remembered that Tichiname once had shown her a similar nettle with serrated dark green leaves. With some plants and their applications both young women were equally well acquainted; for example, with the thorn apple and the henbane used as an anesthetic for severe pain.

Again and again Iriomé made for the forest to look for missing herbs. She not only explored the plant world but also all possible places where she could hide in an emergency.

Guadalupe brought kitchen containers, pots, and crucible for teas, tinctures, and ointments that they prepared, either referring to Iriomé's memory or to recipes from the book of Avicenna. And as Guadalupe was a very talented illustrator, she began to create a directory with pictures of medicinal plants, together with a table for the different names and applications, on large-sized parchment pages from the library.

The hermitage turned increasingly into what Christians would call a witches' brew. From the ceiling various herbal bouquets hung for drying. In the rough stone walls Iriomé carved symbols Tichiname taught her: the spiral as a symbol of infinity and eternal recurrence; the circle for the eternal feminine, the earth, the unity, the perfection, without beginning and without end; the triangle, if it pointed upward, as a symbol of masculinity, of fire and heaven, and with the point down as an image of the female birth organs and the infinite power of Nature; finally the quadrangle, standing for order and maintenance within the four directions. In the cracks between the stones she put black feathers, and in one niche there was the bleached skull of a dog.

In reality, the interior of the cell reflected what was happening deep inside Iriomé. Her true nature, which she had hidden in the rearmost corner of her heart, was pushing out—the intrepid harimaguada who healed people and spoke with spirits—even if this denounced her as a heretic and brought danger.

෬෨

After three months Joaquín came to see Iriomé for the first time. She had not expected to see him again. Working with Guadalupe covered the longing for him, and even in her dreams the young conde became only a rare visitor. Nevertheless, her heart leapt when his visit was announced. She ran as fast as her now considerably grown belly allowed to the office of the abbess, where he was waiting for her.

He seemed changed. The expression of hardness and aloofness she had noticed on him when they first met had returned. His eyes no longer invited her to drown in them. Between them a new wall was built that once had been torn down by their love for each other. Iriomé sensed his condition was not due to her but to the concerns that were weighing on him. She decided to ignore it and infect him with the joy of the imminent birth of their child and the feelings of happiness that went along with it.

It was midsummer now. The sun burned mercilessly on the cracked earth of the Extremadura, which now looked like the skin of an old woman. One of the few cool places in the monastery was the church, so they decided, with regard to Iriomé's condition, to spend the short time of his visit there; however, not in the nave but in the sacristy, where the priests put on their vestments and made preparations.

Joaquín pulled her to a wooden bench, looked her in the face a long time, and thoughtfully caressed her cheeks. "You've never looked so beautiful," he whispered huskily, a little surprised himself by how much he was touched by her presence. Then he laid his hand almost shyly on her belly, drew her into his arms, and pressed her gently against him.

"I've almost forgotten how wonderful it is to be close to you," he said softly when he let go of her. "You alone have the ability to make me feel that there's something out there that's more important than all I formerly thought to be essential."

Iriomé looked at him expectantly. Something had also changed in her. Although she enjoyed his presence, she no longer was dependent on it. She knew his absence would no longer cause her pain.

"But this something often seems to me so fleeting," he continued. "One moment it's there, then it's disappeared again. One cannot rely on it like on one's sword, which one only needs to draw when one needs it."

"Love is the exact opposite of a sword," said Iriomé. "You can rely on it even if you don't feel it at your side. However, you must always prove to be worthy of it; otherwise it will leave you."

"I know." Joaquín lowered his eyes. "I didn't appreciate you enough, but that will change. Just wait and see. We'll find a way to be together." He once again touched her belly tentatively. "The three of us."

Iriomé wished with all her heart that he would succeed in making his words come true. Yet she had her doubts. However, she would find a way to survive alone with her child if necessary. The return to her true destiny, which was the art of healing, had helped her to regain her original power.

Joaquín sent her regards of Ibn Said, who had treated the inquisitor for a while in Trujillo and then one night had secretly disappeared.

"De Lugo's men have been looking for you everywhere," he reported. "And he has watched the médico and me wherever we went. That's also the reason why I haven't come sooner. He even wanted to bring his Excellency Frai Lorenzo de La Huerta to have Ibn Said tortured. But thank god the inquisitor doesn't believe in your magic remedy. He's on the side of the Moorish doctor, whom he wants to stay unscathed. He even promised to put him under his personal protection for his services, in case the Moors are expulsed from Spain."

"Nothing's worse than having to leave one's home involuntarily," Iriomé said wistfully and saw for an instant in her mind's eye the rugged cliffs of her island with the foaming surf thundering against them. But the church bells that called the nuns to vespers, the afternoon prayer, began to ring and brought her quickly back to the hard pew.

Joaquín seemed grateful for this interruption and for not having to talk any longer about this issue. He rose. "I think we must leave the church, and also I have an appointment."

"With your fiancé?" Iriomé could not resist asking.

He shook his head. "Inés of Perreira has traveled back to the Royal Court of Granada. Queen Isabella and Ferdinand are residing there now that the last Emir of the Moors has gone into exile for good."

Nothing remains as it was, Iriomé thought sadly. The stone of destiny could never be stopped. This lesson she had learned. Each rule, as powerful as it might be at some point, would come to an end. Perhaps someday also the great castles of the Christians would fall and their power would be broken? Nothing was made for eternity.

Iriomé accompanied Joaquín back to the monastery gate, where his horse was tied up. A lot had changed in three months; each of them had gone in another direction. More and more Iriomé realized that it was not about holding on to what you possessed, but to give what you could. She thought of this Jesus Christ about whom the abbess and Guadalupe repeatedly told her. He had lived in poverty and struggled alone with the words of love. His Ten Commandments corresponded to what Tara and Tigotan demanded from the Guanches, and Ibn Said's Allah demanded nothing else either. The Christians themselves, however, did not seem to pay much attention to this. They killed and displaced people from their country who had settled there for a long time. And all this they did in the name of their god. He had to be a weak god. Would he otherwise allow such cruelty?

After she shared these last thoughts with Joaquín, their conversation ceased. He did not even try to defend himself. He just did not say a word and stared at the floor. Finally he raised his head and looked her in the eyes. "Maybe we Christians aren't good people and really have little in common with Jesus Christ. But one day we'll rule the world. And then all will understand that our God is the strongest."

⚭

The following night the rain was pouring down. Guadalupe, dressed only in a thin nightgown and with a lantern in her hand, knocked at Iriomé's door.

"Madre Teresa is seriously ill," she sobbed. "It's her heart. I don't know what to do." The tears that were running down her cheeks mingled with the rain. Her black hair lay like a second skin around her head.

Iriomé did not hesitate a moment, threw a cloth over them both and ran with Guadalupe to the main building of the monastery.

"After vespers she suddenly collapsed," Iriomé's friend gasped. "I prepared a tea from hawthorn flowers, valerian, and hop for her and also rubbed her with a brew from lemon balm. But her condition has not improved. I fear the worst."

Soaked to the skin, they reached the main building of the monastery. On their way up to the cells of the nuns they left a wide track of water on the stairs. The abbess lay on a narrow bed made of wood. In the barren, unheated room, apart from a table and a chair there was just an unadorned crucifix on the wall. She was breathing hard. Iriomé laid her hand on Madre Teresa's heart, feeling how abora, the power of life, was ready to escape. She asked the other sisters who were anxiously standing in the hallway to return to their cells. But none of them moved. They stared with a mixture of fear, mistrust, and hope at Iriomé, who with her pregnant belly, to which stuck the wet nightgown, must look to them like the temptation of the devil.

Iriomé closed the cell door unceremoniously. Then she took out Joaquín's amulet, opened it carefully, and let a little of the powder trickle into a cup of water on the table next to the bed. Doing this she whispered in her language, "Tara, Queen of the Gods, Mother of the Earth, your power I invoke. Although I've promised to protect your greatest mystery, I beg you to allow me just one more time to save somebody. I owe this woman a lot and could not bear to stand back and watch her die. Please forgive me."

Only when Guadalupe helped her to support the patient to assist the abbess in swallowing the rescuing liquid was Iriomé was aware of her presence. She had not noticed that her friend had stayed. But her eyes, which confirmed the promise she had given moons ago, reassured her.

After the abbess had fallen back to her bed, the two young women looked at each other in wordless agreement. Then they both sat on the edge of the bed and waited. Outside the door, they heard some of the nuns pacing about restlessly, but none dared to open the door. They were too afraid of the tall strawberry-blonde woman.

Time and again Guadalupe dabbed cold sweat from her foster mother's forehead. It looked to Iriomé as if she counted each of Madre Teresa's breaths. She remembered Tichiname, whose heart had stopped beating in her arms. The medicine woman had used amakuna to save someone from death only once. She obviously had known that the disclosure of the secret would only result in suffering and fighting. But it was impossible for Iriomé to let a person die when she could prevent it. Especially someone who had been as kind to her as the abbess had. After all, she had already enabled Cold Eye, whom she hated more than anything else in this world, and a woman she did not even know to have a new life.

"I think she is doing a little better," Guadalupe said, interrupting these thoughts. She felt the pulse of the patient, whose cheeks had already become a little rosier. Slowly she began to breathe regularly like a sleeping person. Guadalupe reached for Iriomé's hand and squeezed it.

༒

The pitiful screams of a kid were echoing through the pink dawn. Iriomé had gotten it from the shepherd who let his flock graze behind the monastery walls in exchange for an antirheumatic drug for his wife and cough medicine for his children.

She sat in the middle of a small stone circle in front of her hermitage soothing with soft vocals and gentle stroking the quivering animal. Trustfully it stretched out beside her and did not bat an eye as she cut through its throat with a knife.

While she caught the gushing blood from the wound in a clay pot, she whispered in her language, "Tara, Great Mother and Goddess of the Earth, I thank you for the special gift that you have given the harimaguadas. And I swear solemnly to use amakuna from now on only on the shortest day of the year to connect me with the ancestors. Take this as an excuse and as a sacrifice for your mercy."

Iriomé poured the fresh blood in the center of the circle, let a light tone resound from her throat, and lifted her arms to the sky while the dry soil greedily soaked up the red juice. At that moment she felt she was back on her home island again in the days when she had lived with Tichiname and the other harimaguadas in the cave shrine. When she still believed in a happy and safe future.

A short scream brought her abruptly back. At the edge of the forest was an early visitor who was staring at her.

Joaquín.

He seemed stunned. His face expressed horror, disgust, and fear. Even across the distance she felt that he never would be able to stand up to her energy. That he never would be able to love her unconditionally, at least not in difficult times. That he never would recognize her feminine power, let alone appreciate it.

With a jerk, he turned around and ran away, as if a demon was on his heels.

"Akin, stay!" Iriomé shouted after him. He actually stopped. She lifted her dress, rose heavily, and ran up to him.

He did not come to meet her one single step. In his eyes was fear, and when she wanted to take his hand, he withdrew it. "I have thanked my goddess," she tried to explain.

"You've worshipped the devil," he managed to stammer through clenched teeth. "De Lugo and Frai Hieronymus are right. You're a witch. I've been under your spell. By a hair's breadth, I would have been lost."

"Why did you come back so quickly?" Iriomé asked in a trembling voice.

"Do you really want to know?" He laughed out loud. "I stole away from the wedding preparations to hide here, and as soon as the child was born and fit for travelling, to go away with you from here. But God has saved me in the last moment from this stupidity." He went off to his horse tied around a tree without looking at her again.

Iriomé felt a stabbing pain. She called Akin's name, but he had already swung onto the saddle and spurred his horse. He did not hear her—or did not want to hear her any longer.

Desperate, her face contorted by pain, Iriomé dragged herself back to the hermitage and lay down on her fur bed. The time had come. The child that had grown in her urged to see the light of day. She grabbed a clay pot in which Guadalupe had prepared a decoction from the young, green flowers of the wormwood for her and sipped it. Contractions were coming at long intervals, and there was enough time to put out all she needed to survive the birth without anybody's help. But the pain was becoming stronger and nearly drove her out of her mind. She again yelled out for Joaquín and Guadalupe, but nobody heard her cry for help. A warm liquid was running down between her legs. Iriomé went to her knees, squatted on the ground as she learned from the women of her tribe, and pressed as hard as she could. But nothing happened. The child in her did not move.

It seemed to her as if he did not want to see this world. As if he clung to the inner walls of her belly in order to resist the force of the labor pains. Again she was attacked by unbearable waves of pain, and again she pressed. Yet nothing happened. She dragged herself to the door and cried out her pain. Only an owl answered.

The picture of the woman in the dirty hut came to her mind. What if her child lay upside down? It would suffocate without help and she herself bleed to death. The next contraction took her with all its might, and she felt carried away by roaring surf into the realm of the souls. She had just enough strength to open the medallion and lay a few grains of the powder on her tongue. Then everything around her dissolved into darkness.

Chapter 27

"Romy, Romy!"

She looked into Nic's anxious dark eyes and heard his warm voice.

"Thank God, she's regained consciousness."

Romy perceived the scent of aromatic herbs, the essential oils of which were showing her the way to the present time. Sister Felicitas was holding an herb bag under her nose. "Take a deep breath," she said in a deep voice and stroked the hair from Romy's forehead.

Very little time seemed to have actually passed because she was still lying just outside of the ruined hermitage.

"How are you feeling?" asked Nic, who sat next to her on the ground, her head cradled in his lap.

She could not speak. What could she say? That she had just been in mortal agony giving birth in a previous incarnation?

"You've been out cold the last ten minutes," he remarked, worried. "And you screamed as if you had severe pain. Do you feel any pain now?"

She shook her head. "No, I'm fine." This was not true. Iriomé and her pain were literally in her bones, and not only there. When trying to sit up, she was dizzy, and she had to hold on to Nic. He picked her up unceremoniously and carried her back to the monastery.

It was a comforting feeling, and she wished secretly this walk would never end. Joaquín had simply cut and run. The young Spaniard had, in the moment when Iriomé needed him most, taken to his heels like an idiot.

"We'll take care of her; don't worry," she heard Sister Felicitas say as she walked in front of Nic and guided him into a small but bright and friendly room.

He put Romy on a white bed and took her hand. "Get some rest. The doctor has already been sent for. He'll be here at any moment."

"I don't need a doctor," whispered Romy. "Definitely not. I'm fine. Just a little dizzy spell."

"The doctor will determine this, *mi amor*," said Nic.

My love. His words and especially the way he had said them went right through her. She suddenly felt the urgent need to tell Nic everything; to lay Iriomé's feelings and thoughts out before him. To tell him of her strength and at the same time the helplessness which she felt toward Joaquín and the iron men. Perhaps this monastery, where the smell of the past still hung in all nooks and corners, was the right place for it. She was about to ask Sister Felicitas to leave them alone for a moment when Nic spoke.

"I've received an important call and unfortunately must immediately drive back to Marbella. I'm very sorry. I'd rather stay here with you. But as soon as you feel better, Sister Felicitas will call me. Then somebody will pick you up."

Romy nodded, disappointed. Although she was not in mortal danger, he must have felt how upset she was and that she wanted to talk to him. Instead he squeezed her hand, pressed a kiss on it, and disappeared. Only the subtle sandalwood aroma of his aftershave stayed.

Sister Felicitas noticed Romy's disappointment and looked at her encouragingly. "You shouldn't be angry with him. I don't think he wanted to hurt you."

The doctor, a friendly elderly gentleman who arrived shortly afterward, diagnosed temporary circulatory disorder, gave Romy an injection, and prescribed bed rest and especially sleep. Sister Felicitas in the meantime brought her a tea made from amber, which Romy sipped. The nun saw the doctor out and then came back and sat on Romy's bedside. "May I ask you something?"

Romy nodded.

"When you were unconscious, you breathed, pressed, and screamed as if you delivered a child. I've previously worked on the maternity ward and have assisted in a lot of births there. Could it be that you're pregnant? Or are afraid to be pregnant?"

Romy shook her head. She could not possibly tell the nun about Iriomé. As far as she knew, Christianity had little to do with reincarnation. Though Jesus rose from the dead, this was only reserved for him. Normal Christians lived only once and then went to heaven or hell, depending on the life they had led. And ancestor cults, psychotropic mushrooms, and voyages to other dimensions were certainly not Sister Felicitas's cup of tea.

Moreover, the fewer people that knew about amakuna the better. Hattinger was already dead. The mushroom caused as much damage in Romy's life as in Iriomé's: she had put the médico in a situation that had almost cost his life and was responsible for his mother's death; Guayafanta died under torture; and Guadalupe and the abbess probably already had one foot on the stake.

No, Romy would not tell Sister Felicitas. It was better this way.

"You're sure you're not pregnant?" the sister asked again. "Some women have such great fear of childbirth that they have terrible visions well before their time."

Perhaps the sister is not mistaken, Romy thought. That night on the ship no time was wasted on a thought of contraception; she was not on the pill. As soon as she found a pharmacy, she would get a pregnancy test.

"I am doing quite well already," she said, to wipe away the concern from the face of the nice sister.

Suddenly she had an idea: did Sister Felicitas have something to do with Guadalupe? But she quickly dropped this. Not every person she met must necessarily be entangled with the past, although the benevolence and spontaneous sympathy reminded Romy very much of Guadalupe. "I'll just sleep for a while, and you'll see when I wake, I'll feel like a new person."

Sister Felicitas smiled unfathomably. "How good that we're always given this chance again." She stroked her hair and then let her alone. Romy looked at her in amazement but then was overcome by fatigue; the injection took effect.

When she was woken by bright female voices coming into her room through the half-open window, she had slept almost twenty-four hours. And she indeed felt like a new woman. Her clothes hung neatly over a chair so that Romy only needed to slip into them.

It was cold outside, although the wintery midday sun bathed the cloister in bright light. Curious, she followed the sacred sounds and walked through a portal that was left ajar into the church. The chant gave her the shivers—normally Romy was not particularly fond of this kind of music, but this morning the clear voices of the nuns touched her more than her favorite singer. She sat on a wooden bench in the last row and closed her eyes. Certainly Iriomé had also sat here now and then. Romy still could not quite believe that she had ended up in exactly the same monastery where the Guanche woman found refuge more than five hundred years ago and had given birth to her child.

She agreed with Thea. There was indeed something to heal. The story between Joaquín and Iriomé begged for it. Though the young conde had not delivered his beloved to his friend de Lugo, Romy wasn't sure he would really be on Iriomé's side if worse came to worst. Were men of his sort capable of love at all? Had anything changed? Was Nic capable of love?

"How are you feeling?" Sister Felicitas, who had sat down beside her unnoticed, whispered in her ear.

"Thanks for asking. The sleep was good for me, just as I told you," Romy said also in a whisper.

"I'm glad to hear that," the nun said, taking her hand.

"Señor Saratoga called. His driver's already on his way to pick you up and take you back to Marbella."

Romy took a deep breath. Actually, she enjoyed being here. She would have preferred to stay in the monastery, as Iriomé had, and become friends with Sister Felicitas. But another task awaited her. She had to find out whether she could trust Nic and with him get amakuna on the right track. Or if he, like Joaquín, ultimately was only concerned with his own interests, respective to the interests of those in power.

⁓

Nic's driver as well as Romy's personal babysitter—properly dressed in a two-piece suit and with an earpiece—both kept an eye on her the whole way back to Marbella. They seemed to have received strict instructions from Borges. Neither of them felt obliged to speak to her. Romy felt more like a prisoner than someone who should be protected. However, the longer the journey took and the more she thought about Joaquín and his obligations toward his family, the more her suspicions grew. She tried to remember everything she had lived through with Iriomé, while outside the barren landscape of the Extremadura was rolling past.

Amakuna connects the fate of all those who have ever taken it for all eternity in a chain that never breaks, Tanausú had explained to Iriomé shortly before his death. Her worst enemy had been de Lugo, who had stopped at nothing to get the magic potion. But who in Romy's life could be this enemy? He must be responsible for killing Hattinger. Perhaps it was this Gerald Forster, major shareholder of the world company Forster's Health, Nic's boss, and at the same time his father-in-law? Was he connected to Nic by a similar history of guilt as Cold Eye to Joaquín? Did he use Nic the way de Lugo had used Joaquín for his own purposes?

If he got hold of the mushroom, the species of the iron men would certainly not die out, and the world might never heal. Thea's words had been pretty much the same. A company like Forster's Health would keep amakuna under lock and key and sell the mushroom, if at all, only to the richest of the rich at an exorbitant price. The rest of the world would have to content themselves with the remaining overpriced, underperforming drugs.

Tichiname told her pupil to preserve amakuna's secret until humanity was free of greed and abuse of power. It was obvious that the world was clearly not ripe for amakuna. What should she do now? How should she act toward Nic?

As the Jaguar drove up the driveway to the castillo, he was already waiting at the entrance. He opened the door for Romy and helped her getting out of the car. "You look a lot better," he said with a velvety voice and put his arm around her shoulders while he showed her in.

Romy enjoyed his touch, even if she wished this was not the case. She had to constantly remind herself that Nic was one of the iron men. At least the setting helped. Here in the shadow of his stronghold what in the monastery she had perceived as closeness started to fade.

"I can't tell you how glad I am to see you well again," he said as they climbed the grand staircase. "If you're not too tired from the journey, I'd like to show you something in the library up here."

"No problem," said Romy, who after a twenty-four-hour sleep felt fit as rarely before.

The *Liber Herbarum Medicinarum* was presented in the middle of the room on a large table. The large-sized parchment pages were bound in a thick leather binding. Nic smiled at Romy invitingly. She felt a lump forming in her throat. A slight dizziness came over her, so that she clung to the edge of the table.

Nic looked at her searchingly. "Everything okay?"

Romy nodded and gazed raptly at the first page as she opened it. There it was written. The ink was slightly faded, but the words were still legible:

> *Para mi mejor amiga I.,*
> *que se convirtió en mi hermana y*
> *gracias a su conocimiento este*
> *libro podría ser realizado.*

"For my dearest friend I., who became my sister and thanks to whose knowledge this work could be written," whispered Romy. Tears ran down her cheeks. With this she not only had further evidence of Iriomé's existence but also the proof that all that she had experienced on her travels into the past had actually happened.

Nic got out a white handkerchief and handed it to her. "What's wrong?"

"Oh, nothing. It's just such a beautiful book." She just could not bring herself to tell him what moved her so much.

"I want you to have it," Romy heard his voice as from afar. "It could become a good basis for our common project. Monastic medicine is becoming more and more popular. A few years ago in Germany there was a real Hildegard von Bingen boom. This should be possible in Catholic Spain or in South America, too."

Romy couldn't believe her ears. *Our common project. Monastic medicine.* Did he really mean it, or did he just want to take her in, in order to tie her even closer to him than he already had?

It was terrible. Whenever her suspiciousness toward him grew, he did or said something which gave her new hope. Could he read her mind? Or know much more than he showed?

While she turned the large-format pages in awe, suddenly, with a loud noise, the double doors of the library flew open and a blonde Barbie doll in a tight-fitting haute couture costume teetered in on high heels. She flung her arms around Nic's neck and kissed his cheeks.

"Darling, Dad lent me his jet. Unfortunately the air traffic controllers in Madrid were on strike and only three hours ago condescended to give up. Of course I'd have liked to accompany you to Khalifa Bin Kayid, but I see you've quickly found a substitute." She smiled benevolently at Romy. "I've already heard a lot about you. It's an extraordinary discovery you've made. A mushroom that cures cancer. Impressive! After all, the world has been ready for this for a long time."

She held out a hand to Romy while holding on to Nic with the other. "Jennifer Saratoga."

"Romy Conrad," Romy replied huskily.

"And did you already sleep together?" she continued in the same conversational tone. "Nic prefers blondes. You're exactly his type. I unfortunately need a little help." She shook her blonde-colored curls.

Romy stared at her as if she were a creature from another planet.

"My dear, don't look at me so shocked. These days it's the most normal thing in the world when two people are attracted to each other."

"Jennifer, please!" Nic interrupted her flow of words.

She shrugged. "By the way, you don't need to worry. I'm resigned to the fact that I'm married to a born conquistador and am no longer jealous."

"That's enough." Nic shook off Jennifer's hand.

Jennifer made a face. "You're so mean!"

"Take a nap, and don't come back until you're sober," he said, shoving her out unceremoniously.

Romy saw how embarrassed Nic felt. And for his sake she did not immediately leave the library as she wanted to.

"I'm so sorry," he said, pulling her to him.

Romy pushed him away. "I thought I was in the highest danger, and now obviously every Tom, Dick, and Harry already knows about the mushroom," she hurled at him. "I might as well have put the story on the internet." It took all her strength not to go berserk.

"My wife's not just anybody."

"I'm sorry. How could I have missed that?" Romy took a deep breath. "She's the daughter of your boss. Silly me! I want to leave right away. It was a big mistake to come here. Please call a taxi to take me to the airport."

"Romy, please stay," he said in an urgent voice.

But she no longer heard him. How could she have trusted this man even for a minute? All this talk of danger to her life, of working together. He only wanted to talk her into telling him, in a weak moment, where amakuna grew. This was his main concern. She ran to her room, preemptively called herself a taxi on her cell phone and threw her things hastily into her bag. However, when she was sprinting across the entrance hall to the outside with her bag over her shoulder, all she saw were the taillights of the taxi.

Antonio Borges came to meet her with a false smile. "At the moment your trip is off, Doctor."

"I beg your pardon?"

He grabbed her arm and forced her to put down her bag.

"Let go of me!"

"Sure, if you return to your room."

Romy glared at him, rubbing her arm. "You must be out of your mind. I'm not your prisoner!"

"Think of it as a kind of protective custody," he grinned. "I actually have bad news for you. So you will hopefully understand why I can't let you go."

Romy was stunned. They could not keep her here against her will. These were not the Dark Ages.

"Your boss, Hannes Berger, was killed this morning at a classic car rally in Hungary. He wanted to cross the Danube in a swimming jeep from World War II, drifted off, and drowned. This shows how quickly an accident can happen."

Romy froze. What a nightmare! Was there no end to it? First Hattinger, now Berger. *What have I done?* Her stomach revolted, her head was throbbing. She was unable to think clearly. *Who will be next?* She prayed that Thea was safe. The rumbling in her head grew louder, her heart began to race, and an agonizing nausea overcame her. Beads of sweat formed on her forehead, though she shivered. The claw of fear was reaching out for her with all its might. Without Borges having to ask again, she fled back to her room. For nothing in the world would she have compromised herself by fighting a panic attack in his presence.

Adrenaline was rushing through her veins; her throat became tight. A strong dizziness came over her. She had to hold on to the column of the canopy bed to avoid falling over. Romy forced herself to breathe regularly. In, out, in, out. Slowly, she regained her composure and was able to think straight again. Berger definitely had not drowned by accident.

But if he had been murdered, who might be behind it and why? Maybe he had tried to sell the mushroom, which he did not actually possess, to a competitor in order to prevent the takeover of Biotex by Forster's Health? Was this the reason he had to die? One more confidant gone. That's how Nic had put it when Hattinger was killed. Or was Nic behind it after all?

Or was it Tanausú? Perhaps as a holy warrior he considered it his duty to protect the mushroom against today's conquistadors. They said he already had several deaths on his conscience. But the Guanches only killed in self-defense; at least that had been the case five hundred years ago.

Romy breathed deeply. The attack seemed to be over. She went into the bathroom, splashed cold water on her face, and ran her fingers through her hair. She was done with this house. Someone had to get her out of here. She pulled her cell phone from her pocket, but not even 112, the Europe-wide emergency number, still worked. The house seemed deserted and shielded from the rest of the world. Borges probably still guarded the entrance gate like Cerberus.

Desperate, she went back to her room and turned on the computer, but the internet had gone dead, too. She felt completely helpless, like a bird in a golden cage. A view from the barred window increased her hopelessness. Even if she could squeeze through the bars, the smooth sandstone offered no chance, even for a practiced climber like her, to reach the ground safely.

What would they do with her? Torture her until she told them where the mushroom grew? Romy thought in horror of de Lugo and Guayafanta. Tears welled up in her eyes. What should she do now? What would Iriomé have done? She wished she had the strength of the Guanche woman, who had jumped bravely into the cold Atlantic to save amakuna from the conquistadors, while she allowed herself to be lured into a love trap like a naive teenager.

Self-blame, helplessness, and exhaustion made her sink into a fitful doze. She did not know how much time had passed when there was a knock on the door, and Jennifer Saratoga stuck her head in. "Can you spare a little minute for me?"

Romy sat up.

"Oh my God! Have you been crying?" The American sat next to her on the edge of the bed. She had changed her clothes and now wore designer jeans and a tight designer sweater, which emphasized her designer bust.

"I want to apologize to you," she said. "I just don't know what's wrong with me sometimes. Life at Nic's side is not always easy, you see. We have something like an open marriage." She stroked Romy's forearm. "Nic's not even capable of what you might consider romantic love. Neither am I. We were both raised to preserve at all costs what our parents and the generations before them created. Everything else is secondary for us. Nic is, in this respect, even more unscrupulous than I, but he's 100 percent reliable and loyal to his friends. And you're one of them, even if you haven't known him for a long time."

"Why are you telling me this, Mrs. Saratoga?" Romy asked, moving away from her a little bit.

"To my friends, I'm Jen," Jennifer said and held out her hand to Romy.

Although Romy by no means regarded herself as a friend of "Jen," she took it.

"I'm telling you because I want to make it clear to you that you'll miss a great chance if you simply run away now. Forster's Health will offer you all that a young scientist can only dream of. Your own laboratory and unlimited financial support."

"I know."

Jennifer put on the smile of a woman who was used to having her own way. "But have you really thought about what that would mean for you? Total independence and at the same time a safe job. No cheap car that won't start in winter, no cold two-room apartment in Augsburg. Rather, a company car and a villa at the Costa del Sol or at any other place of your choosing. Hawaii, Miami, Acapulco, wherever . . ."

"And for that I'd have to cede amakuna to Forster's Health?" Romy blurted out, no longer surprised that Jennifer obviously knew all the details of her life.

"What would be the alternative?" Jennifer replied in a buddylike tone. "You'd be on the run for the rest of your life, and somebody would find you sooner or later. With Forster's Health you'd have a career and especially security—both personal and professional."

Romy didn't know what to think. All she knew was that the noose was slowly tightening, and she could do nothing about it right now. "Perhaps you're right," she said in an attempt to play for time. "But it's not so easy to turn one's life upside down at a moment's notice."

Jennifer beamed at her. "I understand that. What if we begin with a little shopping tour of Marbella?"

"Unfortunately, I lack the wherewithal for this," Romy said.

"Oh, come on. It would make me so happy to treat you to shopping." Jennifer put her arm around Romy's shoulders. "In pairs it's much more fun."

Chapter 28

The narrow, winding streets and alleys of the old town of Marbella formed a confusing maze with upscale shops, restaurants, and bars. Bougainvillea and geranium were abundantly growing between the wrought-iron window grilles and balconies of the whitewashed two-story houses. Romy's glance took in the wall of the well-preserved Moorish castle as she searched for an escape route. But the two body-guards Borges had sent with them did not let Jen or Romy out of sight for a single second.

Nic's wife dragged Romy into every boutique and persuaded her to try on outrageously expensive clothes. She seemed to really have a knack for it; the noble rags she chose for Romy invariably looked beautiful on her.

Romy felt awful, as if she had already sold her soul to the devil. How could she ever escape from this dilemma? She was already up to her neck in it.

"This is perfect for you," cried Jennifer, when they entered a Jil Sander shop. She pointed to a tight-fitting straight-cut dress of a dark green color displayed in the shop window, an exclusive single piece. "It matches the color of your eyes exactly."

And it was also exactly the color of the dress in which Iriomé had fled from Trujillo, Romy registered in astonishment. She shook her head, but even the saleswoman was insistent that she try it on. She pulled Romy against her will in the direction of the changing rooms.

"Please come with me," she said in an almost imploring tone. She unlocked one of the doors covered with cloth and shoved Romy in.

She was face to face with a pair of deep blue eyes!

"Sit down. We don't have much time," whispered Tanausú.

"You're here?" Romy was stunned. "How did you know that I . . ."

"I need to talk to you. Urgently," he interrupted her. "And we don't have much time."

"How is Thea?"

"She's safe, unlike you. I'll help you get out of here."

"Thank you." Romy composed herself slowly. "But first I need to know what role you're playing."

"Well, you know."

"Yes, but I lack some context." Romy tried to stay calm, even though he clearly perceived her inner tension.

"For ages I've had my hiding place at La Palma, where nobody could find me," he said softly. "When I heard that those mummies had been found in the caldera, I went there on my own during the winter solstice and encountered the mushroom, just as you did. Only one year before you."

"Then it was you who closed the grave?"

"So that no one else would come across it."

"And then you consumed amakuna!"

He nodded.

"And thus traveled into the past?"

"And into the future."

Romy stared at him; then it dawned on her. "The fall in the Karwendel Mountains?"

He nodded. "I foresaw your accident. But because I mustn't interfere with your destiny, all that remained was the mushroom." Romy looked at the strong man in the threadbare military jacket, speechless.

"I've sworn to take care of you," he said huskily. "Forever!"

She swallowed. Even though everything seemed to make sense now, she had to digest all this. She began to realize what it meant for her. Finally she was no longer alone with this incredible story. At last she had found her soul brother in the true sense of the word. She saw

Tanausú being chained to the mast of the caravel in her mind's eye and could not do anything else but fall into his arms. He held her tightly. And Romy would have stayed in his arms forever.

Jennifer's slightly squeaky voice interrupted this special moment. "So? Does the dress fit? I'm convinced you look stunning in it."

"Please, give me just a minute," Romy called back, trying to sound as calm as possible. "What's your plan?" she whispered to Tanausú.

"Forster's Health will not give up easily. And they don't even know yet that the mushroom not only cures cancer but all diseases."

"But how are we supposed to cope with such a powerful company?"

"You've been entrusted with this task. That's why it's on you—and you're also the one who can handle it."

"Who has Hattinger and Berger on his conscience?"

He handed her a CD in a transparent cover. "Here you'll find all machinations and deals that Forster's Health recently made. I'm working closely with Medical Transparency, a volunteer organization that uncovers filth in the pharmaceutical sector and has had it in for Forster's for a long time. They've prevented the approval of Avistan. And they got me the security job at Biotex."

"So *you* actually stole my samples and records."

"Brought them to a safe place, Romy. I'm also responsible for the break-in at your house. Ricardo told me that you possessed a map to the cave."

Romy took the CD and put it in her purse.

"Come back here in three days. I'll prepare everything for your escape. I've told the saleswoman about a romantic love story between the two of us that your family wants to prevent."

Romy smiled. "Has there been one? Did something escape me in the past?"

He shook his head. "You were a harimaguada and thus taboo for all men of our people."

"And why didn't you tell me all this when we first met?" asked Romy. "In the Karwendel Mountains or later in the lab?"

"Because you would have never believed me then."

He's probably right, thought Romy. She found it difficult even now, although she had traveled into the past three times, and the analogies were undeniable.

"*Hasta pronto*, see you soon." He opened the window and climbed nimbly onto the window sill. Then he disappeared like a cat behind the garbage cans in the courtyard.

As Romy watched him, she was reminded of the old Guanche legend about the guerrero sagrado, who reincarnates time and again to fight for the good. That she would come across him in the changing room of Jil Sander's, however, she had not expected. Nevertheless, all he said made sense. The many different pieces of the puzzle slowly added up to a picture, albeit one that was still far from being whole.

Seconds later, Jennifer stormed into the dressing room. "You haven't even put on the dress," she squeaked, disappointed.

"Excuse me, I felt a little bit dizzy and needed fresh air, but it's better now," Romy said, while she closed the window.

"Oh, I'm sorry. You're really looking a bit pale."

It's no wonder, thought Romy while taking off her shoes, sweatshirt, and jeans.

Jennifer helped her into the expensive dress and buttoned it up on the back. Then she danced enthusiastically around Romy. "Wow, you look great. The dress suits you, as if you were born in it."

"Maybe it's a little bit too long," said the saleswoman, who had joined them. "We could alter it, and you could pick it up in three days."

"That would be nice," said Romy.

"Can't you get it done any faster?" Jennifer asked, a little annoyed.

"I'm afraid not. I'm sorry," the saleswoman replied firmly and winked at Romy furtively.

৩৩

Romy excused herself from dinner due to not feeling well. And that was not even a lie. Her head was spinning. She could hardly distinguish between legend and reality, past and present, any longer. It hurt having to give up a man like Nic. But did she have a choice if she wanted to prevent the past from repeating itself?

Another option would be to change fortune, win Nic over to her side, and with his help hit back at the pharmaceutical companies. But would that even be possible? Iriomé had failed to change Joaquín. He had misjudged her, had not even listened to her when she wanted to explain herself.

Romy found it hard to imagine that the Guanche woman and Joaquín had ever been reunited.

In any case, she needed to look at the contents of the CD still hidden in her bag. Was it possible they had installed hidden cameras in her room? Systematically she searched every corner. Above the bed, in the lamp, around the Greek marble goddess in the bathroom, and behind the curtain rod. But she could not discover anything. Having made sure the door was shut, she took the CD from its cover and inserted it into her laptop. It took a while for the list of contents, which was arranged in chronological order, to open.

The first file described the company's history, which began in 1980 with the conversion of Forster's Health into a corporation, the last one was titled with Acquisition of Biotex, Germany. Romy opened it first.

She skimmed through a very personal characterization of Hannes Berger. *Ambitious, but not very cooperative. Tends to overestimate himself. Does not identify with Forster's Health. He clearly lacks a sense of humility toward the hand that feeds him.* When she read this, she almost took a liking to him. He wanted to keep his company and had offered Nic the mushroom for compensation.

But what she then read took her breath away. *Hannes Berger requires final solution after February.* Romy suddenly felt sick. Her stomach turned and the prawn cocktail she and Jennifer had eaten after their shopping trip was searching its way upward. She just made it to the toilet.

After she had rinsed her mouth with water and collected herself, she sat down again in front of the laptop and opened the next file with the headline Action Plan Avistan/European Market. This was about the application for the approval of Avistan with the European Medicines Agency in London. The German approval body had rejected the first request, whereupon the company tried it in London. Romy found the complete profiles of the key decision makers of the EMA, the European Medicines Agency for Drugs, containing their sexual preferences, their hobbies, their affairs, including their illegitimate children. All this information was needed for bribery or blackmail. If Forster's Health carried through the admission there, the pharmaceutical company had a good chance to still score a world best seller with Avistan. She found a memo from Berger to the EMA in which he explicitly pointed out the side effects of Avistan and explained that he had stopped the study for the time being.

Romy leaned back. Was this the reason he had had to die? Perhaps his death only indirectly had to do with the mushroom. She felt somewhat relieved at the thought.

Under the title Further Measures she discovered a file named Infiltration of Self-Help Groups with a complete list of European cancer support groups into which employees of Forster's Health would be introduced as patients to praise Avistan as the new wonder drug, which allegedly had already helped them considerably.

How deceitful and how shameless! Romy thought of Thea, her despair, and how much she had clutched at each straw in her seemingly hopeless situation. As her closest friend Romy had been no less desperate and had even persuaded her to have a go at Avistan.

The next file consisted of a list of top-ranking doctors who should present Avistan at medical congresses worldwide. Among them Romy found the name of Professor Hattinger with the remark *no longer available* added in parentheses. Romy swallowed. That Hattinger had been involved with Forster's was unexpected.

This CD was highly dangerous. She wondered what would happen if Forster's Health learned that it was in her possession. However, there was no reference to any author or distributor. It was a mere text file, and it was questionable whether it was of any legal value at all.

At that moment the phone beside her bed rang. Romy answered hesitantly. It was Esmeralda. She sounded worried. "Could you please come quickly to Señor Saratoga's office? He's not well. You're a doctor, aren't you? The Señora has just left for the city again."

"I'll be right there," said Romy and hung up the phone.

What was the matter with Nic? Her heart was beating fast as she hurried through the endless corridors to his study. He was lying with his eyes closed on the Chinese silk carpet in front of his desk, arms and legs outstretched in an unnatural way, his face completely distorted. She called his name, but he did not respond. His breathing was fitful and he wheezed. The Doctor Conrad part of her brain overtook the Romy part of her heart: *generalized tonic-clonic seizures, unresponsive, could be an epileptic seizure. Or poisoning? Hmmm . . . a panic attack? Intracranial pressure symptoms, a tumor?* No, she did not want to admit this possibility.

Esmeralda had placed a pillow under his head. His face was deathly pale, despite his natural tan. "I've already called his doctor, but he's stuck in traffic. The highway to Marbella is closed to traffic in this direction due to construction," chattered the maid nervously.

Romy tried to stay calm and checked Nic's pulse, but it was relatively normal. "Has he had attacks like this before?" she asked Esmeralda insistently.

She hemmed and hawed a bit, then nodded. "The Señor has forbidden me to talk about it."

"How often?" Romy asked.

"Surely four or five times already. But this time it has stayed quite a long time, so I called you. Please don't tell him that I let you know."

Acute poisoning was out. "No, no," Romy reassured her, putting Nic's head in her lap and stroking his hair gently.

The maid looked at her anxiously. "Is it very bad?" she whispered.

Romy didn't answer. She had to admit that Nic was closer to her than a normal patient and that in this moment she wished nothing more than to be able to give Esmeralda a negative answer. "I don't know," she finally said. "I don't have the ability to examine him thoroughly here."

Slowly Nic relaxed as the spasms subsided. After a few minutes he opened his eyes but was still disoriented.

Esmeralda crossed herself. "*Gracias a Diós,* thank God. Shall I fetch him a glass of water?"

Romy nodded. "Yes, please."

Carefully Nic was trying sit up. His gaze found hers, and slowly he seemed to realize his situation. "First you, now me," he muttered.

"Are you in pain?" Romy asked softly.

He pointed to his head. "I'm terribly sick."

When he tried to sit up farther, Romy stopped him. "Take it easy. First you tell me what you see when I move my finger. Okay?" She held a finger in front of his eyes and then changed its position slightly to the right and to the left.

He answered her obediently like a child that wanted to make no mistakes. On the left side his field of vision was clearly limited. This suggested that something was squeezing on the optic nerve.

"*Buenas tardes*, I'm sorry, but I couldn't make it earlier," a male voice interrupted them. Esmeralda showed in a small, corpulent man in a dark blue suit.

"*Buenas tardes,*" Romy greeted back. "You're Nic's doctor, I suppose?" She stood up and held out her hand. "Romy Conrad. Here's your patient! He is already reasonably stable, but his view is significantly limited on the left. Is he an epileptic?"

"Doctor Cabrero," said the doctor, without answering her question. "Thank you very much for your help. Would you please leave us alone now?"

Romy glanced at Nic, who tried his irresistible smile. Thoughtfully, she headed back toward her room. Through one of the high, floor-length windows she saw one of the security people walking up and down in the garden. Perhaps she was kept prisoner for a completely different reason than she had believed up to now. Romy sat down in one of the window niches in the hallway. Could it be that Nic was seriously ill? Did he perhaps need the mushroom himself? *Please no,* she thought. That would make things even more complicated.

When she came back to her room, the next shock was already awaiting her. Antonio Borges sat in front of her laptop and had just unloaded the CD. "Sorry, but the door was open." He smiled at her deviously. "May I ask who gave you this CD?"

Romy was as red as a beetroot. She had negligently dropped everything and only thought of Nic. "You may," she said curtly. "But you won't get an answer."

Borges took off his glasses and looked at her like a professor at a slow-witted student. "It's not important," he said. "With this CD someone wanted to provide you with insight into the wheels of power. I'm only surprised that this someone thinks you're so naive that you would allow yourself to be manipulated by such banalities."

"Do you consider murder a banality?" Romy replied in a slightly trembling voice.

"Welcome to reality, Doctor. Your distinguished Professor Hattinger and your boss Berger unfortunately did not understand the difference between knowledge and power. Knowledge without power means nothing. Knowledge can even be dangerous, especially for the one who knows too much. He who wants to turn knowledge into power must himself change." His cold eyes looked at her searchingly. "Are you capable of such a metamorphosis, Doctor Conrad?"

Romy stared at him. "Does Nic know the contents of this CD?"

"No, he has more important things to deal with. And it should stay that way." He put the CD into the pocket of his jacket, almost tenderly took hold of her under the chin, and looked her straight in the eye. "Nic and you. This is a great opportunity. As far as I understand, both he and his wife mean very well for you. Moreover, Gerald Forster, the founder and main shareholder of Forster's Health, wants to make your acquaintance. You'll fly to Switzerland tomorrow morning; to Geneva for the annual press conference."

Romy took a deep breath. Now the time had come. She would finally set eyes on the mastermind of it all. The incarnation of evil, the slaughterer of the Guanches. Her hand clenched into a fist, which Borges registered, grinning.

"You should be on good terms with him," he said. "This will certainly contribute to your future career. And . . ." he made a significant pause," . . . would also be in the best interest of Nic."

"What's wrong with him?"

"You mean what just happened?" Borges gave her a condescending glance. "An epileptic seizure. You as a doctor surely diagnosed that immediately. He'll be sleeping for a few hours. Then he'll be fit as a fiddle again. Your plane leaves at nine a.m. And please don't cause any trouble. I wouldn't like to hurt Nic." Smiling, he left her room.

Romy would have liked to smash her laptop out of anger, but she stopped herself from doing it. It was important to keep a clear head. She needed to remember the power of the Guanche woman in her, which now had to be awoken.

⌒⌒

The European headquarters of Forster's Health was located on a plot right at Lake Geneva and was surrounded by high walls on the sides facing land.

A heavy iron gate opened as if by magic as the Jaguar drove up the driveway. Borges followed behind them in a dark Mercedes with two security guards.

Romy sat with Jennifer in the rear, Nic in the front next to the driver. He looked dazzling. Nothing remained of the attack the day before. Romy had had no opportunity to speak to him in private yet. Neither to ask him about his actual state of health nor to confront him with the facts on the CD. But probably he would appease her regarding his health and give her no honest answer regarding the CD.

"The press conference starts in half an hour," said Jennifer. "If you want, you can participate in it, then you can see my father in his element. For your own safety you'd better speak to no one. Journalists are a dangerous pack."

"Should I pretend I'm dumb?" Romy asked with an ironic undertone. She was immediately reminded of Iriomé, who had to act as Ibn Said's mute servant, though for very different reasons.

"Romy knows what she should do," Nic intervened, whereupon Jennifer only shrugged.

The car stopped in front of a pompous white Art Nouveau villa.

"I'll see you later," Nic said to Romy as they left the car. "Don't let yourself be impressed too much. It's only a big show."

The room where the press conference took place, probably in former times a kind of ballroom with crystal chandeliers and mahogany-paneled walls, was nearly filled to the last seat. Romy chose a chair by the window and admired the spectacular view of Lake Geneva and the snowcapped Alps. None of the others present seemed to be interested in her. Most journalists were either talking to each other or busied themselves with their electronic devices, except for a young, sporty guy in a leather jacket who had been watching her for a while and now was coming toward her.

"Michael Timm," he introduced himself. "I write for *Medical Journal*. And you?"

"I'm not a journalist."

"Right, now I remember. Don't you work at Biotex? We met last year at a conference in Baden-Baden with your boss Dr. Hannes Berger."

Romy could not remember the man, but he seemed to be quite friendly.

"You probably already know that he died in an accident yesterday. A tragic accident, indeed, but don't you find it remarkable that Professor Hattinger also died a few days ago? I mean, considering both had to do with the new miracle cure?"

Romy looked at him startled. "What do you mean?"

"Avistan. It's claimed to be the new mega best seller of Forster's

Health. And originally Hattinger was scheduled to speak here today. This stinks of foul play."

"I share your opinion." Romy took a deep breath. So Forster's Health had actually succeeded in convincing the registration authorities in London. Probably by bribery, like the action plan on the CD mapped out. Maybe she could make the journalist investigate these so-called accidents further. "I've got some interesting information for you," she began but was rudely interrupted at that same moment.

"May I ask you to go to your seat now? We'll start in a few minutes." Antonio Borges was standing beside her.

"See you later in the parking lot," she just managed to whisper to the journalist as the Argentine seized her by the arm and led her to one of the reserved chairs in the front row. "Are you mad? Do you want to be next?" Borges hissed in her ear.

Gritting her teeth, Romy sat on the assigned chair.

Two wood-paneled double doors opened, and *he* was entering the hall: Gerald Forster. Small, wiry, with cunning eyes. A bright orange tie under a dark blue suit. An iPad in one hand, he strode swiftly to the lectern. His entourage, all in white shirts and black suits, kept within a few steps distance. The hall instantly fell silent. The camera people standing at the end of the rows were getting ready.

Gerald Forster savored the excitement and like a general let his eyes wander over his army. He waited another few seconds before he gave a sign. The wall gave way to a huge LCD screen. Thereon appeared, accompanied by a Dolby Surround soundtrack, the three-dimensional, rotating golden logo of Forster's Health, an entwined capitalized H and a capitalized F on a stylized map of the world.

The Penguins, as Romy internally named the suits, sat on the podium. Forster paused, casually adjusted the microphone, and began to speak in a restrained, high voice and with a strong Texan accent.

"Every eighth woman is diagnosed with breast cancer today. Worldwide more than 200 billion euros are spent on cancer research annually. Often in vain. But Forster's Health will, in a few months, place on the market a new drug to treat breast cancer that will set new standards: Avistan. This will help us reach a higher goal worldwide: absolute market dominance in this therapeutic area. Forster's Health possesses a powerful sales army all over the world and will turn this new substance into a global success."

Romy could have screamed. But the sense of a piercing look kept her from doing so. When she turned, she looked directly into the cold eyes of Antonio Borges, sitting behind her.

"We will spend more money on further research, marketing, and distribution than any other pharmaceutical company," Gerald Forster continued.

One of the journalists raised his hand. "And what plans does Forster's Health have for the huge money avalanche that's now coming up to the company? Are you going to reduce drug prices in developing countries?"

A smile crossed the angular face of the president of the board. "We have two weeks till the main annual meeting of the shareholders. What do you think?"

Romy did not want to hear the answer. She just wanted to get out of here. Out of this place. Away from Forster and his army, which ruthlessly overrode all rules of decency, honesty, and humanity. And away from Borges, who hopefully would not dare to restrain her here in front of everybody.

In the hall she found an open door and ran down a narrow path that was clear of snow down to the lake. The fresh air was good and cooled down her heated temper. The worst thing to her was her own helplessness. And of course there was the thought of the helplessness of tens of thousands of cancer patients who would take Avistan into their veins despite its horrendous side effects and then die nevertheless.

When she turned around, she noticed someone was following her. But it was not one of Borges's bodyguards; it was Nic who was coming toward her at a quick pace.

Down by the lakeshore they sat down on a bench. For a while

neither spoke a word. Only the quacking of the ducks bustling around was to be heard. They did not look at each other; their warm breath mingled with the cold winter air.

Finally, she could not stand it any longer. "Avistan is still in development. And yet you push it onto the market," she gasped out.

"That was not my decision," Nic said quietly.

"But couldn't you prevent it? What do you owe Forster? Why don't you set boundaries? All that talk of herbal and monastic medicine is just ridiculous. You only wanted to curry favor with me." Romy felt all her pent-up rage threaten to come to a boil.

"That's not true!"

"What else could it be?" she shouted at him. "It's all about profit and about power and nothing else. You don't seriously believe that Forster's Health would make the mushroom available to all people!"

"Romy, we don't even know what effect the mushroom has yet," he said, trying to stay calm.

But I know it, thought Romy, who was, however, careful not to say it out loud.

"Let alone whether its active ingredient is reproducible so that a drug could actually be developed from it."

When he's right, he's right.

"You want to know what you've discovered, don't you? Maybe the mushroom gives you magical powers or even immortality." He chuckled, while a shiver ran down Romy's spine.

"Would you like to be immortal?" she asked him provocatively. He didn't take long to answer. "Yes, so that I can love you for all eternity."

She had not expected this answer. She took a deep breath to evaluate this. "What's the connection between you and Forster?" she asked, a bit more relaxed. "What do you owe him?"

"Nothing," he replied. "But feel free to form a view on him yourself. The press conference is over."

They went back to the villa, where the feeding of the hordes was in full swing. The journalists piled the finest dried beef, fine pastries, and savory cheeses onto their plates. The best delicacies French-Swiss cuisine had to offer served as a treat so that the bloodhounds dutifully wrote what suited Forster's Health.

"The buffet is the only reason they come here in such great numbers every year." Nic confirmed Romy's thoughts and led her through the crowd to the elevator, taking them up one floor.

Romy felt a little queasy. It seemed to her as if she had a rendezvous with the devil himself. Iriomé's fear of de Lugo became hers.

The elevator spat them out directly into a room with high windows, which caused the room to look a little like a medieval knights' hall. Heavy dark chairs ringed a table of at least thirty feet in length, at the head end of which Gerald Forster was sitting as if on a throne. The orange tie hung loosely around the open collar of his shirt; he was gazing at Romy with interest. He didn't seem unfriendly. Yet when he began to speak, it made the hairs on Romy's forearms stand on end.

"Too bad you didn't stay until the end, Dr. Conrad. The applause was gigantic. After all, it is a success for you as well," he began. Without a microphone his voice sounded rather soft, as was common with most people for whom it is not necessary to speak loudly because everyone was trying to hear anyway.

"I've not been involved in the development of Avistan," she replied politely. "I work at Biotex in the Department of Plant Research, and I just started this year. I'm surprised, however, that the drug was approved after it was rejected in Germany."

Forster still looked interested. Only a slight twitching of the corners of his mouth revealed some kind of reaction. "If we had not kept working hard on it, Dr. Conrad, it certainly wouldn't have been approved." He made a dismissive gesture. "But that's water under the bridge. Now that you have discovered this Canary mushroom, we're all very keen to learn more about it," he said in a fatherly tone. "I can assure you, we'll do everything in our power to support you in every respect. Now we only have to stipulate the details by contract. And as you will see, we'll support you handsomely." He laughed for the first time, a shrill kind of laughter that sounded artificial.

Forster seemed to be perfectly sure of his position and not to have the slightest doubt that Romy would kiss his feet if he demanded it of her. "This mushroom almost certainly can't be reproduced in the laboratory. And therefore is probably unsuitable for use as a cancer treatment," she said.

"Let's wait and see. Science has accomplished greater miracles." He smirked. "A carefree future lies ahead of you, Doctor." Forster looked at her with alert eyes. "How fortunate that Nic met you at the right time. Now you belong to us, to those who decide about the difference between life and death." He laughed as if he had made a joke, although he knew he had not.

Romy suddenly was no longer able to say a word. Sweat formed on her forehead, which no one seemed to notice. Her head began to pound, her heart raced, and she felt as if somebody was strangling her. She thought of Berger and was reminded of the little mouse in the face of the serpent that only waited for a single little movement to snap at it.

"When will you fly back to La Palma to get more rough material? I've heard your first research reports and the original samples were stolen from your lab."

"In the next few days," Nic answered for her.

"Very good!" Forster said. "We shouldn't waste any time, because whoever it was will not hesitate to profit from it himself. And then we would be left with nothing. I'd suggest you fly out tomorrow. From Málaga it's only a stone's throw to the Canaries. My son-in-law will be glad to accompany you."

"Of course," Nic said.

"Well, then, I think we've discussed everything. I wish you much success." The interested look vanished from his face, and he made a gesture with his hand as if he wanted to shoo an annoying fly.

Nic pushed her toward the elevator, which was waiting for them. Once the doors closed Romy managed to fend off the panic attack with focused breathing.

Nic looked at her, worried. "You can't stand him, right?"

Romy still could not speak, but she felt the pressure slowly subside in her head, and her heart calmed.

"He's someone who clearly pursues his principles and sticks to them despite all circumstances."

"You mean power principles," Romy said softly.

"What speaks against power? It is and has always been the only means to enforce something," said Nic.

"In one sense, yes, but there inevitably comes a time when power corrupts."

"That's not necessarily so. Unfortunately, power can lead to *absolute* power, which corrupts absolutely."

"Where's the difference?"

"The fact that becoming tyrannical, seeking absolute power, is not a given, and with power you can also do a lot of good."

Romy considered this for a moment before answering. "But then the power is transformed into love, isn't it!?" He did not give her a direct answer. Instead, he pressed the stop button, so that the elevator door did not open, although they had reached the ground floor. He cupped his hands gently around her face. "You're right, Romy. And honestly, love feels much better than power. Free. More relaxed. More familiar! But I haven't felt this feeling for a long time. A very long time. That's why it fills me with fear and joy at the same time."

She had the impression that the narrow elevator cabin was revolving around her. Was he finally opening his heart to her?

"Even if it seems completely unlikely to you at the moment, I love you. I want to marry you, even if that's still a very long way off. But you're the woman I could imagine changing my life for."

Romy could hardly believe his words. What he had just said meant a 180-degree turn. Had he finally returned to the long path they had already walked together once? Would he travel all the way down the path with her this time?

He kissed her. It was a different type of kiss than during their

passionate encounters. For the first time Romy felt peace and a deep
trust, and she found this at least as exciting as the sandstorms. She put
her head on his shoulder and closed her eyes for a moment.

I believe that it is the duty of all human beings to first awaken the
love in their own heart and then in the hearts of others. If people leave
no space in their lives for love, there will be quarrels and wars to the end
of time.

Iriomé was right, in spite of everything. Although her love for
Joaquín could not save her people, she had been on the right path. He
would have been the male partner who possessed enough power to preserve the mystery of the mushroom from the conquistadors. But he had
not been ready then. Perhaps because of his own circumstances, perhaps
because Iriomé had not trusted him completely in the end. *If I trust Nic*
today, will he be ready?

He looked deep into her eyes again before he released the stop button of the elevator. "It's a shame we didn't meet earlier. So much would
have been different in my life."

"Now's the right time," Romy answered and stepped outside.

"What do you mean?"

"Because we have to fulfill a common task," she replied.

"Nic, a journalist from *Spiegel* magazine wants to talk to you; would
you please come?" Jennifer, who was standing in front of the elevator
door, her face expressionless, took Nic by the arm. "Oh, I'm sorry to
have disturbed you two lovebirds, but this is a priority."

She dragged him along. Romy left the building and filled her lungs
with the cold winter air. Her panic attack was over. Nic's words had
sunk deep into her heart and filled it with happiness. The dark, impenetrable forest, as she often saw her future, had become lighter. Still, it
was only imbued with subtle sunrays, but soon it would glisten in a
golden light, and the power of love would resist any tyranny. Romy felt
an unusual strength growing in her, just as if she and Iriomé now shoul-
dered their common goal together. And for the first time in her life
she became aware of the heartfelt craving to return the love of a man.

Against all odds, against all the weaknesses and errors. Simply because he was destined for her.

Still deep in thought, she only noticed the journalist from the *Medical Journal* when he was standing right next to her. "Your guard's busy, maybe you can tell me more about your suspicion now," he whispered to her.

Romy looked around but saw only one bodyguard, who always kept an eye on her from a distance.

"The professor was killed," she whispered, "just as Hannes Berger. And almost certainly Forster's Health is behind these murders." She could not say more, because Borges had obviously been informed and immediately came rushing toward them.

"I'm sorry to disturb you again," said the Argentinean in a cutting tone. "But we need to leave for the airport." He took Romy's arm and pulled her more than escorted her to the car.

Romy would have liked to kick him in the balls.

"You don't think that the man is risking his life to publish your little girl's fantasies. One more such stunt and the two of us will have a serious problem," he hissed into her ear.

At that moment the scales fell from her eyes. It was not Gerald Forster who was pulling the strings, but Borges! He was the one who stopped at nothing, not even murder, and possessed the means to have it look like an accident. However, she was not sure whether he did it on behalf of Forster or on his own account. Whom should she fear more? He had the cold stare of de Lugo. Why had she not noticed this long ago?

She felt his greed and unscrupulousness almost physically. Once again she saw in her mind's eye pictures of the past as in slow motion: Iriomé administering him the powder, de Lugo killing the old mother of the médico and boasting in the ballroom of Trujillo that Guayafanta had been tortured to death. Even today he would not give up until the mushroom was in his hands.

൦൧

The flight back to Málaga was uneventful. By now Romy was almost used to jetting through Europe in a private plane. The pretty flight attendant brought her a pillow and a blanket so that she could make herself comfortable. Her life had changed completely. She felt like Cinderella after the fairy had waved her magic wand. Her hope to pursue this common task with Nic had grown. There only remained the question whether he knew about Borges's machinations. Romy suspected he might.

Romy was still completely lost in thought when Jennifer staggered down the aisle. In her hand she held what was at least her fifth gin and tonic, and she began to rant loudly against her father. "The old man is getting on my nerves," she slurred, in hopes someone would listen, and then sank into the vacant seat beside Romy. In doing so she spilled half of the glass on her white mohair sweater.

Romy pretended to be asleep.

"Well, you wouldn't know that," Jennifer shook Romy's arm. "My mother lives in a clinic in Marbella, and my father wants me to play messenger each time she needs to sign papers for the company."

Jennifer bumped into her, so Romy had no choice but to get into a conversation with her.

"What's the matter with your mom?" she asked politely.

The American tapped her forehead and grinned. "Depression, Alzheimer's, dementia. You name it."

Romy looked to Nic for help, but he was busy with papers and did not look over. Obviously he was accustomed to tuning out all that was going on around him.

"Hey, I'm talking to you!" Jennifer's face was so close to hers that Romy could smell the alcohol on her breath clearly.

"Sorry."

"Okay, then I'll go get me another drink. No one's interested in my life anyway."

Jennifer stood up and this time stumbled over Nic's legs, which were stretched out into the aisle. He withdrew them without even taking note of his wife. His back bent, he stared at his iPad with a look of concentration on his face, taking notes at the same time.

Romy watched him a long time and felt new doubts rise. Presumably, the wish for another life really existed somewhere deep in his heart. But wishing was not enough. Maybe she was something like a bridge into another life for him. But he would have to muster the strength and courage to actually go over this bridge. And that was exactly what she was not sure he had the fortitude to do.

∽

The next day, Romy stared in disbelief at the change of color on the pregnancy test she had bought on the way back from the monastery and carried around in her purse since. She had just peed on it, and within seconds it had become completely pink. She reread the instructions. There was no doubt. The pink coloring meant pregnant.

Romy was sitting on the edge of the bathtub next to the marble goddess, staring out of the window through wrought iron bars onto the garden where well-manicured palm trees were swaying softly in the wind. *What should I do now?* Iriomé's fate seemed to repeat itself in every detail. Joaquín had sent her to the convent, simply disposed of her and left her alone in her darkest hour. But this time it would be different. It was her turn to change the direction. The past must not repeat itself.

The ringing of the phone in her room tore her out of her thoughts. "Could you come to my office? I'd like to discuss something with you." Nic asked.

His voice went right through her. "I'm coming," she said softly. She put the pregnancy test in her jacket, ready to confide the secret she had just discovered to him. Perhaps a child was exactly what he needed to sort himself out and discover his strength. But why didn't he have children with Jennifer? Didn't she want any? Did she not want to lose her figure? Did they even have sex?

Nic received her with a smile. "Have a seat, please." He pointed to one of the elegant chairs in front of his desk.

When she walked across the Chinese rug, she thought briefly of Nic's attack. She must not forget to ask him about it.

"I want to apologize to you," he said in his incomparably charming way. "I've put you in an uncomfortable situation. It's more my style to keep my private and business lives separate. But that's just the way things are at the moment." He pushed a pile of at least twenty closely written pages across the desk. "This is your contract. The conditions are very good. I've just read it."

Romy made no move to take the papers.

"What's wrong?" he looked at her expectantly.

"I thought you wanted to strike a new path with me, or did I misunderstand you?"

"Yes, and I mean it. But I thought you would like to learn more about this mushroom, and that's exactly what this contract allows. And how, pray tell, do you expect to do it otherwise?"

"I don't know yet. I don't even know if I still want to."

"Why?"

"Because the time is not yet ripe, as long as people like Gerald Forster are in power and cooperate with the likes of Antonio Borges. I want to clarify something, even if your friend Borges has forbidden me to talk to you about it under serious threats."

"What would that be?"

"Professor Hattinger and my boss, Berger. Those were no accidents. Both have been killed."

Nic's facial expression showed no change. "What makes you so sure?"

"Borges told me himself."

Nic laughed. "He's put you on. Although I think it's a bit macabre. The pharmaceutical industry has a negative reputation, but it's not *that* bad. Antonio sometimes has a quirky sense of humor."

Romy thought for a moment. Of course, would he say otherwise? He, as always, came to his friend's defense. What had she expected? A confession?

"I can imagine that the two deaths have to do with your discovery, but in no way with Antonio."

Did he think she was stupid, or did he actually believe what he said? Were such actions so normal to him that he was lying automatically? Or did Borges have a grip on Nic so that he was forced to take part in this game?

"Romy," he looked her deeply in the eyes, "I love you and would never allow something that's against your wishes and goals to happen. But Forster's Health happens to have the financial means that such a project involves. What else do you want? Others would give anything to be in your position. Even if the mushroom is not an absolute panacea, you could establish your reputation worldwide. You're thirty-five. Isn't it about time? And isn't it exactly your area? Herbal drug discovery. And it is exactly the branch that I want to expand. Together, with you. Please have a look at the contract."

There was a part of her that even believed him. "Why don't you finance it on your own, without Forster's Health? Your family is rich. We could go through with it together and then jointly make decisions."

He looked at her in astonishment.

"You wanted to change your life, didn't you?" Romy was well aware that by this move she held a pistol to his head, but it was the only way she could imagine a common future.

He thoughtfully picked up the contract. It was not the first time that Romy had brought a man face-to-face with such a decision, but never had she had so much to lose. So far, the men had decided against her and for a safe career. Would it be different now?

"Romy, I bear a heavy responsibility for the continued existence of this company. For thousands of employees and shareholders. I can't bow out overnight and do my own thing with you."

Romy looked at him sadly. He had decided. Just like Joaquín then. Nothing had changed. All her hopes were bursting like a bubble. She put her hand in her jacket pocket, her fingers touching the pregnancy test. She was in the same situation as Iriomé.

He offered her the contract again. "Romy, you put yourself in danger. I, or rather Forster's Health, and really Borges and his men, can only protect you if you cooperate with us. Otherwise, I can do nothing."

"You mean, you can only protect me as long as I'm your lover?"

He didn't answer, but Romy realized how much the question had hurt him. "If I were you, I would finally take your friend Borges to task." She was skating on very thin ice now, and maybe this would seal the end of their relationship, but at this point she didn't care any longer. All or nothing. This had always been her motto.

"I'll check your suspicions, Romy, and will let you know immediately. If you're right, this will of course have consequences."

"If I were in your place, I wouldn't wait too long," Romy said with studied composure.

"You can count on that."

Romy's fingers were clawing at the pregnancy test in her pocket. She was about to place it on Nic's desk, but something stopped her. It was no longer just about her. She needed to protect her baby.

Maybe Nic was not any keener on an illegitimate child than Joaquín. And Jennifer's family was definitely not interested in another legal heir.

"Give me three days." He looked at her for a long rime. "For the sake of love," he finished softly.

Chapter 29

The next morning a cheerful Jennifer was waiting for Romy in the entrance hall of the castillo to go to Marbella and pick up the dress. She wore chic Gucci sunglasses, even though it was cloudy, and her usual designer outfit, this time in olive green with high-heeled pumps in which Romy would not have been able to walk three steps.

"We'll make a quick detour and look in on my mother at the clinic," she said, linking arms with Romy amicably. "I've already told you about her illness, haven't I?"

Romy nodded. She remembered only too well the embarrassing scene on their way back from Geneva.

"I hope you don't mind," Jennifer kept chattering as they went outside where the Jaguar awaited along with the two bodyguards.

"No, of course not," said Romy, which was only partially true. "We just shouldn't be late to the store, to pick up the dress before it closes."

Jennifer laughed. "You're cute! Do you know what this dress costs? No, you'd better not know. For this they'll gladly do without their lunch break and *siesta*. So don't worry."

Romy was worrying, of course, though for very different reasons. She was looking forward to seeing her soul brother today, even if she was unsure if she really would go with him. To be on the safe side, however, she had packed some essentials into her bag.

"By the way, I've heard that you and Nic had a little tiff," Jennifer interrupted her thoughts.

Romy looked at her, startled. "What do you mean?"

"Well. Because of Borges. Just between us girls,. I also think he's scary and asked my father several times to dismiss him with good compensation, but Nic always insisted that he stays."

"Do you know why?"

Jennifer looked at her thoughtfully. "Why shouldn't you know? You actually almost belong to the inner circle by now. Borges saved the assets of Nic's family and was instrumental in the Saratogas not having to leave Panama after the overthrow of Noriega."

Romy remembered reading about the Saratoga family and their position in Panama on the internet.

"Borges's father was involved in the Argentine military coup when he was a colonel and was trained by the CIA. His son maintained a strong relationship with the Americans, too. Without his help Nic's family would have been dispossessed and then expelled."

"That is to say, he owed it to Borges."

"Borges certainly didn't do this out of pure philanthropy. I think he expected something for it. And it worked. They financed Borges through Harvard, and his current position is not too bad if you consider where he came from."

Just like de Lugo saved Joaquín and brought him under his control for the rest of his life, Romy mused. Did his loyalty make Nic blind to Borges behavior? Would everything take a turn for the better when Borges's guilt was proved and he was brought to justice?

"Oh, look. This is awful." Jennifer showed her the morning edition of the *Neue Zürcher Zeitung*. "I knew him. He was also at the press conference in Geneva."

It was just a small item, but the headline made Romy's blood run cold. "*Medical Journal* journalist dead in the bathtub." She should have kept her mouth shut! Feelings of guilt wrapped around her throat. The next victim of Borges.

Jennifer read aloud. "'The well-known German journalist Michael Timm drowned yesterday according to DPA in the bathtub of a Geneva hotel. Timm had, as was confirmed by several witnesses, drunk alcohol extensively the night before at the hotel's bar. The police assume that he took a bath in the early morning and fell asleep.'"

Did Nic already know about this and connect the dots? She wanted to call him on the spot, but they had already reached the clinic.

They drove up the driveway to a stunningly beautiful mansion. Its wooden balconies and bay windows displayed the typical strict old Spanish style. In the entrance hall a huge fire was burning in a fireplace, which made the room comfortably warm. Before it a number of elderly people were sitting in armchairs. Some chatted quietly, others just stared into the flames. Jennifer spoke with an employee and then waved to Romy to follow.

A modern, handicapped accessible elevator brought them to the second floor, where they walked down a long hallway lined with wooden planks.

"She's a bit weird and likes to make up bizarre stories. Just ignore them. People like her are in their own world," Jennifer was whispering to her.

"Don't we all?"

Jennifer looked confused for a moment, laughed loudly, and then knocked on the door with the sign *Señora Ann Forster*. Without waiting for a "come in" or something like that, she opened the door and entered.

A gray-haired, well-groomed lady was sitting up straight in front of a half-open balcony door looking out. In front of her on a table stood a cup of tea and a plate with a half-eaten slice of toast. She did not turn around as the two women came in.

"Hi, Mom," said Jennifer.

No reaction.

"I want you to meet someone. A young scientist who now works for us."

Ann Forster slowly turned her head and looked at Romy, who held out her hand to her.

"I went to college once," she said with a broad, sluggish Texan accent. "But that was a long time ago."

"I don't think Romy is interested. I've got some documents that father wants you to sign."

As she handed over the papers and a pen, Jen's mobile rang and she answered it immediately. "Yes . . . okay . . . wonderful . . . then we'll all meet at midnight . . ." She stepped out onto the balcony to continue her conversation there while her mother, without reading a single word, put her signature everywhere that a small cross demanded it.

"You don't want to at least know what you're signing?" Romy asked softly.

"What for? He does what he likes anyway."

"Gerald Forster?" It was more a statement than a question.

"Do you know him?"

"I met him yesterday for the first time."

"So?"

Romy thought it best if she did not say out loud what she thought of Gerald Foster.

"He once was a really good man," the old lady replied herself. "But that was long ago. Do you want to hear the whole story?"

Romy nodded.

"My father thought a great deal of him and provided him in the early sixties with the financial resources to make Forster's Health into what it is today. I adored him then. His energy and also his social commitment."

Slowly Romy understood. Obviously Forster assumed the name of his wife, who still possessed certain shares of Forster's Health. She took Romy's hand, looking into her eyes sadly. "The power has corrupted him, especially after he started to become politically active. Politics and economics are a powerful alliance. He has friends everywhere. At the approval authority, among the decision makers in health care, in the courts. There one hand washes the other. Do you understand?"

She squeezed Romy's hand so tight that it almost hurt and suddenly spoke really fast as if it was a matter of life and death. Repeatedly she threw anxious glances in the direction of the balcony. But Jennifer was completely preoccupied with the organization of her evening adventure.

"I still remember a lawsuit where a woman sued Forster's Health. Her husband, a policeman, shot himself to death with his service weapon after having taken psychotropic drugs. She was killed in a car accident soon afterward. Thereupon, the trial was stopped. The product wasn't taken from the market until years later when three further suicides occurred."

"Is that why you became ill?"

"No, not because of that. I resigned because I wasn't able to get back the man I had once loved and married—back then when his heart was still open to love."

All of a sudden she let go of Romy's hand.

"And for this I hate myself, you understand? I hate myself for having resigned."

"He's dedicated to the play of power. Nobody could have changed him," Romy tried to reassure her. "You've surely done your best."

Ann Forster shook her head. "I still love him, please understand." She reached for Romy's hand again. "My daughter's different. She doesn't suffer due to her husband. She's been accustomed to it from childhood. She grew up with a father like that."

Romy looked at Forster's wife thoughtfully. She had fled to depression, her daughter to alcohol and parties, and she was about to relinquish Nic and accept Tanausú's offer to help her flee. She didn't know what else to say, but somehow the conversation with this woman had shown her that she was in a similar situation. She loved Nic, but not his social circle.

Jennifer had finished talking and came back into the room. "Well, did you have a good time?"

"Thanks," replied Ann Forster and then turned back to Romy once again. "You're a wonderful person. Please stay the way you are. And stay true to yourself."

On the way back to Marbella it was hard for Romy to be responsive to Jennifer's chatty tone as she excitedly told about a party to which they would absolutely have to go that evening and where Romy would have the opportunity to parade in her new dress. Actually she was not dissimilar to Inés de Perreira. A spoiled rich princess who believed she could get away with anything because of her money. Nic's marriage to her must have a mainly economic background, as had been the case with Inés and Joaquín. It was totally weird how everything repeated itself. There remained only the question whether all this would go on until eternity.

The two women, together with the bodyguards, were dropped off at the beginning of the pedestrian zone, from where they set off for the Jil Sander boutique. Suddenly it occurred to Jennifer that she needed to grab a meal in one of the many street restaurants right away. Romy tried to hide her nervousness as best she could; they were already quite late. The thought of Tanausú was whirling around in her head as in a loop. Would he be there, and what did his escape plan look like? Should she really do it? She had not come to a decision yet.

The third place they went into finally met Jennifer's standards. As there were no free tables outside, another table and chairs had to be brought from the inside, and Jennifer ordered for both of them—grilled prawns and an outrageously expensive white wine.

"There'll be ten of my best friends at this party tonight, all from good families," she continued, getting on Romy's nerves. "I would be surprised if there wasn't someone for you. At least outwardly we must keep up appearances," she whispered to Romy and giggled like a little girl.

Romy looked at her aghast. This woman seemed to have killed most of her brain cells with alcohol. How on earth could Nic stand this?

After Jennifer had emptied her glass of wine in a gulp she got out her iPhone and demanded that Romy narrow down the choices on the basis of the men's Facebook profile pictures. "I've already hooked up several girlfriends, and two of them are even still married," she said proudly.

After half an hour, finally the food was served. The prawns swam in a greasy garlic mayonnaise, the last thing Romy felt like at the moment, but she helped herself bravely. Nevertheless, the large plate emptied slowly, and the wine bottle was still half full.

Romy was on tenterhooks. "I think it's about time to go," she dared to suggest. "The shops will close soon, and I'd really like to wear this dress tonight."

Jennifer looked at her watch. "Okay, although I could call them so that they stay longer, we don't want to be rude and impose on the employees' free time. *La cuenta, por favor,*" she called as she signaled to the waiter, who came rushing eagerly. Still, it took at least fifteen more minutes for the espresso to be served and the bill finally paid.

"Why are you in such a hurry?" Jennifer asked as Romy immediately got up to leave. "Do you have a date?"

"No, no," Romy replied hastily. "I'm just used to being in a hurry."

Jennifer looked at her skeptically but said nothing. "Okay then, let's go."

As she entered the store Romy noticed that something was wrong. The friendly sales woman from last time was not there. Instead, they were welcomed by a young German at her first day of work there. The green dress, however, awaited her on its hanger.

"You want to try it on again?" asked the girl a bit shyly.

Romy nodded and followed her toward the changing rooms. The salesgirl opened the door and left her alone. The room was empty, the window closed. No trace of Tanausú. Had he already been here and gone? Romy looked around attentively. Had he perhaps left a message somewhere? She quickly searched the room but in vain. He will definitely come, she reassured herself.

To pass the time, she put on the green dress and sat down on a chair. But no holy warrior materialized. Cautiously, she opened the window leading to the courtyard. There was nothing to see. Only the putrid smell from the dumpsters reached her nostrils.

At that moment a shot was fired. She winced. Some pigeons flew up, frightened. A male body, dressed in a green military jacket, fell from the fire escape onto the concrete floor of the courtyard. One of the body-guards jumped after him with a weapon in his hand.

Romy felt paralyzed. But then without having to think about it, her flight instinct awoke. She opened the door of the changing room, stormed through the store, past the startled salesgirl and Jennifer, who tried to hold her by her arm.

Romy broke away with all her strength and ran out onto the street where she ended up in the arms of the second bodyguard. As vigorously as she could, she kicked him in the nuts, used the painful moment of surprise, and freed herself from his grip. She ran down the pedestrian zone, almost knocked over a stroller, turned right into a narrow alley, and then at the next intersection went to the left. Like a rabbit on the run from a fox, she darted sideways through the old town. She did not dare to turn around but knew nevertheless that at least one of the two bodyguards was on her heels. And they were surely good runners.

Romy ran for her life. When she came to a square with a small fountain in the middle and a few trees under which blue-tiled benches stood, she paused to breathe. From the alley behind her, she heard running footsteps. Frantically she looked around and saw an open doorway. She rushed in, quickly closed the door and sat breathing heavily on the cool landing. Her heart was thumping like mad. Someone rattled at the door. Romy raced up the stairs to perhaps find an escape over the roof. She wondered if someone in the square might have seen her when she had fled into the house. But she could not remember having seen any-one. After all, it was siesta time, with most Spaniards behind closed shutters.

The front door apparently could not be opened from the outside. Slowly she calmed down. She climbed up to the next floor, where she found a small window from which she could see down on the square. It was deserted. Her pursuers were probably looking elsewhere for her. Nevertheless, she did not dare to leave this safe hideaway. She would wait here on the stairs and later under cover of darkness . . . well, what?

Where should she go? Tanausú got shot. Certainly he was injured, if not dead. He could not help her any longer. The scene as he had fallen from the roof, left a deep impression on her. With all her might she pushed it to the back of her mind and tried as best she could to think clearly. After all, she had gone to school here in Marbella. First of all, she remembered Señor Méndez, her former history teacher. He had been friends with her grandmother, and they had been to his home many times. His wife had always baked particularly sweet cakes decorated with lots of pink buttercream. In addition there was a thin coffee with viscous sweet condensed milk.

Romy remembered that he used to live close to the German school located near the marina. But first she had to make it there. Unfortunately she could not just call a cab because her bag, money, passport, cell phone and credit cards were in the changing room at the boutique, and her shoes as well!

After sunset she ventured outside. Shop and cafe owners had let down the bars in front of their shop windows and hosed the sidewalks with water. It had become chilly. Romy was shivering in her thin party dress. She ignored the surprised looks of the passersby that were directed especially at her bare feet and made her way toward her former school. Finally, a young man took pity on her and gave her a lift on his moped.

The sight of the whitewashed quadrangular building with a flat roof and basketball hoops in front of it awakened long forgotten childhood memories. She thought of her grandmother, who had often picked her up here and given her a wonderful feeling of security. Never would she forget her granny's smile as she waited for her, arms spread so that Romy could dash into them. How good it would be now to have someone in whose arms she could feel safe. She remembered how Nic had carried her from the hermitage to the monastery. Surely he had already been informed about her disappearance and was doing everything to find her.

After some searching, she discovered the small side street where Señor Méndez had lived and hopefully still was. Her heart leapt when she discovered his name on the door panel of the five-story apartment building. She leaned on the doorbell. Shortly thereafter, she heard his voice through the intercom.

"Señor Méndez, it's me! Your former student Romy Conrad," she exclaimed.

"*No me diga. Que sorpresa!*" The buzzer sounded, andRomy pushed the door open. Before she went in, she looked around again in case someone was following her. But except for an old lady letting her pug dog pee on a lamppost, the small street was deserted. She took the elevator to the fourth floor.

Her former history teacher stood in his apartment door and looked at her in disbelief. He still wore a vest and bow tie and had only become a little more corpulent. But his alert eyes were as sparkling as always. "Romy, nice to see you! I can hardly believe it. You're even prettier than before. But why didn't you call ahead?" He looked at her bare feet and the thin dress. "Has anything happened?"

Romy nodded. "May I come in?"

"Of course. Sorry, I'm a bit confused."

The apartment looked the same as twenty years ago. A fact that made Romy feel better somehow. "Where's your wife?"

"Unfortunately, she died two years ago."

So no more cakes with pink buttercream flashed through her mind quite unnecessarily. She squeezed his hand. "I need your help, Señor Mendez."

"First I'll give you some warm clothes. I still have things from my wife. Definitely not your style, but the size will fit." He went into the bedroom, and she heard him open the closet.

"What's the quickest way from here to La Palma?" she called after him.

"The Canary Island of La Palma?"

"Yes!"

"From Cádiz. The next major port," he said, coming back into the room with a bundle of clothes over his arm. "From there you can take a ferry, as far as I know. I can drive you up tomorrow morning, if you wish."

At that moment the bell rang. "Do you expect any visitors?"

He shook his head.

"Please don't open it," she whispered, her voice trembling. She went to the front door to lock it from inside. From the stairs she could hear the voices of the two bodyguards, and an additional one she immediately recognized.

"Open the door, Señor Méndez. We know Romy Conrad is in there," Antonio Borges barked through the door in a hard commanding tone.

Méndez looked at Romy startled. "Who's this?"

She remembered that she had told Nic about her history teacher. He and Borges could obviously put two and two together. "Is there a way to get out of here?" she whispered.

"Maybe over the balcony in the kitchen," the old man replied just as softly.

Romy sprinted into the kitchen and opened the door to the balcony, which led to a small air shaft. While she vaulted over the railing, she heard the front door being forced open.

"Where is she?" shouted Borges. His voice went right through her. Her fingers clutched the bars of the balcony, while her feet were trying to find support on a small ledge. Another sequence from the Iriomé play: de Lugo devastated the house of the médico. Fear clawed up her neck, trying to squeeze all the air out of her. Involuntarily she looked down to the bottom of the shaft. The small concrete square seemed to magically attract her.

Her toes clung to the rough plaster. No, she would not fall. Not this time. She closed her eyes for a moment in order to concentrate completely. Suddenly she felt Iriomé's strength. A strength that was familiar to her and that she always felt when she was hanging on a rock wall being left all to her self. A power that she called psychic turbocharge, driven by an explosive mixture of adrenaline and endorphins. A power that flooded her with courage, self-love, and infinite trust.

Like a cat she jumped sideways to another ledge and in the process grazed her knee, which she hardly noticed. From there she tried to reach the flanking drainpipe by moving hand over hand along the window-sill. For a few seconds this was her only hold. Thirty feet below her was nothing but hard concrete. If her fingers failed now, it would mean certain death. But she made it. Her feet got a grasp of the drainpipe, and her legs clasped it with her last ounce of strength. Her upper body followed, and then she eased herself down slowly.

At the height of the second floor, she reached a balcony with an open door to an apartment. She climbed over the railing and ran inside past a surprised young man with reddish-blond hair—not a moment too soon, because down in the courtyard suddenly one of the body-guards appeared. "Did you see a young woman in a green dress?" he called up to the redhead.

Romy looked at him with a pleading expression and shook her head. "No, I'm sorry," he called down. "Haven't seen anybody around here."

"Thanks," breathed Romy.

"Should I call the Guardia Civil?" he turned back to her.

"Yes, but first I need to get out of here."

The young man eyed her very low-cut dress, which she had rolled up to the hips, and her naked, grazed legs.

"The guys won't rest until they've searched the whole house," said Romy, who was fully aware what fantasies this sight triggered in the young man.

"There's an exit through the bicycle storage room," he suggested.

"How do I get there?"

"In the elevator. It goes right down to the basement."

Romy nodded. "Okay, we'll try it."

He looked at her as if he expected a more detailed explanation of what was actually going on and to whom he had rendered assistance, then realized, however, that this was not the right moment for explanations. He opened his apartment door slightly and looked around to see if the coast was clear. Then he pressed the elevator button, fortunately located right next to his door. Borges's voice was echoing down through the stairwell. "Where did she want to go, Señor Méndez? If you don't tell me immediately . . . "

"As soon as I'm out of here, call the Guardia Civil and help the old man from the fourth floor," Romy said when they were in the elevator. "Please!"

He nodded. In the basement, he opened a heavy iron door, behind which there was a concrete ramp that led up to the back entrance of the house. Romy embraced her helper and gave him a kiss on the cheek. *"Muchas gracias!"*

"Take good care of yourself!" he whispered before she disappeared in the shadow of the neighboring house.

Without thinking, Romy ran toward the marina. She could only hope that she would find a way to get to Cadiz from there and then onto the ferry to La Palma. By now she realized there was no other way than to destroy the mushroom or even the whole cave. Otherwise there would just be more victims, and she would always be prey, just like Iriomé had been. The greed of the conquistadors for power and control would never run dry.

The barrier at the entrance of the marina was guarded by two officials, who demanded an identity card from anyone who wanted to enter. Romy was still wondering how she could sneak in unseen, when next to her a luxury car with tinted windows stopped. The rear side window opened with a soft purr. Romy recognized the pretty Asian woman she had met on the yacht of the sheikh.

"I know you," said the woman in her droll English as she studied Romy from head to toe. Romy nodded. She remembered their brief encounter, when the almond-eyed beauty had warned her about Borges. "Come on, get in."

The rear side door of the silver-gray Mercedes opened. Grateful and exhausted, Romy dropped on the leather padded back seat and pulled the dress over her knees as best she could.

"I'm Zumi." The Asian girl offered a hand. "You and Nic Saratoga were at the party a few days ago, right?"

Romy nodded. "But I've only known him a short while."

"And now you're already on the run from him and Antonio Borges, I suppose," she said dryly.

Romy stared at her, startled.

"Don't worry. You can trust me."

"But how . . . ?"

"I'll tell you later," Zumi interrupted her and told the chauffeur to drive on. The car passed the checkpoint without someone wanting to see an identity card and stopped right in front of the monstrous yacht of the sheikh. Two dark-skinned sailors in white uniforms had already loosened the ropes from the poles and were getting ready to set sail.

"Hurry up, girls," they called out to the two women.

"You're lucky. We sail in a few minutes," said Zumi while they ran up the gangway. "Let's go to my cabin, I'll get you something warm to wear and a pair of shoes."

"Thanks." Romy followed the girl. The interior of the yacht reminded her of the night when Nic seduced her using every trick in the book. Had this been planned from the beginning? She didn't know what to think any longer. Power and money stood between her and Nic, just as they had separated Joaquín and Iriomé. But how could one overcome such a powerful barrier? Especially when it was maintained by the likes of Gerald Forster using every possible means.

"You love him, don't you? Nic Saratoga, I mean." Zumi was studying her intently and then unlocked the door to her cabin, which was almost as large and luxurious as the one Romy had been in.

"What makes you think that?"

Zumi didn't answer immediately, but laid out a pair of jeans and a sweatshirt for her on the bed. Romy looked at her expectantly.

"My best friend Laura dated Nic for some time."

Romy peeled off the tight dress and handed it to Zumi.

"It's brand-new. I've worn it only a few hours."

Zumi looked at it with an expert eye. "Jil Sander. From Nic?"

"No, from his wife."

"How juicy. But I think she doesn't quite know what she's doing anymore anyway. Too much coke and alcohol."

"What happened to your friend Laura?" Romy had a bad feeling.

"She's dead." The well-proportioned face of the Asian woman, which seemed to wear a smile by nature, suddenly expressed fear and grief. She sat down on the bed. Romy noticed how hard it was for her to hold back tears and continue. "Antonio Borges tortured her to death," she said in a flat voice. "This is the reason I'm helping you."

Romy stared at Zumi, stunned. "How do you know?"

"Because he showed me pictures of Laura. Pictures that still keep me up at night. He said that the same would happen to me, if I ever talk."

Romy put on Zumi's clothes and then also sat down on the bed. She closed her eyes trying to give the fear that was creeping up in her no chance. "And why? Do you know why he did it?"

"He thought she was working for another drug company and was spying on Nic."

"And . . . was she?"

Zumi shrugged. "I don't know. She used to study chemistry but then dropped out of college. The way she looked there were easier ways to make money."

"And Nic, he knows about it?"

Zumi shook her head. "He thinks Laura left him and disappeared somewhere."

How could Nic close his eyes to the facts so much?

"You're the first person I'm telling."

"That's very courageous of you," Romy said. "But why?"

"I don't want it to happen again."

"I urgently need to go to Cadiz and from there leave for the Canaries on the next ferry. Can you give me any help?"

"I think we'll anchor off Cádiz to take a doctor on board there.

The sheikh's not doing well. You could hitch a ride back on the boat that brings the doctor."

Romy looked at her gratefully. She had already envisioned having to jump overboard like Iriomé.

"I'll try to arrange that for you," Zumi said wiping away a tear. "But first I'll cut your hair. And I think I've got some black hair dye somewhere. With your long strawberry-blonde hair you're much too conspicuous."

While Zumi cut one strand after the other, Romy could not help but think of the hair-cutting scene in the house of the médico and his poor mother. She wondered if Señor Méndez was okay.

Despite it all she could not imagine that Borges simply did away with him like Cold Eye had with the old woman. After all, these were not the Middle Ages, where the life of an individual was worth next to nothing. On the other hand what Zumi had just told her did not necessarily speak for Borges's empathy with his fellow people. She did not even want to think about amakuna having claimed another victim. Especially not old, kind Señor Méndez.

"May I use your phone?" she asked Zumi, who in the meantime had applied the hair dye and was now washing it out.

"Sure." She wrapped a towel around Romy's head and pointed to her iPhone on the table beside her. "But please don't call Nic; they'll definitely find out that you're with me."

"No, don't worry." Via the directory assistance she quickly got Señor Méndez's phone number and waited impatiently for the ring tone. She was about to hang up when she finally heard his voice on the other end of the line. "*Todo bien?*" she just managed to utter.

"*Sí, sí. Mi niña.* And you? Are you okay?"

"Yes, I'm fine," she said, relieved.

"Who were those men? The Guardia Civil came shortly after, so they disappeared quickly."

"I'll tell you later. I'm terribly sorry about all that. I'll call you again." Romy took a deep breath, put the phone back, took the towel from her head, and looked in the mirror. What she saw was a woman who had nothing, absolutely nothing, in common with Dr. Romy Conrad.

Zumi seemed reassured. "No one's going to recognize you now."

Chapter 30

Romy didn't know what story her new friend had served to the captain. At any rate, the next morning she left the yacht in the motor boat as planned, in the direction of the ferry port of Cadiz.

After a short but rough ride, she was dropped off at the extreme end of the pier. As in every port, it smelled of old oil, saltwater, and indefinable waste. A longshoreman showed her past rows of rusty containers to the service counter area of the Canary Islands ferries. Romy gave him a generous tip. Zumi had handed her a farewell gift of three hundred euros and a small bag with clothes and toiletries.

The departure area was packed with travelers, Spanish families with countless shopping bags, a few tourists with rolling cases, and a group of hippies with backpacks and guitar bags. Romy stood hidden behind a pillar at the very edge of the lounge to make sure she would not be waylaid by Borges or one of his men. If Nic added two and two together, he could figure out that she would try to reach La Palma and amakuna to . . . well, what? Destroy it? The whole cave? But how? All she knew was that it was the only way to put an end to the evil that continued to spread. Perhaps Thea or Ricardo had a solution.

Not discovering anything unusual, she stood in front of the desk of the *Acciona,* which sailed for La Palma via Tenerife. But her restlessness remained. Time and again she looked around. Suddenly she noticed a man in uniform in the back of the lounge going around with a photo in his hand and obviously looking for someone.

"Romy!" a young female voice reached her ear. Startled, she turned

around. Salima, the young mother from the Rainbow family was beaming at her. "I nearly didn't recognize you. You look sort of different. But
it suits you."

Romy was relieved. "Where did you come from?"

"We went to a music festival in Portugal and are on our way back
to La Palma. And you?"

"I'm also on my way to La Palma."

"Then why don't you join us?" She pointed to her friends who had
made themselves comfortable on their sleeping bags with a few bottles
of wine at the edge of the lounge. "If you buy the tickets right before
departure, the line is not so long."

They'd been sent from heaven because at that moment she saw from
the corner of her eye the man in uniform coming toward them with
the photo.

"Yes, I'd like to," she said, following Salima to her friends with head
bent. Between the colorfully dressed hippies she would be less conspicuous than alone. Now she only needed to blend in a bit. "Salima, may I
borrow your scarf?"

"You can keep it; here's my hat, too," she said, laughing, and put it
on her head. Romy gave her a grateful look, now feeling a little more
secure.

She had hardly sat down and greeted some of Salima's friends she
knew from the full moon party in Buracas when the policeman
appeared. He bent down to the group and showed them a photo of
Romy with long strawberry-blonde hair.

Her heart almost stopped. George, with the gold-rimmed glasses,
whom she recognized only just now, gave her a knowing look and
answered for them all. "No, sorry, we don't know this woman. What's
up with her?"

"That's none of your business," the policeman snapped in hardly
understandable Andalusian Spanish and turned away.

George handed Romy a half-full wine bottle. "Here, for the shock.
Is there anything we can do to help?"

She took a big gulp of the cheap red wine, which, however, warmed her stomach in a pleasant way. "I need to get on this ferry without being noticed and leave it the same way on La Palma."

He grinned. "No problem. I'll buy a ticket for you. At the counter they'll already know your photo."

"Thanks." Romy handed him back the bottle. "But I don't want you to get involved, so I'd rather not . . . "

"It's okay," he interrupted and pulled her hat still deeper over her face while she slipped a 50 euros note into his hand for the ticket.

"Have you heard from Sam lately? Do you know how he's doing?" she asked Salima.

"No, I haven't got a clue. We email sometimes, but I didn't receive an answer to my last one. Why do you ask? Is he involved in your problems? Is it about drugs?"

"Not directly."

"It's all right; you don't need to tell me."

That Sam didn't respond did not necessarily have to mean something. People like him surely did not write emails on a consistent basis. But it wasn't a good sign either.

"If you want, we can drive you to Sam. We need to go to Punta Gorda anyway," Salima said.

"That's really nice of you." These hippies were much more willing to help than most of the other people she knew.

Two hours later the lounge came alive. The passengers packed their bits and pieces and gathered in front of the exit. Romy had a moment of shock when she thought she recognized the wiry bodyguard from Marbella, but then she realized that she had erred. The fear of being caught at the last minute made her completely edgy.

Hidden among the hippies and the other passengers, she boarded the ferry, head bent, and followed Salima to the upper deck, from where she would be able to watch the departure.

At the top of the stairs another policeman was positioned with a photo in his hand. Romy turned around as inconspicuously as possible and climbed down the narrow iron stairs to the parking decks in the belly of the ship. Several signs said that unauthorized access was strictly prohibited while the ship was moving, but she didn't care. Quite the contrary. It was probably the best place not to be discovered. Maybe she could lie in an unlocked car until the next stop in Tenerife.

She crept through the rows of cars checking the door locks. None was open. It smelled of exhaust fumes, gasoline, and stale seawater. Romy was about to give up the plan, when from a small truck next to her salsa music could suddenly be heard. She winced. A stocky man with dark, short-cut hair seemed highly amused.

"You don't like salsa music?" he asked, grinning with the typical Canarian accent that swallowed half of the word endings.

"I do," Romy, who had already recollected herself, replied.

"Well, then, sit with me. I have a bottle of good Tinto, so the time will go fast."

"Isn't it against the rules to stay down here while the ship's moving?" she asked as innocently as possible.

He opened the passenger door for her, his chest swelling with pride. "I have an exemption. I keep my eyes glued to my car."

Romy thought for a moment and then climbed into the passenger seat. In the company of this harmless Canario, nothing much could happen to her.

"My name's Carlos," said the man with sparkling eyes and a laugh that exposed two missing teeth. He opened a bottle of wine and handed it to her. "There are no glasses. I wasn't prepared for visitors.

"That's good Tinto, Vega Norte, from Tijarafe," he said, after he had drunk half of the bottle himself.

"It's a beautiful place," said Romy, who knew the neighboring village of Punta Gorda from which Ricardo came.

"I was born there." He took another sip and then fished a crumpled page of a journal from his wallet. The article was titled *La Danza del Diablo*. Beneath it was the picture of a fearsome figure with red eyes and glowing horns from which fireworks sprayed. "This is me," he said, his chest swollen with pride. "And this year for the first time my son will play the devil."

This was all Greek to Romy.

"Have you never heard of the devil festival? It's one of the most famous fiestas in the Canaries; every year many thousands of visitors come."

Romy shook her head. "Never heard of it."

"It's celebrated in honor of the Virgen de la Candelaria, the Maria with the garland of lights. She's the strongest rival of Satan. So it says in the Book of Revelation."

Romy listened to Carlos attentively, although she was not interested in religious festivals. But something told her that it could still be important.

"Before Mary's birth the devil once again obtained power over mankind, until he was finally defeated by the Virgin. That is why we celebrate this festival of joy every year. The good triumphed over the evil. The light over the darkness."

"Is that really true?" Romy tended to feel as if evil had a clear advantage.

Carlos laughed. "Sometimes it's hard to believe, but we must never give up. The Virgin means the best for us in any case."

Romy wished she had the same firm belief as Carlos. She looked again at the picture from which the blood-red eyes of the devil figure were staring at her. "So there's a person in the devil costume who shoots the fireworks."

Carlos nodded. "What do you think I'm keeping back there in the bed? And why I sit down here in my truck? If this explodes here, I don't know what would be left. The devil figure weighs eighty kilos, fifty kilos of which are explosive. And then I've got an extra two hundred kilos for the normal fireworks."

Romy stared at the Palmero while very slowly a plan was forming in her head. Instead of wasting 250 kilos of gunpowder on the devil festival, it could be used to blow up the cave in the caldera—at least so that the grave chamber of the harimaguadas was no longer accessible. The Virgin surely would understand. After all, Romy was fighting evil. How she could put her idea into practice, however, she had no clue.

The ferry entered the port of Santa Cruz de la Palma two days later in the late afternoon. Romy was convinced that Borges's men would check every car and passenger that disembarked. No doubt the Argentinean had flown to the island in the Forster's Health Learjet already, maybe even with Nic.

The safest route would be to leave the waterfront area in the back of Carlo's truck. Everyone knew him, and everyone would know what he was transporting. Surely he would pass all security points without problems.

She said goodbye to him heartily but stayed nearby. When he briefly conversed with someone, she climbed quickly into the back of his truck and made herself as comfortable as was possible between the countless, well-sealed aluminum boxes. Only a few minutes later they drove off.

After they had left the ferry via the ramp, a hot wind like a hair dryer at level three was coming in through the planks of the truck. At first Romy did not understand what was going on. In no time she was absolutely dripping with sweat. Under the tarp it became stuffier and stuffier. She could hardly breathe. Was she really on the Canaries or had she accidentally landed in Africa? She would not be able to put up with these temperatures another minute!

Fortunately, the truck stopped shortly thereafter. To avoid suffocating, she slipped from under the tarpaulin to the outside and was promptly discovered by Carlos. She had no choice but to tell him a hair-raising story of a crazed lover who was looking everywhere for her. Carlos, as a hot-blooded southerner, believed her story and even offered to take her to Punta Gorda. But this time in the cab and with the window open.

"The calima is blowing."

Romy had heard of the hot desert wind that a few times a year transformed the Canary Islands into a baking oven. Even at night, it was said, the temperatures fell only marginally below one hundred and five degrees Fahrenheit.

She leaned back, exhausted. Carlos, grinning, showed his two tooth gaps and handed Romy a slightly dingy towel so she could wipe the sweat from her forehead.

◌◌

"She's back on the island," Tanausú spoke softly into his mobile.

"I can hardly hear you. Are you okay?" asked Ricardo at the other end of the line.

"I've been better. Listen, you need to find her and then take her to the cave where her friend Thea is."

"Okay. And when will you be coming?"

"As soon as I can." He hung up and put the mobile in the breast pocket of his army jacket. Then he unbuttoned his shirt and stroked the spot on his right shoulder where he had been hit. The wound had vanished completely. A smooth penetration. Amakuna had taken care of the rest.

◌◌

"You really need to come to the devil festival. You can't miss out on that," Carlos said to his fellow passenger, dropping her off at the driveway of her former finca.

"Promise," said Romy.

"And here's my phone number in case you need to hide from your boyfriend again." He handed her a piece of paper, grinning like a coconspirator.

She put it in her bag, called an *"Adiós y muchas gracias"* out to him, and then ran down the familiar stony path to the house. From there she followed the small dirt track that led to Sam's cave. She called his name. No answer. Only the familiar sound of the birds and the hum of the bees were to be heard and in the distance a chain saw. Certainly he would be in his cave, because even now after sunset it was still sweltering. Romy was completely sweaty just from the short walk down here.

But the thick wooden door at the entrance was closed with an iron chain from the outside. She knocked hard on the door. Nothing. Her knees began to shake. *Please, don't let anything have happened to him.*

"Can I help you?" A female voice came from the terrace of her former finca, obviously rented out again.

"I'm looking for Sam. Do you happen to know when he'll be back?"

"Haven't you heard?" cried the older woman, who was in her underwear, excitedly. "He drowned yesterday and was washed ashore at the Lomada Grande."

Now Romy really felt as if someone had pulled the rug out from under her. She staggered to the small bench in front of the dragon tree. She had drunk tea here with Sam only a short while ago.

"Are you Romy Conrad?" She heard the woman's voice as if from far away.

"Yes," she called back weakly.

The woman had slipped into a colorful sundress and now came down the little path. "He told me to give you this," she said, handing Romy a small jar and an envelope. "It's funny. When he gave it to me, it seemed almost as if he knew that he wouldn't come back. Are you related to him?"

Romy shook her head and took both. She did not need to speculate to know what was in the jar. Sam had given his life for it.

The woman was standing somewhat helplessly in front of her. "Would you like to come in? In the house it's perhaps a little cooler."

"I'd prefer to stay here, but thank you," Romy managed to reply barely audibly.

"Well, you know where to find me," she said and went up the small dirt track back to the house.

Romy looked after her until she was gone. Then she opened the envelope in which there were a few, hastily written lines on a page that had been torn from a book.

Dear Romy,
Yesterday two guys came, who pestered me with questions about
the mushroom. I didn't tell them anything. You were right. The
stuff is dangerous. I'll disappear for the time being. Hope to see
you soon. Sam

Romy reread the lines several times, but this didn't bring the hippie back. She was at her wit's end. In desperation she went to Sam's outdoor kitchen, got herself a glass, filled it with water, and let the tiny remainder of amakuna from the jar trickle into it. Perhaps she would find a decisive clue about how to go on from here from a different time.

Chapter 31

"Iriomé, Iriomé!" cried Hermana Guadalupe. Panting, she stopped in front of the hermitage where Iriomé nursed little Tamanca in the last rays of the evening sun. He had Joaquín's dark hair and Iriomé's bright, blue-green eyes.

"You must leave!" gasped the young nun. "They're here and want to search the whole convent."

"Who?"

"Frai Lorenzo de la Huerta. He's in charge of the Inquisition Tribunal for this area now. He's been informed that the abbess wants to build a chapel in honor of the Virgin Mary to thank God for her miraculous recovery."

"And this reminded him of me?"

Guadalupe nodded. "You have to go right now and hide in the forest, you know where. Once the danger has passed, I'll let you know."

Iriomé took Tamanca, who began to cry immediately, off her breast and wrapped him hastily into a cloth. The two young women embraced briefly, and Iriomé could not help wondering whether it might be the last time.

With the child pressed close to her, she ran as fast as she could across the meadow up the hill to the forest to go into hiding in the protection of the trees. In the distance she could already hear male voices and dogs barking.

To confuse the dogs, she waded across a stream, jumping from stone to stone. Breathless and soaked, she reached the rock face in which there was the entrance to a tunnel she had discovered gathering herbs, which had once served as a smugglers' hiding place. With the cloth she tied Tamanca firmly to her chest, pushed the bushes aside, and squeezed on all fours through the narrow entrance. The narrowness and the shape of the tunnel dampened all noises, but now and then a howl reached her ears. Yet she could not distinguish whether it was the wind or the pack of hounds.

Trembling with cold, she crouched on the hard rock holding her child close to her to offer him any warmth her body was capable of giving. After she had nursed Tamanca again, she sank to the ground and fell into a restless sleep, exhausted.

Only the crying of her son woke her up again. In the darkness of the cave it was impossible to discern how long she had slept and whether it was day or night. While she breastfed her child, she realized how thirsty she was. She remembered that Tichiname taught her to put a small pebble into her mouth when she had no water and to suck on it to stimulate salivation. She groped her surroundings in the dark until she found a stone of the right size, cleaned it, and put it into her mouth.

Thus hours, probably days, passed between dozing and waking. She was plagued by gnawing hunger, thirst, and increasing weakness. Eventually she believed she could neither sit nor lie any longer. She knew that she and her baby would die of thirst if she stayed here any longer waiting for Guadalupe. Her limbs stiff, she crawled out of the hole.

The glaring sunlight hit her like a blow. It took her a while to get accustomed to it. From the position of the sun she was able to tell that it was early afternoon. Except for the chirping of the birds, nothing could be heard. Carefully and always in the cover of a tree or shrub, she crept down the hill slope toward the monastery. Its valley lay peacefully, and from her location she could clearly see that no horse was tethered in the courtyard in front of the church. The danger seemed over. At least for the time being.

After she had assuaged her burning thirst drinking water from the brook, she crept cautiously along the back of the monastery and then took the path past the barns to the main building. There was no one to be seen, nothing unusual for this time of day in midsummer. Most of the nuns took a siesta until vespers.

Iriomé entered the entrance hall and walked into the office of the abbess. She knocked on the door, which was slightly larger than the others, and entered the room after having heard the familiar, *"Entra por favor."*

Madre Teresa looked at her in astonishment; then her eyes filled with tears. She did not need to speak. Iriomé knew that something terrible had happened. Wordlessly the abbess rose behind her desk and signaled Iriomé to follow. They set out for the church. Iriomé pressed her son closer as if to calm her pounding heart.

Inside the church it was pleasantly cool. The sunbeams looking in through the colored windows spread a flickering light. The abbess went to one of the side altars with dragging feet, took two of the burning altar candles, and handed Iriomé one. Then she opened a narrow wooden door and climbed down a steep stone staircase. Iriomé had to bend to follow her. It smelled damp and musty, as if no one had been here for years.

In a sort of cave with a circular vault, Guadalupe was laid out on a pedestal of white stone. The abbess held the candle so that Iriomé could see the oval face, framed by the black veil of her habit. Her lips were burst, her left eye was only a blue-violet lump of flesh.

"We found her in the forest. She has been tortured to death," said the abbess in a flat voice, which echoed dully from the rough-hewn stone walls of the tomb. "She didn't want to reveal your secret."

Iriomé trembled, and the little boy in her arms began to whimper faintly. "Cold Eye?" she whispered. "De Lugo?"

"This bears his signature," the abbess said bitterly. "But we probably will never be able to prove it. His connections to Lorenzo de la Huerta will always prevent his being found guilty."

Iriomé felt helpless and guilty. As when Inés de Perreira had stolen the amulet from her, an irrepressible wrath welled up in her, and she felt the desire to kill.

"Let's go back upstairs. This is no place for an infant."

Iriomé handed her the bundle with the child. "'I would like to stay with her for a moment," she said softly.

The abbess looked at her, grieved. She took the child from her and left the tomb without another word.

Iriomé knelt down. She pressed her forehead against the stone pedestal, took Guadalupe's cold hand, and closed her eyes. Revenge and retribution always provoked new misfortune. Even the Christian god said that. But at the sight of her dead friend, she found it difficult to stay in love.

Guadalupe had given her life for her. Iriomé let the time since she and Guadalupe had become friends pass in her mind. They had realized how similar they were to each other. Both were outcasts; both were special children of Mother Earth with the gift to heal people. But in this country this gift brought only suffering and death.

Over the body of her sister-at-heart, Iriomé swore to never use amakuna again for medicinal purposes. She would pass the amulet down to her son and no longer make use of it herself, no matter what happened. She decided to gather all her strength to return to Benahoare. There it would be possible to bring her son up far away from intrigues and violence.

She didn't realize how much time she had spent in the tomb; she heard her name being called from above. Slowly she rose, took one last look at the battered face of her dead friend, then turned away for good. The abbess awaited her at the altar in the church above, took the dripping candle from her, and laid her son into her arms.

"You have visitors from Trujillo. The conde and his companion are waiting in my office for you. I'll go for a walk in the meantime. You know the way."

Joaquín! He had come despite it all. This shot through Iriomé, triggering a mixture of fear and anger. Guadalupe had broken to her gently that he had married Inés one day after the birth of his son. And since that day he had never returned to the monastery.

When she opened the door to the office of the abbess, she saw, however, not Joaquín but two friendly old men who rose immediately. Iriomé recognized both at once. One was Joaquín's father, the other the thin man with the big nose, who could allegedly eat no pork due to his upset stomach.

"Sit down, my child," said Joaquín's father. "I am the Conde Ernesto de Alba y Santa Barbara, and this is my treasurer and friend Aaron Soreon, who has found out by incredible serendipity what's happening here in this monastery."

Alarmed by the rumbling voice of the old count, Tamanca started screaming.

"I suppose that's the powerful voice of my grandson," he continued in a friendly manner. "Unmistakably an offspring of the de Albas."

Iriomé nodded shyly. What did they want from her? The old conde rose to take a closer look at the little screamer.

"He's hungry," said Iriomé, unbuttoning her heavily soiled linen shirt and giving the baby a breast without shame. The two men remained in respectful silence for a moment.

"I'm old and have been suffering from a war injury for many years, a stab wound that will not heal. And I don't know how much time I have left," interrupted the conde over the faint smacking noise of the infant. "That is why I want to make a suggestion. I want to give your son a name. My name. He shall be baptized and live together with you in Trujillo. There you'll be safe."

Tamanca seemed to have had enough, and Iriomé patted his back a couple of times, so that the air he had swallowed could escape and not cause a bellyache. Then she arranged her clothes and gave the old conde a sad look.

"Your offer honors me. But I can't accept it. I want to return to my home island. My son shall grow to a man there."

The old man shook his head slowly. She recognized compassion in his eyes. "I understand that well," he said. "But it's a long and arduous journey to your island, which would put you and especially the child at great risk, especially when he's so small. I can only ask you, also on behalf of my grandson, to accept my protection, at least for the time being. You can't stay here. De Lugo will not stop looking for you, and he has the Inquisition on his side." He snorted.

Iriomé knew he was right. "And in Trujillo, we'll be safe? As far as I know, the conquistador's a well-liked guest at your castle."

"Well liked he was never with me. Rest assured, this lunatic will never set foot in my castillo again."

"But what will your son think about it?" she asked with a hint of resentment in her voice. "Or his wife?"

"Let me worry about that," the conde replied calmly. "I'm still the lord of Trujillo and decide what happens there."

When Tamanca was shaken by a violent coughing fit and she felt his hot head, Iriomé realized that she had to accept this offer. Her son had caught a cold in the damp tunnel and was feverish. What he needed was rest and warmth. "All right," she said softly. "I'll come with you."

"I'm glad, my child!" The conde stroked his grandson's head lovingly. "You'll see, he'll get well soon. And when he's a bit older, you can still follow your plans to go home." He nodded to his treasurer, who rose and helped the conde to get up also. He held out his hand to Iriomé as if they had made a pact. "Everything will be fine, my child."

Thoughtfully Iriomé went back to her hermitage to put on the green dress she had worn on the day of her arrival at the monastery many moons ago and to pack the little she possessed.

The abbess sat on the bench in front of the stone house looking at her sadly. "My daughter, I don't want you to leave, but in Trujillo you'll be safer than here, at least at the moment. Since the marriage of the young conde the castle is under the personal protection of the Queen."

Iriomé sat next to the abbess and took her hand. "Why's he doing this, the old conde? Tell me! Out of love for his grandson?"

Maria Teresa de Angelis shook her head sorrowfully. "I don't think so. Rather for the continuance of his lineage."

Iriomé looked at her blankly.

"I told you that only a few children of the de Alba family have managed to survive their birth. This is because noble families intermarry repeatedly in order to not only preserve their lands and their property for their offspring, but to increase it if possible. The de Albas need fresh blood!"

Iriomé understood. On Benahoare the women often married men from other tribes, which sometimes was not easy but was unavoidable.

The abbess sighed. "These men know no love. What the young de Alba has felt for you only lasted a short time. Eternal love you will ultimately only find in the Almighty. Of course there is nothing wrong with searching for it here on earth, but it's fatal to fall for its caricature, infatuation. The art of looking behind people's masks has a lot to do with experience. And it's especially difficult to look behind the mask of a man who comes from a foreign country and grew up with a different religion."

Iriomé knelt before the abbess. "You're a woman, tell me: Have you never met a man whom you loved with every fiber of your body?"

"No, I haven't. Maybe I missed something on the other side; I have thus spared myself much suffering. "

"I want to thank you for your honesty and for all that you have braved for me and taken upon yourself."

The abbess had tears in her eyes, and her face was a little redder than usual. "And I want to thank you for what you have set at risk for me."

Iriomé stood up and laid her hand on Madre Teresa's back. "Only love can defeat the fear of any kind of power," she said quietly and stepped into the hermitage, her son in her arms.

The abbess followed. Iriomé opened a chest in which she kept the green dress.

When Madre Teresa tied the bodice, she again felt nearly suffocated. "You'll get used to it," said the abbess, smiling.

"I don't think so," Iriomé replied, "but it will constantly remind me that I'm a prisoner and maintain my desire for freedom." For the last time, she looked around the hermitage where she had lived so long and which held so many memories, especially of Guadalupe. She wondered if she should take something with her to remind her of this time of her life. Then she decided against it. There were two people who had become valuable to her in this place, and she would always keep them in her heart.

One last time Iriomé ran her fingertip over the lines of the spiral she had carved in the rock above her resting place. "The sign of infinity and eternal recurrence! It will give me the strength to return to my home island."

The abbess smiled. "I wish you all the very best. May God be with you."

Iriomé insisted on riding on Karima's back to Trujillo. The mare had become a true friend to her and would always remind her of Ibn Said. She had been a long time without news from him and did not know if he was still in Spain or had been forced to leave the country to save his life. The abbess had told her that both Moors and Jews were now persecuted fiercely by the Christians. It was not about the different gods but about power. About suppressing the weak and taking everything from them without their having the right to protest, a thought that was foreign to Iriomé. On her home island those who fared better cared for those who had less and did not take the little they had from them, too.

She took her mare behind the church where the two men were already waiting for them in a carriage. The conde insisted that the sick infant travel with him in the carriage, and Iriomé agreed after some hesitation. It was Aaron who especially reassured her and whom she finally trusted. He was a fugitive like her and the médico. This united them in a sad way.

After she handed him the bundle with the infant, she sat on the horse, clicked her tongue softly, and guided Karima with slight leg pressure in the right direction. Her hair came down to her shoulders by now and was blowing red and golden in the wind. The carriage with the arms of de Alba, crossed swords before the rising sun, also started to move and followed her.

They took a much shorter route than on the way there and passed through a village that Joaquín had then avoided for safety's sake.

Even from afar Iriomé perceived a strange mood coming from the village square, as if there was a kind of folk festival taking place. She smelled fire. The closer they came, the louder the voices of the people gathered around a blazing fire were. When she heard the first piercing screams of women and men and the smell of burning flesh rose to her nose, her heart cramped with horror. She made Karima gallop in the opposite direction. Until that moment, she could not have imagined that the stories of Guadalupe about the auto-da-fé, the burning of non-Christians at the stake, was reality. But now she had seen it with her own eyes.

Although she had put some distance between herself and this horrible place, she could still hear the agony of the dying. The disgusting smell almost turned her stomach. She felt like riding in the direction of the coast in a flash, in order to find a ship to take her back to her island. But without her son she neither could nor wanted to leave the country.

So she made Karima break into a full gallop and reached Trujillo at the same time as the carriage. As at her first arrival, the drawbridge was lowered and the gates opened with a squealing noise. Karima seemed to remember and trotted fearlessly onto the roughly cobbled patio.

First they were met by the castellan Roberto de la Torre, who took her horse by the bridle and helped her dismount. He looked into her face a moment longer than necessary but did not show whether he recognized her.

But Iriomé took his hand. "I'd like to thank you again for saving me from the stable lads last time I was here."

He smiled almost imperceptibly. "I'd do it again. And not only from stable lads."

The carriage had also driven into the courtyard. Two attendants came running, tore open the doors, and placed small pedestals in front of them. Aaron Soreon smilingly handed Iriomé her sleeping son, who seemed to have recovered from his high temperature. The old conde offered her his arm and led her into the inner rooms of the castle. This time she felt welcome and respected. Yet the high entrance hall, from the ceiling of which a mighty iron chandelier was hanging, still gave her the feeling of being small and insignificant. Gloomy oil paintings with stern-looking men in full armor adorned the walls. The old conde sensed her discomfort and gave Iriomé an encouraging smile. "Don't worry, they look more grim than they were. Besides, they're deader than they look."

Aaron bid farewell respectfully by bowing deep before Iriomé. "Whenever there's something that I can do for you, do me the honor to consult me."

Iriomé thanked the friendly Jew and followed the conde up stone stairs to the side wing with his personal chambers. Twice clapping his hands made two young maids appear dressed in simple brown clothes, white aprons, and tight-fitting hoods.

He ordered them to immediately prepare two rooms for Iriomé and her son. Both threw her a deprecatory look that turned into hostility and fear. However, this did not keep the conde from hurrying them along even more. "Go, go! Are you asleep on your feet? The Señora has had an exhausting journey."

Heavy brocade curtains were opened, pillows fluffed, and blankets, tablecloths, and toiletries fetched. One of the women the conde called

Ana brought a brightly painted wooden cradle, which she placed beside a bed with a massive canopy. After she had also equipped the cradle with a pillow and blanket, the conde told Iriomé to settle his grandson therein.

"This was once Joaquín's cradle," he said softly. "It was manufactured especially for him. Since then, never again has a child slept in it," he continued with deep sadness in his voice. The other servant had lit the fireplace and now retired discreetly.

Awestruck, Iriomé ran her hand over the white pillows and bedding made of fine, shiny fabric, which felt pleasantly cool. The fire soon gave the room pleasant warmth. The conde looked at her benevolently. Iriomé felt that he respected her and would not harm her. It could have been a beautiful moment if she had not foreseen the raven black clouds that promised no bright future.

The old conde got up groaning, leaning on his crane, and said goodbye for the day. "I'll have you sent something to eat. It's certainly in your interest not to spend the first night in the circle of the family, especially since they've only just heard of your arrival," he winked at her. "You are beautiful. We should marry as soon as possible to give the boy a legitimate father. There's not much time left for me. After that you and your son would be without protection. I'll organize his and your christening for tomorrow."

"What's this I hear? Do I perhaps get a say in this?" It came from the door. It was Joaquín.

He wore a white ruff, a tight doublet of leather, short green- and red-striped bloomers, and beneath them tight-fitting bright trousers. Iriomé had never before seen him in such finery. During her stay in the convent she had met only a few men, and they were farmers in plain, mostly grubby work garments. But what seemed strangest to her was the smell that came from Joaquín. It was the same that had caused her such nausea when the disbelievers on the marketplace had been burned.

The old conde looked at him coldly. "While you're cozying up to this fat Dominican, the greatest sycophant the church has, and even attend these hideous executions, I have performed a real act of humanity."

Her nose had not fooled her. Iriomé was stabbed through the heart. What had happened to him? Why was his heart closed? Although they had not seen each other in such a long time, he did not deign to look at her and pretended she was nonexistent.

"I've only done my duty," Joaquín said.

"And I've made sure that your son will get our name. You should be grateful."

"Grateful?" Joaquín laughed. "You just want to get a young woman into your bed. You should be ashamed of this at your age."

"Are you tormented by jealousy now?" replied the conde. "After you left this wonderful creature of nature at a monastery months ago?"

"Of course not!" snorted Joaquín. Finally he looked at Iriomé, who at that moment could see right into his soul. She realized that behind his anger and his new mercilessness a great shame was hidden. He would never admit that he had betrayed their love and instead had allied with power. He thought he could show opposition and strength to his father in this way. However, it was a strength that was not marked by responsibility and benevolence but by cruelty and violence. All this triggered a deep sadness in her.

"If I marry Iriomé and adopt her son, he's your little brother of whom you can officially take care. Don't you understand what possibilities this opens up for you?"

"And my heritage?"

"Keep silent!" The old conde barked at him, looking him up and down as if he were a stupid little boy. "As my second son," he said, "he'll get a mere trifle after my death, so your inheritance, and also that of your unborn son is not in danger."

Iriomé winced. So they were expecting a child. A legitimate child.

Joaquín turned away.

"That's best for us all, believe me, my son." The conde patted him on the shoulder and was about to leave the room. "At least have a look at your offspring. A beautiful boy. I hope he doesn't have too much of his father in him," he chuckled, walking into the hall.

"Oh and by the way," he came back again. "What do you think of the name Enrique? Enrique de Alba y Santa Barbara. Sounds impressive, doesn't it?"

For the family de Alba everything seemed to be settled, yet not for Iriomé. But at the moment they had her in their grip so she could not do anything. In addition, her son was half de Alba. Could she deny him this name and growing up under the protection of the Christian god? Here in this country this would probably help him more than anything else. Who knew when she would ever be able to return to her island?

Joaquín hesitantly approached the cradle, as if Iriomé were a wild animal and would pounce on him at any moment. Iriomé took the sleeping Tamanca carefully from the cradle and laid him in Joaquín's arms. He held the baby a bit awkwardly, yet the hint of a smile showed on his face. Iriomé realized that loving feelings were trying to come to the fore, but he did not allow it and handed back the infant hastily.

"I named him Tamanca," she said softly.

Joaquín stood ramrod straight.

"Your father is a wise man. Only as his wife will Tamanca and I be safe from your friend de Lugo."

"He would never hurt you. He only wants your magic remedy. Why don't you just let him have it?" Restlessly, he walked up and down the room. "I don't know what spirits or demons you're connected with, but I know one thing: I want nothing to do with it."

That was clear enough! Iriomé's last ray of hope for protecting amakuna together with him was extinguished forever. Tichiname's forecast that the mushroom would eventually meet its destiny only by the true love between a man and a woman would not prove true. She must have been mistaken. Until now, the relationship with Joaquín had only caused trouble.

"Your friend has tortured a young nun to death," she said in a low voice.

"These are only rumors, Iriomé."

"I saw her. She was found in the woods, and she was battered."

"Wild dogs," he muttered. "I have to go now; I'll see you tomorrow at the christening."

Chapter 32

The Chapel of Trujillo was filled to the last seat. Joaquín and the condesa were sitting stony-faced in the first row. Inés wore a black dress under which it could clearly be seen that she was pregnant.

Iriomé looked away quickly. On her island the loyalty of a man toward a woman who had born him a child was one of the most important values, especially among the tribe members of superior rank. But here other rules applied. She wondered inwardly that Inés did not recognize in her the assistant of the médico. But with her white, waxen doll face she just looked straight through her. Joaquín definitely had not told her the reason this christening was happening or who she was.

The one, however, who immediately recalled her, was the Franciscan Frai Hieronymus. He gave her a look as if he wanted to see her at the stake. But Iriomé knew that he was subordinate to the conde, and as long as the old man was at her side, he would do nothing against her. Yet there were more than just enemies here. Ernesto de Alba y Santa Barbara sat in a magnificent gold-embroidered doublet beside her and took her hand soothingly. Aaron Soreon, as well as the red-bearded castellan, both smiled at her when she entered the chapel and paid her compliments on her beauty. Gradually she got accustomed to the tight clothes that enhanced the status of a woman here, at least in the eyes of the men. She had been brought a robe from Joaquín's mother, this time in bright blue, that became her even better.

The old conde signaled the Franciscan, who wore a red robe decorated with golden braids, to start the ceremony. "Let us pray."

The residents of the castillo rose. Iriomé did the same, firmly pressing her son to her body.

"*Pater noster, it qui in caelis: sanctificetur nomen tuum. Adveniat regnum tuum. Fiat voluntas tua, sicut in caelo, et in terra. Panem nostrum supersubstantialem (cotidianum) da nobis hodie. Et dimitte nobis debita nostra, sicut et nos dimittimus debitoribus nostris. Et ne nos inducas in tentationem, sed libera nos a malo. Amen.*"

"Amen," repeated the little community.

Iriomé knew the prayer from the monastery, but the verse about forgiveness she did not understand. Why should she forgive de Lugo, who had given the order to slaughter her people?

Why Joaquín, who had lied to her and betrayed her? Why Inés de Perreira, who had accused her of theft and was a thief herself? As far as she understood it, the Christian god redeemed his children from all evil, so that they could commit new crimes whitewashed. For this they were neither downgraded in the hierarchy nor cast out, as the tribal customs on Benahoare prescribed and as Tara and Tigotan had determined. She couldn't possibly stay here.

"Peace be with thee," said the monk. He nodded to the old conde; however, he avoided looking into Iriomé's eyes. "Please step forward."

Supported on his cane, he rose and gave Iriomé a sign to come with her son to the baptismal font.

"I question you now, Ernesto de Alba y Santa Barbara: You are the godfather and at the same time the father of this child. What shall be his name?"

Iriomé noticed Joaquín slightly wincing.

"Enrique," the conde stated firmly. "After Enrique El Segundo, the illegitimate son of Alonso XI, who proclaimed himself king against his half-brother. He defeated him in the famous battle of Montiel, cut off his head, and thus established the House of Trastámara, from which our beloved Queen Isabella of Castile and our beloved King Ferdinand of Aragon descended. A name that fits this child and takes him in the duty of his ancestors to God and the Holy Mother Church."

"What do you desire from the Church of God?"

"The faith."

"What does the faith grant you?"

"Eternal life."

The Franciscan blew gently three times into the face of the child to baptize him. "Be gone, evil spirit, and make way for the Holy Spirit, the Comforter." Then he put his hand on the head of the child, saying, "Let us pray. Almighty and eternal God, Father of our Lord Jesus Christ, look graciously down upon this thy servant Enrique de Alba y Santa Barbara, whom you have graciously called to the beginnings of faith. Take all blindness from his heart. Tear all shackles of Satan, by which he was bound. Open to him, O Lord, the doors of your fatherly love. May the sign of thy wisdom penetrate him, so that he is free from the blight of all evil desires, will serve you in your Church joyfully, attracted by the scents of your teachings, and let him go forth from day to day through Christ our Lord. Amen." He scooped baptismal water, poured it three times in cross shape over the child's head and spoke the words, *"Ego te baptizo in nomine Patris et Filii et Spiritus Sancti ad nomine* Enrique de Alba y Santa Barbara."

Inés de Perreira y de Alba gave a sharp cry of pain and fell from the pew. Joaquín jumped up and held her just before she hit her head on the stone floor. A murmur went through the chapel.

The two maids of the condesa came running. One fanned her hastily; the other held a smelling bottle beneath her nose, after which she regained consciousness. But her eyes were filled with fear. She reached with her hand under her dress producing it smeared with blood and held it as a silent accusation against the conde. "Look what you have done!" she screamed shrilly. "It's not right to grant a bastard the favor of our Lord in this way." Then her voice failed.

"Quick, get a médico!" Joaquín shouted, carrying her out of the chapel, not without throwing his father a withering look. But the old conde kept his composure.

"Continue!" he barked at the monk. "We are not at the end. The woman must be baptized also."

With a slightly trembling voice the priest ended the christening with the concluding prayer. After the last words died away, Iriomé quickly took her son and was about to leave the chapel. It was all too much for her. The christening seemed to her like one big lie. A betrayal of Tara, her ancestors, and her faith. But the conde held her back and whispered in her ear, "If you want to survive in this country, then you need to play this game. . . . Go ahead, christen her!" he ordered the Franciscan.

"I cannot reconcile this with my conscience," he replied in a low voice. "She's a witch. I witnessed it myself."

"You know only too well that all this is utter nonsense. If you don't immediately administer your office, I will chase you from the court in disgrace and ensure that no castillo throughout the Extremadura will have a warm meal for you."

Fear flickered in the eyes of the monk. "Then she must first confess."

Slowly the old conde reached the end of his rope. "She has nothing to confess," he said louder than intended. "She was until yesterday in the monastery. I warn you, monk!"

The courtiers had become restless. Only the hope of filling their bellies and getting drunk at the expense of the conde during the following celebration kept them on the pews.

"Well, I'll do it," Frai Hieronymus relented. "But solely on your responsibility. For the Lord never leaves something like this unpunished."

"Of course, on my responsibility, what else," the conde growled, upset. "Now get on with it."

"And what shall her name be?"

The conde hesitated for a moment. "So there you have it. Irina de Alba y Santa Barbara. Impressive, isn't it?"

Frai Jerome sighed and dipped his hands in the font.

The table for the subsequent christening party was only half as long and by far not as bountiful as at the festival Iriomé had watched from the small chamber. This time, however, she was no secret listener, but the guest of honor sitting on a raised chair beside the conde.

After all wine jugs had been filled, he raised his jug and introduced her as the Princess of the Island of the Blessed and as his future wife. Exactly at this moment Joaquín appeared at the table. "The condesa sends her apologies," he said in a loud, reproachful voice. "The bleeding has stopped, but she now needs to stay in bed until the day of the birth and can't even get out of bed to relieve herself. The excitement of the last twenty-four hours was probably too much for her."

The old conde kept a straight face. "Well, then she's in her chambers in good hands and can't spoil our mood here."

Joaquín wanted to answer back to his father, but Iriomé stopped him. "Is she in pain?"

"Yes, but a woman from the village gave her something. She's sleeping now. I've sent for Ibn Said. He's said to stay in the vicinity."

"Hopefully, it's not too late then," Iriomé said softly.

Joaquín pulled her aside. "What do you mean by that?"

"Sometimes the skin, in which the child is lying, comes off early. Painful bleeding can be a sign."

"And what does that mean?"

"Maybe nothing." Iriomé felt that he would have liked to grab her and drag her to his wife, but in front of all the domestics he could not afford such a scene.

"Could you help her with your magic formula if it should come to the worst?" he whispered into her ear instead.

Iriomé remembered the oath she had taken at the coffin of the dead Guadalupe. She would never use amakuna for healing purposes again. "No, I won't," she replied.

"Go to hell," he hissed.

The old conde grabbed him by the wrist. "I must insist that you behave appropriately toward my future wife and the mother of my son," he reprimanded Joaquín.

"I'm not going to celebrate with you while my wife is suffering," Joaquín said, so that everyone could hear it.

"When I gave birth to your son, it did not bother you to celebrate your wedding. I've heard there was a glittering celebration," Iriomé said, but so softly that only he could hear it.

His face flushed with anger. "I'll send a messenger to His Excellency Lorenzo de la Huerta. Let's see what he has to say about this farce!" he shouted, outraged.

"Well, if you have to," the old conde said, still calm. "But I will refuse him admittance. I am still the lord of Trujillo."

In his anger Joaquín knocked over a wine barrel as he marched out, so that the wine spilled on the stone floor like blood. Immediately, two maids came running in order to clean it up.

"What did he want from you?" The old conde leaned toward Iriomé. "Did he offend you?"

"No, he's just very angry."

"He's mad at himself, and he has every reason to be. Because he still loves you. Only he can't show it and cannot not live it. Only in the later years of life we see through to the true nature of things and understand what really counts." The conde struggled to his feet. When he stood upright, he towered even over the standing servants. "Come on, let's raise our jugs regardless of rank and name. Just as was the custom once in the good old times in the castles of the Extremadura." All agreed with him loudly and raised their pitchers. "To the health of the young Enrique de Alba y Santa Barbara."

"To the health of the young Enrique de Alba y Santa Barbara!" the servants repeated his words and went for food as if they had been starving.

Iriomé's appetite was gone. She thought nostalgically of the last feast with her own people. Even there they had had more to eat and drink than usual, but nobody stressed their body to such an extent as the people did here. Most of them could hardly sit straight after a very short time. Iriomé watched some of them going outside and sticking their finger down their throat, just to pile new food onto their plate. They seemed to have completely lost touch with themselves, follow only their desires, and think of nothing else. Thus they could escape reality, a life they had no command of. A life that now was also allotted to her. Iriomé longed to return to Benahoare with every fiber of her heart. She felt a pain in her chest, making it impossible to sit here any longer, so she apologized to the old conde, saying she wanted to retire as it was time to feed her son.

"Go on. I will come and look in on you later," he said gently.

Stepping outside, she enjoyed the cold night air and went quickly over the unevenly cobbled courtyard to the archway that connected the side wing to the main building. When someone caught up with her and pressed her against the wall, placing his hands on either side of her head, she knew immediately that it was Joaquín. She smelled his breath. At that moment she was glad of her tightly laced dress enclosing her like armor. His heart that once had beaten in unison with hers had reverted to its old rhythm. The velvet-brown eyes no longer invited her to be lost in them. On the contrary, his gaze was marked by fear, arrogance, and brute force he would not hesitate to use if he considered it necessary. And yet she felt the warmth of his body, his knee against her legs, his groin protection, which pressed against her lower body. The smell of his fresh linens mixed with the smell of his sweat. Gently, like the flicker of a candle flame, his lips were stroking her neck.

"I sleep alone at the moment. My chamber is in the round tower above my father's. You only need to climb up the stairs."

Iriomé did not know what to think. Lust and anger fought against each other.

"Will you be coming tonight?" he asked. "Shall I stir the fire and wait for you?" He let go of her and gave her a nod, as if they had sealed a trade. Then he disappeared into the darkness. Iriomé knew she was lost. She was not only caught up in this castle, she was also just like him, a prisoner of her love and passion, which could not breathe here between the high walls.

When she walked past the silvery shining loopholes to her chambers, she felt that her skin was burning in the moonlight. She imagined that Joaquín was lying naked on his bed waiting for her. Iriomé had just fallen asleep when Ana roused her. "Señora, please wake up. The old conde . . . he's not well. He calls for you and also for Frai Hieronymus for the last rites. I think the end is not far off."

Ana's words ensured that Iriomé came wide awake at once. She looked helplessly down at her nightgown. Certainly it was not suitable to leave her room only wearing this. But Ana held out a cloak of green silk. She slipped into it and rushed to the apartments of the conde.

Outside the window, dawn was breaking. Iriomé beheld at the conte's bed her old friend Ibn Said. Under other circumstances, she would have been glad to see him again, but the serious look on his face made her stop. He had just removed the dressing from the leg of the conde. The smell of pus and rot coming from a huge ulcer that covered his whole thigh stung Iriomé's nose. Ibn Said moved his head pensively from side to side.

"I can't do much for you, Señor. The pus has finally poisoned your blood. Even if we cut off your leg, this wouldn't help you."

"I lived with it for over ten years," the conde said, his voice brittle.

"You were really lucky there," said the médico.

"It was rather strong will than luck," Ernesto de Alba whispered, his voice trailing off.

"It's her fault!" cried Frai Hieronymus and brought a candlestick so close to Iriomé's face that the flame would have set her hair on fire if Ibn Said had not pushed him aside.

"Do you want to burn her right here?" he barked at the monk. "In the face of a dying man?"

Frai Hieronymus took a step back. "I have warned his Excellency. He forced me to baptize this witch. But the Lord doesn't stand for any nonsense."

The conde registered Iriomé's presence and tried to grab her hand. "You need not be afraid," he whispered. "For you and little Enrique are taken care of." Then he turned to Ana, who had remained standing behind Iriomé. "I want you now to wake up all and bring them here. My son, his honorable wife, should she be able to come, the castellan Roberto de la Torre, and my treasurer and dearest friend Aaron Soreon."

The médico rose to retire discreetly. But the old conde stopped him with a movement of the hand. "I ask you to stay as an independent witness for my last will." He closed his eyes and opened them again when Joaquín and his wife, who was leaning on him, appeared shortly afterward, both wrapped in precious dressing gowns. They sat at the foot of the bed without looking at Iriomé. Aaron Soreon came running, his beard wild and unkempt and with a worried expression on his face. He wore only a thin silk coat, while the castellan that was right behind him was already dressed for the day in a dark overcoat, black breeches, and shiny boots. His working day had started long ago, organizing the daily routine of the castillo. He smiled reassuringly at Iriomé.

The breath of the dying man got faster as if he needed more air for what he now had to say to those present. "My loyal friend, Aaron, I want you to pack your things right away and leave for Augsburg in Swabia first thing tomorrow morning. There a powerful merchant family lives. They call themselves the Welser. I've met Anton Welser once, a righteous man, in his commercial settlement in Seville. He helped me with one hundred silver thalers in an extremely precarious situation. I don't want to die without having paid back my debts. It's important that you go as soon as possible, because, as you will know yourself, you won't be able to travel in this country unmolested much longer. Take three well-armed caballeros along with you for your protection."

Iriomé saw tears well up in the eyes of the Jew. It had to be hard for him to lose not only a good friend, but also his home. She could more than sympathize with his sorrow.

"I'll accompany you part of the way," the médico chimed in and put a hand on Aaron's shoulder. "I possess a ferman, a passport, personally issued by His Excellency the Grand Inquisitor Frai Lorenzo de la Huerta. With this we should pass each control point without problems, at least up to the border of Aragon. They've got no such strict laws against Jews there, and you'll be safe for now."

Aaron looked at him gratefully. Iriomé guessed that the conde's main concern was not the repayment of old debts. Ernesto de Alba could now no longer protect his friend or save him from the persecution of the Jews that was getting more and more cruel. Iriomé still heard the cries of the victims meeting their death at the stake in the small village. Hopefully Aaron would be spared this fate. From Joaquín no help could be expected. He had allied with power and would hand the old man over to the Inquisition without batting an eyelash. The little speech had cost the conde a lot of energy. He was lying on his pillows, face pale and eyes closed. But then he straightened up, as if he knew that he had little time left.

"And you," he turned to the Franciscan, "will now marry me to this young lady, and now before I breathe my last breath. For I'm a man who always keeps his word." The last sentence he could only whisper, then his voice failed, and he fell back on his bed.

Frai Hieronymus smiled. This time he felt clearly in the stronger position and was enjoying it visibly. He shook his head. But Ernesto de Alba y Santa Barbara did not realize this. His eyes were closed; he was breathing heavily.

Frai Hieronymus lit the death candle and placed it next to the bed of the old conde, who once again lifted his head and looked his son directly in the eye. "I want you to swear to me to respect and protect little Enrique like a brother and his mother like a sister."

Joaquín hesitated, hoping that death would come quickly and spare him such a promise. But Ernesto de Alba y Santa Barbara was still looking at his son expectantly, just like all the others present. Finally he could not delay it any longer. He raised his hand and said softly. "*Juro!* I swear."

Inés uttered a similar cry as in the chapel and collapsed again. Ibn Said jumped up and carried her with the assistance of Aaron out of the death room.

"De la Torre, you have to testify as a witness to this promise," the conde said with his last strength before his head fell back onto the pillows, this time forever. He breathed his last breath and passed away.

Ana opened the window, letting the cool morning air in, and then retired. The candle went out. Since no one else did, Iriomé closed the eyes of the dead and folded his arms over his chest as she had seen done in the tomb where Guadalupe was laid.

Joaquín stared into space. In his eyes not a single tear showed. His feelings were buried deep in his heart. Neither the death of his father nor the existence of his young son could bring them to light. There was not much else that could touch that soul. He was lost. Iriomé sat down beside him. He seemed to her like a cold rock.

Frai Hieronymus spoke the funeral prayer, giving her a triumphant and at the same time devastating look, but she ignored it. Joaquín seemed to perceive nothing and looked up only when one of Inés's maids approached him with a worried expression and whispered something in his ear. He jumped up and signaled for Iriomé to follow him. No sooner had he closed the door behind him than he grabbed her by the shoulders.

"You have to do something at once; otherwise my wife's going to die and also the child. The médico can't help her anymore! I'm going to lose everything my family has built up over several generations. Queen Isabella will blame me for the death of her favorite cousin and no longer take Trujillo under her wing."

His words, uttered in a harsh commanding tone, fell on deaf ears. "I can't help you. I told you so already!" Her voice sounded so cold that she was frightened of herself. She knew that decisions made out of hatred usually were not good decisions. But she wanted, under no circumstances, to break her oath. In addition, Joaquín had humiliated her too often; he had too often put his own interests first, and she no longer felt compelled to make an exception for him. He had exposed her to situations for which she had not been prepared and brought her into the position of a supplicant. After all, she was a harimaguada, the successor of the great Tichiname, who had appointed her guardian of the amakuna.

Iriomé turned away without another word and walked through the door back into the room of the conde in order to bid him farewell a last time. Although his main concern had been his noble family, he had showed himself obliging and generous to her. Unlike his son he had not been driven by fear but acted out of self-assurance and true assertiveness. She opened the door and nearly collided with the castellan, who was about to leave the death chamber.

"How is the countess?" he inquired politely of Joaquín, who, however, only stared at Iriomé full of hate and quickly walked away.

"All this must be very confusing to you," the castellan said to Iriomé sympathetically.

"I've been through worse," she replied softly, then moved past him to the bed of the conde. The windows of the room faced east, and the morning sun cast his first rays on the body of Ernesto de Alba y Santa Barbara, as if even the sun did not want him to get cold. She sat down on the bench at the foot of his bed. Frai Hieronymus's still ongoing funeral prayer was only perceived as a monotonous murmur.

Perhaps the abbess had been right, and the only true love was the love for the gods, the spirits, or the ancestors. Maybe people were only capable of this great, comprehensive feeling for a short time, then sank back into their existence, overshadowed by greed, jealousy, avarice, and other ugly characteristics.

Chapter 33

Inés and her child died a few hours after the conde. Joaquín brought Iriomé the message while she was playing a little game with her son in her bedroom. She swayed a cord, on one end of which she had knotted a pearl, back and forth in front of the infant, who could already follow its movements with his eyes and who stretched out his small hands after the pearl.

First she said nothing at all, just kept playing with her son.

Joaquín fetched a stool, sat down beside her at the cradle placed at an open window, and watched the two.

"What do you want?"

"You."

Iriomé paused and looked at him in disbelief.

"It's just the two of us now. Fate has chosen us. You know that as well as I. We belong together, against all odds. And our son will one day be the lord of Trujillo."

Iriomé wondered if she had heard him correctly. She put the pendulum aside and picked up Tamanca, who promptly began to cry because his play had been interrupted.

"I can understand that you were jealous, but there's no longer a reason for it. I'll marry you. Officially."

Iriomé was at a loss for words.

"Yes, I'll marry the mother of my son," he repeated firmly.

"I was already the mother of your son," she said softly.

"But now the situation has changed."

"Right. Now you're afraid you will never have an heir. Because in your family there've been too many stillbirths. Now suddenly I'm good enough! Now suddenly our son is no longer a risk!"

"Iriomé, I beg you. You must forgive me. I was wrong. I've let myself be blinded by the splendor and glory of a cousin of the Queen. I thought I had to prove to my father that I'm able to preserve the family property. And that was only possible through this marriage. I had no choice. But the truth is and always has been, I love you and finally want to live with you, as destiny planned for us."

Iriomé could not distinguish whether he actually felt this truth or only wanted to ingratiate himself with her. But it no longer made a difference. Even though Joaquín offered her what she had yearned for, her heart was closed to him. And it would not open up for him again. Not in this life. She now felt nothing but contempt for this man.

"I'll never marry you. And you won't get my son," she said firmly. "If he grows up here, a heart of stone will be beating in his breast just as in his father's. We'll return to my island."

Joaquín collapsed. Similar to their first farewell at the monastery, he looked like a tree without leaves. Perhaps he loved her, but even so, it was a love that could not withstand the storms of life. He would always give in again.

"Is this your last word?" he rasped.

Iriomé nodded. "I'll pack up our things today."

Joaquín's face hardened. "And how are you going to do this? Turn into a bird and fly across the sea to your island?"

"Aaron and the médico will allow me to travel with them to the coast. There I'll find a ship to bring me home."

"I won't permit this." He stood up abruptly. The little stool on which he had sat noisily toppled over, and Tamanca began to scream, scared.

"The goddess will show me a way," Iriomé said softly and cradled her son in her arms, who thereupon stopped crying immediately. Joaquín paid no attention to the stool and turned toward the door.

"Your goddess?" he laughed. "You'll see where she will get you."

Iriomé learned what that threat meant just a short time later. There was a knock, and two caballeros she knew as gate guards harshly asked her to follow them. When she did not immediately respond, they grabbed her by the arms and pulled her from the chair.

"Order of the conde. Bring a cape because it's not very warm where we're going to take you."

What was Joaquín up to? Did he want to take revenge on her for not obeying him?

The two men let go of her so that she could put a cape around her shoulders. She looked around quickly. The only escape was through the open window. From there she could let herself down the wall, but not with an infant in her arms. She went to the cradle to pick up Tamanca but was abruptly stopped by a female voice.

"The child stays here!" Ana, who had until now hidden behind the guards, moved the cradle out of reach. The guards took Iriomé between them and dragged her to the door. She screamed. Tamanca cried. But their cries met only the rough walls of the castillo, which swallowed them like a predator.

It took all the strength of the two men to haul Iriomé down the stone steps into the cellar to the dungeon. They almost slipped on the wet ground. This offered Iriomé a possibility to escape, but they caught her robe and pulled her back. Both flung themselves at her. After a brief fight they pushed Iriomé into a dark, moldy cell. The heavy, iron-studded wooden door was locked from the outside.

She was breathing heavily. Blood ran down her temple. Her legs were scraped and burned where she had been dragged over the rough ground. She felt her left eye swell up. As the guard predicted, she was cold. She tucked up her legs and tried, as best she could, to cover herself with the thin cape, but it was of no use. From high above scant light was coming through a small hole, enough to be aware that she was not alone down here. She shared this eerie accommodation with a crowd of rats that were coming toward her curiously. Iriomé let them. In contrast to most people, these animals seemed almost amiable to her. She got in touch with them in her very own way and convinced them to stay away.

Eventually, Iriomé even slept a little. She heard the key being turned in the lock, and then the door opened. She hoped it was Joaquín so that she could convince him to let her out. But standing in front of her, a lantern in his hand making his gaunt face look like a demonic mask, was her worst and most hated enemy: Alonso Fernández de Lugo. Behind him the two guards had taken position and would not let her out of sight.

De Lugo closed the door with a smile and leaned against it. His face was sunken, deep wrinkles between his mouth and nose notched into his skin. He had become even skinnier than she remembered.

"So we meet again! It's a long time since you've saved my life. And so far I've had no opportunity to show my appreciation," he said. "But now I will."

Iriomé did not know what was worse; the voice or the eyes of this man.

"For I'm going to save your life, just like you once saved mine."

"My life's not in danger," she said. "Joaquín wants to marry me."

"Yes, and then he will put you away and marry some noble woman who's related to the royal family. It won't matter if she bears him a son or not. Because he's got one already! How convenient. And our mutual friend, His Excellency Frai Lorenzo de la Huerta, whom you already had the pleasure of meeting, will kindly ensure that small Enrique will be recognized by the Queen as Joaquín's legitimate son. In return Joaquín will immediately offer him his full assistance in setting up his Inquisition tribunals on his own lands."

Iriomé stared at him, her mouth open.

De Lugo laughed scornfully. "How soon do you think you will end up at a stake there? For this will be the easiest way for Joaquín to get rid of you, and quite a legitimate one, too. He saw you in the monastery of Santa Maria del Valle—just think about it, in a convent!—paying homage to Satan and offering him a goat sacrifice. And don't believe he will save your life again. You've forfeited that chance. Once and for all." His laugh turned into a coughing fit. "And if that's not enough, I'm going to testify against you. And should this still not be enough, we also have the abbess of Santa Maria or the young mother from a small village north from Cádiz whom you brought back to life."

Iriomé was shattered. So she would burn. Just as Guayafanta predicted.

"But you can avoid all this if you prepare your magic potion for me exactly in the quantity I need. So what do you say? Thus all would be satisfied." He laughed throatily. "Think about it. But not for too long."

"May I see my son? He must drink," Iriomé asked in desperation. She got no answer. Cold Eye had already left her prison.

One of the guards brought her a pitcher of water and some stale bread and a blanket. Although she felt no hunger or thirst, she ate and drank. She needed to stay in good health if she wanted to extricate herself, no matter how, from this wretched situation. Neither a life according to de Lugo's wishes nor death were an option.

The only friends she had would set off tonight to save their own lives. She had little hope they would get her out of here. Nevertheless Iriomé stayed awake all night. She paid heed to each sound, each voice. She heard each single cry of the night birds, the howling of wolves in the distance. When the new day was dawning and a thin beam of light fell on her in her dungeon, she was still sitting on the stony ground. The only creatures that occasionally had looked in on her were the rats.

What tormented her far more than the cold, the hunger, or the fear of death by fire was concern about her little son. She missed him. He was the one who kept her alive and gave her comfort when solitude lay over her like a gray cloth. When she had lived in the hermitage of the monastery and she and Guadalupe prepared medicine from herbs, she had at least felt useful and connected to the task Tara had meant for her. But now she seemed to have lost touch with her goddess completely. The rats that lived down here and ate the waste of the castillo served their purpose in life more than she currently did. She was not only outwardly a prisoner, her soul was imprisoned as well. She could not make a free decision. Perhaps there was no more for her.

The day passed without Joaquín or Cold Eye seeking her out or receiving a message from her friends. Slowly Iriomé lost all hope that her fate could still take a turn for the better. When she became aware of this, she cringed. She touched the amulet that she still wore around her neck. Nothing in life came in vain. Everything she suffered had something to do with amakuna. And all of a sudden she understood. The realization hit her like a bolt of lightning. Tamanca was the key. With him the door to the future opened. He would be the next keeper of the mushroom. His descendants would ensure that the secret would be kept and only be revealed when the time had come. That was what Tichiname had wanted to say.

Joaquín had been destined to be the father of her son. Because only as his son would Tamanca have the power to protect amakuna . . .

Iriomé had dozed off briefly when she thought she felt a touch on her shoulder. Assuming it was a rat that had come too close, she tried to shoo it away with her hand and instead pressed her hand against Roberto de la Torre, who held it.

"*Rapido!* Come quickly," he whispered.

Iriomé was promptly wide awake and on her feet.

"I've saddled your horse. If you ride fast and always keep to the northeast, you'll overtake your friends by tomorrow evening. They couldn't take you with them, because the conde searched every corner of the carriage. They'll wait for you near the village of Tabla de la Reina on a farm belonging to a certain Paco de Oriega."

The castellan was a true friend. This was now the second time he had come to her rescue.

"Gracias," she whispered and followed him as noiselessly as possible up the stairs and across the courtyard, always in the shadow of the castle. When she looked up the steep wall, light fell into the night from her former quarters. "I can't go without my child."

He stopped and turned to face her. The moon lit his face. Iriomé could read the compassion in it. "That's impossible! Two men guard the door and the maids of the deceased condesa and a nurse from the village are in that room. You'll be lucky if you make it out of Castile and the orbit of this insane monk. He was appointed Grand Inquisitor and is now—spurred on by de Lugo—also interested in you."

"Please! Lend me that!" She reached for the dagger that he wore in his belt. "Don't worry, you'll get it back," she said as she took off the thin cape, rolled it together like a thick rope, and wrapped it around her waist. There she also stowed the dagger.

De la Torre watched her, puzzled. "What are you up to?"

"I'm going to get my son while you distract the guards in front of the door. The women I can handle." She grasped the first protruding stone of the coarse masonry over her head and pulled herself up. Her toes found a firm grip, and her eyes already were scanning the wall for the next projection.

"Your horse is waiting for you at the door to the secret passage," he called up to her and hurried to reach the west wing.

Iriomé had already climbed up the wall some length and almost reached the window. She used the belt of her cape as a loop and threw it over the stones that were too far above her to reach with her hand. Then she pulled herself up on it. Inch by inch she approached the lighted windows. Every now and then a small piece of the masonry broke loose from under her feet, but she always managed to find a grip. She felt the skin under her soles crack but did not care. What awaited her demanded all her concentration. She had survived in the icy sea for many hours, had escaped her worst enemy more than once, and would also make it this time.

When her fingertips finally reached the window ledge, she had just enough strength to pull her body up onto it. She crouched in the window niche and waited until her heartbeat and breathing calmed. Through a chink in the curtain she peeked into the room.

The cradle was still near the window. But Tamanca was not in it. Iriomé felt frightened. What if he was kept elsewhere? Maybe down in the village in the nurse's house. How could she find him then? But at that moment a woman approached with the infant in her arms. Iriomé pressed deep into the niche so she would not be discovered, then dared only a peek through the curtain.

Tears of relief welled in her eyes. Tamanca was lying peacefully on his back, a thumb in his mouth, sleeping. Her original plan to bind the child with the cape around her upper body and then climb back the same way was abandoned. It was too dangerous. If she fell, this would end his young life. This must not happen.

She smashed the glass with the handle of the dagger and opened it. Shrill cries penetrated her ear, but she didn't care, she grabbed the child and tore open the door. The long hallway was empty. De la Torre was reliable. She rushed down the stairs, the infant pressed close to her body. In hurrying past she saw one of the guards lifeless on the ground. The other, however, suddenly appeared at the end of the long corridor. Someone seized her by the arm and drew her into a large room. De la Torre pushed her behind a heavy curtain that reached to the floor—and not a second too soon because already the second guard stormed into the room. "Where is she?"

"Gone."

"It was you who helped her escape," he shouted.

De la Torre shook his head. "Are you mad? She has freed herself! I've followed her up here."

"And now?"

"She has vanished into thin air." He opened the window and looked outside. "She truly is a witch, as the rumor goes."

The guard turned pale.

"She bewitched your friend. I saw him lying on the ground next to the stairs. We'd better stay out of her way before the same happens to us."

The guard looked suspicious and frightened at the same time, but he saw nothing unusual in the room. Willingly he followed the castellan. Iriomé waited a few heartbeats, then climbed out the open window and ran as fast as she could with her son to the stables.

In the castle all the lights came on. The women had sounded the alarm. Dogs barked. Men shouted orders out to each other. She recognized Joaquín's voice among them. Having safely wrapped Tamanca into the cape and tied it around her upper body, she pulled herself by the mane of the gray mare up on her back. And as if Karima knew exactly what she should do, she walked without hesitation into the dark passage.

"Good luck," she heard the castellan say while barring the wooden grate again. She had had no opportunity to give him back his dagger, but perhaps situations were lying ahead of her in which she would be glad to have it.

It was still dark when they trotted out of the tunnel. She was guided by the stars and steered Karima to the northeast. Only after she had finally emerged from the shadow of the castle did she feel her soul could breathe again, unfolding its wings like a butterfly. Never again would she come back here, to the place of her greatest humiliation.

Without treating herself or her mare to a longer pause, she kept riding to the east, toward the rising sun. She stopped only to nurse her son and once when they crossed a brook so that Karima could drink. She herself felt neither hunger nor thirst, only the urge to put as much distance as possible between them and Trujillo.

Eventually, she heard in the distance the drum of hooves and the barking of dogs and drove the mare on. But it was only a hunting party more interested in a boar than a runaway young woman and her child.

The rest of the day went by uneventfully. When the sun was low and everything appeared in a reddish light, she reached the village of Tabla de la Reina and asked the way to the farm of Paco Oriega.

At first glance, everything gave a very peaceful impression. A blackbird was singing in one of the fig trees, under which a few chickens were scratching the ground. Iriomé's glance went over the hives, a pigsty, a few goats, two cows, and a calf. She rode cautiously past a shed and a half-ruined farm building. Not a soul could be seen. She got off the horse and tied Karima to a tree near the entrance of the whitewashed main building.

Suddenly a colorfully dressed shape came out the shadow of the shed. Iriomé fell to her knees—partly from exhaustion, partly out of gratitude for finally seeing her friend. Ibn Said helped her back on her feet and embraced her. When he saw that she had brought Tamanca, he was the one to get on his knees before her. "I knew you'd do it!" he said admiringly.

"Without de la Torre it wouldn't have been possible," she replied almost shyly. She was no longer used to being met with such respect.

"He's a good Christian, one of the few," Ibn Said said, standing up. Worriedly he looked at the gate. "Are you sure no one's followed you?"

Iriomé shook her head. "You've given me Karima with great foresight. Who could be able to overtake her?"

He smiled. "That's true. Nevertheless, we need to continue our journey immediately. Now not only de Lugo is after you, but also the young conde."

Iriomé wanted neither to remember her ugly last encounter with Joaquín nor what Cold Eye had suggested to save her life. Therefore she told Ibn Said nothing about it. He probably could imagine what had happened anyway. After all, he had lived for a long time in this country and knew the people. She looked at him, her eyes tired.

"I have ridden almost without interruption. Let me sleep a short while; otherwise I'll fall off my horse before long."

He pointed to the barn. "In there you can sleep in the hay. We'll get everything ready and wake you once we're finished."

She looked worriedly at her mare that was just as exhausted as she was.

"I'll take care of Karima," Ibn Said reassured her.

Iriomé squeezed his hand and disappeared with her child into the barn. While she nursed him it occurred to her that it might not be such a good idea to travel with her friends. Joaquín and Cold Eye would certainly follow this track. Her exhaustion was, however, stronger than her fear, and she fell into a deep sleep.

The smell of a hearty meat broth woke her. Aaron was standing there smiling. "Here, eat this, and then join us outside; we're ready."

Iriomé gratefully accepted the bowl with the soup. Some vegetables swam in it and even a few small pieces of meat. She scraped her bowl and then discovered that Aaron had left her a bundle with plain peasant clothing.

She was still wearing her house robe. Iriomé took off the soiled shirt and washed herself with water from a rain barrel in front of the barn. She did not mind showing herself undressed in front of the men, who were already sitting on their horses waiting for her. It had remained a mystery to her why nudity should be something inappropriate and why everyone in this country covered themselves from head to toe, no matter how hot the day was.

Back in the barn, she decided to wear the new clothes but not the medallion. She pulled it over her head, shortened the chain by a knot and put it around the neck of the sleeping Tamanca. He was now the new guardian of amakuna. Once he was old enough, she wanted to tell him what the secret of the powder was. And in case she was taken prisoner, no one would discover the magic agent on her.

In order to move faster, Ibn Said had decided to leave the carriage in which he and Aaron had traveled up to now on the farm and continue the voyage by horseback. The contents of the gold chest had been put into three sacks, which the three caballeros who accompanied them for their protection had strapped behind their saddles. Nobody asked any questions about why Iriomé suddenly rode with them. And she didn't want to know what Aaron had told them.

From the start they kept a rigorous pace and kept riding northeastward until the sun was vertical in the sky the next day. According to Ibn Said, it would be possible to slow down a bit as soon as they reached the border to Aragon. There Ferdinand of Aragon was reigning, not Isabella of Castile. And neither the Conde of Trujillo nor Alonso de

Lugo nor the fat monk possessed any powers there. Currently, however, they were at least two days' ride from Soria, the first Aragonese town across the border.

At the height of Segovia, with its Roman aqueducts standing out against the blue sky already perceptible from a distance, they stopped for a while to water the horses. Ibn Said reveled in historical remarks and reported that his ancestors had conquered the city that once had belonged to the Roman Empire in the eighth century but had then lost it two hundred years ago to the Spaniards.

Although Iriomé understood by now that the calendar of the Christians was based on the birth of Jesus and the year was 1493, she had no concept for such a long period, especially not for the many lives that had been lived and ended again, often violently. On Benahoare no conquests were known until the arrival of the Spaniards, who had destroyed a whole people, together with its customs and traditions. Although small disputes between the tribes flared up, this had never led to the complete destruction of the weaker party. She wondered once again why it was so difficult for the people here to share what they had and why everyone was afraid the other would take something from him.

Deep in thought, she realized only at the last moment that the caballero at the front raised his hand and stopped his horse. Ahead a mounted *hermandad* approached, five men in royal colors. They had spotted the small travel company and rode straight toward them. There was no time for Iriomé to hide. Worried, she pressed the infant to her body and pulled the cloth up high so that at first glance no one could see what was in it. Aaron reminded all to stay calm, and the médico searched his pocket for the "miracle paper" that supposedly convinced all officials and kept them from asking further questions.

"Where are you bound?" said the captain of the troop. In his belt he had a scimitar, his alert eyes seemed to pierce each of them.

"We are on the way through to Augsburg in Swabia on behalf of the Conde of Trujillo in order to settle debts there. I'm his treasurer," Aaron replied with a calm voice.

"You're a Jew!" cried the captain, pointing his finger at him. "You know that Queen Isabella has issued a decree that all Jews who have not converted to the true faith must have left the country by the end of this month."

Aaron still remained calm. "I'm not going to come back but will from Augsburg leave for the Holy Land to be buried there in the soil of my ancestors."

"I hope you'll make it there." The captain grinned derogatorily and then pointed to Iriomé, who had stayed in the background with her child as inconspicuously as possible. "And who is she?" he barked.

"My wife. She comes with me and won't return either."

The Spaniard sized Iriomé up, turned his horse next to hers, and pulled the cloth from her face. "A little bit too young to die, and also too young for you. Don't you think so? And far too beautiful. Where do you come from, beautiful child?"

Ibn Said felt the time had come to intervene. He shoved the ferman right under the captain's nose. "I'm the personal physician of His Excellency Frai Lorenzo de la Huerta, and these are my friends, whom I accompany to the border. His Excellency is, as you surely already know, the uncle of the Condesa of Trujillo. I don't think he would appreciate it if you interfered with this mission of his nephew by marriage."

The captain looked at the paper closely. Iriomé and the médico exchanged a knowing look. The captain seemed to recognize the seal of the inquisitor, for he handed the paper back to the médico with a nod.

"You could have told me at once." He gave his horse the spurs and gave his *compañía* a sign, whereupon they all disappeared in a cloud of dust.

Iriomé gave a sigh of relief. Yet it did not escape her that one of their armed companions eyed her suspiciously. He guided his horse beside her. "You're changing your plans quickly, Señora. Didn't you want only a few days ago to marry the old conde, allegedly the father of your child? Then it was rumored that the young conde wants to marry you, and now you're suddenly the wife of the Jew?"

Ibn Said, who as so often was there for her when Iriomé got in difficulties, rode to her side and glared at the man furiously. "I don't see how that's any business of yours. Your sole task is to guarantee our protection and the protection of the gold. Don't forget that."

The caballero looked at him disparagingly. "You can't tell me what to say, Moro. I usually don't even talk to the likes of you. If God had found your people worthy, he wouldn't now send you back into the desert. You moros have taken by force what was not yours, and now you pay the price. I'll ride back and inform the young conde what's going on here." He turned his horse and spurred it so brutally that the maltreated animal stood on his hind legs in shock and whinnied loudly before he galloped away.

Iriomé, who had just recovered from the encounter with the hermandad, looked after him startled and then to the other two armed companions, who, however, showed no inclination to follow him. She rode up to them, bowed, and thanked them by laying her hand on their shoulders.

"I'm Francesco de la Torre, and this is my brother Adolfo," one of them said. "Thank our father. He has made us take an oath not to depart from your side until we have reached the border."

Iriomé sent silent thanks to the castellan of Trujillo once more. It was a good feeling that even in this country where naked fear ruled, people were willing to take such a risk for her.

"We'd better not stop until we have reached the border," warned Aaron. No one disagreed, although they all were saddle sore and needed sleep.

The sun was still burning in the sky, and they made little headway. Every time they came near a village, they kept well clear of it to leave no trace. The landscape became barren. There was very little green for the horses and even less water. Iriomé's heart bled when she looked at her mare during a short rest. The ribs were clearly visible under the hair that had become rough, and over the normally fiery eyes lay a veil of exhaustion.

Time and again Iriomé looked over her shoulder as if she expected, at any moment, to discover a cloud of dust in the distance from which their persecutors would emerge. But no one was to be seen. The flicker of the differently hot air layers was the only movement on the horizon.

After another two days they reached the border town of Soria in late afternoon with the last of their strength. The city gates were still open, and Ibn Said's ferman worked wonders again. The médico had already been here once and led them to a small inn where they could sleep with few questions asked.

While Aaron and Ibn Said went to bed in a dormitory, exhausted, the portly host assigned Iriomé and her child a small chamber with a simple but clean straw bed. When she was nursing little Tamanca, she saw through the window Francesco, one of the castellan's two sons, keeping watch. In order not to fall asleep, he walked constantly up and down, never losing the plain they had just crossed out of sight. He gave her the good feeling of being safe. For the first time in a long time she did not fear that she would wake to look into the cold eyes of Alonso de Lugo.

Chapter 34

The next morning they rode off at sunrise to reach Zaragoza before dark. They crossed another barren plateau on which the sun was burning down mercilessly and where they found only a few shady spots to rest. Man and beast were fatigued by the exertions of the trip to such a degree that they were progressing slower than planned. In Zaragoza Aaron had friends; there they would be able to rest for a while. From there they would continue their journey in the direction of a seaport with the name of Barcelona where their ways would part. Ibn Said promised Iriomé to help her find a ship that would take her and her son back to her island. Then he wanted to return to Castile and stay as long as possible in the service of the inquisitor so that he would not have to leave his beloved al-Andalus. Aaron planned to take a boat to Marseille and then struggle to the northeast in many arduous one-day distances to the Duchy of Swabia. He had shown Iriomé some drawings in which he had highlighted their itinerary, together with the places to be passed. But just as she had no feel for the length of time, she was not able to reckon the distances and how long it took to cover them. While she often had walked around Benahoare in a month's time, this country seemed to extend to infinity. This was also one of the reasons she felt so uncomfortable. Anyone who went on a journey here might never know whether he would finish in his lifetime.

They reached the walls of Zaragoza after dark, so the gates were already closed. Thus they had no other choice than to spend the night in a hostel once more. Aaron suggested celebrating the successful completion of the first part of their journey in the taproom with wine and a hearty roast goat. Ibn Said agreed and was fishing for sympathy showing his waistband, which flapped loosely around his still well-rounded belly. Everyone laughed. There was something liberating in this, a feeling that Iriomé had not had in a long time.

In the parlor a crispy goat was soon roasting on a spit over the fire. Its smell made their mouths water and their hunger go sky high. Ibn Said called in the guards, who were just as starved, then kept his seat in front of the roast until it was ready to be eaten. Two kitchen assistants cut the delicate pink flesh into slices with sharp knives. The meat juice, which dripped onto the floor, was licked up by two well-fed black cats. Iriomé did not like these animals, although she now knew that they ate mice and rats and were actually rather useful. Somehow the idea had settled in her that they brought ill luck, so even now she could not help having a bad feeling. But finally sense prevailed. They were outside the influence of the Inquisition, a thought that reassured her. She even managed a smile when one of the kitchen help, with an unmistakable wink, put a particularly large piece of meat on her plate. It was served with strong brown bread and gravy seasoned with laurel, a spice that Iriomé knew from Benahoare and that reminded her once more of how much she was missing her home island.

The host put a large pot with red wine on the table from which Aaron filled a tin cup for each of them. Ibn Said raised his cup to them. "*Salud!* To a successful journey!" All raised their cups and then pitched into their meal ravenously.

Suddenly the clatter of hooves, spurs, and harsh commands in the language of Castile were heard outside. Ibn Said dropped his fork, a hunk of goat meat slipping off it. The cats under the table scattered. Aaron turned pale. Iriomé jumped up, grabbed Tamanca, who was sleeping in a basket on the stove bench, and ran toward the kitchen to escape through the back door. But ten men stormed into the room, their swords drawn. The first recognized Iriomé's intention immediately and caught her before she could run past the startled kitchen maids.

He dragged her back into the taproom, smacked her face so brutally that she fell to the ground, and snatched the infant from her. At this moment the old fencer of his youth awakened in Ibn Said. He reached for his sword that he, in the traditional manner, never took off even while eating, and threw himself with a Moorish battle cry on a Spanish caballero, taller than Ibn by at least two heads. Since he was adept at human anatomy, he knew exactly where to stab. The man collapsed like a felled tree. On his back was emblazoned the blood-red flower behind a golden trellis, the coat of arms of Frai Lorenzo de la Huerta.

Francisco and Adolfo de la Torre tried bravely to defend their charges, but there were only two of them, and they stood no real chance against the Santa Hermandad of the Grand Inquisitor.

Iriomé regained consciousness and ran right through the thick of the battle outside, chasing the man who had wrested her son from her. She reached him just as he was about to mount his horse, and he struggled with the roaring infant in his arm. It would have been easy to snatch Tamanca away, but the caballero that stayed outside to guard the horses grabbed her from behind and pulled her back. Before he could knock her out, the médico leaped between them out of nowhere. He was bleeding from several wounds. Iriomé realized quickly that another hand-to-hand fight would be fatal for him. So she pulled Roberto de la Torre's dagger and rammed it into the Spaniard's left eye. With an anguished cry, he went to the ground. The other had now mounted his horse and disappeared with Tamanca in the dark. All she heard was the quickly receding clatter of hoofs, mixed with the angry cries of her son.

The rest of the men now also stormed outside. Ibn Said, despite his injuries, had succeeded in untying the horses. He was already getting on his horse and shouted in Arabic at Iriomé, who was still looking in the direction her son had disappeared, stunned. "*Yalla, Yalla!*"

At last she awoke from her stupor and jumped on her mare, who automatically galloped behind Ibn Said's stallion. Tears ran down Iriomé's cheeks, and deep sobs shook her body, so that she could barely hold on to the reins. But she had no choice. The pursuers were close on their heels. Iriomé gathered all her strength and adapted to the rhythm of Karima's smooth movements. Like an arrow they shot through the night. The full moon showed them the way, and Iriomé wished nothing more than to dissolve in this pale light forever. She had lost everything.

Ibn Said held on to the reins with ebbing strength. They had made a huge detour around the city walls, and he now turned his horse to the large main gate, in front of which beggars and poor pilgrims that could not afford accommodation in the city encamped.

The gate was guarded by Aragonese troops, in the presence of whom they would be safe for the time being. The Castilian hermandad could not capture them here in front of everyone.

Only now Iriomé noticed that the two brothers were no longer with them. There could only be three reasons. Either they were dead, had been captured, or had ultimately changed sides. Deep in her heart she hoped that it was not due to the former, that more had not died because of her.

Ibn Said had lost much blood and was so weak that he fell from his horse more than that he dismounted. Two young men, woken up by the horses' hooves, helped Iriomé to lay him next to a fireplace. At her request they brought water and heated it so that she could boil some scraps of fabric, as she had learned from her mentor. After they cooled down a bit, she dressed his wounds. From the medicinal herbs she still carried around her neck in her leather pouch from the time in the monastery, she prepared a mush, which she applied on the deepest wounds.

Meanwhile Ibn Said had lost consciousness. She felt the power of life begin to leave him. She took his hands and tried to let some of her own energy flow to him. He was her best friend. He just could not die, especially not for her. The mere thought of it was unbearable. While she was dressing his wounds with the clean scraps of cloth, she remembered when the two of them had been waiting before the walls of Cadiz to slip through the gate. Even back then she had foreseen that one day he would give his life for her. Had the time come now?

The two young men who had helped her retired, leaving her alone with the injured man. Iriomé took his hand and in desperation asked

Tara for assistance, but deep in her heart she knew that even the goddess could not help anymore.

A heavy hand lay on her shoulder. She looked up. It was Aaron. He also had a bleeding cut on his face, but otherwise seemed unharmed. "How is he?" he asked quietly.

"Not well," Iriomé answered.

"The Inquisition is relentless. Nothing can stop them. No border and no law. One of the men of the inquisitor babbled something about a magic formula you allegedly have."

Iriomé shook her head violently. "If I had such a remedy, don't you think I would have given it to Ibn Said? All this is utter nonsense."

"I thought something like that," he said and then looked around searchingly. "Where's Tamanca?"

Her concern about Ibn Said had covered the pain of losing her child a little, but now the thought went straight to her heart like the stab of a dagger. She had no more tears and just looked at the old man sorrowfully. He took her hand and held it tightly for a while.

"He's now going to be a conquistador," whispered Iriomé. "Like Tanausú foresaw."

Aaron shook his head. "He's still half your son, and this he will remain. No one can deny where he comes from."

"You mean I'll see him again?"

Aaron shook his head slowly. "Someday or another for sure."

Iriomé looked hopefully toward the horizon where the first silver stripe announced a new day.

"At first light when the gate is opened, we'll go in with the first pilgrims. The house of my friend Nathan and his wife is not far from here."

"Ibn Said can't ride. Perhaps the two young men who helped me before are willing to carry him into the city. But won't this attract attention?"

"On the contrary. Many pilgrims bring their sick to the Holy Virgin."

Iriomé looked at him quizzically.

"Tomorrow a great festival will take place in honor of the Virgin del Pilar. Thousands of believers will pass the Virgin, who stands on a column, and ask her for mercy. Thus we'll surely attract no attention."

Aaron sat next to her. Iriomé cleaned the gash that ran across his cheek with the last clean cloth. "This virgin," Iriomé began to speak. "Could she perhaps also help Ibn Said, or is she only there for Christians?"

Aaron twirled his long white beard between his fingers thoughtfully. "She probably won't help him because he doesn't believe in her any more than I do. We all have our own god."

"And where are they now, your gods?" She looked at Ibn Said, whose eyelids fluttered and who threw his head back and forth in pain.

"I don't know. Since the Christians persecute us and the Jewish people have to endure so much suffering, I sometimes doubt whether any god exists at all."

Iriomé looked at him, startled. "I couldn't breathe without knowing that Tara loves and guides me and helps me in distress and that abora, the power of life, comes from her."

"Sometimes it's hard for me to think this way," said Aaron, "but maybe God wants to test me in such times to see how strong my faith really is."

Iriomé could not and did not want to follow a conversation in this direction. She had never really had any doubts about Tara, and Tara had never doubted her. Their relationship was pure mutual love that would never end. What the goddess decided was right. This would never change. Even if she decided to take her only friend and her child from her, she would never question Tara's love.

At sunrise Aaron ensured they could leave their horses for a small sum in a shelter. After the gates were open, the two young men carried Ibn Said into the city. They managed to pass the guards unchecked and were dragged along by the pilgrims moving toward the Basilica del Pilar. Most of the travelers were poor people in rags, including many lepers, old people with crutches, and mothers with several children in tow. In all their eyes Iriomé read hope: hope for a better life, hope for health, and hope for a little prosperity.

When they reached the square in front of the Basilica, Iriomé stood still in amazement. She had never seen the like of this before. Flower arrangements in all imaginable colors formed a huge colored carpet. Purple, pink, white, red, orange, yellow. People came in flocks and constantly added new bouquets and flower arrangements.

Amidst all this, Ibn Said did not notice a thing. He was still unconscious. Iriomé was seriously worried. He had lost a lot of blood, and the wound on his chest was still bleeding. Before they set off, she had changed his bandages, but already they were soaked again. If they did not reach the house of Aaron's friends, where he could lie still, soon, he would die here among the people. She made Aaron hurry up. It seemed like an eternity before they turned into a quiet side street and the Jew stopped in front of a big two-story house. From his expression, she immediately realized something was wrong. The doors and windows on the ground floor, where once a store or goods office seemed to have been, were boarded up. In the upper stories the curtains were drawn.

The two young men leaned Ibn Said cautiously against the house wall. "We must go back to our family," one of them said, shrugging his shoulders regretfully.

"Good luck," murmured the other. "Perhaps the Virgin can still help."

Iriomé thanked them, crouched down in front of the wall, and took Ibn Said in her arms.

"Nathan and Rahel have probably escaped," suspected Aaron. "Since Queen Isabella's marriage to Ferdinand of Aragon, Jews may no longer be safe here either."

Perhaps Aaron had not been so wrong, and the god of the Jews had actually left his children. Suddenly Iriomé was shaken by the thought that Tara might be only a memory now. She remembered being with Guayafanta at the holy well, and they had not been able to contact the goddess. She had been silent, as had Idafé, the speaking soul stone of her people.

Maybe she just did not want to admit that a new era had begun. Iriomé wondered about a time without gods, in which people were left to their own devices . . .

"I'll go and see if maybe the back door is open," Aaron said indecisively. "The guest and pilgrims' hostels are crowded, and besides, they'll be looking for you there first."

Iriomé only nodded, holding Ibn Said.

When Aaron came back shortly afterward, he seemed more confident. "Let's carry him inside," he said. They picked up the médico and dragged him more than carried him into the backyard. Aaron had made it into the house through a small skylight and opened the kitchen door from the inside.

There it looked as if the inhabitants had packed their belongings in great haste. Used dishes stood on the kitchen table, as well as leftovers mostly eaten up by rats.

In one corner there was a simple bed on which they settled the still unconscious médico. While Aaron lit a fire in the stove, Iriomé carefully took off the bandages to clean Ibn Said's wounds again. With some water from a jug she cooked the materials again and hung them on a line above the stove.

In one of the rooms on the second floor they found blankets and fresh towels, clothes the former inhabitants had left behind, and a pair of scissors. Once again the time had come. Iriomé had to sacrifice her hair and turn back into a man. She exchanged her dress for a pair of trousers and a coarse linen shirt. Then she ran down to the kitchen, holding out the scissors to Aaron with a pleading look. He understood immediately and in no time she looked like the servant of the médico again.

The rest of the day she stayed at the side of Ibn Said, who seemed to feel a bit better. The wounds had stopped bleeding, and he fell into a fitful sleep. Aaron had fallen asleep beside the stove in sheer exhaustion. His snoring filled the room, which was sparsely lit by the fire and a single candle. Barely a noise made it through the boarded-up window. The hours passed without anything happening.

When it was almost dark Iriomé stirred. She went out of the house to fetch fresh water at the city fountain and to perhaps find something to eat. Despite her disguise, she looked all around before she stepped into the street. But no one seemed to take notice. She followed a woman in dirty clothes carrying an empty jug at a distance and was thus led to the city fountain surrounded by many people. While waiting for her turn, she overheard a conversation between a servant and a washerwoman that worried her supremely. Although the Aragonese dialect sounded strange to her ears, she understood more or less what it was about. There was unrest in the city because a Castilian nobleman had appeared before the Viceroy of Aragon and said he was looking for a tall fair-haired slave. The alguaciles, the town constables of the bishop, were searching for her everywhere, and the nobleman had announced that no matter who brought her to him alive, they would receive three gold coins. Iriomé froze. The thick washer woman standing behind her nudged her. "Come on, boy, it's your turn. We don't have all day!"

Iriomé recollected herself as best she could, looked away, and filled her pitcher with water. And without turning around again, she ran back to the house of Aaron's friends. She shook the Jew awake. He had been lying in the same position before the stove for hours. He woke with a start and at first did not know where he was. Iriomé stroked his shoulder reassuringly and handed him a mug with water.

"They're looking for me. And whoever finds me will get three gold pieces."

Aaron had to take a sip of water to get over the fright. "Did anyone recognize you?"

She shook her head.

"You need to leave Zaragoza tonight and ride in the direction of Barcelona."

"I can't do that. I'll never abandon Ibn Said."

"Yes, you will," the médico commanded in a weak voice from the other end of the kitchen.

Iriomé immediately ran to him. "How are you feeling?" she cried, happy to see he had regained consciousness.

"What do you think?" he said softly. "The end is fast approaching. I'm going to die here, little Iriomé, but you're too young for that."

"But . . . "

"No buts. I don't want all we have done to be in vain."

Aaron came over to them and looked anxiously down at Ibn Said. "I'll take care of him," he said to Iriomé. "I know another Jewish family that definitely will accommodate us."

"And if they had to flee?"

"I'll figure it out." He took another sip of the water and went to the back door. "This may take a while. As far as I recall, they have a gold-smith workshop across town in the district of the Jews."

"Good luck," Iriomé muttered and turned back to Ibn Said. "Do you want a drink?" He nodded. Iriomé supported him and held the water cup to his lips. He could hardly swallow, and the water ran from the corners of his mouth. Even breathing was hard.

Every two hours she changed his bandages and tried to get him to eat some flour soup prepared from a few ingredients she had discovered in the kitchen.

Outside it was getting dark, but Aaron was still not back. Iriomé feared something was wrong. She would have liked to go looking for him but did not dare to leave Ibn Said alone. His breathing became more and more flat. She believed he may already be hearing the high-pitched voices that summon all to the other world. His pulse rate was less than half of hers. Tears filled her eyes, and her breast felt con-stricted. Why did all those who had remained steadfastly at her side here in this strange world and kept faith with her have to go so early?

She thought of Guadalupe, who had offered her a new purpose in life in the foreign world of the monastery. She had become a victim of amakuna, just as the médico was. But she would not burden herself with more guilt, because the mushroom was no longer in her custody. Had she failed or was it part of the great plan that amakuna now was in the possession of her son?

In the morning, when she awoke from a short sleep, Ibn Said was dead. Iriomé put her forehead against his and said good-bye to him in her own special way. She began to strike the high notes of the harima-guadas to show his soul the way, even if she did not know if the soul of the Moors might not travel in other ways. She remained by her friend until she was sure she could let him go. But what to do now? Ibn Said had told her that the mortal remains of a Muslim must be buried on the day of their death, in a quiet place, in virgin earth with his head facing Mecca, the most important sanctuary of his people. She needed Aaron's help. Yet how could she find him in this huge foreign city without running into her enemies? She had no choice, because she could not have brought herself to leave the body of her friend lying here unburied after he had risked his life for her repeatedly.

It was noon now, and the sun was high in the sky, so that no shadow was to be found in the narrow streets. Iriomé noticed that far fewer people were in the streets than the day before and that the stores that had offered their goods out of doorways now were closed. It had to be Sunday, a holiday for the Christians. Whether the hermandad of the inquisitor also rested on this day she did not know. Probably not. She recalled every word Aaron had said before he left: a goldsmith at the other end of town in the district of the Jews. That meant she had to traverse the center of the city where the great basilica stood. And from there she had no clue.

Without thinking she moved in the right direction. Once she had walked a way she did not forget it because her memory of the color of a particular house, the shape of a roof, and the nature of the soil never left her.

Suddenly there were loud hoofbeats. Iriomé squeezed into a doorway. Not a second too soon. The hermandad of the inquisitor dashed recklessly through the narrow streets. Anyone who did not jump out of the way in time was in danger of being hit by the hooves of the horses. Trusting her inner feeling, Iriomé followed them at a reasonable distance.

Before a building of enormous proportions, its canopy pillared by countless thick columns, they dismounted and handed the reins of their horses to two young boys who eagerly came running. Yet one of the riders remained sitting on his horse, his back bent and with a downward gaze. As one of the boys tried to help him off his horse, he was shaken by a coughing fit so loud that you could hear him on the other side of the wide street.

Iriomé's blood ran cold. De Lugo! He had actually followed her here. And now she understood why. He was mortally ill. After the coughing attack was over, he croaked hoarsely, "Did he say where she is?"

Iriomé instantly recognized the seriousness of the situation. They had seized Aaron and would try by all means to press out of him where she was. As they had done with Guadalupe and Guayafanta. What should she do? She could not let her friend down if he was still alive. But if she went in there, she would die here, in the same city in which Ibn Said breathed his last a few hours ago. Was this her fate? If Tara had really left her, then she wanted to follow this fate. What sense was there still in life?

She took a deep breath, crossed the street, and walked to the gate of the palacio. "I want to speak to Alonso de Lugo," she said in clear Castilian to the guards in front of the heavy iron-shod gate.

Yet they did not deign to look at her and only made a gesture to shoo her away. "I'm the slave he's looking for," she tried again and took off the small woolen cap that she had discovered in the house of the Jewish family.

One of the guards looked at her and grabbed a breast that was difficult to hide, especially since she no longer nursed Tamanca.

"Indeed, a woman!" he shouted and seized Iriomé by the arm. The other guard also wanted to grab her, but Iriomé struck at his hand, so that he howled with pain.

"Just wait." He gave her a slap that almost floored her.

"If you strike her dead, no one will get something out of it," said the former almost reproachfully and held her. "Have you forgotten? Three gold coins to who brings her to the Castilian alive."

The second stopped immediately. "You're right."

They studiously wiped the dust of Iriomé's pants and shirt. Then one of the two grabbed her arm and dragged her inside the palacio while the other took his post again.

Unlike outside, it was dark and cool in there. Iriomé entered a long hallway with wooden doors on both sides. Behind one of the doors she heard a muffled cough. De Lugo! The guard knocked at the door. Iriomé closed her eyes. "Vacaguaré!" she whispered. It would not be an easy death. The torture could drag on for days, even weeks, and end inexorably with death by fire. But there was nothing that still held her to this life.

The once cold glance of de Lugo was clouded and dull. He was sitting bent forward at a wooden table. Opposite him was Aaron. His white beard was bloodied, the face marked by abuse. Iriomé felt the suffering, the burning and aching caused by his wounds, in her own face. A taste of what was in store for her.

It took Cold Eye a moment; then he recognized her. He rose staggering and stumbled toward her, his arms outstretched. But before he reached her, he toppled and fell to the ground right in front of her feet. No one came to his aid. Like a drowning man, he clung to her knees, trying to pull himself up her trouser legs. Iriomé stood, her face emotionless. She felt neither hatred nor compassion, nor any kind of satisfaction. There was nothing that would strike a chord in her again. Her heart was cold. Petrified lava against which beat the waves, sometimes gently, sometimes violently. Nothing would move it again.

Slowly the bony fingers that had managed to claw up to her hips loosened their grip, and the emaciated body of the conquistador slumped to the ground. He wheezed one last time; then blood oozed from his mouth as the water had from Ibn Said's the day before. He twitched, and his eyelids fluttered. Then he lay there on the ground, his limbs unnatural. The two men of the hermandad who were also in the room and a man with coarse features and a leather apron stained with blood shuddered.

"Bruja. Witch," one of them whispered, staring fearfully at Iriomé. But no one made a move to seize her. Before they could change their minds, Iriomé dragged Aaron from the bench and ran outside with him as fast as she could. The guard who had brought her in let them pass. A look at the dead Castilian had probably been enough for him. From him he would no longer get even a single gold coin. Better to steer clear of this weird woman.

In front of the palacio Iriomé and Aaron once again joined the fresh stream of pilgrims, this time being swept to the Basílica del Pilar. Even from a distance the fervent prayers of the faithful could be heard. Although Iriomé held Aaron's hand as tightly as possible, they were separated by a group of young pilgrims who quite ruthlessly fought their way through the crowd as if it were a race.

Eventually, she lost all feeling for the progress of the day. Iriomé found herself in the huge cathedral. Hundreds of columns seemed as if they not only held the roof of the church, but also the entire sky. The small statue of the Virgin Maria del Pilar stood at a silver pillar, looking patiently at the long rows of people who had come to worship her and implore her help. Iriomé learned from a mother who was just explaining it to her little daughter what the legend of the Virgin was all about. The mother of Jesus was said to have appeared here to one of his disciples named Jacobus after his crucifixion. She had been standing at a column. And that's why they had built the basilica around this sacred place.

She joined the long line and waited patiently until she finally arrived at the foot of the column and looked into the golden face of the Virgin. For the first time in a long time she was overcome by a feeling of peace. To her it was not the mother of Jesus looking down on her but Tara, the Earth Mother. In fact there was no difference. Iriomé thanked her, glad that she was still alive, and promised to never again doubt the existence of the goddess. The look she received back spoke of forgiveness and mercy, that there was no sense in making others responsible for one's own destiny and thereby experiencing suffering and creating new suffering time and again. And it spoke of the fact that in spite of it all, the only feasible way was love—love for oneself, love for the people, and love for the gods.

Chapter 35

Romy opened her eyes and looked into Ricardo's worried face. He had changed so much that at first she hardly recognized him. He was deeply tanned and had grown a full beard. "We need to go, as soon as possible," he said, took her hand, and pulled her up from the small bank under the dragon tree.

Romy had great difficulty standing upright. Her knees trembled. She was still too caught up in Iriomé's experiences. A look at the entrance of Sam's cave, however, catapulted her back to the present. Sam had died for amakuna, just like Iriomé's friends in the past. This must have an end.

The mushroom had brought nothing but misfortune and would again. Humanity was not ready for it and would not be in the near future. "This Borges, he'll kill us all," she whispered.

"Don't worry, Tanausú's on his way here. He will know what to do," Ricardo said.

"What did you say?" She clearly saw before her mind's eye the picture of the strong man being shot at in the alley behind the shop. "Tanausú is not dead?"

Ricardo shook his head. "I was on the phone with him this morning. He is a guerrero sagrado. Do not forget that."

Romy was suddenly no longer sure in which time she actually was, especially since Ricardo looked like a Guanche with his beard. "Who are you?" she asked softly, remembering how much she had distrusted him when they first met.

He smiled, put his forehead against hers, and bowed. "Chusar

Axhoran, Magoc e Cel. Hail in the face of the earth, the moon, and the sun."

Romy was now completely lost.

"I'm a friend of Tanausú's," Ricardo said with awe in his voice. "He once fell in a barranco in the caldera and broke his neck. But he has returned to us."

"Healed?" If what Ricardo said was true, the only logical explanation was that the eco-activist had the mushroom with him and had cured himself—in the caldera as well as in Marbella.

Ricardo nodded. "He's our leader, and he will be forever."

"Leader of whom?" There were no more Guanches in the twenty-first century. Romy felt as if everything was revolving around her. Images from the past and present mixed in her mind's eye. She needed to sit down again.

"I belong to a group that calls itself Corro Benahoare, and only its members know of its existence . . . and now you. We are committed to ensuring that the island is preserved and the old traditions are not lost. Tanausú is our leader. He knows everything about the life of the native Canarians and has taught us a lot. We often spend time in the caldera and try to resurrect the past."

Romy understood slowly. Tanausú seemed to have built a kind of environmental battle group with Neo-Guanchen. And they saw him as their immortal hero. Which he was in a way. *What am I then?*

Romy had to start getting accustomed to a new way of seeing things. Nothing seemed to be like people imagined or desired. Most of what people acted out was only personal manifestations of patterns they were spoon-fed from childhood—by parents, at school, at college, and by society. And then suddenly something happened that turned everything upside down, as if the channel of life was changed via remote control at a moment's notice.

"We have to go," Ricardo interrupted her thoughts. "I'll bring you somewhere safe now, where no one can find you. Thea's waiting there for you."

This took a load off Romy's mind. She had missed her friend so much. "How is she?" she asked anxiously.

"Fine! She's getting used to her new life in the north of the island. As far as I know she has made friends with an old wisewoman from Garafía. And she also treats a number of women in Santa Domingo."

Thea was living her old life as a harimaguada again. Did Ricardo know that? Did he even know of amakuna?

"My bike is up there in the driveway. We should really be going now," he urged, "for whoever comes looking for you will definitely be looking here first."

The hot desert wind burned her skin as they drove to the north of the island, with Romy closely pressed to his back on the moped.

Borges and his men were the conquistadors and inquisitors of the present. They could, as the hermandad of Lorenzo de la Huerta, turn up anywhere at any moment. Iriomé's fate had become hers. The goddess had literally, in the last moment, seen to it that Cold Eye met his maker. But would she ensure it in this life as well?

Somewhere in the middle of nowhere the paved road ended, and they rolled along an ever narrower sandy track, meandering between dry, prickly plants toward the coast. It was dusk when Ricardo finally stopped and turned the engine off. "We'll have to walk the rest of the way," he said, while hiding his Enduro under a few bushes so it could not be spotted easily.

They stood on a huge rock plateau. In front of them lay the majestic cliffs of the north coast, against which the sea was thundering. The landscape lay in a slightly yellowish haze that was caused by the sand that the Calima brought from the Sahara.

Romy could not detect the slightest trail, but Ricardo knew exactly where he wanted to go. Without speaking she followed him to the edge of the cliff. The hot wind and the roar of the sea made verbal communication impossible. After a while he stopped so abruptly that Romy nearly knocked him down. Before them a hole was gaping in the ground, so large that a person could squeeze through. Around it the undergrowth had been ripped out. Romy could tell from Ricardo's alarmed face that this was not a good sign. Nevertheless he climbed carefully down into the hole feet first and was gone shortly thereafter. Romy had no choice but to follow him. Her feet found a grip on the side walls from which a few stones protruded. She let herself down into the earth well little by little, until she was on firm ground. In front of her was a tunnel with holes in the right sidewall through which a little daylight came in. Here it was nice and cool. When she looked through one of the openings, she found the white spray of the Atlantic splashing up to her from at least fifty feet below. Thus, the puddles on the ground.

Suddenly Ricardo was standing beside her and took her by the hand as they moved on. With a flashlight he lit their way along the cliffs from the inside. Eventually a huge living cave opened before them; it was partly glazed on the sea side; offering a stunning view of the Atlantic and the steep cliffs. But there was no sign of Thea. But someone seemed to have been here before them. And this someone had clearly been looking for something. The furnishings had been completely destroyed; boxes opened; blankets, clothing, and food scattered all over the floor; seating overturned; mattresses ripped open. In one corner Romy discovered Thea's turquoise dress and her shawl.

She sat down on one of the boxes, staring down into the wild spray that spilled out onto the rocks just to withdraw again into the vastness of the Atlantic. Had Thea drowned? Had Borges tortured her to find out about the location of the mushroom?

"Here, look at this." Ricardo handed her a sheet printed with capital letters.

WE HAVE THEA AND ARE WILLING TO EXCHANGE HER FOR ROMY CONRAD.
TRANSFER AT THE DEVIL'S FESTIVAL IN TIJARAFE.
NO POLICE, OTHERWISE SHE WILL DIE.

"Can you tell me what they want from you, and who they are, anyway?"

He seemed to know nothing about amakuna. Tanausú apparently had not told his friends. He was definitely wiser than she.

Ricardo grabbed her by the shoulders and looked into her eyes, but Romy could not bring herself to say it. "I don't know," she lied and could tell he did not believe her. "I'm sorry, but I can't say. Tanausú will explain everything. I just can't." Romy had tears in her eyes. On no account did she want to run the risk of jeopardizing yet another person. This, of course, did not satisfy Ricardo, but he didn't press her.

She reread the few lines. It was strange that Borges, or whoever was behind the kidnapping, had picked this festival. He probably planned the transfer during the spectacular fireworks. Unfortunately, those would take place elsewhere. Her idea to blow up the cave with Carlos's fireworks still seemed a possible solution. She hoped from the bottom of her heart that Tanausú would arrive soon. He was the only one who could help her now. The Holy Warrior! If she only had believed Sam the first time he had told her of this legend, things would have turned out differently.

"Be that as it may, you can't stay here," Ricardo said in a calm voice. "We're going to my house."

The motorcycle was fortunately still in the same place. Ricardo took off his shirt and put it over the seat, which had become so hot one could fry eggs on it. Romy thanked him and got on the bike. Her mind rushed. *How can I get Carlos's explosives? Will Tanausú help me at all? How can Thea be freed before the fireworks are launched?*

When they had almost reached Tijarafe, Ricardo turned from the main road into a small side street in the direction of the coast that led directly to his finca, an old one-story Canary house with wooden balconies, around which stood several smaller cottages made of natural stones. Under some almond trees hens pecked their food and a few well-fed cats were lying lazily in the sun. From a kennel resounded deafening barking of dogs. Only after a sharp command from inside the house peace was restored to some degree. The front door opened, and none other than Carlos came to meet her, beaming.

"*Hola guapa!*" He hugged her and planted a big kiss on her right and left cheeks. "We know each other from the ferry," he told his astonished son, "and passed the time with a good bottle of wine. If I had known she's a friend of yours . . . "

Romy could not believe it. Someone was massively pulling the strings making sure that everything took its course. It could not be a coincidence that she had ended up at exactly the place where the truck with the explosives was! Could it be that Tara had her hands in it? Romy spied Carlos's truck under a vine-covered tin roof. "So you've brought your dangerous load home safe and sound?"

"All's well." He gave his son a pat on the back. "Ricardo will be the greatest devil Tijarafe has ever seen."

Romy was under the impression that the young man shared his father's enthusiasm only to a limited extent but deferred to tradition. She just hoped that Tanausú would arrive as soon as possible so that they could discuss her plan. They probably wouldn't be able to get around letting Ricardo in on it.

Carlos laughed and clicked his tongue a few times in order to calm the excited dogs that pressed themselves against the grill of the kennel trying to get his attention. "These are podencos. The best hunters in the world, quick and perfect tracker dogs," the Palmero said proudly. "You don't even need a rifle. They fill my freezer every weekend. And then we're having *conejo en salsa* or *con ajo*." He ran his tongue over his lips. "I think there are some leftovers from the weekend."

Romy laughed. Carlos really was a connoisseur, and although she was actually not in the mood for roasted rabbit, she was persuaded to eat a bit.

"Well, how's the jealous lover?" he asked, when they walked over to the house together. Ricardo gave her a skeptical glance.

"I think he's still behind me." She winked at Ricardo conspiratorially, who fortunately understood and picked up the thread immediately.

"I offered for Romy to stay with us for the time being," he said. "I know her and her friend from a recent vacation here on La Palma."

"You'd better watch out; otherwise you might have a knife in your back before long." Carlos laughed. "I'm only joking. Of course, you can stay here," he said. "The señorita can sleep in one of the caves. When the Calima blows, the caves are the pleasantest place to be anyway."

Although this was the second time she was on La Palma, the idea of sleeping in caves still needed some getting used to, even though they were much more comfortable nowadays than in the times of the Guanches.

As they entered the house, they were met by the smell of delicious food. In the kitchen they encountered a small, slightly lumpy woman of at least eighty. She wore an apron that was far too large for her over a black, almost floor-length dress, and her white hair was tied at the back in a small bun.

"*Abuela*, we have a guest," Ricardo shouted in her ear.

She turned around, and Romy looked into a thin, deeply lined face. She beamed at her. "I'm Rosa, Carlos's mother. How nice to have such a pretty woman here in our humble home," she said with an almost maidenly voice, embracing Romy. She only reached to Romy's chest. "Are you thirsty? Oh, those men! Didn't they offer you anything?"

"We've only just arrived," Romy came to the men's defense.

"Men today have no manners." She handed over a large glass of water, which Romy downed in one gulp. "My husband was quite different in this."

Ricardo laughed and tugged her ear. "Abuela, you haven't seen your husband for fifty years. How do you know what he's like today?"

"That's true. The scoundrel!" Rosa turned back to her stove and was busy with her pots, from which more delicious odors ascended. Ricardo also helped himself to a glass of water and sat next to Romy, who had taken a seat at the kitchen table. "My grandfather migrated to Cuba in the sixties when there was a true famine here to try his luck, like many others. Since then we never heard from him again."

Romy had read about this. Cuba had long been considered the eighth of the Canary Islands. "But most of them returned or got their families to join them as soon as they had made a bit of money, right?"

"That's true." Rosa laughed scornfully. "But some of them also looked for a new wife, a younger one. Just as my José, the bastard!" she said.

Romy grinned; Rosa seemed like she could easily stand on her own. Here in this cozy kitchen she relaxed a bit, feeling more like a human being and not like a chased rabbit. "But now you have these two wonderful men. Not everybody is so lucky."

"That's right," Rosa confirmed. "And I thank the Lord for it every day."

In order not to put her foot in her mouth, Romy stopped herself from asking about Ricardo's mother, but the old woman seemed to be able to read her thoughts. "My daughter-in-law also left us and never came back. She was from the mainland and eventually could not stand it any longer here on the island. Carlos has never tried to find a new wife," Rosa mused. "History repeats itself. And sometimes it takes many generations, until a pain is overcome."

Rosa is a wise woman, Romy thought. Iriomé's love story spontaneously passed through her mind. Then Nic's face with his warm eyes appeared before her inner eye. She had not thought of him for quite some time; rather, forbidden herself to think about him. And now she shooed the thought of him away quickly while helping the old woman set the table in the *comedor.* The wood-paneled dining room with the old sepia-colored photos on the walls gave the impression of being rarely used. In Romy's honor Rosa produced a white tablecloth and laid out the best china, as well as fancy silverware.

"You really don't have to do this," Romy tried to hold her back, even if she had to admit that she enjoyed the caring atmosphere and at least for a short time felt safe.

The rabbit was tender like butter and could easily be removed from the bone. In addition *papas arrugadas,* wrinkled potatoes cooked in brine, were served with mojo, the famous Canary chili sauce, and a strong red wine from Garafía. But when Romy was about to swallow the first mouthful, she suddenly felt the urge to vomit. With an apologetic gesture she rose.

Just in time she made it to the bathroom, opened the toilet lid, and threw up. *Right, I'm pregnant,* flashed through her head. In all the excitement she had completely blocked out this fact. After she rinsed out her mouth, she went back to the comedor, hoping that no one would take notice. Rosa was still railing against unfaithful and unreliable men, obviously not for the first time, because neither Carlos nor Ricardo seemed to be listening. They were busy carefully removing the rabbit meat from the small bones with their teeth without swallowing one.

Ricardo threw Romy a searching look when she sat down, which even his father noticed. However, he interpreted it wrong. "You'd better watch out!" he said with a grin. "Jealous lovers possess no sense of humor."

Neither do people like Borges, Romy thought and scolded herself. Her mere presence endangered this nice family. And she did not like that at all. *But what can I do?*

Ricardo's cell phone rang. "Yes, she's here with me."

Tanausú! It was a load off Romy's mind.

"We're coming." Ricardo pocketed his phone and stood up. He gave his grandmother a peck on the cheek. "The meal was *muy rico* as always. Unfortunately, we need to go," he apologized for their abrupt departure.

Romy also said thank you and followed Ricardo outside. She breathed a sigh of relief. Finally she was no longer the only one responsible for everything, for all the evil that had already happened or for the decisions that had to be made yet.

On the motorcycle they roared back north but changed direction just before Punta Gorda and drove up into the mountains. The road zigzagged its way up in uncountable curves. The temperature increased with every meter in height. While normally it was always cool and windy at high altitudes and sunny and warm at the seaside, the exact reverse was true in the Calima season. The hot wind contributed to the fact that Romy eventually no longer knew whether they were moving forward or backward. The mixture of sweat and sandy wind was unbearable. Her eyes burned, and she had to narrow them to slits. Even when they were driving cross-country through a forest with huge pine trees, there was no drop in temperature.

Finally, they stopped in a small clearing where an old stone house stood. Romy was glad to get off the bike. She felt like a breaded and fried cutlet. Shaking the sand off her clothes caused new sweating.

Ricardo gave a whistle combination Romy knew from Iriomé, and indeed Tanausú appeared shortly thereafter in the low entrance of the little house. He had to stoop so that he did not bang his head on the door frame. Romy got goose bumps when she saw him. He looked tired, he wore a three-day beard and his green army jacket was ripped. First he greeted Ricardo in the manner of the Guanches, by placing his forehead against his friend's and muttering the old greeting; then he did the same with her.

"Are you okay?" Romy stammered.

Tanausú nodded. "*Perdona*," he apologized, "that I let you down in Marbella. That was not planned. But obviously you managed to get here without me, about which I had not the slightest doubt, by the way." Then he asked Ricardo to leave them alone for a moment. Without protest Ricardo walked away to use the time to clean his completely dirty motorcycle with a rag.

"You already know all that will happen anyway," Romy said in a slightly provocative tone. She still found it difficult to believe the story of the Holy Warrior.

"Unfortunately not. Just as you always experience only certain time periods in the past, it's the same with me in the future. It's like in a TV series. When it gets gripping, it stops, and you have to wait for the next episode."

"And why is it that the mushroom causes you to look into the future and I travel into the past? I mean, am I the harimaguada, or not?"

He smiled. "Because amakuna always makes everyone see what's best for their development in the moment."

"You want to say, the mushroom is an animate being and thinks for itself?"

"You could say that. Yes."

She thought for a moment before she put into words what had been on her mind for quite a while; namely, that she could not have endured all this without Iriomé. She felt connected with everything stronger than ever. For the first time Romy felt this awareness as the greatest gift of the Creator to humankind: to feel life in all its intensity, in all it had brought forth; to look deep into the living nature, to perceive it and feel secure in it; to be aware of the god's creation—and not to simply stomp blindly through it. The earth kept her grounded, the trees offered protection, the air allowed her to unfold, and the wind gave answers to many questions; water transferred its power, and the drifting of the clouds reminded her of change and transience. She felt forearmed for what was awaiting her.

Tanausú smiled. Romy assumed that he already knew all, even before she had found the right words.

"I feel the same," he said. "It's a very special force that enables us to do things of which we are only capable if we can see behind the curtain of time. But maybe it's also the reassuring thought that our souls will always return." He looked at Ricardo, who stood with his back to them and was still busy with his motorcycle. "Did you tell him about amakuna?"

She shook her head. "I was about to, but I didn't. I don't want to endanger him and his family as well. The mushroom has brought about enough evil. Now Forster's people have also abducted Thea. I'm sure that this Borges is behind it." She got out the note they found in Tanausú's hiding place and handed it to him.

He read the words with a serious expression on his face. The scar on his forehead turned dark. "At the devil's festival," he murmured. "An ideal occasion. People come by the thousands from all the islands to watch this crazy spectacle."

"I know. Ricardo's father has brought a whole truck full of fireworks from the mainland." She took a deep breath and grabbed his forearm. "What if we blow up the cavity with it or at least destroy the entrance, so that no one will have access any time soon." Anxiously she awaited his response.

Tanausú took his time answering, so she got the impression he was playing through the whole scene in his mind.

"It's the only way to put an end to all this madness," Romy stressed.

"I think you're right," he said. "The mushroom once had the task of allowing the harimaguadas a look into the future or let them go back in time to better understand the occurrences of the present, but not to save humanity from death. The time for this has not yet come. Maybe someday in another life amakuna may save this planet. Then certain people will know where it can be found."

Romy became aware for the first time that in this present life one could take on responsibility beyond and into the next. "So you agree with the idea?"

"It's your decision, Romy. You are the guardian of the mushroom. I'll talk to Ricardo to see if there's any chance he'll help us. The devil's festival takes place tomorrow." He grinned. "After all, he is the devil."

"Won't you need to tell him about amakuna?"

"Yes, I'll have to. He has made an oath to respect and protect the tradition and the customs of the Benahoarias forever. He's a good guy and deserves to become one of us."

The next day Romy woke early. When she opened the wooden gate of the small sleeping cave, there was still a hot wind blowing, even though the sun had not even come up. Her body yearned for water, and her teeth needed a toothbrush. She ran along the small dirt track past a steep cliff to Carlos's finca. All was still quiet. She crossed the parched yard but kept well clear of the kennel to keep the dogs from barking. On the outer wall of the kitchen she discovered a faucet. She turned it on and recoiled. Even now, in the early morning, the water came out boiling hot.

"*Buenos días,*" she heard Carlos call from a small wooden balcony on the second floor. "Wait, I'll come down and open the door for you; then you can use the bathroom."

Romy turned the faucet off and followed his invitation gratefully. When she looked in the mirror in the plain but clean bathroom, she frightened herself by what she saw. Her normally darker hair had bleached and was sticky with sand and dust, her face was deep brown, and her blue eyes sparkled as never before. It was the Guanche woman who was looking at her from the mirror—Iriomé as she had looked before the amakuna ritual, face and hair rubbed with ash and clay. Romy would now assume her task as guardian of the mushroom and accomplish it with all that it implied.

Tanausú and Ricardo had spent the entire night making explosive devices from the fireworks. Once they were done, the former leader of the Guanches intended to set off to the caldera and place them in a way that the entrance to the tomb cave of the harimaguadas would be completely blocked up. When Thea had been exchanged for Romy at the devil's festival, she would lead Borges and his men to a specific location in the Cumbre, a small mountain range above Los Llanos, where the Corro Benahoare—the secret society—would free her. Although the plan seemed foolproof, Romy had a strange feeling. It was not fear, but rather disappointment or a deep sadness.

Not that she regretted not becoming the new Alexander Fleming of the twenty-first century. Rather she was hurt by the thought of the countless people, especially children, with deadly diseases growing weaker and weaker in the hospitals of the world. With the complete destruction of the cave her original idea to make the mushroom available for all humankind as a comprehensive cure was dead, at least in this life. It was a fact that the doctor and scientist in her did not like at all.

But her decision was irrevocable. And maybe the médico had been right in saying that humans, with such a magic remedy, would interfere with god's plans and thereby only cause mischief, which had already been proved in the past as well as in the present.

Chapter 36

At the Danza del Diablo literally all hell had broken loose. In the narrow streets and on the Plaza of Tijarafe people danced and celebrated. The young people wore flashing red horns on their heads. Countless stalls served wine and beer. On a stage a salsa band of ten was playing, while from various pubs other music reached the street. In addition there was the roar and the songs of the drunkards. People mainly communicated by shouting or via hand signals. Tanausú and Romy pushed their way through the crowds to the main dance floor. Couples of all ages were moving to the rhythm of the music. Time and again, the band played a song that had been composed especially for this occasion and encouraged the people to sing along. *"Diridiridiri el diablo está aquí."* Yet the devil could not be bothered. And only with his appearance would Borges turn up, when all were distracted and had abandoned themselves to hysteria and ecstasy.

After what felt like three hours, the time had come. A monstrous figure, at least two men high, black with glowing red eyes, appeared on the dance floor. Romy admired Ricardo for how he coped. She knew he was wearing a suit of asbestos under the costume and a breathing mask. The crowd went wild. The band played the devil song now at triple volume. A deafening drum solo followed. The crowd cheered, shouted, and tried to flee from the immediate vicinity of the devil. Some young men took off their shirts in anticipation of the first fireworks that would be shot from the head of the figure—a test of courage and of course to impress the girls.

And indeed the first rockets hissed right into the middle of the screaming crowd. Romy looked at Tanausú, startled. "Why? Didn't you . . . I thought . . . "

"The Chinese Shop in Los Llanos still had some illegal fireworks in stock," he shouted in her ear. "But they'll only last a maximum of three minutes; after that the party is over."

At that moment Romy felt a jolt. She was ripped from Tanausú's arms and seconds later found herself in the iron grip of Antonio Borges. Just out of the corner of her eye she caught a glimpse of Theay whom Tanausú now was holding in his arms.

The Argentine dragged Romy more than walked with her to the edge of the dance floor. She had not the slightest chance to twist herself free from him. Between the stalls, where meat was fried under a cloak of smoke, two other men showed up to receive Romy.

"It would be good if you could cooperate, Doctor. We don't want to spoil the party for the people," Borges hissed in her ear.

But even if she had screamed her head off nobody would have heard anyway or seemed to find it strange that she was downright dragged along. On the road, the noise level was even higher than in the plaza: one car parked behind the other, equipped with giant speakers sending their own sound through open hatches into the street, around which small or large groups had gathered drinking cheap alcohol they had brought along from paper cups. They had no mercy for Romy and laughed when she tried to defend herself tooth and nail. Finally they turned into a slightly quieter side street, at the end of which two large jeeps were parked.

Romy could not believe what she saw. Leaning against one of them was Nic. *So he is part of it!* He was the one who was holding the strings in his hand, who was the head. Only after a second glance, something seemed funny to her. Nic seemed not to be standing there of his own free will. The man in black paramilitary clothing right next to him had a revolver in his hand, which was directed at Nic.

"Listen to me carefully," Borges hissed in her ear again. "As you can see, there's your friend Nic. But he's not well. Not well in the least. He suffers from a brain tumor and will die in a few months. And your child will grow up without a father."

Romy froze; she was not sure whether she had understood Cold Eye correctly, because there was still a lot of noise. A Spanish tearjerker singing about *amor* and *ojos negros* echoed through the small alley.

"You left the pregnancy test in the bathroom," Borges shouted, trying to drown out the music. Although at first she hoped he was bluffing, she now realized that Borges was telling the truth. That's why Nic had the seizures. It was not epilepsy, but a tumor that caused them. "You don't want to have to tell your child someday that you let his father die in the streets."

What should I do now? Tanausú was already on the way to the caldera to blow up the cave and finally destroy amakuna. She broke away from the men, ran to Nic, and flung herself into his arms. Suddenly nothing counted anymore. She loved this man. She did not want him to die. She wanted to save him, even if Borges's plan would then work out. Iriomé once believed that love was the strongest force in the universe, but she had despaired of it and had shut her heart against Joaquín. It was Romy's destiny to overcome these doubts in order to fulfill Tichiname's prophecy that the mushroom must be protected by a loving couple.

"Borges is behind all this," Nic whispered in her ear. "He wants to sell the mushroom to seriously ill billionaires acting on his own. You were right. He's responsible for the murders. And when I confronted him with it . . . " He raised his hands, which were bound with cable ties. "He'll stop at nothing."

"I love you," she said. And it was the first time in her life that she said these words with so much conviction.

"*Te amo también,*" he said, barely moving his lips. And for the first time in her life she believed a man. "That's the only thing that matters. I'm going to die, Romy; I'm very sick, but I know for at least for a short time I was blessed to have known your love." He caressed her face with his bound hands and wiped the tears from her cheeks with his thumb.

"I'm sorry that I must disturb this moment of deep intimacy, but it's time to leave," Borges said with a cynical smile.

"You must, on no account, show him the location, Romy," Nic called to her while Borges pushed him into the car.

"I don't think she will listen to you; am I right?" he grinned at Romy. "As an expectant mother one no longer bears responsibility only for oneself."

Nic looked at her surprised, desperate, and at the same time full of love. A look that went right through her and that aroused all the feelings in her that had lain idle for years. Borges, who did not want to allow sentimentality, dragged her to the second jeep, which also stood ready for departure. He sat beside her on the back seat and gave the command to drive off.

Originally the plan was for Romy to have lured the whole group into the trap carefully prepared in the Cumbre by the Corro Benahoare. She now had to reach the cave before Tanausú if she wanted to save Nic's life.

Again, it was love that brought her to exactly the same situation as once had been the case with the Guanche woman. Was she about to make another mistake? Would they all be doomed again? She put her hand on her belly. Perhaps it was only about the child that was growing in her. Perhaps he or she had the task to protect amakuna, like Tamanca, and it was not important at all to save Nic's life. Perhaps he had done his duty by fathering the child. But what about love? Iriomé had shut her heart out of disappointment and humiliation, even though she had once believed so much in the most powerful of all powers. Suddenly she saw the eyes of María del Pilar in her mind's eye and felt the look she had given Iriomé.

"Where to?" Borges barked at her.

"To the caldera," she said firmly.

Borges stroked her cheek. "At last you've come to your senses, Doctor. But actually," he hesitated for a moment, "I knew from the beginning that we would eventually agree." To him the world seemed to act like clockwork and people like puppets whose strings he pulled or let loose according to his whim.

Romy pushed his hand away and closed her eyes in order to focus on her soul brother. Just as Iriomé was once connected with Tanausú, he should be able now to sense that the tide had turned. Certainly the holy warrior possessed something like telepathic abilities. Despite the tense situation, she smiled to herself. How much she had once looked down on such forces, and now they might save her and Nic's life.

※

Something was not going according to plan. He felt Romy wanted to convey a message to him, but he didn't understand what it was. His ability to receive messages without the help of the modern means of communication was quickly deteriorating. As much as he focused, he did not understand what she wanted to tell him. He tried to get the maximum speed out of Ricardo's motorcycle, forcing Thea, who was sitting behind him, to be pressed ever more closely against him.

At the parking lot at the Barranco de las Angustias he parked the bike. Thea put her hand on his shoulder. "Romy is not on the way into the Cumbre. She is coming here with Borges and his men."

"What!?"

"You need to call your friends from the Corro Benahoare. There will be a battle again. Just like once before."

Tanausú looked at her—surprised only for a moment—and then took out his cell phone. "And we'll win this time?"

※

Romy grew more and more restless. Tanausú seemed not to hear her. She hoped that he would not think she had changed allegiance when she suddenly appeared with Borges's people in the caldera.

"Where to now?" The driver's rough voice pulled her from her thoughts.

They had arrived at the parking lot. Romy spotted Ricardo's motor-cycle at the farthest end of the parking lot.

Borges followed her gaze. "Can it be that someone has gone collecting the mushroom before us? I don't need to tell you what this would mean for you and Nic." He opened the door of the jeep and let her get out. "I think from here we'll have to walk."

The second jeep parked right behind them. When she watched Nic get out, Romy felt a stab in the heart. Their eyes met. No, these were not the eyes of a greedy conquistador. How could she just have been so skeptical all the time? These were eyes full of love and warmth in which there was a plea for forgiveness.

It was hard to watch as one of Borges's men pushed a gun in his back. She wanted to run up to him, but the Argentine seized her by the arm and pushed her along. "After you, please, Doctor," he said in his inimitably affected way. "I think we have no time to lose."

The small party moved off. In front went two men with automatic weapons, then Borges with Romy. Behind them followed three other gunmen with Nic in their grip.

Under a full moon, the caldera was a wild tangle of light and shadows among the rocks, suitable for an escape. But it was not the muzzle of the gun in her back that kept Romy from fleeing but the one that was directed at Nic. He was a victim of Borges, just as Joaquín once had been used by Cold Eye. This storyline must not be repeated. Everything could be changed. Nothing remained forever! This life offered a chance. Why else had they all met again, if not for the reason that they could finally clear things up?

Suddenly there was a rumbling sound. Romy spun around. The man who was the last in the row had gone to the ground. His skull was smashed. A medium-sized boulder rolled down the hillside. The rest of the men drew their weapons and rushed to cover. One of them switched on an LED flashlight and systematically illuminated the rock walls, while another was trying to locate the attacker via binoculars. Several times they shot at indefinable objects. But except for the echo and a little debris that came down, they didn't achieve anything.

Once Romy thought she saw the shadow of a man vaulting over the rocks clinging to a long stick as the Guanches used to do. But perhaps her imagination was playing tricks on her. Was there a new battle breaking out? Was this the chance for the Guanches to take revenge?

"Whoever it is," Borges, squeezed next to her against a rock, hissed in Romy's ear, "tell them to stop it; otherwise . . . "

"Otherwise what?" she hissed back.

"You know what I mean," he snorted. "Let's go!" he called out to his men. "We'll deal with him later." He kicked the dead man against the rock wall with his boot.

Shortly before they reached the Cascada de Colores the next man was hit. A wooden lance bore into his back that must have been thrown at close range. He fell forward to the ground. Blood was coming out of his mouth. One of his comrades tried to remove the huge weapon from his body, triggering another surge of blood that now gushed from the wound. He groaned one last time.

The men refused to move on; they were all on high alert. This had nothing to do with what they had learned during their training as security guards. This was a guerrilla struggle of the first class. For this they were neither prepared nor equipped.

"If one more of my men is attacked, Nic's going to die. Here and now." Borges gave a sign, and Nic was thrust to the ground at her feet.

Borges pointed his gun at Nic's head and looked at Romy, prompting her. She had no choice. She pursed her lips and gave a whistle in two different keys, which reverberated from the caldera as an echo. They came so naturally from her lips, as if she had always communicated in this way. The first whistle meant "stop." The other meant "mortal danger."

No answer.

"What's that supposed to mean?" barked Borges, who in contrast to his normally controlled and smug attitude was getting more and more nervous.

At that moment a long-drawn whistle came back. "They'll stop," Romy said.

"And who are 'they'?"

"The native inhabitants who protect their sanctuary."

Borges laughed. "Don't tell me stories. They went extinct ages ago."

"You mean, they were eradicated by guys just like you."

"Antonio. I beg you!" Nic struggled to his feet. "There's no point in all this."

"No point?!" Borges stepped close to him. "For me there is a point. I'm fed up. Totally fed up. This mushroom is the chance I've waited long enough for."

A very long time, thought Romy.

His eyes flashed with anger. He grabbed Nic by the collar. "You think you've got a monopoly on luck. But that's over with now. You didn't keep your promise to promote me as your partner."

"It was an extorted promise, Antonio."

"A man is true to his word. But one probably knows nothing of this when he is born with a silver spoon in his mouth."

On a signal from Borges, Romy was dragged away by a stout guy, so that she could no longer hear what the two men were saying.

"Who are these natives, and how many are there?" the burly man asked her with a Russian accent.

"I don't know," Romy said. And this was actually the truth.

"Even if they don't outnumber us, we have no chance here," he continued. "We don't know the terrain. They can kill us off like flies."

Romy looked thoughtfully into the coarse but good-natured face of the man. Perhaps it would be smart to recruit an ally among Borges's men. Someone who would be on her side when the Argentine completely freaked out.

"This was going to be my last job. I'm not prepared to put my life on the line. After all, I'm going to be a father."

Romy smiled in spite of the seriousness of the situation. "And I'm going to be a mother. Nic Saratoga is the father. Take care of him, and I will ensure that you get out of here alive."

He took her hand and squeezed it. "I'll do that. My word is my bond. By the way, my name's Slatjo Kamiriew, and I come from Chechnya."

"Okay, Slatjo" Romy said. "We have a deal."

Just then Borges came up. "Can we go?"

She nodded. "The Guanches will remain quiet. As long as you don't make a mistake."

Now the moon was shedding her light on the caldera such that they no longer needed flashlights.

Time and again Romy believed she recognized one of Tanausú's friends following them in the shade of the rocks. It was reassuring and frightening at the same time to know they were really close. If they started another attack for some reason, that would mean Nic's death. But they reached the cave shrine without further event. Romy pointed silently up to the entrance of the great ritual cave, which seemed in the semidarkness of the moonlight like an ominous maw. "There it is," she said to Borges.

He followed her gaze, and it seemed to Romy as if he was suddenly undecided. "Is there no other way up there, except this cliff?"

She shook her head.

"My men are not equipped for this. Therefore you will climb up there and get me the mushroom."

"Without a rope?"

"You'll manage it!"

"And if I don't come back?"

"You will come back." He glanced at Nic. "Love is a powerful force, Dr. Conrad, isn't it?"

Romy was reminded of Cold Eye begging for Iriomé's help in his last death rattle. She felt anew the power of the Guanche woman, while she walked up to the entrance in the rock face. Nobody followed her, but all night vision glasses were on her and at least one weapon.

The hooks from her tour with Sam were still there, and Romy pulled herself up to them. She still remembered the route they had climbed the last time and felt reasonably safe even without a rope. Though the excitement of the past few hours had gotten on her nerves, the claws of fear did not grip her this time, did not bore into her breast, and also did not choke her. It was as if she had defeated fear. Once and for all.

When she reached the top, she pulled herself over the edge and sat there for a while to catch her breath. Then she got out the flashlight she had brought in her belt and entered the cave. She could have gone blindfolded; she recognized each branch, each stone she had to step over, each overhang where she had to duck her head. It seemed to her as if she was led by Iriomé.

When Romy entered the rock cathedral, she saw that from the hole at the top of the ceiling a rope was hanging down. Tanausú must have entered the cave from up there.

"Tanausú?" she called into the darkness. And once again, "Tanausú?"

No answer. She worked her way through the narrow passages until she reached the one with the grave chamber of the harimaguadas. It was broken open. The stones that she and Sam had closed the entrance with lay on the floor. She grabbed the rope that hung there and climbed up as she had done before. With her flashlight she inspected the grave. Not a single mushroom was growing on the ground. Instead small packages with explosives were neatly deposited in all four corners.

"Why have you brought them here?" she suddenly heard Tanausú's voice from a rock niche. He flashed a torch in her face so that she was blinded by the light. "You're making the same mistake all over again!"

"Nic needs the mushroom. He's fatally ill."

"Amakuna is not meant to cure people. It may only be used by a harimaguada and those who follow her. It's your job to protect the mushroom until the time for your successor has arrived. I thought we agreed on this."

The last thing Romy wanted was to start a quarrel with him, yet somehow she had to make her position clear to him. "Woman alone can no longer shoulder this task. I don't know if you're aware of it, but Tichiname said shortly before her death that the mushroom can only be protected by the love between a man and a woman."

"And you seriously believe Nic Saratoga, CEO of Forster's Health, is this man?"

She nodded. "That's what my heart is telling me, and I believe in it more than in anything else in this world."

"Iriomé was mistaken in Joaquín de Alba y Santa Barbara. Isn't that so?"

"She wasn't. The era she lived in was against them. It was too early. But the world has moved on. Today we stand on the threshold of a new way of thinking."

"I hardly think so," Tanausú replied harshly. "The struggle between those who exploit and those who are exploited has remained the same. And believe me, I know what I'm talking about."

"When love gets no chance there will always be fighting. And nothing will ever change. Is that what you want? Keep on fighting for all eternity or until nothing is left of this world?" she asked provokingly.

He looked at her thoughtfully. "We've been down this road before. And you see where the world is today."

"I'm still not giving up. Iriomé had no chance then. I think today we have one."

"Maybe you're right. But I can't help you anyway. Amakuna won't grow here again until the winter solstice in December."

"What?!" Romy looked at him desperate. "By then Nic won't be alive," she said in a low voice. "And everything . . . "

At that moment she was interrupted by two male voices coming from inside the mountain.

"Borges's beagles," whispered Romy.

"Come quick." Tanausú dragged her with him into one of the side passages. From there they passed through a tiny blind shaft directly into the cathedral.

Obviously the two mercenaries had managed to follow her and then had gotten lost in the maze of the passages. But none of the two sounded like the Chechnyan. That meant Nic was only guarded by Borges and Romy's new friend Slatjo. Romy felt a surge of hope.

"Come on, you first." Tanausú handed her the rope and held it tightly, while Romy climbed up. She propped herself with her feet on a rock face, praying that they would have enough time before the two appeared on the scene.

It was already dawn when Tanausú got to the top and pulled the rope up—right at the very second when the shadows of the two soldiers appeared.

"Where's Thea?" Romy whispered when he had gotten his breath back.

"In a safe place, from where she will blow up the whole thing via remote ignition at exactly five in the morning. He looked at his watch. "Well, in exactly ten minutes."

"When Borges hears the explosion, he will kill Nic." Romy knew that Slatjo was with him, but the Argentine would also put his own man out of action if he was in his way.

"Can we make it to the healing cave in that time?" She looked at her soul brother pleadingly. "Pray! We must help Nic."

"If I do not come with you, would you do it alone?" Tanausú asserted rather than asked. "It's my task to protect you."

This took a load off Romy's mind. She admired this man who against all his experiences and his attitude toward men like Nic Saratoga still remained at her side. He handed her one of two jump bars that had been hidden in the bushes next to the rock hole.

"You still know how to do that?"

It was her only chance to arrive below before the explosion. Romy took the rod, looked out for a suitable spot on which she could land, and rammed it into the ground there. She took a deep breath and swung downward. Automatically she pulled it out again and repeated the whole procedure until she had traveled a few hundred feet difference in altitude within a few minutes. Tanausú, who had followed in the same manner, overtook her and showed her the way across prickly scrub and loose scree to a small platform above the healing cave. From here they could perfectly observe what was happening down below.

Borges held a walkie-talkie in his hand and was just informed by his men that they had found a cave packed to the brim with explosives.

A mushroom or similar plants were nowhere in sight. He hurled the device on the ground and pointed the gun at Nic, who leaned next to the cave entrance, his hands bound.

"I'm dying anyway," Nic said softly.

"It will nevertheless give me great satisfaction," replied Borges.

Romy held her breath. As in fast-forward the images of the past ran through her mind. How Iriomé pulled Joaquín aside when Guayafanta was about to kill him, and vice versa how Joaquín saved her life by challenging Cold Eye to a duel on the ship. Now it was obviously on her to come to his rescue. She turned to Tanausú for help, but he was gone.

As if she now was led by Iriomé, she bent down quickly and grabbed one of the boulders lying on the ground in piles. She felt an unprecedented power rise in her, targeted the back of her mortal enemy's head and threw with all her might.

The stone hit him full force. Borges collapsed, but in falling was still able to trigger a shot that echoed off the rock walls. Romy winced. She tripped, slipped, fell down the slope, came to her feet, and continued sliding. Her heart raced. Had Nic become a further victim of Borges in these last minutes?

Bleeding and scarred, she reached the cave. Borges was lying on the ground and would not get up again. At the place where Nic had leaned, Slatjo now stood, cradling his shoulder covered in blood. "A through and through, but I'll be okay," he said.

"Nic?" Romy was so out of breath that she could hardly speak.

The hulk of a man smiled and moved aside. Behind him there was Nic, and he was uninjured. When she closed him in her arms, it was the most beautiful and intimate moment she had ever experienced. His kisses, his breath, his smell surged through every pore of her body. This feeling alone made all she had taken on worth it. She had finally arrived. The enemy was destroyed. Love had won. "You must hang on. Only till the end of this year, then the mushroom will grow again," she whispered in his ear. At that moment an enormous blast rocked the caldera. Nic yanked Romy into the small cave as in front of it stones and boulders came falling down.

Thea had done it.

"It's better this way," Nic said softly, gently stroking her matted hair with his still bound hands. "Otherwise everything starts all over again."

"Romy!" It was Tanausú; he sounded worried. "Everything okay?" Even though he did not look like the last leader of the Guanches in his military jacket, his figure, his gestures, his gait, and the proud look conveyed this impression. Romy felt connected to him in a deep way and wanted to preserve this for all eternity. Yet the look he darted at Nic was anything but friendly.

"I'm glad to finally meet you in person," said Nic as he held out his bound hands to him.

Tanausú ignored the gesture. "Unfortunately I can't share in this joy."

"He's on our side," said Romy, trying to relax the situation as she freed Nic.

"A little late, isn't it?" said Tanausú.

"Not really. I was from the beginning."

"That's true. But I had no trust," said Romy.

"I want to make you a proposition." Nic looked Tanausú straight in the eye. "As you have perhaps already heard, I won't live much longer. And I know you're planning to take legal action both against Forster's Health and against two other pharmaceutical companies," he said with a quiet voice.

"So?"

"I can give you all the inside information and will officially testify, if we can manage that the whole thing doesn't drag on too long."

Tanausú looked surprised and incredulous at the same time. "In the face of death many become pious."

"I understand your cynicism, but I'm serious." Nic again held out his hand to Tanausú, but he again did not accept.

"And why this change of heart now?" he asked.

Nic looked at Romy a long time before answering. "I'm doing this for my child and for a better future. Whether you believe me or not won't matter." He looked Tanausú in the eyes. "I admit, it took me a while before I understood what direction this world must follow so that it doesn't go entirely to the dogs. But better late than never. Also if I don't have much time, I'll do all in my power to put a stop to some people's games. I can help you achieve your goals, perhaps by different means than you're used to, but believe me, they will be effective."

Tanausú looked him searchingly in the eye, then reached into the inside pocket of his jacket and handed him two small mushrooms.

"Those were the last."

Romy fought back her tears. Now everything would be fine. She had made the right decision when she followed the call of love against all adverse circumstances. Nic had been meant for her from the beginning. But it was Iriomé who had prepared the way for her. Without the Guanche woman and her fate, she would never have had the courage and strength to continue on her chosen path. For quite a while Romy stood between the two men, lost in thought.

Only the call of an early falcon lured her out of the cave. He circled over her, again and again. Did he want to tell her something? She looked up, and suddenly understood. Iriomé had sent him to tell her that she had now forgiven Joaquín. She had cleared the way for Romy's love to Nic. She was finally redeemed. She now only needed to put her soul on the wings of the bird. It would bring her home.

The next moment, against the brightening sky in the distance, the slim silhouette of a woman appeared, who slowly came closer. Thea. With her now regrown, thick hair she reminded Romy inevitably of Tichiname. Behind her was a group of men with beards and long sticks in their hands. The two friends locked in a loving embrace. They were finally reunited. Amakuna had appeared at exactly the right time. The first step was taken. But the struggle for a better world had just begun.

Epilogue

According to the Christian calendar more than ten years had passed since Iriomé had last seen her home island.

In Barcelona Aaron could not find a ship for her that would have brought her back to her island, so she had traveled with him to Augsburg and found accommodation with the Welsers. There she was held in high regard, not only because of her beauty and her special charisma, but also because of her knowledge about her home.

Fortuitously, the Welsers' famous trading house planned a mission to the newly discovered islands to acquire land for the cultivation of sugarcane on Benahoare, now called La Palma. It was like a twist of fate that Iriomé was invited to come along and thus could finally travel home and do so in a quite comfortable manner. The ship was twice as large as that of de Lugo's; she had her own little cabin and was allowed to eat with the captain, the officers, and the client: Anton Welser. The merchant, who even after a month-long voyage still looked just right in his baggy trousers and his black, close-fitting jacket, had from the beginning seen her as an expert consultant. Iriomé was well aware of this and deeply regretted that she had not been able to open her heart to him. She still felt as if wrapped in a cloth of gray sadness and allowed no one to pull it off.

He was standing expectantly beside her at the railing as the ship, under light wind, slowly approached her island. But Iriomé could not and would not share her feelings with him. Her gaze was fixed on what she called the island of her ancestors, but she already knew that nothing would ever be the same again.

After she had thanked her benefactor and said goodbye to the crew, she set foot on the island again for the first time. On the side where the sun rose, a small town and a harbor had been built in which several ships were bobbing up and down. Everywhere there was hammering and construction going on. It seemed to her as if half of the Spanish population had settled here. Only very rarely a lighter hair color flashed in the crowd. Iriomé hoped that she would find someone she knew who could tell her whether Nesfete and the people she had left in the volcanic crater a long time ago were still alive. But no familiar face crossed her path. She heard that most had left their caves and now worked for the new landowners. The young girls made mooneyes at the Spaniards, hoping they would marry them. Exactly what Tanausú had foreseen had come true. Their people would disappear in the next generation or the one after. Only now she understood completely why the voice of the old medicine woman had failed when she foresaw the fate of Benahoare. Iriomé wanted just one thing: to go where time stopped forever.

She asked one of the sailors for a shirt, trousers, and shoes, in which she would get along on the stony and narrow streets and in the wild canyons.

The sun had reached its zenith when she approached the place of the sacred well. But where was the familiar rippling, which always had been heard from a distance? Even the small birds that used to keep watch here had disappeared. The well had dried up. No trickle dripped from the rock face. Where wild ferns had once burgeoned around the water-filled stone basin, there was only dry scrub. The spiral that had been carved into the rock many generations ago had lost its power. Even the sun that shone down brightly on Iriomé could not bring it back to her.

For the last time she ran her finger along the lines of the spiral, this time from the outside to the center. Then she stopped. It was over.

There was nothing for her here anymore. The enchantment, the magic of nature, the spirits—they had left the island for good. Iriomé had no option but to follow them.

She sat down on a rock, closed her eyes, and tried to stir her imagination to dive into that space Tichiname had always brought home to her as the actual world, the world with which the soul of humans was connected. Only there could one understand oneself and others. It was the beginning of all and the end. Her thoughts wandered to her son. What kind of life would he have before him? Would there be anything that connected him to his forefathers and their way of thinking?

She got up and continued her way to the cave shrine of Aceró. The dragon tree Tichiname had grown in front of the big cave was no longer there, the wooden ladders between the cavities had disappeared. She gave a whistle, but only an echo answered. No one was left.

"Vacaguaré!" she murmured softly and then climbed up the steep rock wall to the final resting place of the harimaguadas. She opened the grave chamber and closed it again from inside. Then she crouched in a corner on the rocky ground, closed her eyes, and entered upon her last journey, feeling the wings of a strong falcon bringing her into the rising sunlight.

Romy was sitting on the boxes from the moving company that would transport her stuff to Spain. On the one hand she was sorry to abandon her apartment and job in Augsburg; on the other hand she was looking forward to her new family life in her beloved Spain.

Nic wanted to come in the evening to fly out to Marbella with her. They had not seen each other for two weeks because he had been busy up to his ears splitting up with his wife and especially Forster's Health. Jennifer and her father put every possible obstacle in his way, but he refused to be thrown off track. Without caving in once, he indefatigably pursued his new path. Romy admired him for this. She would have preferred to spend the evening with him alone, but Thea insisted that they both attend the opening of the new Welser museum, of which her mother was the patron. Romy's best friend had reconciled with her mother and by this had surprisingly encountered the last piece of the puzzle that had been missing to complete the picture of Iriomé's life. And tonight she wanted to present it to Romy.

Thea's mother, an extremely well-groomed elderly lady in an ivory sequined dress, greeted each guest with a handshake that evening. Thea herself was nowhere to be seen among the crowd of everybody who was anybody in Augsburg. Far back in the corner of the foyer of the Welser museum Romy even spied Anton Feistner with his wife, whom she made a mental note to avoid.

Nevertheless, Romy enjoyed wandering with Nic through the simple rooms where various exhibits from the history of the famous Augsburg merchant family were on display; for he was not only familiar with the history of Spain, but also knew much about the period at the end of the Dark Ages in Europe.

Suddenly he stopped dead, as if struck by lightning and stared at an old, slightly faded oil portrait that showed a woman with an enigmatic expression who wore her reddish-blonde hair loose, which was completely unusual for the period. Instead of folding her hands in her lap, her thumb, index, and middle finger formed a spiral. Speechless he looked from the picture to Romy and back again, as if he needed time to organize what was going on inside him.

Romy was no less surprised, even though she more quickly iden-tified the coherence. Thus Iriomé actually had made it to Augsburg alive and had obviously stayed there with the Welsers! And she must have made such an impression that they had her portrait painted.

"I know this woman," Nic said softly to Romy. "And even if you think I'm completely crazy, I need to tell you a strange story . . ."

Closing Remarks

Alonso Fernández de Lugo, the great conqueror of the Canaries, is a historical figure who in 1492 seized La Palma on behalf of Queen Isabella of Castile. However, he did not die, as invented by me, in Zaragoza of consumption, but in 1525 in San Cristobal de la Laguna on the island of Tenerife. In September of 1492 he succeeded in achieving an agreement with a part of the twelve tribal leaders in Tazacorte without conflicts breaking out. They showed themselves ready to both convert to Christianity and to recognize Queen Isabella as their sovereign.

After a few battles the remaining chieftains capitulated in April 1493, except for Tanausú, who held the line in the caldera, the large volcanic crater. In May 1493 de Lugo offered him a truce, to which he agreed. However, when Tanausú left his territory for negotiations, he was lured into an ambush and captured. He died during the passage to Spain by refusing to eat.

After the successful submission of La Palma, on February 2, 1494, Queen Isabella entered a new contract with de Lugo for the conquest of the island of Tenerife. However, this was only successful at his second attempt. There he lived as governor until his death in 1525.

Also historical is the figure of Francisco Pizarro, who was born as the son of a swineherd in Trujillo. Whether he ever met de Lugo is not authenticated. Living in the Age of Discovery, he was lured by the adventure to take part in the conquering of the New World. He was mayor and magistrate of Panama City and earned a small fortune there. In 1522 he learned of the existence of the Inca Empire, and tantalized by Hernán Cortés's conquest of the Aztec Empire, he dreamed of a similar success. In 1524 he committed himself to finding the legendary gold country of Eldorado.

In the second volume of the amakuna saga he is going to play an important role.

The period in which Iriomé arrives at the Spanish mainland is characterized by the consequences of the Reconquista, the recapture of Spain from the Moors, whose last bastion, Granada, fell in 1494.

One of the first actions of the new authorities was the introduction of the Inquisition. Jews and Moors were persecuted and executed in the famous auto-da-fés (burnings at the stake).

Even in the present portions of the story there are many parallels to reality.

The field of the research of psychotropic mushrooms has lately gained new knowledge that is constantly integrated into drug development. And where the dubious practices of the pharmaceutical industry are concerned, reality is certainly far ahead of the fiction.

❦

The endless fight between love and power will be continued by the children of the heroes from *Daughter of the Dragon Tree* in the next volume of the saga.

❦

For more information about the amakuna saga, visit
www.amakuna-saga.com